MERECÀ

JOHN BENNY DOLGETTA

John Dolgetta
50 Palmer Ave
Bronxville, New York 10708
Copyright- © 2021
Library of Congress Control Number: 2021910357

All rights reserved. No part of this publication may be reproduced, stored in a retrieval system or transmitted in any form or by any means electronic, mechanical, photocopying, recording or otherwise, without prior permission in writing from Rebound Press.

Designed and typeset by KDP
Printed and bound by KDP

www.johndolgetta.com
johndolgetta@yahoo.com

Dedicated to the City of Sarno.

To the gentle way the town administration took an American kid into its care, making me an instant citizen and opening the door to a wonderful public-school education at the Guido Baccelli Middle School. To the friends who exposed me to the beauty of my ancestral culture while nurturing in me a profound respect and love for the simple joys and passions of a Southern Italian life.

To the townspeople and their addictive and enduring character. *Gaetano*, the deli owner, just outside my home, who made me my *mortadella panino* each morning on my way to school. *Giulillo*, the zeppole guy who moved me to the front of the line at his stand to take my order for the most perfect zeppola filled with tomato sauce, fresh mozzarella, and shredded pork, then fried in olive oil to a golden brown … one was never enough. My cousin Tullio, his smile, his comedy, his never-ending affections, and his honest and genuine love. My greatest friend Carminuccio, without whom my life in Sarno would have been a mere vacation. My classmates Mimmo and Raffaele who eased me through, providing priceless instructions in language and the social graces. To the colorful, theatrical vendors at the *mercato*. Sarno encouraged me to blend my American and Italian cultures into a more delicate, more refined product. I came home to New York bi-lingual and bi-cultured, and lovingly indebted to my charming, seductive and fascinating Sarnesi. Un abbraccio!

Contents

TABLE OF CONTENTS

Introduction

Prologue

CHAPTER 1	BACKPEDALING	7
CHAPTER 2	SARNO	14
CHAPTER 3	VIA UMBERTO I	28
CHAPTER 4	TULLIO	38
CHAPTER 5	SCUOLA GUIDO BACCELLI	48
CHAPTER 6	CARMINUCCIO	73
CHAPTER 7	FIRST CHRISTMAS	95
CHAPTER 8	IL GIARDINO	106
CHAPTER 9	PRIMO BACIO	120
CHAPTER 10	STELLA E ELISA	148
CHAPTER 11	ESTATE	161
CHAPTER 12	AMORI PROIBITI	173
CHAPTER 13	MANCANZA DI EQUILIBRIO	187
CHAPTER 14	QUANDO IL DIAVOLO TI ACCAREZZA	194
CHAPTER 15	IL DESTINO NON ….	223
CHAPTER 16	ADDIO	282

MERECÀ

Previous Page – Sarno City Coat Of Arms

MERECÀ

Introduction

I was eleven when my parents decided to move the family back to their hometown of Sarno in the province of Salerno, Italy in 1967. We lived in the Bronx, the Little Italy section where life was an American version of an Italian village. I understood and spoke my parents' Neapolitan dialect alongside my English. As an only child, Pop made the tough decision to move the family back when his mother, my nonna Nunzia fell ill. She had been diagnosed with intestinal cancer and needed our care.

In a small town struggling to break into the twentieth century, time took its time. It stymied us at first, as we tried to tone down the adrenalin from the more energetic existence on the streets of the Bronx. When the place started to grow on us, we allowed the history, the ancient agrarian culture, and the theatrical lives of its inhabitants to produce a glimpse of what life would have been if my parents had never left for the allure of America.

This is a fictional story based on my experiences overcoming the initial shock of being so clinically uprooted, to finding a way to acclimate, and to ultimately fall in love at first with Sarno, and consequently with an entire country. I used the names of my closest male friends as a tribute to their kindness and brotherhood. Actual people I encountered helped me to define the main female characters, Elisa and Stella. Chapter four is dedicated to my cousin Tullio who became our willing instructor in all things Sarno. Not only were our days filled with his laughter and love during our move back, but in subsequent years we spent entire summers together at numerous venues on the Amalfi

MERECÀ

Coast. He married hi love Clotilde, together raised three amazing children, and stayed true to his hometown. Sadly, this beautiful man passed away, but his legacy lives on, never to be forgotten.

So, there are fictional characters based on real people I either met or learned about, as well as many who left their marks on an American kid discovering his heritage. In that coming of age, I absorbed the subtleties of living Italian, a wide range of academics, and both the Italian language and an addictive Neapolitan tongue. In the book I incorporated both languages in support of the English narrative. As I read through chapters, I pleasantly concluded that the reasonable repetition of Italian and Neapolitan words would have the reader gain a level of fluency to put those words and sentences to personal use. What a wonderful way to learn enough of a foreign language to be able to belt out a few words, maybe put together a sentence or two without having endured the delusion of learning nothing in three years in high school Italian.

As far as style goes, I decided on the unorthodox. Purists will be upset at my use of contractions and everyday expressions. I prefer to write the way people speak, the way they express themselves on certain topics, and the unexpected reactions that do not exactly identified with stereotypes. I may have neglected some of the norms of political correctness simply because the world I grew up in was not concerned with it.

Ultimately, the novel is the story of a teenager coming of age in an unexpected place, with an unexpected language, and unexpected people. It took me off my Bronx streets, out of my Catholic elementary school, away from my comfortable friendships, with all the anxieties of a true immigrant. Sarno and its people took us in, eased us through assimilation, granting us the respect earned by those like my parents who left to seek out opportunities abroad, but who never severed the umbilical. I turned our two years into four years to push toward the end of high school and an age when we were old enough to define our world in stronger personal terms to create and typify the conflicts in the book. Our first encounter with alternative sexuality, in a world convulsing with liberation movements, asked us to understand it, show compassion, and to shelter and support those who had staked their claims to live as they desired. We lived on the edge of that revolution, deciphering reasons why some humans were socially marginalized so that empathy would prevail over tragedy. Despite the willingness to engage, to make a difference, we lacked the power to fully prevail.

MERECÀ

Prologue

Most of the reasons I was asked to acknowledge and understand the changes that came my way during my "Italian" life were non-dramatic, caused small amounts of anxiety, and were easily absorbed. What was unexpected and less digestible were the lives and the friendship of Stella and Elisa. I was my own main character until the girls took over.

Stella was the local girl from the short side of life, hailing from the housing projects of Sarno, the town in which my parents were born. Elisa, the daughter of the town's only aristocratic family with a deep heritage, and a traceable history to the year 1486, when the Tuttavilla family inherited the feudal title to the earldom of Sarno. The Tuttavilla family had strong ties to the Mussolini government prior to World War II. They owned several textile factories in the area that were refitted to produce military uniforms, backpacks, and ammunition bags during the war. Elisa's father was never a member of the Italian Fascist party, but after the war he was falsely labeled a closet fascist, accused of cooperation with Mussolini's government in support of Italy's entrance into the war. The accusations stuck with the post-war government and the allies who were in control of the country. The Tuttavilla family was consequently stripped of its aristocratic title, its properties, and liens placed on bank accounts for a period of twenty years. They were ultimately cleared of charges during my stay.

The family retained possession of their villa in Sarno, and acreage on the outskirts of the town rented to famers to produce San Marzano tomatoes. Just after the war, they had managed to transfer some funds to connections in London. Stella made frequent trips to England, enrolled in summer classes which produced fluency in English, and where she cultivated close friends and honed her knowledge of progressive politics. In Sarno, she remained a quasi-recluse inside the villa where she received instruction from a private tutor. She ventured out with her grandmother on short trips to shop for necessities.

The fear of being targeted by left wing groups still bent on punishing aristocrats, kept her from interacting with local teens and from being enrolled in public school. When her father needed to prop up the family's finances in the early 60's, he sold an acre of the villa property to my parents. My grandfather brokered the deal, and immediately had a small building with five apartments built on the land with money my parents had been funneling to Sarno from America. It was because of that sale that I met Stella. The stone wall erected by my grandfather to separate the lands only increased my curiosity of what was on the other side.

Stella and Elisa may never have become acquainted if not for my ability to get her to venture outside the villa and into the town. Their first encounter was enough to initially spark an infatuation which quickly evolved into a tender love affair.
Eli (the short version of Elisa) had no inhibitors that would have delayed expressing her affections for Stella. The girl from the projects (*palazzine*) may have nurtured some inkling of her sexuality, but it was Eli's liberated sense that gifted her a deeper, more convincing awareness of herself.

The story explores the unconventional coming of age of an American teen when he is forced to experience it in a foreign setting, as well as the powerful dynamic between two women from opposing classes determined to consummate their love in the difficult setting of a small southern Italian town in the late 60's. Stella's path is littered with consequences almost impossible to navigate. He father, Carlo, is the director of the local office of the Italian Communist Party office. His wife had been the town beauty won over by the up-and-coming politician. Staying true to the socialist cause, Carlo and Adela live on the edge of poverty. As director his stipend is at best subsistence, and they rely on subsidized housing. Adela still retains a matured beauty in her mid-forties, but she is haunted by a life that could have been, and which has taken its toll making her appear worn. She lost all love for her husband as his fanaticism for the communist cause destroyed the marriage. She denies herself the power or conviction to start a new life without him. She tows the line, plays the part of the submissive spouse, and comes to despise her life. It's only a matter of time before Adela falls into the arms of another man. Carlo remains oblivious to his wife's needs, dismissing her as a background prop to his egotistic, but delusional rendition of a man with a powerless title.

The party wants to expand its influence into regions further south. They enlist Carlo to travel to the remote region of Basilicata to scout out locations to set up a base of operations. Two party secretaries are dispatched to oversee his work. They spend most of their time in Sarno , traveling to the region secure a place, furnish it, and stock it with necessities. One of them, Amadeo is a younger operative with experience jumpstarting new districts. Carlo takes a liking to him, deciding he would be a good match for Stella. The prospect of marrying an older, established man (he is twenty years Stella's senior), living in a large urban center in the north with stable work, incomes and modern conveniences are reasons employed in the ill-fated attempt to convince their daughter to submit. Amadeo finds the opportunity to wed a young, beautiful woman of southern origin both personally satisfying, and a choice that the party will approve of as it moves to spread its influence in the south. Stella would become a convenient tool in accomplishing that goal.

The reaction from the girls is expected. Stella rebels against her parents, chastises Amadeo for even trying, while plotting for a way out of the mess. Eli can only give advice, urge caution, and wait for outcomes.
Amadeo is slow in dropping the marriage question. When he is spied in an uncompromising position by Stella and friends, blackmail becomes the desperate choice in fixing her world.

| MERECÀ

Carminuccio and Merecà (Americano) are the two males who, with Stella and Eli, complete the list of main characters. The boys are at first perplexed about the budding lesbian relationship. With time they come to understand, and accept, creating the space in their natures to invite a newer, more amplified definition of love. They also become the counterweight to Eli's naïve insistence on sidestepping the protocols in a less than cosmopolitan, heavily traditional existence of her small-town lover. The boys caution that Stella could never openly advocate for her sexuality without suffering the predictable consequences. They insisted that her father's violent reaction would stem from protecting his reputation, and from his hatred of the aristocracy … claiming the corrupt practices of the rich were designed to manipulate and promote his daughter's sick proclamation. In his mind, irrefutable cause to seek revenge for political and personal reasons.

Stella eventually finds herself at a fatalistic crossroads, forced to reveal herself to Amadeo to give him the most convincing evidence that a marriage would never work. Once the word gets out, the girls must scramble to find a way to calm the approaching storm.

The town is not immune to the spasms. The clannish character of its inhabitants must meet the challenge of either extending its benevolence to the unconventional love affair or support the hypocrisy of rejecting it. The soul searching is initiated en masse by the town's youth, pressuring adults, authorities, and the church to deal with the convulsions of change. These contending forces will either meet head on to staunchly advocate for their views or find cause to advance a more common application of their humanity.

MERECÀ

PHOTOS:

Page 1- My fifth-grade class photo at Mount Carmel Elementary. Last class before moving to Italy. Me: bottom row, seated, third from left.

Page 2-My eight-grade photo at ScuolaGuido Baccelli in Sarno. Me: kneeling, first from the right with the American sneakers, Mimmo standing far right, Carminuccio kneeling second from left, Raffaele kneeling fourth from the right.

Page 3 My best friend Carminuccio.

Page 4-Nonna Nunzia and Nonno Domenico.

Page 5-My amazing aunt (zia) Assunta.

Page 6 Our home in Sarno-Mom and my sister on our balcony. The 500 Lire nonna gave me to spend out with my friends on Sundays.

(Veduta della città di Sarno e delle sue antiche fortificazioni.)

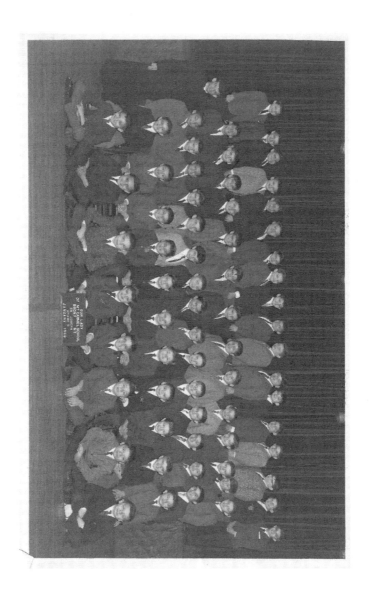

MERECÀ

MERECÀ

MERECÀ

I

MERECÀ

MERECÀ

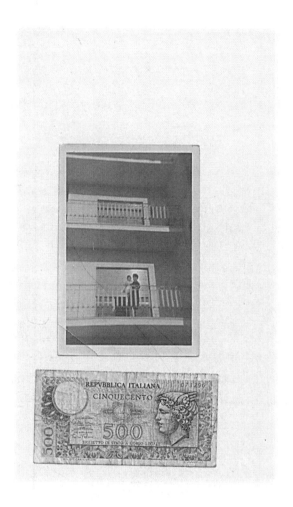

CHAPTER 1
BACKPEDALING

My parents were finally making good on the promise of coming back to America. Four years earlier I witnessed the sale of everything we owned in the Bronx and boarded a transatlantic ship for Naples. My father's mother was the only surviving grandparent when her second husband died. As her only child, Pop's reaction was predictable, but his decision to quit his American life came as a total shock. Nonna (*grandma*) had been first widowed when her son Giuseppe was hardly a year old. It would take years to overcome the small town, southern Italian stigma that came with taking another spouse. Her husband's three brothers would have made their displeasure known had she attempted to replace her dead spouse's place in her bed too soon. She wore black forever.

To my father, my grandmother was not only the object of a powerful affection, but his strongest connection to a father he had never known. If my grandfather Giovanni had not been such a revered figure in the austere, interior Neapolitan town, then Pop could have kept his feelings suppressed, having little need to know his father more intimately. From what I learned, *nonno* Giovanni's good nature stimulated the affections of many. From his sharpshooter reputation as a hunter; to his orthodox work ethic; to his loving generosity which wove its way through so many of the local families; to his incorruptible honesty, and to the pride with which he donned his military uniform as a member of a cavalry unit… Giovanni was the ideal gentleman of southern Italian culture. Pop absorbed the images on the few photos that existed, and the stories handed down by his mother, relatives and *paesani* (locals*)*, like a schoolboy listening to a teacher's first reading of *Robinson Crusoe*. With each trip to the cemetery, I watched him paralyzed at his father's grave-conjuring images of a life that might have been, aware there was no opportunity to make up for lost time. He shed tears during those visits … the heavy, regretful tears of a little boy who never had the chance to know his father. His mournful sadness drenched me like a dark, pounding rain … often I had to just walk away. How he identified with the kind of person his father had been in life, had much to do with the way he treated his own children. His loving and delicate manner made sure that the three of us would never have to wonder about a father's affection. In so many ways he recreated the relationship he imagined he would have had with his own father. Considering all we learned about my grandfather, Pop succeeded in that entirely.

    Our Alitalia flight pulled up to its gate at JFK airport on an early summer afternoon in 1971. My grandmother's condition had stabilized, so she remained behind in the care of close relatives. Manhattan was covered in the usual haze allowing only the tips of the tallest buildings to capture the rays of the setting sun in the western sky. I was intrigued by the paradox that I was returning to America as an *American born* immigrant, and that the view from the Whitestone Bridge was the same one so many true immigrants had first experienced. I was ready to reclaim my place, but I argued that in some way I had to earn it back. We had been away long enough and feeling much like one who did not belong, was an uncomfortable first reaction.

    We had many relatives, but the size of the committee at the airport attracted silent stares. There were uncles, aunts, cousins and even neighborhood friends gathered in the main lobby of the International Arrivals Building. We emerged from Customs into the waiting arms of my mother's sisters Rosie and Silvia and her brother Benny with their shrieks turning us all into instant celebrities. The hugs and kisses flowed uninterrupted, ignoring the demands of airport personnel to move away from the greeting area … nothing was going to budge what had become one huge, odd geometric structure of interlocked human beings. Finally, my father injected a dose of his usual good sense, warning everyone that the airport security people would not tolerate much more, and that it would be wise for us to leave for home. My father's words had the usual desired effect: a flawless, appealing delivery, and an undeniably sound argument as galvanizing as a Sunday morning sermon.

We left the airport in a caravan of cars, and when we slowed before the toll booths that landed us on the other side of the Long Island Sound in Bronx territory, I struggled to appreciate the blurred, hazily familiar sights. Then, just beyond the tolls, I could decipher from a distance the friendlier: Bronx River Parkway North. In earlier years, as a kid sitting in the back of my father's Fiat, I knew we were close to home when that sign appeared, signaling that I only had to hold my pee just a little longer, and if I could keep myself from wetting the back seat of the car, I could avoid being the cause of my father's rare displeasure.

The parkway took us to the Allerton Avenue exit. I struggled to connect to the curious neighborhood; it did not look like the Bronx I was trying so hard to recall, so I abandoned the attempt. We were back, and it was all that mattered. The summer day melted away into a receding, muggy twilight as we approached the building that was to become our new home. It was around the time when people escaped the heat of their apartments to claim their favorite sidewalk lounging spots. The mostly elderly crowd had positioned their folding beach chairs to take in the cooler evening hours and any sight that may lead to some tantalizing bit of gossip. These were not the same mothers and grandmothers we left behind in the more familiar Italian neighborhood. They did not speak the old language and they weren't as quick to ask about us. These kept to themselves, looked us over while they whispered a cryptic procession of comments that floated quickly through the group, followed by inquisitive stares. There were no greetings, no salutations, hardly a welcoming smile. This was a weighty departure from the customary "*buongiorno, buonasera, and ciao* we used obligingly among family, friends and even strangers back in Sarno. We remained puzzled when we failed to receive a response to our greetings ... strange, I thought at the time. It kept me leery at first, but with time I would come to understand and appreciate those differences.

MERECÀ

My mother's dear brother, and my godfather uncle Benny, graciously accepted the task of rehabilitating us and, not being able to resettle our family back in Little Italy, we found ourselves in a different section of the Bronx; it could have been a different country. The size and the territorial nature of New York's segregated neighborhoods were unforgiving to anyone who did not quite fit. We climbed the flights to our two-bedroom apartment, and I sensed, as we passed through the door, the uninvited and unappealing new chapter in my young life, and this time around I was old enough to resent it. Once inside, we interacted sadly with crumbling plaster, an older, stained carpet, aged furniture with no antique quality to it, and a kitchen that could not escape the staleness of its decaying odors. I walked into our bedroom and within seconds my younger brother's eyes welled with elliptical tears that struggled to empty from his puffy eyes. I remained fixed in my spot feeling a sudden, deep teenage melancholy. Everything looked ugly: the room, the beds, the chipped dresser, the gated windows, the rusting fire escape, the roach crawling along the wall above the molding of the narrow closet, the warped, lumpy, and pallid linoleum floor, and the lone light bulb dangling from the ceiling fixture. My brother rolled over into a fetal curl on one of the beds and remained there until my mother finally persuaded him to eat something. I hardly touched any food struggling with the attempt to rewind life back to Italy ... hoping that we could turn a corner and find ourselves in our Italian beds, waking to the delicate trickle of the water fountain; to the addictive aroma of a brewing *caffelatte*; to my grandmother feeding the chickens, and my father pruning hazelnut trees ... all this to the sound of hundreds of sputtering scooters whiningly ferrying people to the market or to their jobs.

The short, rapid nostalgias were suddenly and rudely shattered by the rumbling sound of the elevated train only a block away; making it clear that not only would our conversations be interrupted, but so would our more soothing thoughts. I gazed out the living room window catching a glimpse of the last compartment of the stumbling heap of metal decorated in the latest graffiti on its way to the South Bronx. While my first reaction was

MERECÀ

to find the graffiti artistically appealing, I couldn't help but feel there was something onerous and untamed about it, ultimately striking a dark fear in me as I made out the crosses, skulls, and headstones. Several of the relatives who had been at the airport remained with us through dinner keeping the mood as festive as possible-at least for the adults. I engaged my cousins in conversation, realizing all along that the years apart had brought on diverging interests. We had left each other as goofy adolescents and returned as budding teens. I had little affection for much of American pop culture having been away from it too long. A four-year absence represented a greater gap than it did for my parents-a gap that would take longer to bridge. Getting into the music, the art, the street life and the slang would come eventually, but those first few months were characterized by a powerful longing for the Latin life we left behind, and a youthful curiosity in rediscovering the world we had been born into.

  I stretched out mummified in bed that first night, while my brother tried hard to deal with his anguish brought on by the Italian experience that had molded his definition of a life that was difficult to give up. I wanted to scream the same violation, but there was little sense in competing with him; he became the spokesperson for the way we both felt ... his scorn carried more weight. There was little incentive to sleep, staying awake in the hope that my parents had thought of a way to steady us through this new bump in the road. That first morning I got up first and strolled into the kitchen only to be greeted by a roach crawling close to my fingers feeling my way to a light switch. The brightness only revealed more of the undesirable tenants as they scattered to the sound of a human intruder. In the frenzy of just being grossed out, I grabbed a magazine and started swinging, knocking over boxes, cans of food and some dishes and glasses into the sink. My parents and my younger sister came running, and before they could react, I, in an uncommon display, went off in my angry Neapolitan: *"Perchè sa da vivere accusì? Non se poteva truvà nu posto miglior? Aggio' perdut' tutt' I cumpagn' e na vita che me stave bene. Mo' sa da cumincia' ro 'cap' senza che v'interresate e nuie. Chest' nun è na casa!"* The youthful

indignation spilled over into a series of stinging questions and selfish observations. *"Why do we have to live here? Couldn't you find a better place? Why didn't we stay in Italy? How many more times are we going to move? I keep losing my friends and a life I was good with! Now we are starting over ... again! You just don't care what happens to us! This is not a home."* Italy had clearly spoiled our tastes for what we considered normal. My father left the room dejected to slouch on his bed as one who had made an irretrievably wrong decision. My mother looked at me motionless, while tears flowed down her soft, swollen cheeks betraying her fears: *"Chest'era l'unica scelta. Già se sapev' ca fosse stata difficile, ma era necessaria e turnà ... papa non lavora ra' quatt'ann. Ti cride che a vita è facile? Nun voglio che iss' nge sent', ha già suppurtate tropp', e nun addà sapè che nun site cuntent'. Sa da preocupà sull' e truvà nu lavoro."* Mom spilled her sentiments at my feet admitting they had no choice. In her words: *"I knew it would be difficult, but we had to come back ... your father hasn't worked in four years! You think it is easy for us? I do not want him to hear! He has been through enough, and the last thing he needs right now is to know that you and your brother are not happy. Finding work is the only thing he needs to worry about."*
I gathered what she meant. In Sarno we had been living off minuscule rents my parents collected from tenants living in the three leased apartments in our building. The money was hardly enough to support us and the increasing costs of my grandmother's medical expenses. The solution was America, the only place where they knew how to earn a living. I walked away and into their bedroom where my father continued to unpack. He took the magazine from my hands and slumped into a chair rubbing his forehead in silent desperation. For the first time in my life, I found him powerless to fix everything-that he too would have to confront situations with unclear outcomes. We were in for a rough ride and our parents carried the added burden of keeping us from a total meltdown. The argument lost its power quickly since no one was in the mood to hold a grudge.

In the following weeks, I made numerous sorties into the kitchen and the closets to squash as many roaches as I could. I never did quite eliminate all of them despite uncovering most of their favorite hiding spots. It took several attempts at fumigation to finally make them an unpleasant memory. Killing roaches was only one of the many gritty and distorted New York diversion that compounded the heartache of leaving our more delicate Italian lives. Hopes of returning were soon dashed when Mom rattled off figures of how much it cost to move back to the Bronx. The time had come for Pop to return to the work ethic forced on him when he first set his immigrant feet in America. He understood it, accepted it, and I could tell he was itching to get back in the game. My parents knew what was expected of them on a less forgiving American stage and shaking off the malaise of the small-town life had become a pressing priority. I recalled admiring their drive. Within a few weeks my father was back on a truck moving furniture and my mother had only to make one phone call to alert her old bosses in the sweat shop before she found an empty seat to fill in front of a Singer sewing machine. I had listened to all the stories of how they were unable to get beyond the third grade because of World War II, hiding out in the mountain caves beyond their town, catering to the Germans while they controlled the area, then to the Americans and the British when the Germans retreated north towards Rome. Somehow, they made it through, and it was that instinct that allowed them to survive and thrive in New York as they blended again into the American subculture. We were back where it all began, but our hearts had refused to take the trip, staying behind in our little Neapolitan town.

MERECÀ

CHAPTER 2
SARNO

1967 had seen us gather up our belongings destined for my parents' birthplace. As toddlers, Sarno, a thirty-minute drive to the Amalfi Coast, had been nothing more than a one-month summer vacation and an opportunity for Mom and Pop to reconnect with their parents. In late June, each year before my sister was born, Mom would load up herself and her two boys on a trans-Atlantic liner bound for the bay of Naples. Pop stayed behind to mind his business, eventually making the trip sometime in July. We knew our grandfather's huge country home simply as *Quattro Funi*. As my Italian improved, and I became more aware of the nature of local things, I would come to understand that *quattro funi* meant *four ropes* … the four ropes that were used in the absence of gates to stop the flow of traffic at four intersections while trains transited through the "*passaggio a livello*" or *the street level crossing*. The term had even become the address for the area as *Via Quattro Funi*. One of the four crossings was the entrance to my grandfather Domenico's estate. The road leading to his home was known as the *stradone*, the *long road*. The huge house only came into view about halfway up the *stradone* just beyond the elegant hazelnut trees and the towering walnuts. The final stretch was lined with a pageantry of evenly spaced orange and tangerine trees dense with dark, oily leaves. Even in the summer months, the citrusy scent gathered like a hallucinogenic in one's nostrils, carving out a permanent spot in my memory of things Italian. In the coming years, I would add a complete portfolio of nostalgias, caringly donated by the ancient culture of my ancestors.

MERECÀ

That steamy last day of August we sailed out of New York harbor wondering if it would be our last crossing to Naples. I kept my confusion and fear disguised. I was a fourteen-year-old New York native bidding farewell to his blue-collar Italian American life on the streets of the Bronx. Would I ever see my friends again? Would I ever flip the sports pages of the Daily News again, to read the play-by-play summary of how my beloved Yankees homered the opposing team to death? What about my adolescent first girlfriend who shared half of her Bazooka bubble gum, her Coke, and her bag of Wise potato chips with me on those summer days lounging on the concrete lips of the sidewalks that lined the school yard. This was not an easy choice for my parents, but it was downright painful for me and my twelve-year-old brother. My sister was a playful five-year-old immune to any anxieties; she would go willingly if her costume jewelry and dolls went with her.

My schoolyard athletics were finally being taken seriously. I had worked my way into the top ranks of the summer evening schoolyard softball games, and it had become a sweet sound when my name popped quickly off the lips of the older guy who won the *first pick* coin toss, and I never disappointed. Hitting stickball home runs over the fence had become second nature. When we were not pounding Spalding balls into submission, I had come up with the best way to spend a dime at Rocky's Candy Store-often walking out with twenty pieces in a small paper bag, choosing only the two-for-a-penny deals. Life was urban, chalky, dirty, and graffitied in an immigrant neighborhood that had evolved into our safe, medieval fortress with clearly defined borders. The Third Avenue elevated train, Southern Boulevard, Fordham Road, and Tremont formed the quadrant boundaries of our city state. The brutality of the gangster beatings and killings were enigmatically balanced by the compassion of an occasional good neighbor and the honest, blue collar nature of its inhabitants. We all spoke English first, but Mom and Pop dished out instructions in Italian to their children and engaged in the mother tongue with any encounter on the streets, in the shops and even at the Savings Bank. Little Italy in the Bronx was an American attempt at

MERECÀ

recreating a village in the old country, and life ran on an Italian schedule within an American time zone. Gentility and respect grudgingly characterized few relationships. The deep-rooted instincts of the *paese* were kept at bay in an American landscape that fostered suspicions of the guy next door, and whose immigrants were kept busy working at mostly manual, long hour jobs chasing the opportunities they so craved. There was little time and few occasions to genuinely care for others. Beyond the superficiality of the Sunday Mass, one hardly engaged in communal efforts unless there was some personal profit in it. Profit had been the American incantation and the practice defined life. Pop logged countless hours on his rickety truck roaming the streets and basements of buildings buying up scrap metal and old newspapers for resale to refineries. Mom sat at her sewing machine pushing out completed dresses to the machine gun sound of that needle, whose image blurred at supersonic speed each time it laid down a straight line of stitches.

My parents had always been financially stable. They had money, but we never knew how much. Mom, however, made it clear we hardly had enough, even when we carried home bags full of groceries from the *mercato* on Arthur Avenue. She never used the word *poor*, but somehow, we were still penniless when Pop drove home in a brand-new Fiat. And we were practically destitute when we bought the building we lived in. Since the evidence was weak, my brother and I could not help but wonder whether we were middle class or something between that and starvation. Mom's claims of scanty finances remained unconvincing despite the drama and facial expressions taken from a Great Depression screenplay. She taught us that no one needed to know our business, especially when it came to money; that claiming low funds was the best way to spend less and get more. Little was spent on anything that was not an absolute necessity, which made us feel that we were only "luxury" poor. Going out to dinner was strongly discouraged because it just did not make sense in an Italian home. Pop would always set aside our restaurant curiosities by using his trademark line in Neapolitan: *"O mangià e casa è semp meglio, 'i risturant te fann' carè malate"* (home-cooked is always better, restaurant food will make you sick). Mom and Pop were both excellent cooks. The food on our plates never backfired and sidelining the restaurant thing until we were old enough to start going on our own, was hardly a burden. Any new furniture was meant to last countless years. Sofas and lounging chairs covered in plastic were as common as the decorative *Capodimonte* porcelain lamps that housed no light bulbs-they were showpieces not meant for their intended use. We never went cheap on furnishings because it harked back to the *"bella figura"* (make a good impression) mentality, and the need to recreate the lives they wished for themselves back in Sarno. We had a car, but it was a no frill, manual shift, no air conditioning, four-cylinder two tone, red body, black top Italian import. When we first saw it, my brother and I confessed to be embarrassed, thinking they forgot to paint the top. Our clothes were basic, everyday quality from the most affordable stores like *Alexander's* and *John's Bargain Store*. Mom reinforced our jeans and pants with added stitches to help resist the harshness of our concrete schoolyard play, in the hope of adding a few more weeks of life before turning them all into dust and mop rags. She would avoid patches because they gave credibility to all the make-believe poverty talk. Our Sunday and going out clothes were of the highest quality Italian fashions. My brother and I always cringed when Mom took her sweet time dressing us up-it was painful because we knew the outcome. The clothing made us too Italian and less Bronx, and we could only handle the creepy looks and the comments from the kids in the schoolyard with a threat to start throwing punches. A good fight was the only way of re-establishing the status quo and have them overlook the funny foreign clothes.

The fridge always had a bottle or two of *Hammer* sodas (no one else on the block had ever heard of Hammer, but we would get a dozen delivered every two weeks-they tasted something like Coke, Pepsi and 7Up, and we never complained). There were some cold cuts, cream cheese, and the Arthur Avenue fruits and vegetables that made their way onto the dinner table each evening.

MERECÀ

Welch's grape jelly was a favorite since the jars turned into drinking glasses once empty ... we had the complete Flintstones collection. We never saw a jar of peanut butter-Mom always thought it nasty and too American. Cups of MY-T-FINE chocolate pudding were a welcomed dessert, and small fights would break out when it came time to lick the spoon. Mom always insisted on cooling down the pudding; she had devised some story about how hot pudding could damage your stomach, and the intensity with which she told it, put enough of a fright in us to respect the cooling process until she gave us the green light to raid the cheap, chocolate, kid delicacy. Sliced white bread made enough toast to get us through breakfast, and Italian bread with a few slices of salami was enough to sooth the hunger pains till dinner.

In later years, in biographical discussions with my mother, I learned that in affording properties, a new car, airline tickets to Italy each summer, college tuitions, growing up funds for three children, and providing for basics, my parents had still been able to save an impossible forty percent or so of their gross income-it was never how much was spent, but how it was spent. I asked how much she saved for every dollar they earned. She would answer forty, maybe fifty cents. I found it believable considering that anything less would have had them borrowing money. I did not see a credit card until we were well into our twenties. Loans were never a consideration except for real estate. Tuitions were always paid in full, in cash. Cars were always purchased in full, in cash-no debts. They married off three children with gifts that allowed each of us to purchase our own homes within a year or two of our weddings. The lessons on money were stark and sometimes painful, but the immigrant discipline, a nurturing clan of relatives, and the still believable American Dream kept us tolerating our realities while calibrating our hopes around the notion that the future would deliver on some abstract promise of wealth.

Leaving behind America and the Bronx streets I considered home, soon came to pass. The small building and the car we owned sold quickly. Pop gave his business gratis to his cousin, and Mom got some decent money for many lesser assets, with any unsold belongings packed away in steamer trunks. The trip down to the New York City pier was quick and numb. We were all too preoccupied with boarding the baggage and ourselves to become emotional with the relatives who came to see us off. Once on the ship, we gazed down at the crowd waving white handkerchiefs. Mom finally broke down, wiping tears as quickly as they streamed down her puffy cheeks. She had first stepped foot in America as a spunky sixteen-year-old accompanied by a mental list of her teenage curiosities. The countless opportunities to experience a world within a world, kept Mom firmly grounded in all things New York. She reveled in the city's hustle and diversity, signing up for evening English classes, befriending as many "Americans" as possible to quicken her stride to assimilate, and spending any free time in the local stores learning as much as she could about once unimaginable products. Mom's grief as the ship pulled away from the pier had less to do with losing contact with family and friends, and more to do with the heartbreak of a young, progressive woman who had found her stride in the New World, and who's aspirations were now being defeated by unforgiving circumstances. Mom never had any intentions of moving back. The unavoidable outcome for me was to take all those early experiences in my Italian American life and unload them at the port of Naples, wondering whether I would be able to protect them as part of my own legacy, or would I lose them to a new and possibly permanent Italian life.

Naples appeared nothing less than total chaos to the sensibilities of a kid accustomed to the neat ethnic neighborhood existence of New York. The Bronx had its share of noise and crowds scurrying about, but there was less confusion, people waited for their turn at things, and life had a busy predictability to it. America insisted on the rule of laws, while the Neapolitan habit was to make rules seem useless-even foolish. As we filed off the *SS Michelangelo*, relatives rushed up to us, dodging disembarking passengers, competing for first embraces and sloppy kisses, completely ignoring the security personnel who seemed to routinely fall away from any attempt to keep order ... content to just let things happen. I understood in those first delicate Italian minutes, that a word or two, a specific facial gesture, and the methodical, frenzied gesticulation of arms and hands like mad puppets, could subvert any regulation, belittle a uniformed employee's authority, and in some cases even influence a judge's ruling.

My nonno (grandfather) Domenico had died almost a year earlier. Nonna (grandma) Nunzia was the first to greet us. My father softly poured himself into his mother's arms-both lacking the power to check the flow from their watery eyes. I wondered whether they were happy reunion tears or was my grandfather's death more the catalyst. My aunt Gianna held my mother's face in her rough, chapped hands, greeting her like a newborn baby. Within seconds they gave way to the rest of the relative cohort. Conversations were loud and jumbled, forcing me to absorb only the words I understood in helping to decipher the emotional exchanges. Mom recounted how we spent three of the eight days on the ship dodging a huge storm in the North Atlantic. The word for life vests (*salvagente*-literally people saver) stood out, as the faces of those listening added all the dramatic effects along with the biblical convictions that Jesus (*Gesù Cristo*) had interceded, guiding us safely to port.

I was left alone long enough to slip away, to lounge on one of our bloated trunks as I nervously wiped away the saliva puddles from my face still wet from uninvited kisses. In my self-imposed silence, I focused only on those more native Italian expressions. So much more was being said beyond the words. The body and the facial distortions had morphed into languages of their own. In dialogues, as one person spoke, the listener validated what was being said with compelling, wordless expressions ... there was no passive retention of information, only the active locomotion of upper body and facial muscles. I was not involved, but the clamor kept me disoriented, dazed, and tired, finding just enough space on that battered trunk to lay my head down. I fell into an exhausted, crippling sleep that only slackened when my loving aunt Assunta nudged me gently in the back seat of a Fiat 1100, my head slumbered on her lap. I awoke as the car came to a sudden, sliding stop along the gravel road in time to avoid a stray goat that had wandered too far from a nearby flock. The nervous shepherd peered into the windshield, cradling his wooly property while adding another string of wordless gestures to the collection forming in my head, thanking us for not reducing his numbers by one. My uncle Alfonso was not the best of drivers. His habit of breaking frequently, grinding gears, and rhythmically stepping on and off the accelerator had us hoping we would reach our destination sooner than later. I recognized our destination as I glanced out the rear window through the clouds of thin dust kicked up from the parched *stradone,* the recognizable long dirt driveway that guided us to my grandfather's huge country home that had retained its welcoming appeal. The day had been hot and dry, and the thought of a cold pitcher of water from the well had me ready to bolt from the car. The caravan of vehicles which included a miniscule, bubbly, oval-shaped *Ape* (literally *bumble bee,* and best described as a three-wheeled scooter truck) came to a stop in the parking area that ran up to the *portone (the large portico covered by a tall, stone archway).* Nonna Nunzia shifted her attention to the preparation of food. As I stood stretching and yawning, fixed on the familiar sights, my nostalgia took me back to past summers recalling the *contadini (farmers)* trekking back to their homes, leaving their fields to the care of dense, star-speckled nights and custodial moons. I could read in their muted joy the anticipation of a country meal, the goodness of which would have been enough of a reward for a day's labor. It was that food that I now craved.

    The evenings and the cooler summer nights sponsored a complete set of rituals; it was not a time to wind down and pack it in. Nonna rushed through the usual routines in her kitchen, housed in a separate, smaller building. I followed close behind recalling, as a little guy, how much I marveled at the way she lined up her cookware like obedient soldiers ready to cradle their precious cargo of simmering and hissing velvety and pungent tomato sauces, and garlicky oils. The temptation was always too much to handle, so dipping a scrap of bread ripped sloppily from an unsuspecting loaf through that crimson brew had become a sneaky habit which nonna tolerated with a loving smile that exposed the mock anger struggling to take hold of her expression. The surrounding air filled with the smell of ancient wood logs and splinters burning cleanly in the cast iron stoves as I studied the liturgical preparation of food and absorbed the powerful peasant aromas. Diced fresh tomatoes with garlic bulbs pulled from the dirt, and oil squeezed from the stone crushed flesh of green olives sizzled and bubbled over red and yellow flames expertly tamed into a consistent heat with wedges of kindling. The pasta water boiled outdoors in a bloated, black pot. Potato fillets sautéed patiently in a grassy colored olive oil, sprinkled with tiny, coarse rocks of kosher salt. Mom and her sisters had joined us ready to do their share of the work, and to follow any instructions from the head cook. There was an Amazonian hierarchy that governed Neapolitan cooking. The eldest female ran the show. The next generation of women and wives moved pans from hot to cooler spots on the stove and vice-versa. They filled pots with water or skillets with oil and sprinkled julienned vegetables with salt and spices. The youngest females apprenticed, fetching supplies and setting tables. Nonna decided when to start the cooking. She would run her palm over her caste iron arsenal to detect the intensity of the heat. When all was right, large half-moon cloves and crushed red peppers were tossed. That familiar bouquet would carry on droplets of roasted oil erupting upwards from enraged, crackling pans. Seconds later handfuls of *broccoli rabe*, sweet red peppers or eggplant added their own fragrance. Skillets came off the stove briefly in measured intervals, allowing nonna the time she needed to maneuver the contents with her venerable wooden spoon. Mom and her sister snapped the foot-long barrel shaped *zitoni* with their hands into three-inch offspring, skillfully spilling them into the salted, boiling water, stirring up a whirlpool that had the pasta swimming like a school of sardines. That first day the tables were stacked end to end with seating for every relative that made the trip to Naples. Demijohns, topped off with local wine, bobbled in antique brass buckets filled with cold well water, while two of the ladies spilled a pot full of tomato sauce over the *al dente* baby zitoni. Nonna waited with an oversized steel ladle in hand to scoop out heavy amounts into deep pasta dishes. The assembly line started with *zia* (aunt) Silvia drowning the pasta in sauce, then handing them off rugby style to a queue of ladies completing the process on a short journey to the hungry tables. I marveled at the pleasure that punctuated the chores as the women urged each other to get the plates delivered before the contents cooled. The table conversations were loud and lively, with storytelling and laughter filling the pauses between the consumption of food and drink. I learned in those first months that being hungry had the least to do with eating. Food in my Italian world surpassed most other pleasures. Beyond the good cheer, the midday *pranzo* had a more serious, more complete character to it. The quantity and quality of the food was meant to replenish and to gratify. It also served as fuel to send the *contadini* back to their fields later in the day working until the retreating sun signaled an end to their labors.

With a belly full of pasta, I decided to take a friendly journey into the past when we first set foot on my grandfather's property as curious adolescents. Nonno was still with us when, on those late summer evenings, as the long daylight hours gave way grudgingly to the darkness, I would watch quietly as relatives trekked back from their fields barefoot, with workpants folded above their ankles, burdened with a variety of field tools carried military style on their shoulders. I recall being overcome with a youthful, sad bewilderment as they lowered their dusty and dirty feet, with dark crevasses exposed on their heels, into basins of fire-boiled water, and washed with amber colored soap bars the size of bricks. Once the dirty water was tossed, and the basin refilled with new water, that same bar of soap was worked into a lather along the front and back of their necks and faces. The final cleansing washed away the detergent with quick, upward hand scoops of water splashed about to reveal their clean, leathery skin. The late evening *cena* was less of a supper, and more of a casual, finger food treat, and it became my favorite meal for the variety of cheeses, fresh *mozzarella di bufala*, dried meats like *prosciutto* and *sopressata*, as well as pickled eggplant, sundried tomatoes, olives, mushrooms, with slices of dark, grainy bread dipped into infused oils. While most of the male adult relatives kept no account of the amount of wine consumed, I recalled that my grandfather kept his wine-drinking to no more than a glass at any meal. It was a lead the youngest of us followed, learning to consume alcohol in measured quantities, avoiding excess. As the cena always came to a satisfying conclusion with a steamy cup of espresso, I again ventured back to how nonno would savor his last Camel cigarette of the day, puffing methodically, shaking off the ashes with a flick of his pinky, always extinguishing his smokes when half consumed.

All the day's sacraments would shut down on time for the precious hour or so of television viewing. We all took our places on our favorite chairs or sofas; my habit had always been to cozy up to nonna on the daybed, leaning up against the smooth, earthy scented skin of her arms, anticipating with youthful wonder the unusual programming. During those summer stays I had come to accept the sad fact that Italian television started its schedule only in the late evening, and that most of it could hardly excite an American kid accustomed to hours of Saturday morning cartoons and sitcoms like the *Munsters*. The *Telegiornale* (evening news) which came on right after the *Carosello* (best described as advertisements touting products in short story, musical vignettes), signaled the end of everyone's day, and the time when the *masseria* (homestead) was prepped for the overnight hours. Nonna had her kitchen swept and cleaned, with every item returned to its resting place. Nonno followed a well-practiced epilogue of tasks that ended with the oversized skeleton key locking the grotesque and weighty doors to the main hall with a cavernous thud. Nonna followed us with a bucket of water in one hand and two bed pans in the other, as we climbed the creviced and worn stone stairs to the second-floor bedrooms. The water was used to flush the hallway toilet, while the bed pans were placed strategically beneath the beds within easy reach during the night.

MERECÀ

My many attempts at using mine only ended in desperate frustration, in most cases with my pee sprinkled about, some landing in the ceramic pot, some on the stone floor, and still some forcing me back into bed with wet pajamas. No amount of practice ever turned me into a pro. The nights seemed purposely shadowy despite the amount of moonlight, as they hosted the eerie, mysterious pulses and voices of nocturnal country creatures who also seemed to speak Neapolitan.

A deep sleep in the embrace of the large, marshmallow beds kept us kids slumbered till mid-morning, while the adults busied themselves with the ancient tasks that jumpstarted the life of a southern Italian country home. The routines took a pause on Sundays when nonna took in the early Mass, still dressed in the black outfits that marked the passing of a first husband, two brothers during the war and other close relatives. Nonno drove her to the parish church of *Santa Maria delle Grazie*. There, she would join the legions of local women that packed the church, while her husband passed the time talking business and politics with other landowners at the café'; sometimes getting in a quick game of cards. That last summer vacation with nonno, my curiosity got the better of me, so I insisted that Mom explain how my mother's father and my father's mother were living together. Despite the Catholic upbringing, we exercised very American values such as expressing curiosities, and demanding answers even on topics that may have been taboo. We were never afraid of asking questions of our parents, and they only refused to respond when the information could wait. She motioned me over to a quiet corner under the lemon grove where we sat on stone benches my grandfather had built. She ripped a leaf from one of the vines, cracked it in half and moved it to her nose to breath in the citrusy mist. She then held it out urging me to do the same. It would become an easy habit I would practice often with pleasure. She then paused, gathered her thoughts, and with a sober, but gentle look, decided it was time to reveal the facts best learned from a mother than from locals or relatives. "*Nonno e nonna so marito e moglie. Nonno è papa mio e nonna è mamma di tuo papà. Si sono sposati dopo io e papà*". I

MERECÀ

looked beyond my mother's face toward the grove. I knew her own mother Maria had died when Mom was about fifteen, and that Pop had grown up never knowing his father, lost to Typhoid Fever a year after his son's birth. There was little more to explain and, with my snoopiness satisfied, I learned to live with the fact that my mother's father had married my father's mother after both had lost their spouses and after my parents had wed. Mom worried that I would draw unhealthy conclusions, but I was too young to apply an orthodox view of relationships. In my mind, the fact that they were married was enough to validate the union. We walked away from the grove, sensing that Mom had again found a way to shelter her children from unnecessary traumas. She was so good at it, that she could only be defeated by a death in the family ... there was little she could do then to keep us from that anguish.

We had landed in Naples on that Saturday, and as the day faded into the next, there was little time to lazy around the *masseria*. After a quick, rustic breakfast of *taralli* (bagle size hard bread) floating and softening in a bowl of *caffelatte*, we were suddenly moving all our luggage back onto the shaky Ape (nonna called it *Aparella*-little bumble bee). The fearless three-wheeler, so much like the smallish, powerful people it served, was forced to carry more weight than was intended, stacked top heavy, wobbling as if drunk as it navigated through imperfections on roads still wearing the scars of war. We started off toward the downtown area of Sarno where we would meet our new home. I watched as relatives and friends packed into their toy cars (in my mind there was little room to consider the tiny Fiat 500's as anything more than cousins to the bumper cars that showed up once a year at the church fairs back in the Bronx), and convoyed with us on the twenty-minute drive attracting curious stares on the way. As the scenes of Southern Italian life floated by, I understood that our new reality would soon make unusual demands on us, and that finding a way to fit in would be the key to at least some small amount of happiness.

MERECÀ

CHAPTER 3
VIA UMBERTO I

I plastered my face to the backseat window of zio Alfonso's car scanning every image that came into focus. In that glass frame I wondered how the procession of women we passed along the way could balance the huge baskets of produce on their heads without the use of their hands, as they straddled the stone road within inches of our cars. Then I gazed down to lose myself in the incomprehensible image of their bare feet covered in white stone dust floating over pebbles, in step, one behind the other, without losing stride. I rolled down my window to capture the complete image of these slender, shoeless women, and the lone young girl, in a thin, colorful cotton dress protected by a worn apron. My youthful intuition tried to make sense of what I believed was obvious pain on their heads and on the bottom of their feet, mostly because I saw no evidence of it on their happy faces. For so many *contadini,* Sunday did not qualify as a day of rest. The produce had been harvested from their fields, and the overflowing baskets would sit in a cold cantina until early Monday morning when the women would once again position them on cloth buns flattened like bird nests into the wavy grooves of their thick, dark, Mediterranean hair to carry it off for sale in the local market. I continued to nurture an admiration of that sight even as we added years to our Italian lives.

As we left the countryside behind, I could finally decipher where it ended, and where the town began. The crowds grew thicker, the lyrical Neapolitan dialect, and the rhythmic chugging of small engine scooters, cars, and Api (more than one Ape), filled the air around me. It all tangled me up in a bundle of unusual feelings, coming to terms with that foreign version of urban sounds. There were differences, but what may have been nothing more than a painful cacophony to the natives, was nothing less than a newly composed symphony to my ears. On our approach to the first block of stores, we came to a Sarno version of a traffic stop brought on by the passage of a small herd of water buffalo. I was first dumbfounded by the amount of dung dropped by one of its members, only to start giggling uncontrollably as my brother pointed and prodded me to take a second look, cautiously whispering, "*that's real cow shit*", into my ear. It was the authentic and impromptu nature of a sight we never would have witnessed on the streets of Little Italy that caused the radical reaction, with the word "shit" being as common to our schoolyard ears as the *Our Fathers* we recited as penance for our sins. Just beyond my fascination with the animal spectacle, my eyes fixed on the long, metal billboards attached to each side of the massive, wooden medieval doors that typically protected the entrances to the centuries old stone buildings that lined the main road into town. These foyers had now become storefronts and those billboards, attached to the inside of the doors, and exposed to consumers as they swung open, lit up my adolescent brain with displays of inconceivable Italian versions of all sorts of ice cream selections. The images were not of simple swirly vanilla or chocolate soft serve. There were no cones dipped in hard shell chocolate syrup, no vanilla ice cream sandwiches, no Popsicles, and not a hint of anything with sprinkles. The figures seemed more like a tease, of fictitious prototypes that might someday become real, and in my thoughts, I questioned if it were possible to taste one. I read the name of the company quietly to myself. I wanted to make sure I would remember it when the time came to explain to Mom what it was that I craved. *Algida*, written in large red and yellow letters, stood at the top of the billboards like a mother hen looking down on its hatchlings. The name of Italy's largest ice cream distributor would become as common to my eyes as the red and white Coca Cola signs back home. This menu was dressed to kill. Everything about the images screamed high class, gourmet, and out of your league stuff you cannot afford. The ice cream ads that graced the windows of the Howard Johnson's restaurant on Southern Boulevard was the closest American version, but still no competition for the Italian lineup. Cheap, mass produced ice cream at Rocky's candy store on my block was a weekly consumption if you had a dime; Carvel cones, shakes or sundaes could be a

MERECÀ

monthly treat when we had a few extra quarters in our pockets ... mostly during the holidays. Howard Johnson's, with its *Wonderful World of 28 Flavors,* would have to wait till most of the kids in Little Italy were old enough to earn their own money. Mom and Pop avoided even driving past the iconic orange roofed mecca of cheap, blue collar food on the upscale side of a dollar. Howard Johnson's had become the fancy place to eat for millions of America's emerging middle class. Problem was that most of the people in my part of the Bronx had no idea what class they belonged to, so claiming middle class status was hardly a consideration-the perfect excuse Mom and Pop needed to avoid even that affordable menu.

Algida transported me beyond blue collar America, even beyond the faded hopes of strolling through the large glass doors of Howard Johnson's. But all that was suddenly so silly. There was no worrying about being able to afford the Italian delights. Nonna was a willing enabler when her tiny purse (*borsellino*) emerged like a phoenix from her apron pocket. She would carefully fish for two twenty lira pieces, placing them onto the counter. She spread those coins across the surface to make sure she parted with only two. Years later, as I looked back nostalgically on my grandmother's habits, I made sense of the practice of a southern Italian widow who never could allow herself the accidental loss of money. Whenever she spent, the coins always lined up like foot soldiers ready for roll call. Those copper and silver-colored pieces lived precariously, piled in short pyramids at the bottom of that *borsellino* until her slender fingers jostled them around, picking only those that would complete the purchase. The loose-leaf size of Italian paper money supplied all the reasons I needed to understand why she kept them folded like love letters nestled in the safety of her cleavage, and those bills got counted with licked fingers several times before handing any of them over to a vendor.

As we approached the middle of a long block with houses still humbled by the effects of bombs and bullets, I heard my aunt Gianna make a point that our new home's address would be Via Umberto I, number 62. Zio Alfonso maneuvered the Fiat through a narrow portal *(portone)*, past a rectangular courtyard, and down a steep driveway, coming to a stop in a small parking area bordered by a marble tiled patio. The parking area was enclosed by an iron fence that separated it from about an acre of land we would come to affectionately call *o'giardin (*the garden*)*. It was filled with hazelnut and walnut trees that shed their products abundantly once a year, providing an easy snack as we cracked them open with small, sharp stones. Learning to climb to the top of the many fig trees to pluck those that ripened first, closest to the sun, became a welcomed habit. We dared each other to bare-handedly pick the most scarlet-colored prickly pears; each of us shedding a comical tear or two when our amateur attempts supplied little more than wounded fingers. When we did manage to make off with several, plopping them into nonna's apron as she held it up by the corners to make like a basket, to watch her expertly peel away the booby trap skin so we could finally enjoy the blood-colored fruit deposited into the palms of our cupped hands.

    With age, the *giardin'* would become less of a playground, and more of a loyal refuge. There I would spend hours imagining who had built, and which army of invaders had ruined the town's medieval Norman castle perched on the hill overlooking our property. Those ghostly grey turrets hovering over the town, no longer capable of offering protection to its inhabitants, had me imagining scenes of knights covered in armor, slashing, and cutting through flesh and bone, beating back Saracen invaders. Covered in enemy blood, they would drag their long, heavy swords to the pinnacle, once again raising the crusader flag in victory. In our century I pictured American fighter planes suddenly appearing from beyond the distant mountains, swooping down over the castle strafing German soldiers scattering for cover in the narrow streets. The tall stone wall that separated our *giardin* from the one that belonged to the Count of Sarno, provided the imagined stage setting for a Napoleonic era noble dressed in a colorful military uniform with a sabre by his side, dismounting his war horse at the entrance to his mansion. I was helped along by images from my elementary schoolbooks, but my surroundings were ancient enough to jumpstart my fascinations. It was merely a beginning, but the history that shaped Italy would douse me so completely, exhorting me to romance life in every moment, in each encounter with people or nature, in every breath of that primeval air, absorbed in the sounds of life playing out as they had done for centuries, and ultimately in the aromas and scents that swaddled us like an early morning fog thick with droplets of a lush culture. It seemed so spastic at first, but with the passing of days, all became one endless poetic celebration of life. I understood that displays of affection with hugs, joyous, impromptu smiles, and the double kisses, were as genuine and organic as all the other simple ingredients that defined my new world. And I became a willing participant- baptized into that seductive civilization.

    Mom urged us to follow her upstairs to the first-floor apartment. The smell of fresh plaster hinted at the newness of the building; the hallway and apartment walls welcomed us with bright, cheery pastel hews. The marble floors and the beautiful, ornate furniture caused some anxiety, forcing me to suddenly accept the possibility that we were about to start living way above our means. The whole layout was borderline rich, which challenged my plebeian comfort zone. Back in the Bronx we lived in aesthetic comfort, but hardly upscale. Even new furniture in our American lives appeared unfashionable and cheap compared to what stood before me that first day. Used pieces that my father would sometimes inherit on one of his jobs, were not out of the question. On Crotona Avenue in the old neighborhood, it was never a question of shame. Shame only became an issue if you couldn't feed your family. These living room walls, in contrast, had been professionally wallpapered. The chandelier reminded me of the ones that hung in the lobby of the Loews Paradise Theater on the Grand Concourse in the Bronx. It was during our third-grade school trip to see Disney's Fantasia on the big screen that I got my only glimpse inside.

    The awe stuck around for days, as we explored our new surroundings and settled into a home that seemed more like a resort. I asked Mom about the building, and she explained that they had saved and transferred money for years to have it built. She made it clear that we were the owners, and that we would all need to chip in with maintenance. It may have been very modern, but

MERECÀ

nonna insisted that we keep a hen house in the garden. It would become a morning ritual to weave my way past the clucking and indignant inhabitants, to steal away their warm brown eggs; at times having to do battle with a particularly stubborn one who would peck at my fingers as I searched for booty.

That first day I ventured into the deep end of the garden to peer back for a complete view of the building. Each of the first and second floor apartments had full, wraparound terraces which added a certain pomp to their appearance. Getting onto the terraces meant lifting the heavy *persiana* (oversized, floor to ceiling Venetian blind made of wood) that covered the large glass doors. Once on the terrace, the entire *giardin* came into view, and in the distance a tall mountain that seemed to be missing its cone. My uncle Luigi placed his hand on my shoulder and in his raspy voice he mouthed "V*esuvio*". He gazed out into the distance and explained "*Chill'je o Vesuvio, o vulcan' che tant'ann fa' a distrutt tutt' Pompei. Poi, dop'a guerr, s'e' scetate nata vota."* I locked onto his face where each expression added another short chapter to his story, providing the props to decipher the severity of what had transpired so long ago. I was curious about our town, so I asked: "*e Sarno, non era distrutt"?* "*No"*, he answered, "*sulament' cenere. Tutt'a citta'... chien' e cenere... chiu' e nu metro alto, fin a ca'"* as he placed his hand to his chest indicating how much ash had covered the area. Mom, listening nearby, explained that Vesuvio had destroyed the city of Pompeii many years ago, and that the last time the volcano had erupted was in 1944 at the end of the war, covering Sarno in several feet of black ash. She lifted her brows, and with her eyes wide open, she gave me her folklore rendition of the event: "*Tutt'era nirr, nirr, e nun se vedev manc'o sole*". As she re-lived the episode, she added more detail: "*E nun se potevan'lava' manche i pann cu tanta cenere dinta l'aria*". To make sure I understood, she switched it up, and gave me some of it in English: "*Everything was so dirty-the houses, the streets, the cars, the faces of the people. The American soldiers told us to cover our nose and mouth with a handkerchief, and to stay inside our houses. They also told us to sweep the ash off the roof because it was hot enough to start a fire. No noise, no cars, no scooters, nobody in the streets.*

MERECÀ

You remember how quiet it was on our street in America when it snowed?" I nodded willingly, while quickly turning back the pages to the one storm I did remember when the snow blanketed every inch of life. When we were able to sled down our street for hours without interruption from any type of vehicle, and when the boys could dive for touchdown passes in the schoolyard, landing safely on a two-foot cushion of fresh flakes. Then Mom brought me back as she continued: *"The ash made everything so quiet like the snow, and for many days we only heard the sound of the American tanks and the trucks with the plows helping to clean the streets. Two of nonno's pigs died, and some of the chickens too. I had a little black cat named Fiamma (oddly enough Mom's cat was named Flame)... I thought she died, but a few days after the volcano calmed down, I found her behind the wine barrels in the cantina."* The thought of Mom finding her little cat brought a smile to my face, letting me set aside horrors I could never have imagined back in New York.

We spent the remainder of that first day finding convenient corners and out of the way spots for all the luggage, and the gargantuan trunks. As Mom pried open one of them, I spied the brown paper bag I had used to store my beloved comic books. It was still wrapped tightly with about a dozen rubber bands ... I dreaded the thought of losing even one of them, and I hoped I would never grow tired of the stories, even if it meant reading them backwards. I had seen Italian versions in the stores, so I wondered how long before I knew enough of the language to take on the local ones, leaving my American versions to finally gather some dust.

The room I would share with my brother did not quite seem like home, but it had newer and friendlier furnishings with wide, rectangular windows that framed the distant image of the now familiar volcano. It was late afternoon when my brother and I met with a torturous level of frustration attempting to find anything to watch on the T.V. ... Italian television had not improved from our first trips. The two RAI channels offered little to entice us. T.V. schedules were useless since you only choice were classic American movies mostly from the decades before the war, the famous *Carosello* and the late evening *Telegiornale*. It would become a matter of potluck as we beseeched the black screen to pitifully grace us with anything related to the antics of a Tom and Jerry cartoon or, God-forbid, some Bugs Bunny and the Looney Toons family. Despite Mom cautioning us that we were wasting our time, we would make that once daily attempt to learn if there was any hope for two American kids yearning for some home cooked television, wondering why the evil people at RAI would so deliberately torture Italian kids. The tube could do little to entertain us, so we spent much more of our time outdoors, reading or taking up new hobbies … a silver lining as it happened.

I picked up my precious cargo of comic books and headed for the day bed in the corner of the guest room. With my back to the wall, and before flipping my first page, I was caught up in a short whirlwind summary of my first experiences: how incredibly delicious my first gelato had been; the chances the volcano would erupt leaving all of Sarno once again buried in black ash; wondering if chickens laid eggs every day; anticipating the stares and gossip as we ventured beyond the *portone* and onto the streets of our new hometown; and stressed that I would soon end up sitting in an eighth grade Italian school room with all the dread associated with having to overcome the inevitable initiations.

Moments later, and a few pages into one of my favorite Archie editions, the doorbell rang. I could hear Mom greeting someone and urging him to come in. The voice hinted at someone young. They continued talking as Mom called out several times for us to gather in the kitchen. As we entered, I gazed at a skinny, meat and bone eleven-year-old with a long chin, dark hair, and jet-black eyes. Mom made the introductions: *"This is Tullio, your cousin. He is zia Gianna's son. I want you to become friends. He doesn't speak English, so you have to learn more Italian if you want to understand each other".*

I looked at my brother who rolled his eyes, ready to abandon the kitchen without speaking a word, when Mom reeled him back in, threatening him with the loss of his collection of miniature classic sports cars. Tullio had learned our names from his mother, and he couldn't wait to show it off thinking he had learned to speak some English. He looked at me and uttered a friendly

MERECÀ

"*Joahnnee?(Johnny)*". He then turned to my brother and worked a bit at trying to get it right "*Jovheee?(Joey)*". We could not hold back, so our reaction was uncontrolled laughter which irked Mom to no end but did little to dampen Tullio's spirits. As she filled three glasses with *aranciata* (orange soda), Mom had laid the foundation to what would become a powerful lifelong friendship with our unique and unforgettable cousin.

MERECÀ

MERECÀ

CHAPTER 4
TULLIO

 Tullio embodied not only the genuine affection of a curious relative, but the very Italian customs that humbled and tamed our American energies. He lived just beyond the gateway to our property in the large courtyard that housed several connected buildings of varying sizes and shapes. All had an unappreciated antique quality that made them seem just plain old and worn, with peeling plaster exposing faded, amber colored bricks, and rusted terrace railings yearning for a good paint job. His was a two-story structure, home to his parents and two siblings. Tullio was the youngest by years to his brother Alfredo, and his sister Lina. His parents owned an Italian version of our American candy store. It was oddly referred to as a *Sale e Tabacchi (Salt and Tobacco Shop)*. The term had its origin in a time when government monopolies controlled the sale and prices of popular staples like salt and tobacco. Eventually the stores could add other consumer products including impressive inventories of candies. It was a short block to the store, and my brother and I would make frequent sorties to buy up our favorite Italian sweets. Much like the ice cream, Italian confectionary also had an exotic look and taste to it. We raided nonna's borsellino with impunity, transferring those funds into our relative's cash register. Despite the kindness, business was business, so at the Sale e Tabacchi there were no freebies, except the ones that Tullio could sneak out in the pockets of his shorts.

 Our good cousin was the first to instruct us on the southern custom of *favorite* (pronounced fahvoreeteh), or the act of offering to the others the first bite of food. The morning following our first night in Sarno, Tullio showed up carrying a fresh panino concealing two thin slices of *mortadella* (Italian baloney), wrapped in brown paper. He had made his usual quick stop at Gaetano's *salumeria* (delicatessen) to pick up his breakfast sandwich. My brother Joey and I sat silently on the terrace on straw chairs dazed from our travels and the penetrating newness of our surroundings; our energies finally succumbing to the abrupt mutations, when suddenly Tullio's excited, high pitched voice echoed through the apartment:

"*Buongiorno zi' Maria! ... na bella giornata, 'riscite a verità. Zi Pepp', Buongiorno! Ve salut' mammà e papà. Stann' do' negozio. Gianni e Johwee addo' stann'-e voglio saluta'"*. He greeted aunt Maria and uncle Pepp' (short for Giuseppe), delivered salutations from his parents who were at work, and asked excitedly about me and Joey.

Gianni (short for Giovanni) was close enough to Johnny, so Tullio eventually abandoned the need for the tongue twister pronunciation settling on the easier Italian version. He insisted, however, on conquering the *Joey* thing. He would manipulate the pronunciation acting it out as if he had been an American all along-it seemed more like his rendition of whatever English he had heard in movies. He added a comical twist to it, exaggerating to the extreme, sucking us into his silly, boyish laughter. He was closer in age to my brother, and his insistence on the name had much to do with paving the way to a quicker and more sincere friendship. Tullio had inherited a deep rooted and venerable Southern Italian trait to please other human beings. He lived it every day, and practiced it with an intuitive, unrehearsed devotion.

As he slipped onto the terrace, his next *buongiorno* was loud, and as crisp as the early morning breeze that sailed in from the *giardino*. His voice washed over me like one of those playful waves at Jones Beach back home, riding it to the shore, gliding and tumbling onto the sand. I yearned for the company of a young person, and Tullio's smile and the way he insisted on me taking the first bite of his panino, raised my spirits. He stretched out his arm in my direction and invited me to eat. *Favorite, ja, mangia*! Practically, *com'on, take a bite!*

My brother found our cousin's good cheer intrusive and made every attempt early on to avoid him. In the Bronx, friendships were acted out in schoolyards, on sidewalks, or in classrooms. The insides of our homes were usually off limits, and the most we could do was to imagine what they looked like. Joey was having a more difficult time assimilating to all the niceness. Admittedly, we had been accustomed to less intimate interactions with the kids on our block. It was easier to share our interests in a common street culture than it was to create more intimate acquaintances. There was a superficiality and a certain coldness to the lives we shared with neighbors, despite the abundance of time spent in each other's company. We were all friends in a world that recognized clear boundaries and space. Tullio was about to shatter all that, forcing us to learn to live in a more common space with others, and where barriers were easily swept aside by the power of human compassion and altruism; by hugs, kisses, and inviting smiles. While my brother ignored Tullio, I couldn't get enough of his inquisitiveness. He laid down a string of questions about America and being American. He wanted to know what it was like living in a great city like New York, having little understanding of the microcosm existence in a place like the Bronx. He asked about *"beisbol"*, and the unusual practice of hitting a ball with a long piece of wood, giggling at the thought of players turning those bats on each other in the event of a dispute. *"Ma quann'non vann' d'accord'… se pigliano a mazzatt'?* By contrast, he made the point that in soccer the most damage any player could inflict on another was to kick him. He then asked about the *"guantoni"*, the large gloves that players used. We had packed away our little league equipment, so I excused myself to rummage through one of the trunks finding a glove and one of the balls. His reaction was a predictable awe at the bloated size as he comically attempted to slide my glove onto his right hand. The glove dangled like a lifeless puppet at each attempt to make it fit. And, as the task became a lost cause, he broke down and gave up, weakened by his own laughter. I willingly joined in, while my brother finally softened to reveal a slight grin with a few short chuckles escaping through his buckled lips. That was the episode that broke the ice for all three of us, and we became one. Tullio had earned himself all the reasons he needed to boast about his American cousins, and to confidently stroll through those gates inviting himself into our lives.

MERECÀ

      We would eventually be sitting in an Italian classroom, but those last few weeks of summer had Tullio instructing us on the nature of life in Sarno. My brother and I expected to find an Italian version of street life, but on that first trek outside the gates, our good cousin made it clear there would be no Italian -*Bronx*- life. There were no schoolyards, no candy stores with red stools, black and white tiles, and egg creams; no cops standing on corners twirling a baton, and no American sports. There were, however, things that intrigued us like those 11th century ruins of a Norman castle perched at the top of a craggy ridge overlooking the town, rumored to have a treasure of sorts buried beneath it, the huge cul de sac nets dangling from a single hook in front of the Sale e Tabacchi holding about a dozen soccer balls-a huge temptation for any Italian kid, and Tullio's introduction to a sweet snack as we ventured up the narrow path cutting into the stunted, balding hill behind our building. That afternoon we accepted his invitation to the short hike. Halfway to the summit, we paused to look down on our new neighborhood, when Tullio walked over to a tree with what appeared to be very dark, shiny ribbons about the length of the pretzel rods we bought for a penny at Rocky's, dangling from its branches, swaying to the will of a soft breeze. He plucked one cleanly, approached us and invited us to take a bite. The unappetizing burnt complexion and the three equally spaced camel humps protruding from under the leathery skin, caused some deep suspicions. We pulled away from the oddity that, upon closer observation, looked more like a flattened cigar with a polished shine to it. Our reactions gave us a second dose of that throated laughter that would become our cousin's calling card, and with that he took his first bite. We watched, ready to run for help or to drag his lifeless body back down the trail. As he chewed, he sucked the juices out of the vegetation and, enjoying it, he reached for a few more extending a handful in our direction. With his second and third bites we noticed he was still standing and breathing, and with what had already become his signature smile, he urged us to give them a try.

-*Dai, provate, queste, se chiammano sciuscelle ... sono dolce comm'o mel' e non costano manc' na lira!* He insisted that we give

MERECÀ

it a try, and that they were as sweet as honey without costing a lira. He called them "sciuscelle" (best pronounced *shooshealeh*). I found that word so playful, learning that it was also used to describe girls that had a certain sweet character.
I finally gave in and cautiously ripped a small piece of the bizarre crop into my mouth. The texture was hard and toasty on the outside with a soft nougat feel on the inside, like the inside of a Three Musketeers bar. Within seconds I had a mouth full of honey infused saliva, and it went down as easy as the juices of a Bazooka bubblegum. I had missed the short lesson on spitting out the hard matter after all the juices were gone, so I kept chewing guessing at when it would be fine to swallow it all. Then Tullio finally implored me to spit and not swallow. *Sputa, sputa, Gianni!*
I let the goo drip out of my mouth, only spitting the last pieces stuck to my lips at the very end of the strange trauma. *Queste le danno a mangiare ai cavalli. Ma i cavalli non sputano.* I understood the word *horses (cavalli),* and with my brother's help, we figured out that the food was also fed to horses, and that they had no need to spit it out since to them it was a complete meal. Later that day Mom would explain how horses love sweets, and that the *sciuscelle* were a favorite used mostly to reward the animal's labors.

    As we made our way back, the three of us laughed it off as Tullio poked fun of our "NewYorkness" sensing how alien his version of life was to us. He readily expressed his amazement that there were things the *Americani* knew nothing about. Tullio's mythical America had always been of a place and people with no limits on wealth, knowledge, and power. America's foreign policies projected decisively in Italy's post-war life, with all the propaganda that guided the country's fledgling republic, with promises of stable governments and healthy economies. Tullio's generation had been mostly indoctrinated with American music, blue jeans, Hollywood Westerns, images of larger-than-life cars with rocket ship fins, and skyscrapers that rose to the heights of passing planes. My cousin's America was a land of heroes and complete possibilities; if you could think it or imagine it, Americans could make it happen. Hardly a surprise then, that he

MERECÀ

viewed us in the same way ... anything less than super-human abilities would have made us all too common, and Tullio needed us to constantly feed the myth.

My brother and I were mostly comfortable with the label, and often we did not disappoint. When it came to sports, the super Americans ran faster, jumped higher, dribbled circles around the local kids with a basketball, and even learned to play soccer as well as those who had been kicking since they were babies.

The Bronx gave us schoolyards with concrete baseball diamonds and basketball courts. The opportunities to play, but to also develop skills, had become a part of growing up. If you gave us a basketball court, we would become good at it. If you gave us baseball diamond, we would master that game; if you built a pool, we would bring home Olympic Gold. We had Little Leagues and volunteer adults providing the organization that allowed us to practice and perfect those skills almost daily as the sporting seasons shifted from baseball to football to basketball, to stickball with the cycle repeating itself yearly. Sarno had none of these. A dirt field was the best the kids could manage, dodging rocks, small boulders, wilted shrubs, and the occasional *Aperelle* that used it as a parking lot. Some were seriously off limits with huge posters warning of unexploded World War II bombs and other ordinances all pictured on large, colorful posters made to attract the attention of children. To us they seemed more like movie posters announcing the next feature at the RKO cinema. Only when we learned of a seven-year-old who had lost his life running through one of those fields, did we start taking them seriously. Tullio, like many of our new Sarnese friends, had limited athletic ability, but his competitive nature would have him engage combatively in any game. When he found it difficult to keep up, he would always blame the superman factor: *E sì, se capisce… mo me mett'a giocà comm'o merecà… a cap nun v'aiutt. Gianni ten e cosce e nu gigante e cert'i piere lungh comm' na paranz'e pane!*

Often, he gave up, admitting that he could not play like an American, claiming I had the legs of a giant and feet the size of bread loaves. We did wear our Keds and Converses, and when matched up against the locals with thin, flea market canvas shoes, ours looked abnormally huge. We did not disappoint with academics as well. Our stern Catholic school upbringing with stiff classroom lessons and corporal punishment made memorizing multiplication tables, writing impeccably neat compositions with accurate punctuation, and completing nightly homework assignments a must. Failure to do so unleashed the wrath of Brother's paddle or Sister's sadistic yanking on your ear. Those lessons had been rough, but when it came to performance in an Italian classroom, even the *professori* were amazed at how advanced we were in the basics. One even commenting that it was no wonder America was such a great country. I did not quite understand the connection between good grades and a great country. When it came to the arts and literature, I found myself a complete illiterate. Ancient Greek and Roman texts, Renaissance literature, and Mythology would never have been part of the curriculum at Mount Carmel Elementary.

    Tullio provided his best lessons on walking the streets of a town with few sidewalks, following his lead on how to get the vehicles to respect your space. Sarno had one traffic light, used mostly on special occasions and emergencies-and one was not entirely sure when to obey it since there was little consistency … it was mostly ignored by all, including the police.

As we moved about the town on foot, our good cousin taught us the discrete act of peering into a car crawling along in traffic to catch an erection inducing glimpse of a female driver's exposed legs. We may have been on the verge of that adolescent hormonal time bomb exploding, but Tullio had conspired to rush that process a bit. In an era of miniscule, low to the ground cars, and miniskirts, he kept a keen eye, insisting on not looking away because with every gear shift, the chances of eyeing a little bit of panty would have been a bonus. *Nun te gira', guarda che quann' canj'e marce, se po' vede' pur'e mutantine. Guardate, chest' tene e mutantine rosa! Maronn'non ngia faccia, mo me ven' na cosa!* He urged us to keep looking, pointing to an unsuspecting female exposing more and more leg, even her pink panties with every gear shift. Scenes like those had him declaring it was too much to take, adding stage-quality Neapolitan dramatic effect when the color of undergarments came into view. The poetic carnal pang of being too young, was believable, since, with practice, Tullio had mastered the art of stealing away short, erotic episodes so very dear to a pubescent womanizer.

Our American sense of the opposite sex was stuck in making out and copping a feel. The barriers that separated us from older women were being shattered by a more continental standard-one influenced by troubadours and Renaissance lovers. In the Bronx, adult females were either mothers, nuns, close relatives, or candy store clerks; it hardly dawned on us to attach any sexual sentimentality to them. Young Italian males had none of those inhibitors, and their attitudes seemed universal. I came to notice, beyond the first months, that the less than discreet act of locking onto those exposed female legs was being practiced by boys opportunistically at every intersection. Some even crossed in front of cars to slow them down, often to grant themselves more audience time. It inevitably became infectious when my brother and I understood it was a chance to liberate a curiosity we always harbored. I expected the usual moral backlash, but it never came; the coming-of-age antics were gracefully tolerated by Italian women. Females had successfully imposed limits on male behavior. Tullio knew he could sneak that peak, but that is where it ended. It was also true of older men. The occasional stray cat that took it too far was rare, the transgression shunned by women and men alike. It was common for Tullio to scold a friend for infractions that placed a female in an uncomfortable position. *Macche' fai? Che scem'! Cretino, n'hai visto che chell' si offende?* He would mouth off about how her body language should have been enough of a rejection to get him to stop. I was sensitized to the way males checked each other's behavior to protect the delicate romanticism that bonded the sexes. Male courtship of the female was still a powerful norm with the understanding that it had to end if the female showed no interest.

Respect for others extended to all age groups in its own unique way. We knew that the words *zio* and *zia* meant uncle and aunt. When we noticed our cousin using the titles for the elderly around town, I marveled at how many relatives we had. I expressed the curiosity, so Tullio had to set me straight by pointing out that it was common to refer to the elderly, relative or not, as zio and zia. He taught that the habit would pass from generation to generation to instill from the youngest age an awareness of the value of older members of the community. This was a radical departure from the marginalized elderly in our Bronx world. Except for close relatives, the old were treated suspiciously, and if poor, even demonized like the witches and goblins of Halloween. Southern Italians had no illusions of the role played by parents and grandparents in the lives of offspring. The bond was powerful, and it extended naturally to an entire population. I found it appealing since it was invited behavior, and it brought a smile and a willing reaction from the recipient. There was a simple, harmonious, and comfortable feeling in creating that bridge between generations.

    Tullio would remain our early instructor of gentile manners. We followed his lead, and before long, we became acculturated in many things Italian. The process that would take the better part of our first year in Sarno, diverted our upbringing onto a path that might have been otherwise predestined had our parents never left for the allure of America.

MERECÀ

MERECÀ

CHAPTER 5
SCUOLA MEDIA STATALE GUIDO BACCELLI

In early October I was informed that I would spend two Saturdays per month at the American School in Naples to keep my English fresh, then Mom walked me down to the public middle school Guido Baccelli to enroll my sad face into the eighth grade (*terza media-literally third year middle school*). I said nothing, but with a heavy anxiety and a fatalistic flutter in my chest, I wondered how in the world was I to walk into an Italian school, weave my way around desks filled with inquisitive and critical tweens who spoke a different language and followed a completely different set of social norms, and make like everything is simply fine. For Mom it was the least of her concerns, and I was hardly sure my agony made her list. The bad stuff flash cards shuffled through my mind like the scenes of a sweat inducing horror flick. I anticipated being made fun of for: not speaking Italian correctly; for not being cool; for not wearing the right clothes; for keeping my mouth shut, afraid to speak; and for the killer stares from the girls turning me into some laughable work of abstract foreign art. I had lived safely on the other side of that formula back at Our Lady of Mount Carmel, recalling how the newly arrived Italian immigrants caught the raw end of the deal when it came time for them to assimilate. The tougher Bronx kids were brutal, unforgiving, and consistent; hardly allowing a day to pass without torturing some poor off the boat soul. Bullying was a way of life in Little Italy. You took it and lived with it it. If you could land one good punch somewhere on your tormentor's face, you had the best chance of being left alone. Getting him to spill a little blood from the mouth or nose was usually enough to move you up a notch into "leave him alone/don't mess with him" territory. If you had it in you to keep punching out one face after another, you had what it took to become the bully.

As we approached the building still riddled with bullet holes from the war, I looked up at the faded sign. Mom looked my way and translated: Public Middle School Guido Baccelli. Our Catholic schools were named after the saints, Jesus, Joseph, and Mary. Our public schools were usually named after dead presidents. Although the name sounded comical to me, I figured Guido Baccelli must have been someone important enough to have a school named after him. The quick connect back to America was hardly enough to console the heavy anxiety. I slipped into the main office hoping I had somehow become invisible, gloomily knowing that I could not even hide behind my mother's frame, since I had grown to match her height. After some paperwork had been hastily completed, and a hard look given to my passport, American school records, and birth certificate by the school principal (*preside*), a nod of the head and a handshake sealed my fate.

    The *preside* greeted me with a smile and a long, curious probe into my eyes ... I thought perhaps he was wondering how long I would last before wanting out, into some private school. *"Allora, Giovanni, benvenuto alla nostra scuola. Qui c'è Mimmo che ti accompagna alla tua classe"*. Mom's betrayal was complete: I was being handing off to some teacher's pet named Mimmo chosen to show me the way to my classroom. I panicked and started drooling in an angry whisper. *"Mom, you didn't say anything about staying here today, I didn't even know school had started. I can't stay, take me home!"*. She tried putting a cute spin on it, motioning with her eyes to calm down or else! *"Why you no want to stay. Look, all these people, they happy to have a boy from America in the school. Make friends with Mimmo ... go"*. I loved Mom's fragmented English, but I wasn't buying the message, so I repeated the same line, just a bit more forcefully. Mom had no idea of the calamity that befell the dead kid walking, condemned to take those heavy strides into a classroom full of unfamiliar faces, staring you down, engaging in bloated gossip hovering above the room like vultures over roadkill. It would have been explosive for a local kid, I imagined it was about to be an atomic blast for me. The desperation took me back to my fourth-grade class when Sister Mary Immaculata introduced a new kid. *"Boys and girls, this is Salvatore who has just arrived from a small town in Calabria, Italy. If you recall our geography lesson, Calabria is the toe of*

Italy". Frankie Fusco, who sat behind me, leaned over, and whispered what he had learned from his grandfather about Calabria. *"My gramps always says that Calabria is the shithole of Italy, and this kid looks like a shithole. Look at those pants, they hardly reach his ankles, and I think he has something dead attached to the bottom of his shoe. This kid doesn't have a chance around here"*. It did not take long for the girls to start their usual chainsaw buzz, judging everything they considered ugly or weird about the immigrant. Not understanding the language was a big plus for the new kids, since the Bronx girls' chatter could dry up anyone's last drop of dignity. I lacked the insight or the fortitude to shelter or ease their pain, instead wandering off into a momentary daze thinking how lucky it wasn't me.

As I came out of it, I was reminded again at my mother's insistence, that I was soon to become *that* kid. *"You have no choice; you have to go to class. You already missed two weeks. I will come back to pick you up"*. Then the unbelievable happened: she left. I felt a sudden weakness in my legs, wanting to crumble into a million pieces like the Turkish Taffy bars we slammed against the red brick schoolyard walls. All the instructions, the directives and the discussions going off around me like little Italian firecrackers increased my bewilderment. I understood only a handful of words trying to figure out why this Italian sounded different from the one my relatives had been speaking. Around town the Neapolitan dialect dominated all forms of speech, while inside government buildings, particularly in schools, only official Italian was allowed. The formal Italian did seem rigid, but crisp; and as I paid closer attention, I was able to understand more of what was being said. With my head drooping in despair, and my chin cradled in my chest, Mimmo compassionately placed his hand on my shoulder urging me to follow him to be introduced to the students in my class, while attempting to pacify my fears of receiving too much attention. *"Dai, non avere paura, adesso ti faccio incontrare I ragzzi della nostra classe"*. I eased into his kind manner, thinking perhaps this would not hurt so much. At the end of a long corridor, we stood at the threshold of a classroom with about a dozen students, seven two-person desks, and a

MERECÀ

gloriously courageous blackboard that had refused to die a noble death, proudly displaying deep, powdery battle scars and war wounds. As Mimmo walked over to the teacher with a quick explanation, I looked away ignoring my audience falling into a short trance imagining German soldiers holed up in that room, hunted down by American and British troops during the war. My John Wayne mind saw bullets ricocheting off that blackboard, slate shrapnel flying around ready to cut into some poor guy's flesh, and Nazi soldiers blown to pieces by a hand grenade. The history book version of war had me in conflict with the Hollywood counterpart, but the adolescent American patriot in me made it easy to believe the movies. Then I understood that I was suddenly living in a place where it had been so very real; a place where the damage was still evident on the facades of the buildings and on the faces of those who had witnessed it. As I learned more about those harsh war days, I would come to lose my infatuation with the movie versions.

It had only taken seconds for me to wander off into that imagery when Mimmo kindly asked the *professore* if he would permit him to introduce me. Back in the Bronx our teachers took titles like Brother, Sister, Father, Mr., Mrs. And Miss. Every teacher at the Scuola Baccelli was referred to *as professore* for males or *professoressa* for females. It all had me feeling like some college kid, so it took a little getting used to. Mimmo then asked to verify my last name. *"Allora, il tuo cognome è Dolgetta"*? He understood my hesitation, so he came back to me with the same question in English. *"Your name is Dolgetta, correct"?* It was a pleasant "wow" moment that had me reward him with a smile and a quick "yes", eventually learning that Italian kids started foreign languages instruction in the sixth grade. As I stood at attention, avoiding eye contact with the other students became impossible, as I gauged their reactions to Mimmo's monologue.

"Vi presento Giovanni Dolgetta, nuovo studente appena arrivato dall'America". Mimmo had been briefed by the *preside* about me, my background and why were now living in Sarno. *"Se mi permetti, vorrei chiamarti Gianni"*. As he faced me, he repeated the question in English. *"Please your permission to name you Gianni"*. I granted him that same smile. Gianni sounded exactly

like Johnny, and it softened me up enough to add a few extra words. *"Yes, in New York my friends called me Johnny".* The quick burst in English gave me instant celebrity status with giggling girls and males urging me to keep speaking. Mimmo explained it all when he asked me to say something else in English. *"Okay, well, I really didn't want to come to school today, but my mother forced me to stay".* My translator turned to the class and explained my dilemma. The girls felt my pain, while the boys brushed it off as just another annoying thing expected of mothers. They wanted to know more, so Mimmo obliged. *"Gianni naque nel Bronx, contea della città di New York. Genitori sono Sarnesi emigrati in America nel dopoguerra. Sono tornati a vivere qui a Sarno per ragioni personali".* He explained my Bronx origins, and my parents' immigrant background, and that personal reasons had caused us to return to Sarno.

One of the girls, Stella, insisted on knowing what would motivate us to leave a place like New York for Sarno, which she unapologetically referred to as a -purgatory-. *"Ciao Gianni, mi chiamo Stella. Perdonami la curiosità, ma come mai lasciare una grande città come Nuova York per questo purgatorio"*? I understood the general meaning of her question, but I still looked to Mimmo for reassurance. He laughed at her "purgatory" remark, agreeing with her assessment. *"Si, hai ragione Stella; né inferno, né paradiso, proprio un purgatorio, aspettando I miracoli".* At Mount Carmel, lessons on heaven, hell and purgatory were powerful and most of my generation believed them to be real places. So, according to Mimmo, Sarno was neither heaven nor hell, but, agreeing with Stella, a very real purgatory with all of them waiting for miracles. I smirked, unable to disagree.

Mimmo came back to me asking if I still wanted to answer. I nodded, smiled, and took a deep breath. *"My grandmother, my father's mother, is not well. Her husband died when my dad was only a year old. My father is the only one my grandmother has, so we came back to take care of her, and so we left New York to live in Sarno".* After Mimmo's brave translation, Stella's expression turned apologetic, asking how that decision had affected me. *"E tu, come te la sei presa sapendo che devi ora vivere in questa piccola città? Non assomiglia affatto al tuo Bronx"*. She made the point that there was no comparing the two places, and that the change must have had some effect on me. *"Yes, I do already miss my street in the Bronx, I miss my friends, I miss the Yankees, I miss my girlfriend Debbie, but I don't miss my school."* The Yankees did not surprise Mimmo and a few of the other boys. The team logo had become a symbol of things American. One of the other boys, Antonio, had a small collection of Yankee paraphernalia he received as gifts from relatives living in New Jersey. What caught their attention in the translation was the name Debbie. Stella could not get enough of the American kid's story. *"Ma tu hai una ragazza in America? Hai detto 'girlfree-end' significa fidanzata, vero? Mimmo, come l'ha chiamata"?* Puzzled, Mimmo turned to me to ask about Debbie, since Stella was curious about the name and recognizing the word-girlfriend-. Soon she had the information she was looking for. *"Si, Gianni mi dice che lui ha una ragazza nel Bronx che si chiama Debbi…"*. The other girls began to show an interest in the girlfriend thing, and so their soft chatter once again dominated the space in the small, but cavernous room. Despite Mimmo revealing all he learned about Debbie, Stella remained inquisitive, thinking the name to be strange. *"Mi sembra un nome strano … ma proprio Debbi"?* Finally, the professor, who had allowed the interactions to work themselves out unhindered, came up with his best explanation. *"Stella, il nome Debbi sarà forse un soprannome o una forma corta del nome Deborah … mi ricordo di averlo sentito in un film Americano".* I paid close attention to his connection between Debbie and Deborah, and it worked for me since that was her real name. Satisfied with that explanation, Stella finally backed down.

  The *professore* thanked me for the autobiography and asked me to fill the empty seat next to a very dark skinned, bushy haired, skin and bone male with an attentive eye, and a whimsical smile. He made sure I had plenty of room as he nudged a bit to his side, fixating on all of me. My instinct was to sit quietly, look up at the front of the room, and pay attention to the teacher. Any deviation from that behavior in my American grammar school days would have invited a rough reprimand, with the possible

MERECÀ

punishment of having to que up in the hallway outside Brother George's room after school with other outlaw males to receive the mandatory paddle bruising. Brother's favorite number was seven, and it was his habit of counting them out quickly, sentencing the hapless souls to feel the pain, with little time for the butt to mitigate the sting of the previous shot.

My desk mate, however, had no intention of sitting quietly, peppering me with a chorus of questions in the local dialect. *"Ma o'ver' sei americano? E secondo me, sei pur assai intelligent, e tinite assai dollari. E quann' stiv'a merica, tiniv' pur na casa grande cu'na Cadillaca"?*

Mimmo leaned over from his spot to make the point that Raffaele's questions were all silly, and that I should ignore him. I refused to brush aside his friendly approach, insisting on Mimmo's help to decipher. I learned of Raffaele's refusal to believe that he was sitting next to a real American, of his conviction that I must be intelligent, that we were rich with dollars, and that we once owned a huge house and the iconic Cadillac. I was only then beginning to understand the stereotype, but I had no plan to counter it. The advertised model to the Italians was the clean-cut, all-American one that stood to convince them that the blueprint could work the same magic in their country. Many Southern Italians had no idea who their president was, but a portrait of John F. Kennedy adorned many living room walls side by side with that of the Pope.

I couldn't have explained the complicated American class system with the hope of debunking their notion that we represented the rich images of American life that spilled across television screens and in Hollywood movies, until I could say it clearly in Italian. I had lived my young life with the conviction that we existed on the edge of poverty. I had also seen the rich neighborhoods we sometimes drove through when my parents started living the American dream; it didn't escape me, even at that tender age, that there were people with a lot of money, the kind of money difficult to fathom. I wanted to tell them the truth, but it had to wait.

  Suddenly, the *professore* announced that it was time for *merenda (recess snack)*, reminding the class they had twenty minutes, then exiting to take his own break. I thought it odd since

MERECÀ

there was no way that the sisters back at Mount Carmel would ever leave us alone even for a minute. I did not need a translation when I noticed each of the students pull paper bags from their desks, unpacking a host of different snacks. Mom had failed to give me anything: no snack, no notebook, no pen. I sat there feeling so naked, I hardly knew what to do with my hands. Then it happened, the first time I heard the word that would define who I suddenly had become and would be for the remainder of my days in Sarno. Raffaele laid out a small handkerchief on his side of the desk and lined up a pear, two walnuts and a piece of stale bread neatly side by side. He pulled out a small pocketknife and sliced the pear into quarters. He grabbed the two walnuts and squeezed them together in the palm of his left hand with overlapping pressure applied by his right hand. The nuts cracked as planned and he surgically picked out the pieces of meat, cleaned off the skin, and returned them to the cloth. The shells ended up in his jacket pocket to be discarded later. The bread was sliced down the middle in halves. Once the ritual was complete, he looked up at me and delivered his invitation: *"Dai merecà, favorite",* as he motioned with his hands to share his meal. My hesitation did little to discourage him. *"Merecà, mangia, che tenimm nat' doi ore è scuola, mietette na cosarela ndo' stomaco, tien na faccia accusi' stanca!".*
Anticipating my look, Mimmo assured me it was the right thing to do. *"Gianni, he want you to eat the food. Please, good for you. He say you look ... stanco ... aspetta come si dice in inglese?".* Not sure of the correct word, he pulled out his English language textbook and looked up the translation. *"Si, allora, you have tired face."* I tried to remain cordial, but the problem was that I did not consider it good food. Pears with bread and walnuts were not my idea of a decent snack. I was used to the nuns selling pretzels, chocolate cookies and bags of chips during snack time to those who had the money, since we were not allowed to bring our own snacks. I asked Mimmo the meaning of *"merecà"*, to which he explained that it was the local way of saying *Americano*.
The only decent thing to do at that point was to reward his kindness by trying his food. He then showed me how to do it right by placing a walnut on top of the pear, popped them together into

MERECÀ

his mouth, followed quickly by a brawny bite of the very organic, brownish colored bread that had shriveled with age, turning the process into a challenge for teeth and jaw. Slowly, I followed his lead. By now the entire class had turned our interactions into a show worthy of a fan club. As I chewed cautiously, I came to understand how that weird trio could turn into a revelation of appealing tastes. The juiciness of the pear blended piously with the dry bread and walnuts, producing a nutty sweetness that turned on taste buds I didn't know I had. The bread was added for bulk, a way of killing the hunger. The grainy taste added even more flavor. It all went down with an abundance of satisfaction. I remained stunned as a smile lit up my face, while the others came with samples and offerings of their own food, begging me to *"favorite"(pronounced fahvohreeteh).* The word was a standard, and it carried the common invitation to partake of another's food.

By the end of the day, they had all picked up on my new nickname, and within minutes I had heard it dozens of times: *merecà*. Mimmo supplied a more detailed explanation. He wrote the word Americano on his pad, then he crossed out the *"A"* and the *"no"* at the end of the word. What was left *"merica"*, was close enough to come to terms with Raffaele's invention. In the Sarnese pronunciation, the "i" became a soft "e", and the ending had an accented sound. So, *merecà* was born, and that's the way it stayed and spread. Before long, the entire school, friends and extended friends turned it into my nickname. Gianni would still be an option. Sometimes, to be more exact on the question of my identity, kids could be heard saying: *"Gianni, o'merecà"*, or Gianni, the American. Whatever my titles, all the students in that classroom, that first day, showered me with a natural benevolence and compassion unknown in the Bronx. What humbled me the most was the universal character of that affection-it came from all of them. They all offered their food, their help, their guidance with no expectation on my part. I did little or nothing to create that feeling in them ... it had always been there.

Class was dismissed at 1:30 p.m., and Mom was out in the courtyard anticipating an encounter with an irate child. I had lost my antipathy for her actions by that time, and since I knew the way home, Mom allowed me to take the trek on my own. Mimmo, and the rest, however, would have none of it, offering to walk me the entire distance. It may have been part concern, and part curiosity about my destination, but it all offered an added stage to the developing friendships, along with an inviting relief that there would be little hardship in my assimilation. We had become a small parade on the path home attracting the attention of the few street vendors still packing up their produce. The outdoor market shut itself down for the afternoon as the Mediterranean world set off to enjoy their midday meal (*pranzo*). Their oversized early afternoon version of lunch was difficult to handle at first, but then it began to make sense to have more food to burn off earlier in the day, as my father explained it. It may have also been the reason why so many of the Sarnesi were skin, meat and bones. Being overweight was rare. The only group to suffer an occasional, playful insult were those who had a few extra pounds on them. Most insults, however, were followed by quick apologies and sometimes a strong hug and a face caress. The guilt in having wronged someone was another of the social covenants I invitingly allowed to grow on me, yearning to be a participant. The lessons on the interplay of human feelings were as old as the volcanic dust that covered the area. And like the abundance of produce born of that rich soil, there was an equal amount of irrevocable goodness in the tribal kinships; and it became infectious.

    The noise we made on the way home caught the attention of persons still about the streets in the early afternoon. I said little, attempting to pick up on the lingo and the body language, hoping to shorten the time it would take to fit in. Halfway home, Stella locked arms with me, intent on monopolizing my attention. "*Ma tu adesso devi dimenticare quella Debbi, perché ormai sta troppo lontano, e se tu resti qui per sempre, non la vedrai mai più. Allora, devi avere una ragazza qui a Sarno*". With a level of bravado uncommon for most girls, she advised to forget about Debbie because she was too far away, and that if my destiny was to remain in Sarno, then I needed to find a local girl. By this time, I had been friended by another student named Carminuccio (a diminutive of Carmine, pronounced *carmeenewcho*), who provided some wisdom of his own, hinting that if I still cared for my American girl, then I should ignore Stella since she was trying to replace Debbie. "*Merecà, se tu la vuoi bene a questa Debbi, non dai retta a Stella, perché quella vuole essere la tua ragazza*". Stella became instantly enraged, and forgetting her Italian, she mouthed off a blistering condemnation in dialect, even cutting short his name. "*Carminù, ma tu si scem? Comm'te permitt' e dice ste fesserie"? Ma si proprio nu cretino! Chi o'vo o'merecà, chenn'o faccio"?* Mimmo could not take it, and along with Francuccio (diminutive for Franco), cracked up laughing at Stella's castigation. I asked for an explanation, and Mimmo gave a dignified translation that she had no intentions of becoming my girlfriend ... he then added apologetically that she had "no need" for me, explaining that she used the harsh response to protect her dignity. I was learning that, despite the influx of American liberalism, women in Italy were still heavily influenced by traditional norms and exposing one's attraction to men held the potential to be labeled, no matter the age.

We all kept pace along Via Umberto I until we reached the gates to our property. The girls tailed off a bit, cautious of the reaction they would get from my parents. The boys itched at the prospect of discovering how an American lifestyle would play out in the town light years from the streets of New York, so they tumbled down the driveway and onto the landing. The sudden, awkward silence was followed by a string of rapid questions, with each one waiting his turn. Mimmo's translations gave most of them a common theme: was the entire building ours? Carminuccio had to ask the question twice in disbelief. "*Merecà, ma il palazzo è tutto vostro? Non solo un apartamento, ma tutto il palazzo"?* As the meaning became clear, I asked Mimmo to confirm that indeed the entire building was ours, not just an apartment.
That revelation spawned a reaction I wasn't ready to handle, given my blue-collar Bronx upbringing. It drew some of the kids away, leery of the apparent class distinction. The building created an instant gap that appeared to undo the smooth and easy track things had taken. I had suddenly become the "rich kid" from the opposite side of the proverbial tracks. They had little exposure for the American middle class ideal, and the conviction that working hard

and saving enough income would create assets. My parents had locked into that formula back in the states, and the abundance of work and profit, along with very frugal routines, delivered on the dream of home ownership. Granted, the building was a bit more than even they had expected, but investments in Sarno allowed for it. Dollars bought millions of Italian *lire,* and millions of *lire* had much buying power in what had become a developing country.

      Whenever it came to the end of a stretch when things that had started out well suddenly turned sour, Mom always found a way to inject one of her collection of antidotes to make it all good again. While some of my new friends lounged along the concrete trestle that lined the driveway, and those that had felt a tinge of discomfort pulling back into the courtyard, Mom made her entrance in her simple dress and an apron that announced she was one of them. No fancy clothes, no pearl necklace, no diamond earrings, and no makeup. She engaged instantly, killing the stereotype, and speaking her native dialect. *"E vuie site tutt'studient da stessa classe? Ma site tutt' bell! E tu comm'te chiamm'"?* Mimmo was the tallest and a bit rotund, so he easily became her first target asking his name, after learning they were all in my class, and claiming they were all so beautiful. *"Mimmo, cche bello nomm'! Allora o nomm' tuo è verament' Domenico"?* She exposed his birth name (Mimmo being the nickname for Domenico). She paused for a few seconds granting him a little more attention than the rest by connecting his name to that of her deceased father. *"Sai, Domenico era o'nomm di mio papà ... e se vede che sei proprio speciale."*. Mimmo shared my grandfather's name which made him instantly special, and as the months passed, he would become a regular at Via Umberto I where he freely practiced his English.

Mom's approach was reassuring enough to have the others rejoin us. The atmosphere became further relaxed when they were served fruit and pastries. Pop joined us and came to find out that we were related to one of the girls, Carmela. She shared the same maiden name as his mother-*Marchese.* Her grandfather (nonno) and my grandmother (nonna) were cousins. When my sister and brother joined us to complete the family portrait, it added more familiarity,

MERECÀ

bringing us back down to their earth. I yearned to be just one of the many, feeling a strong discomfort in being thought of as richer or better. While conversations flowed, and my classmates made numerous friendly gestures towards my entire family, Carminuccio slipped his arm into mine, and invited me to take a walk with him into our garden (*o'giardin*). Mimmo couldn't help himself, following close behind. Carminuccio had taken a sentimental liking to the American family, and he needed to express it.

"*Gianni, sai che durante la guerra* (he extended his arms and turning his fingers into the image of a gun, he made the *boom, boom* sounds to have me understand he was talking about the war), *mio padre, appena diciassette anni, divenne prigioniero e trasportato in Germania dopo l'armistizio con gli alleati. I Tedeschi presero molti soldati e giovani maschi italiani qui, mandandoli in campi di concentramento. Dopo due anni, papà era quasi morto. Poi arrivarono gli Americani nel 1945. Il soldato americano a liberare mio padre era di origine italiana. Si chiamava Pietro Santino di Filadelfia e parlava anche italiano. Fu lui a dare papà da mangiare e panni puliti da indossare. Alla fine della guerra, Pietro aiutò papà a ritornare in Italia. I genitori di Pietro erano di origine Napoletana, di Castellammare. Oggigiorno, si scrivono ancora e l'anno scorso Pietro venne a trovarci proprio qui a Sarno ... se avessi visto come piangevano tutti e due, proprio come bambini.*

I understood it was about his father, it involved an American soldier named Santino, somewhere in Germany, and the prisoner of war talk-crossing his wrists and placing them behind his back each time it came up. Mimmo filled in the blanks with an emotional story about Carminuccio's father who had been taken prisoner by the Germans as a seventeen-year-old after Italy surrendered to the Allies, and of how he had been liberated by a G.I. named Peter Santino from Philadelphia. Peter spoke Italian, fed Carminuccio's father, gave him clean clothes, befriending him completely. They stayed in touch and Peter even made a visit to Sarno the previous year to re-connect. Once again, the war came alive on the faces of those who had lived it in some way. It would be one of so many stories to settle in my heart during my time in

Sarno, and they finally shattered the one-sided Hollywood heroism that filled the huge screen at the Bronx Savoy Cinema on Saturday afternoons. We walked out of the double features play acting the exploits of John Wayne and Henry Fonda in uniform, even jumping on a hand grenade to save a platoon of soldiers. Carminuccio fell silent as his eyes fixed on mine looking for a reaction. I placed my hand on his shoulder giving it a slight nudge followed by a reassuring pat that I wanted to share his truth. There existed a vague air that America and Americans were unconcerned with the rest of the world, that the ocean parting the old continent from the new was too extensive to be bridged philosophically, and that Americans owed sympathy to no one. I was learning that Italians extended much affection towards others, but that they needed the reassurance that all that love was acknowledged. Reciprocity had no importance; there was no expectation of pay back. As Mimmo would eventually explain it, respect for each other wasn't enough; that the only way to add value to respect was to endow it with love. The Sarnesi were no different from the rest of a country that implored its citizens to live a sincere *amore* for each other. An Italian's universe found alignment and harmony only if guided first by a benevolent humanism. As the months passed, the variables that defined one family from another melted away and thinking of Sarno as one large family, seemed so natural.

    We made our way back to where the others continued to lounge, carrying on cliquish, innocuous conversations about school, an escalating war in a place called Vietnam, and the threat of nuclear holocaust. I found my classmates much more aware of global issues, particularly those that involved Western Europe. Our Catholic School history books had stark images of the evils of Communism that denied people the choice of religion and the existence of God. As a Catholic, one could even question the role of the church, but there was no questioning God. Jesus, Mary, Joseph and the Holy Ghost were mentioned more often than friends, family or the president. Our strong sense of democracy and the notion of individual freedom and free-thinkers kept us from being brain-washed when it came to religion.

MERECÀ

    To some of my Italian classmates Christianity had become a political party. Being Catholic and believing in God made many adults members of Christian Democratic politics, and a vote for the party line was a vote for God. The children owed allegiance to their parents, and in most cases to the same political ideal. A good two thirds of the class identified with their parents' unusual combination of democracy, religion, and socialism. These urban blue-collar kids whose fathers worked mostly at government jobs, quietly stood with their dads, hardly ever joining in any vocal confrontation with those kids whose fathers were white collar doctors, accountants, lawyers, or businessmen. There was a clannish fealty each had for their own side, but it did not create barriers of association; medieval class distinction had faded decisively in the post-war republic. The only measurable distinction was between those who dwelled in the town and the *contadini* (farm families) in the periphery. The differences were visible in the darker, sun drenched skin tones, the less than fashionable clothing, and the worn and dusty shoes. There may have been some banter, a slightly disparaging remark, but considering that so many of those urban kids had parents or grandparents who had emigrated away from farms, prevented a full-blown culture of prejudices. Italians would eventually move en masse away from rural lives to seek higher paying jobs in urban centers, but respect for the nobility of farm work remained a constant.

    I moved through the group becoming more familiar with all my new friends. Francesca, Mara, Chiara, Elena, and Giulia were outspoken, and therefore easier to befriend. Besides Mimmo, Carminuccio and Raffaele, Matteo and Marco shared similar curiosities about the *merecà*. I mingled willingly taking advantage of Mimmo's help in clearing the communication channels with his now labored and comical English translations. I defaulted to my habit of stepping outside of what was happening around me to view things from a different perspective. A few hours earlier I had fretted over being the new kid in the class, afraid of becoming the target of an expected brutal hazing. That afternoon, instead, I and my family had become the subjects of a collective curiosity that had pleasantly morphed into admiration. The least probable outcome to a Bronx kid was nothing less than a common cultural reaction for the Sarno kids. Through them I was gaining a deeper understanding of the motivation behind the many acts of kindness that bound my parents to our neighbors and relatives back in the Bronx. Mom and Pop dedicated countless hours in the care of others with volunteer labor, impromptu meals, free babysitting for single mothers in a bind, and loans to those who had fallen on hard times. They were at once anomalies and the objects of much affection in a neighborhood of heterogeneous souls. It was common for me to encounter an adult who would ask if I was the son of "*those wonderful people who owned the yellow brick building.*" My response was always a proud "*yes, those people are my mother and father.*" I may have always been aware of the good deeds, but until my days in Sarno, I never quite understood the motivations. Had we never left the Bronx, it may have escaped me well into my adulthood.

      Life on my native streets, even for a kid, was rough. You learned early, either through your own tribulations or those that bloodied others, to avoid becoming a constant victim of abuses. The *West Side Story* type gangs were common, with fist fight battles waged to protect territory the size of a few blocks, while turning younger kids, taken by the heroic gang images, into easy recruits. American neighborhoods had an identifiable ethnic character, but they were not hamlets. Suspicion was the immediate norm, even within one's own group. Trust was hard to come by, and years living next door to each other was not a measure of how much acceptance had been earned. Looking back, survival had become exclusively a personal challenge for the immigrants that crossed my path, so for them there was no village effect, no easy empathy for hardships, and in many cases, no extended families to interact with or ask for favors or solutions.

Sarno, instead, had a system of support. One invested time and favors in the care of others as a form of social security. It was employed often enough to attract my interest. I was curious not so much about the process, but rather the proletarian nature of the system-it created a good amount of social equity, bridging the gaps

MERECÀ

in wealth. There were certainly those considered richer than others, but the greater part of the population seemed to live similar lives when it came to the home, comforts, and putting food on the table. No formal claims were made for assistance-people understood and rose to the occasions. Newly married couples, the birth of children, the need for housing, debilitating illnesses, and ageing were all motivators that qualified for those homegrown social services. Families responded first, followed by friends and townspeople. Parish priests and small charities also played a hand in alleviating hardships. Modernity, bureaucracies, and the global economy were years away, so the only choice was to internalize needs and respond with traditional practices. My conversion to these powerful instincts came easily as I overcame my street inclination to ignore the plight of others.

I catalogued the self-imposed social lesson, turning my attention back to what was going on around me. While the boys helped themselves to the remaining pastries, the girls followed Mom upstairs. She gave them the tour they secretly desired, through rooms, around furniture, and ultimately to flip the pages of an album that revealed our history in photos of naked butts, toothless smiles, cone head birthday parties, and Catholic confirmations. The images stimulated quiet giggles and, as fingers pointed to cultural oddities they could not explain, they attempted once again to cushion their inquisitiveness. Stella showed the most affection, scolding the others before their chatter could turn into insults. Mom enjoyed the girls, sharing an account of her childhood in Sarno. They paid close attention, smothering her with questions, fascinated by what seemed to them a lesson on ancient history. The war years were only two decades old, but Sarno, as well as the rest of the country, felt a need to distance itself from the past without losing its lessons. It seemed that containing it was the best way to usher in a new age, and young Italians yearned to be a part of the new order.

When the group finally blended again in the courtyard, they shouted out reminders that it was getting late, and parents were probably wondering about them. Stella appeared comfortable in her mother hen role, and since the others did not mind, she was the first to nudge everyone along. "*Ragazzi, ve ne siete accorti a che ora siamo arrivati? Lasciamm' in pace sta' gente, jà, tutti a casa"*. She used an unexpected combination of Italian and dialect to make her point, asking if everyone had taken notice of the time and to make their way home leaving us in peace. I found her mannerisms, and the words that flowed from her plump lips engaging, creating that little tingle that ricochets through your veins igniting that primitive hormonal combustion, awakening the young male heart to the noxious allure of that standout female.

      They filed out into the courtyard with hesitations, looking back, waving, and filling the air with heartfelt salutations. Mimmo lingered a bit, then scampered up the driveway, trailing the group out onto Via Umberto as he looked forward to seeing me in school the following day. His words faded as he drew further away: "*Ciao Gianni! Ci vediamo domani a scuola. Ciao Carminu*'". Carminuccio lived a few blocks away, so he decided to stay. We sat on the stone bench under the persimmon tree as he urged me to look forward to the coming weekend. Mom had explained earlier about Sundays being the only day we were free. Saturday was a regular school day which I did not lament; getting out at one o'clock every day, a full two hours earlier than the dismissal bell at Mount Carmel, was no hardship. My classmates avoided speaking to me in dialect at my mother's urging, grasping the need to learn the official version of the language. Carminuccio then used his best Italian to propose an invitation. "*Gianni, sai che domenica sera si va a passeggio sul rettifilo. Ci saranno gli altri di scuola. Possiamo fare un gelato e una partita a biliardino"*. He described his words with hand and body gestures to make certain I understood that Sundays were set aside for socializing with an invitation to go strolling when he used two fingers to mimic a person walking and licking an invisible ice cream cone to hint at. It sounded like billiards, but the foosball gesture was a complete enigma. The table game had yet to make an appearance in the Bronx, so there was no way of understanding what was meant … the closest I came was the hand movement on the accelerator of a scooter. I asked Mom where the *rettifilo* was. She described it as the town's main street near the *Municipio (town hall)*. I nodded, recalling that we had crossed it on our way home from school. The word alluded to something straight and linear. Understanding the literal meaning of the word months later, I made the connection to the straight (*retti*) nature of the road that ran linear (*filo*) for about a quarter mile with no bends or curves. *Rettifilo* became the stimulant that would have me investigate the nature of all words and their applications to everyday life. The intricacies of language would continue to intrigue me into my adulthood.

    I walked Carminuccio out to the *portone* on the edge of Via Umberto. He gestured to follow him down the street to the small public park known as the *villetta* (little villa). The palm trees gave the place a feeling that it did not belong, that somewhere in Morocco would have worked better. We strolled the perimeter while my friend pointed to items speaking their Italian names: *panchina* (bench), *fontana* (fountain), *palma* (palm tree), *ragazze* (girls), *scemo* (idiot) pointing to his cousin.

    He was friendly with the girls, so we approached. Marianna and Betta (short for Elisabetta) extended a cordial smile while Carminuccio explained my American background. They also expressed disbelief while looking me over, spying any sign that would make me different enough to change their minds.

"*Si chist' è americano', falle dice na cosa in americano*", insisted Marianna. "*Non si dice americano, parlano in-gle-se in America*", asserted Carminuccio in clear syllables. She insisted on my speaking some words in American, when Carminuccio corrected her, explaining that we spoke English in America. "*E va bene, ja, comm'se'chiamm'sto ragazzo*" added Betta. Her friend cut in asking my name. "*Gianni*", he replied slightly exasperated. Betta looked into my eyes and insisted in the slow, lazy syllables that one would speak to a foreigner to say something in English.

"*Gianni, se tu sei a-me-ri-ca-no, dici qualcosa in in-gle-se*". I picked up on the tough spot we were in, so I overcame the discomfort of being different, blurting out a few words in English about the Bronx and some friends I missed. The girls stared, then looked at each other, and fell silent for a second before agreeing … amazed that I was for real. Betta could not resist the obvious, wanting to know how I ended up in Sarno. It was sad to think that the locals would find it unusual that any outsider would choose to live in their town. "*Carminù, ma perchè sta a Sarno?*". My new friend steered the conversation away from details. "*Ci sono circostanze di famiglia. Lascia stare, ormai si trova qui e stiamo diventando amici*". "There are personal reasons. Anyway, now he's here and we are becoming friends." She turned sassy and suggested a different reason for my being in Sarno. "*Allora, Gianni- mo te lo dico io. Tu stai qui a Sarno perchè t'hai trovà na bella ragazza come me, nge sposiamo e poi ritornamm' in america. Facciamo così- noi ci sposiamo qui, facimm nu viaggio di nozze bell' sule nuie e poi mi porti con te.*" She received a quick response from Carminuccio calling her crazy for conveniently proposing that I had come to Sarno to marry a nice local girl like her. She went on to imagine a wedding and a honeymoon before taking her back with me. "*Ma a cap nun t'aiut? ... prima di tutto o'merecà nun ten intenzion'e se spusà cu un e Sarno, e specialmente cu te*". He continued, concluding that she would have been the least likely to be chosen as a wife. The girls finally settled into my reality, sprinkling me with more questions about America. I answered in my spotty dialect only those that I understood. My pronunciation generated frequent, apologetic chuckles which I found charming. I complimented their energy with laughter of my own, feeling no disrespect. They invited me back to visit pointing out that they lived in the same *vicolo* (alley) as Carminuccio. We left the serenity of the public garden through the large iron gates and onto the thin sidewalk that buffered us from the noisy and unsettled street. A short distance from the *villetta,* we turned into *Vicolo San Gennaro*. The street was extremely narrow bordered by two story buildings on either side. Some showed signs of being repaired, others still scarred from the war. Only the smallest of vehicles could navigate the space wisely enough to avoid scratching up against walls and doors. The girls skipped away into a *portone* across from where we stood, projecting a smile and a promise to seek each other out again at the *villetta*. A dozen or so feet further down, Carminuccio's pace slowed to peer through the thin cracks in the beaded curtains that shielded the entrance to a small store that sold children's clothing. He then turned to me and blurted *"Teresa"*, pointing towards the curtain. The name was close enough to the English, so I understood that someone named Theresa was in the store. He gently parted the curtain in the middle with both hands and called out to the girl seated behind the counter. *"Teresa, ciao... stai sola?"* He asked if she was alone. Convinced she was, he entered, and I followed as Teresa leaned over the counter planting her lips on his. A slight angst overcame me believing her parents to be lurking nearby ready to pounce on their daughter's disobedience and my friend's transgression. My sympathies for young love had not been liberated enough to avoid the doomsday scripting; I was certain we were all about to suffer some explosive adult thrashing, and that somehow it would all make its way back to my parents. Teresa absorbed my nervousness, distracting her from her boyfriend's lips. *"Carminù, Ma chi è questo?"* *"Teresa, questo è Gianni, un amico arrivato poche settimane fa dall'America".* Her question had become my introduction with each encounter through town: *chi (pronounced key) è questo?...* who is this? The question would be asked often enough for it to become the easiest Italian to roll off my lips. Upon learning I was a newly arrived kid from America, Teresa pulled a 45-vinyl record of the Beatles song *She Loves You* from behind the counter and positioned it on the turntable that sat dusty in a corner behind some gift boxes. Beyond the first few scratches, the song played flawlessly. She swayed to the music, clearly enchanted, haphazardly singing some of the words. The effect of her pronunciation was to find her irresistibly adorable-I understood Carminuccio's infatuation. Midway through, she pulled the needle off the record, looked at me and asked for a translation. *"Gianni, dai, dimmi cosa dicono, cosa significa. So già che il titolo significa Lei Ti Ama ... però il resto non ci capisco niente.* I turned to Carminuccio who led me part of the way probably employing his entire portfolio of English words. He squeezed out: *"Teresa ask what significato the musica?"* Gazing back at her, he had to deliver the sad news that a translation with my limited Italian was not forthcoming. *"Senti, Gianni non parla italiano abbastanza per farti na traduzione".* Teresa became reconciled and returned the needle to the record. As the Beatles song faded into that repetitious thumping sound at the end of the record, she wrapped her arms around Carminuccio's neck and planted another kiss. As she pulled her lips away, with her arms still cradling his neck, her mother caught a glimpse of the act as she crashed through the beads brushing them aside trying to keep the parcels she carried from escaping her embrace. Italian mothers, including my own, always sent a shiver down my spine when they were silently enraged. The woman stood there clearly understanding what was going on, said nothing at first, placed her bags on the counter, and with the accuracy of guided missile, planted five fingers across Teresa's left cheek with her right hand, sending the poor girl to the far end of the counter and onto the floor. The stinging sound echoed into the high ceiling of the store bouncing off those walls coming at me like an irate ghostly spirit. Then it was Carminuccio's turn to feel the wrath when she turned to him and chased him out of the store still engaging him with the same fury. *"Tu, te ne devi andare, mo' subbito! Truovete na via e ascepiett' ca parla cu mammeta! Ste scemenze nun se fann' a chest'età… e nun te fa vedè cchiu dint'o negozio!"* A very dejected young man made his way toward the door, inviting me to step out first. I did not need a translation: the echo, the red face of anger, the five finger marks on Teresa's face, and the troubadour's defeated look, said it all. I deciphered the ultimatum to never show his face in the store again, the admonishment for committing acts not normal for their age, and the ultimatum that my friend's mother would soon get an ear full. I could not get the sound of her hand slapping poor Teresa's tender and beautiful cheek out of my head. I had witnessed a few good beatings in my young life, but never upon the face of a girl with that much ferocity. I was puzzled and bothered by it enough to hate the woman.

   I walked Carminuccio to his *portone* where we were greeted by the rest of his huge family. Mother, two younger sisters and a younger brother hung over the iron railing of their aging terrace each belching out a different topic to their brother below. It was one huge shouting match that had me turning away and back into the alley. I waved and shouted a very native *ciao*, feeling a certain satisfaction in sounding Italian. I made my way back through now familiar streets, yielding to my curiosity as I slowed my pace passing in front of the store. Turning to look in was a dangerous act, I thought, but I found it impossible to resist. Teresa stood behind the curtain, her face dissected by the strands of beads. I stared in bewilderment, employing another, seldom used sense to detect the possible presence of her mother. Teresa managed a slight smile, signaling perhaps that she was fine, or to deflect the embarrassment-I wasn't quite sure. Mindful that even a lingering second could make me the next target of her mother's rampage, I picked up the pace, and found my way home.

  I caught up with Mom, and I narrated the incident. She appreciated my turmoil, so she took me aside and explained what I found difficult to understand. *"Teresa's mother didn't slap her because she kissed Carminuccio, but because she was protecting the daughter ... her reputation".* I had only previously understood reputation as it applied to a person's job or maybe the president, but Mom had to explain further if I wanted to understand its application to a young girl. *"A girl is supposed to wait until she is engaged or married before she can kiss a boy".* I challenged her theory. *"Did you wait until you were engaged to kiss Pop?"* *"P'ammor e Dio! (For the love of God) I kissed your father the first time on the day we got married".* With that, she pulled out her wedding album and showed me the picture of that first kiss. I had never seen that heavy, camel colored leather album thick with photos. It had stayed behind in Sarno with nonna after the wedding. The sepia images of Mom in her elegant and lacy wedding dress harnessed with a train the length of an American station wagon, required several women on either side to get it to keep pace with her steps. In his traditional black tux, Pop looked more the part of a Hollywood star attending the Oscars than the son of humble *contadini*. Mom was the youngest of five sisters, so nonno Domenico went all out as he married off the last of his daughters to a local boy raised by a single mother who was well known and respected in the farming community. It was 1954, and in many ways that young couple, beautiful and progressive in their appearance represented much of what Italy was becoming as the country recovered from the exhaustions of a punishing world conflict. Some of the photos showcased a sizeable crowd surrounding the newlyweds as they exited the church of San Francesco and into the waiting horse and buggy. I asked Mom if they were all relatives. *"No"*, she said, *"those were all people from the town"*. As Mom pulled away into the kitchen, I sat silent, studying those faces with their honest expressions of approval caught in that instant, with all eyes fixated on the two people that would become my parents. To know them in that capacity, before any of their children came into the world, was a sweet revelation that turned Mom and Pop into superheroes.

    The day finally ended with short replays of the curious events. Except for the slap across Teresa's face, I recalled good feelings about my new friends, the appealing nature of my unusual classroom, and the unpretentiously rustic nature of the town. The earlier premonitions of maltreatment had given way to the good omens that promised to fascinate me. My only concern, as I laid awake listening to the last of the gurgling scooters making their way home, was that the novelty of being the *mercà* wouldn't wear away too soon.

MERECÀ

CHAPTER 6
CARMINUCCIO

 His truer name was Carmine (*Carmeeneh*). The nickname, Carminuccio (adding *uccio* to the end of any name), made him younger, innocent, and childlike. Growing older did not necessarily return a person to his birthname. He would remain Carminuccio throughout high school. While Mimmo would make frequent visits to our home and the other boys in my class remained occasional good friends, Carminuccio would become my constant companion. The proximity to my *portone* had much to do with cultivating the relationship. Early mornings he would stroll up to our gate and softly call out to my window signaling it was time to start off for school, asking me if I was coming. "*Merecà, vieni?*" His voice penetrated the *persiane (floor to ceiling window shutters)* like an inviting alarm clock, prompting nonna to demand that I make haste. "*Giuvà (trucated Giovanni), jamme bell'e mamm'… sta Carminuccio fore che t'aspett … scinn' che t'aggiò preparat' o'café cu'i tarall'."* Most of the time breakfast was the usual *taralli* (hard biscuits) floating around in an oversized mug of scalding *caffelatte* with their deceitful simplicity that I never tired of. They were surprisingly alluring as they turned spongy, drenched in espresso coffee, dissolving in your mouth, releasing those early morning aromas into your nostrils. I never refused a second helping, the rich taste staying with me as we weaved our way through town.

Nonna never failed to invite Carmine to the breakfast table, which he politely refused each time, conscious of not creating any *fastidio* (imposition). This is how I was introduced to the art of *non dare fastidio (*create no imposition or hardship*)*. People unselfishly considering the discomfort of others before accepting an invitation was hardly practiced in my Bronx life, where imposing did not happen apologetically, and where invitations were rare, but usually accepted. Survival was not a communal affair; people did not share

MERECÀ

the same genesis of a small Mediterranean town. Despite the insular feel to a Bronx neighborhood, traditions hardly took root, and those that did were superficial at best and contemporary to newly settled immigrants. Altruistic practices disintegrated with the departure of American born generations seeking the greater experience beyond the neighborhood, to perhaps resurrect them if they landed in some small, upscale suburban town which informally imposed a code of behavior.

The continuity of homogeneous cultural habits in Sarno, passed down through the ages, had been woven conspicuously into the social fabric. Each thread stood as a blueprint to be applied as situations arose. I found the process unusually comfortable. Unusual because it conflicted with my limited understanding of common culture, comforting because it offered an anthology of mutual behaviors whose applications created a casual harmony. I took to that harmony, quickly understanding the benefits of acculturation. I was becoming more willingly *Italian* as the days rolled by.

    Carminuccio had also become my conduit to more language, music, the budding Italian pop culture scene that mimicked Anglo and American models, girls, and sex. He played the piano, guitar, and drums. His cherished collection of forty fives spun with few interruptions on the older turntable inherited from his father who earned his living as a musician in a local band playing feasts and weddings, visibly spending a good part of his earnings on instruments or anything related to the music business. It was common to see father and son belt out tunes on the same stage. Carminuccio may have embraced his father's itch for the arts, but he never lost sight of the value of a degree. His mother was the steady breadwinner as an elementary school teacher, a reminder to take his schooling seriously enough ... consistently performing above average.

    I had avoided talk of his Teresa, sidestepping any reference of the beating she endured. The sadness of watching a young girl suffer that level of violence, kept the images fresh in my mind, and the trauma alive. Her suitor may have been put on notice to stay away, but our round-trip excursions into his *vicolo* were calculated to allow the lovers glimpses of each other when she could stand at the entrance to the shop uninterrupted. It became a routine that turned into a lesson on romancing a female, with facial expressions that generated unspoken words, hand gestures and body language. As they became more familiar, I was able to decipher a host of communications: *I'll be back in a few minutes. Where's your mother? Where were you?* (if she hesitated to show herself at the entrance on time). There were hand and facial movements that asked where and when they would meet; sent messages of love; and begged to show her panties. She only complied once for his birthday. Often that request would be met with Teresa's right hand fingers coming together in the shape of teepee tapping her forehead to let him know he was crazy to keep asking. The forehead tap was the silent gesture that told others they had lost their minds... basically, you were nuts.

   There was more sexual play than actual sex. Understanding the difference was another cultural refinement pressuring me out of my adolescence, and Teresa had been an unsuspecting accomplice as she allowed her femininity to act out almost unhindered. It had also been the case with several of the girls in class. Stella and company circumvented the censorships for girls with impetuous, veiled teasing that got puppy love reactions from several of the boys. As I grew older, I looked back with fondness on the amorously mature nature of schoolboys hardly into their teens. It was another cultural bonus that erased the superficial, childish nature of our lives around girls in a Bronx schoolyard. Italian girls had no interest in being the tomboy equals of the boys. There was an aura of sixties liberation, but it was not open rebellion against the establishment. Rather, a skillfully subversive resolve to act out their female instincts was more the norm, exposing nothing to the scrutiny of adults. The commitment was cultish, the results legendary. The good Catholic girls contributed callously to the developing fantasies of young boys, yet able to stifle their expectations at will. The process was as theatrical as any other Italian discipline, keeping them in suspense into early adulthood. For boys becoming men, courting the female became a lengthy, labored, but pleasurable ordeal with love letters, short poems,

MERECÀ

playful gifts, and those ubiquitous hand and facial signals, with each becoming experts at keeping to their secrets. It would take most of my first two years to absorb a working catalogue of those signals. As a foreign actor, however, I lacked the indigenous flair, with hand and body gestures that did not come off entirely as natural.

    This was the effect Teresa had on Carminuccio, and just the mention of her name brought on a lovesick sigh and an impassioned smile. He would answer my questions about her with a serious look that defied his youth and made him appear much older. "*Merecà, tu devi capire che io non posso stare senza Teresa. Ci conosciamo da piccoli e siamo cresciuti con un certo affetto*". We were approaching Christmas, and my passion for the culture had me learning the language with a lively urgency. I understood the adolescent agony that kept him respecting the limits of his age in asking me to sympathize with his need to be with Teresa, and that knowing her since they were children had caused them to develop a certain affection.

    The constraints of living in the *vicolo*, the concert of lives acting out in such proximity, and the commonality of destinies, had people locking into each other for emotional support from the earliest years. I started using my Italian with less fear of butchering it in pursuing the nature of the kiss. I had witnessed the energy they both contributed to their locked lips, and it seemed more like love than just making out. "*Come ti senti quando tu baci Teresa?*", I asked. I could sense the sweet thoughts running through his heart. "*Mi devi credere che mi sento il ragazzo più ricco del mondo. Le sue labbra sono morbidissime e poi, non so, la sua faccia ha un profumo dolce che porto via con me e lo sento anche quando sto solo.*" They were the words of a kid who had grown beyond his years. His account added a level of seriousness I couldn't wrap my boyish head around when he described how the softness of her lips and the sweet perfume of her face made him the richest kid in the world-her scent lingering even when he was away from her. There was nothing erotic about his description; it was *amore* in its purest, most innocent form. It struck a chord, making me yearn for the same sentiment, the kind I wanted to feel for Stella. This was puppy love Italian style.

      The currents of mutual dependency offered a way of validating lives that would have otherwise been sacrificed to an archaic existence. They wasted no time in granting each other the power of affections with their impulses to offset the mundane. The courtship may have been contemporary to our time, but it had historical roots in the best schooling of Italian Romanticism, and it seeped into their lives from the earliest age. Carminuccio would explain that demonstrating one's affections was greater than consummation, greater than the kiss. The kiss was meant to be a hard-earned reward for persistence and sincerity. I was eager to know if the persistence was meant to last forever. He smiled and gave the only answer he could: *"Gianni, siamo troppo giovani. Questo fatto con Teresa dura per adesso ... per il futuro non si sa. Non significa però che non possiamo occuparci di noi due, anche se non dovesse esserci un futuro"*. He gave it the seriousness it deserved. Teresa's life had been too intricately connected to his for him to treat her as a coming-of-age hobby. He was good with an unpredictable future that may or may not have kept them together, but it could not diminish the need to act on the present; to take what it offered while advocating for Teresa's emotional wellbeing. I recall the weirdness of it as an unselfish kind of selfishness, or a selfishness that needed justification through some form of compromise, some limitation. It made sense at the time, but I knew I would have a tough time explaining it. I started thinking of age as cubicles of time with characteristics of their own. Carminuccio had delivered a profound lesson on living time as it pertained to a certain age. If all you could experience at fourteen was the tingle of sharing a space and a time with a girl, when the best reward is your first kiss, then one needed to invite it to happen and to live it. This was a radical departure from the simple-minded concept of time as measured in sport seasons and holidays. Our American cubicle contained footballs, baseballs, Halloween candy, Christmas gifts, and kissing only because we were curious of how it felt. We blissfully practiced the rituals of life, but the thought that we could fall in love with life at fourteen completely escaped us.

MERECÀ

The altruism exercised by my Italian generation also forced me to re-balance my sensitivities. Rare was an occasion when it was not practiced. Safeguarding another's happiness required a level of altruism I would have forever been convinced did not exist if we had never set foot in Sarno. Carminuccio was a young teenager with the compassions of a well-adjusted, functional adult aware of the complexities of human interactions. This was not a trait a kid in Sarno picked up by chance or exclusively through parental upbringing. His inclination toward Teresa was mostly a result of cultural breeding. The breeding took place everywhere: at home, in school, strolling down the *rettifilo,* in the cafés, in church, and on the streets, and there were common denominators that ran through each of these institutions. Participation was universal except for the few that chose to be unaffected.

Music and the soapy lyrics played a huge part in the build up to a romantic experience. His collection of forty fives kept me in touch with some of the pop music that played on our Bronx jukebox, Saturday afternoons in Sal's Pizzeria where we spent our weekend allowance of fifty cents. We had enough for a slice and a small Coke. The leftover dime sat snug in our pockets to be spent later at the pastry shop for an Italian ice. Sal loved the music as much as the kids did, so he kept the volume high, filling the space with the songs we would keep singing or humming all week long. In those early teen years, we focused more on the sound than on the words. There were strong hints of boy meets girl stories, but they lacked the deep attachments of Italian songs. The tunes would rush through my head bringing me back, as Carminuccio purposely rattled off titles in his exaggerated English pronunciations to keep me entertained. *"Gianni, questa la conosci: Dah-oon (*Dawn*) cantano Frankie Vahlli e Fo-oor Say-ah-sons (*Four Seasons*). E questa: I gett A-roe-uhnd (*I Get Around*)? E questa: Preh-tty Vooh-man (*Pretty Woman-most pronounced the "w" like a "v" when followed by a vowel). The fascination with things American or British was strongest in the choice of music. English language songs were constantly in the top ten hits list and were standard in many collections. Original Italian hits had an appeal all their own, so when he played a Bobby Solo tune *Una Lacrima Sul Viso,* I was

MERECÀ

listening to an Italian Elvis, and I was smitten by the melody and the easy lyrics. I then asked him to play only Italian songs. Each urged you to listen again, and to sing along. After a third time around for Bobby Solo's song, I not only knew what the title meant (A Tear on my Face), but I was able to individualize the words and use them independent of the title. Since a good number of English words spoken by my friends were processed with the help of music, I decided I could do the same by listening to Italian songs. It did not take much prodding to convince Mom to invest in a turntable and a half dozen forty fives. The songs played from a vendor's van all morning on Sundays at the outdoor market, so the free listening was not only an enjoyable pastime, but it had become the prelude to a spending frenzy. Enriched with my grandmother's stash of coins, Carminuccio and I would spend the better part of the late morning sorting through the songs and making mental lists of those we wanted. Minutes later we were in the *cantina* (basement room), rewarding our efforts with the best acoustics, and the only place we could steal away to with our purchases to play as often as we wanted. We didn't tire of an inventory until we returned with a newer batch a week or two later. I was becoming familiar with the artists, so when they spoke about *Rita Pavone, Gigliola Cinquetti, Patty Pravo, Celentano, Gianni Morandi* and others, I could relate and even rattle off the titles of their hits. Our summer days together became one prolonged foray into the vast pop culture scene. Beyond the music, we sought comic books, contemporary literature, the poetry of the Beatniks, the lyrics of the Hippies, and the sermons of young priests who were saying Masses in Italian, not Latin. The Saturday pilgrimage to catch the latest feature at the Cinema Augusteo had become a welcomed habit even when the American movies was horribly dubbed in Italian. Carminuccio had also found a way to have us pay a small premium to the clerk to turn a blind eye to gain entrance to more adult-only movies-those labeled *Vietato Ai Minori Di 18 Anni*. (prohibited to those under 18). Sunday evenings were spent devising strategies that would have us dedicate as much time in the company of the girls that owned our hearts. The staging was the venerable *rettifilo* where the greater part of the population gathered to check out the neighbors, engage in the latest gossip, window shop, snack on the many vendor delicacies, or offer to buy others an expresso and pastries.

The first time I could spend a Sunday evening with Carminuccio, became a rough lesson on grasping the appeal of strolling round trippers from one end of the thoroughfare to the other. When he slipped his arm inside mine and held me like a girlfriend, I looked for a way out. In catching on to my discomfort, he found an explanation to rid me of the culture shock. *"Gianni, non ti preoccupare che non è una cosa strana. Guarda in giro, vedi che gli uomini anche vanno braccio in braccio come le donne. Non è usanza in America"?* He diminished the strangeness by pointing out how many men were walking around arm in arm. When he asked if it was practiced in America, it gave me the chance to defend my unrefined reaction. *"No, in America non si fa questo. Solo con una ragazza. Se lo fai con un ragazzo, ti danno I pugni".* In my cautious Italian, I gave an emphatic-no-answer in support of the notion that one did that only with a girl, and that attempting it with a man would lead to a fight. The old neighborhood made same sex anything taboo and unacceptable, limiting my exposure and understanding of homosexuality. The one outstanding opinion spoken by the kids who ruled the streets, was to label any emotionally physical contact between men as simply *homo*. Catholic teaching added another layer of disapproval, even sinfulness, so it ranked right up there with serious stuff that kept us blindfolded. As youngsters in a tough environment, we carried a heavy burden when it came to unacceptable social behavior. There was no grey zone-everything fell cleanly into absolute right or wrong. My reaction then, had been an expected extension of that upbringing, and it would take some time trying it out to finally lift the stigma and smooth the transition to acceptance and a greater understanding of differences. Walking arm in arm with Carminuccio would eventually become a Sunday routine.

Back on the *rettifilo,* Teresa acted out her part by latching on to two girlfriends and pacing in the opposite direction meeting us face to face at some midway point. In that flash of time, without stopping and without the slightest pause, with her parents not far apace, poems, sonnets, and love songs were exchanged between the lovers without a word spoken. The eyes, facial expressions and head movements did all the talking. I could only guess at the messaging codes in the early days, but like so many of the nuances, I would come to decipher their meaning, without quite owning them ... much of me could aspire to become more Italian, but hardly a natural. The interactions were subliminal productions of love making. What the body was not ready to embrace, the mind improvised. It was an operetta employing the romantic folklore that spawned a portfolio of secretive gazes and signals. These ranked right up there with all things saturated by a culture passionate about rituals. The carefully contrived recipes in nonna's kitchen; the love in having your senses aroused, seated at a table inhaling a bouquet of freshly sliced prosciutto and aromatic antipasti; the common pleasure of watching the barista's habitual intercourse in prepping the perfect cup of espresso, adding to the anticipation of that first creamy sip; and the courtship of women were all examples. There was genius in everything propelled by genuine love. Every passion was to be lived, and life's mandate was to promote and sustain that drive. Italians needed to inject this ideal in every twinkle of life; to ignore it was nothing less than an ignoble betrayal of one's own birthrights ... to breathe was an invitation to seek out and inhale instances of love detected in everyday life.

Carminuccio lead by example and with words. *"Gianni, se a te piace Stella nella nostra classe, devi trovare il modo di fargliela capire."* He had locked into my feelings for Stella, and the easy advice was to promote the relationship by urging me to let her know how I felt. *"Ma non è facile, non so come dire le parole giuste e ho paura."* I admitted to not knowing what to say, and that my fear made it too difficult to find the words. He insisted: *"La paura è nella tua testa. Perché dovresti avere paura di una ragazza come Stella? È una ragazza come tutte le altre, e anche lei ha bisogno di apprezzare qualcuno e di essere apprezzata."* I probably agreed that the fear was in my head, but I disagreed that Stella was a girl like any who needed to be appreciated and that

MERECÀ

she also had a need to express an affection for someone. I was not sure I could be the object of her affection, since she had once announced that I would be useless as a boyfriend, and the fact that she paid me little attention in class. *"Stella non è come le altre ragazze. È molto più ... come si dice ... forte?* "I looked for a way of justifying my fear by labeling her as tough, but my limited vocabulary couldn't come up with the right word. *"Vuoi dire prepotente, forse?"* I pulled out my dictionary to find the translation. Under *prepotente* I found the English *bully and authoritarian*. I smirked at the accuracy of the descriptors, then turned to Carminuccio and gave him an energetic *"si"*.
"Allora, se per te è una ragazza sfacciata, si capisce che hai paura. Ma devi capire che tutte le ragazze, le donne, anche le mamme fanno la faccia dura, ma di sotto sono tutte torte morbide... come le sfogliatelle ... croccanti di fuori, ma pastose dentro. Tocca a te trovare il modo di farla perdere quell'antipatia." I had to read between the lines, but I caught his meaning that all females are capable of that tough exterior, but that most are soft and cake-like on the inside (I understood it more when he mentioned the *sfogliatelle* pastries with their crusty exteriors and creamy insides). His monologue caused a slight giggle, but it did little to convince me I had the power to act out with Stella.

    In school I paid a boyish attention to her, mastering her mannerisms, losing myself in her profile. Her words came easy, and conversations were hers to start or end. She projected sentiments from joy to anger in her genuine traits, never masquerading the truth no matter the pain it could cause. It did not escape Carminuccio's notice that her big weakness was *cioccolato alla nocciola* (hazelnut chocolate). One pack per day, sometimes several, was all she brought for snack (*merenda*). Breaking down the bar into small squares, she gave them no attention, slipping each into her mouth hardly pausing her conversations. During one of our snack breaks, Mimmo had to make a point of how much of my gaze fixated on her. *"Stella, ma ti rendi conto che o'merecà guarda solo te? Povero ragazzo s'è fissato ... e tu non gli dai retta."* Mimmo had played his card challenging Stella to acknowledge my crush. The two had competed for notoriety since I arrived. Mimmo using his wit, intelligence, and chauvinism in his attempts to break down Stella's feminism, while Stella countered with stinging lines about male stupidity, Mimmo's weight, and the useless nature of relationships. *"Parlamm' chiar' e comm'ta'fatt'mammetta. Ma tu ti si fatt' ancora più scem'e cretino? Comm' ti permiett' e parla' acussì? Che cazz' me ne fott' se o'merec me guarda. Si chill' s'è fissat, che nge pozz'fa? Chist'so problemi suoi ... tant' non è che mo mett'mbraccia e mo port'a casa! Ma che ti si mise ncapo che io e o'merecà simm' nammurat'? Mimmo, sta'attient' a come parli, si no faccio venì a cugineme o' meccanico e cu duie cavece te fa arrivà fore a Foce! (Foce was an area on the outskirts of town known for its natural spring waters).*

The rage was clear for the tone and the use of her dialect. There was no way she would convey that kind of anger in her cleanest Italian. This was classical *Sarnese (*slight difference from the Neapolitan*)* dialect, and the words punctured my ego like the sting of Brother George's paddle on my unblemished butt. She prefaced her reaction by speaking "as her mother made her", that is, to use the dialect first learned. The locals did this when it was felt that using the standard Italian was an artificial or unnatural mode of letting loose with your true feelings. If they wanted to be real with each other, then it had to be in the language born into. She resented his attempt at matchmaking, threatening him with her older cousin who, with a couple of swift kicks, would exaggeratedly send him flying all the way to the Foce part of town. Mimmo was thrown back on his heels, not expecting such a violent response. *"Stella, ti sei impazzita?"* He refused to call up his dialect, asking if she had gone nuts. *"Stiamo parlando solo di sentimenti, e tu sei una ragazza, e mi sembra naturale che qualche ragazzo potrebbe trovare anche una come te piacevole."* He injected a dose of sarcasm as he explained that being a girl, it was only natural that someone could find even one like her appealing. She was too sharp not to pick up on it, coming at him in a louder, more determined tone, and using her Italian to match his snobbery. *"Una comm'a me? Cretino che non sei altro! Io sono un te-so-ro! Hai capito? Un*

MERECÀ

te-so-ro! Chi si fa amare da me sarà il più fortunato del mondo! Invece, povera a chell' che se pigli'a te! Na vera e propria condanna! She pumped up her worth by calling herself a treasure, pounding it out in clear syllables, and declaring that whomever she fell in love with, would be the luckiest guy in the world, and that any woman falling for Mimmo would be damned. A simple adolescent crush had ignited a war of the sexes, and the combatants were equipped to take it to extremes. I struggled with all the fuss, since I had not taken any steps in acting out my feelings towards Stella; I never uttered a word. The hope was that it would wane and just wither into a forgotten classroom drama, but Stella had to take it to the source, reducing the heat a bit and shifting her energies to get her point across, looking me in the eyes. *"Merecà, parlo Italiano perché forse mi capisci meglio. Tu devi toglierti questi pensieri dalla testa, non te scimunì pure tu!"* (Bringing all five of her fingers together in the form of a pyramid and tapping her forehead). *Noi siamo amici e così deve restare. Come ti faccio capire che non sei mio tipo? Tu un giorno forse ritorni in America e ti sposi a quella tua ragazza ... come si chiama, Debora? Vedi, tu in America e io a Sarno, e così deve essere."* The Italian worked. I understood all she said and, as much as I wanted to apply an alternative conclusion, I slid back into my seat as the recess ended. While the *professore* prepared his lesson, I took a minute or two to process her words. She insisted on being just friends and to not lose my head over her; that my life and destiny were probably in America, and hers in Sarno ... in her world; it was as things should be. The jab that stung the most was the revelation that I was not her type. Not sure what she meant, I chalked it up to being American.

    After school, me and some of the boys decided to hang around in our favorite café to play a few rounds of *biliardino* (foosball). December in Sarno was more like October in New York... the weather remained pleasant, so lingering about the town finding some recreation to beat back the stiffness in the classroom, had become a sought-after escape. The teen showmanship was still fresh, so Stella dominated our discussions. Mimmo tried his best to put a positive spin on things and provided reasons to get me to let it go. "*Gianni, credimi, per me non vale la pena avere alcun affetto per una ragazza come Stella. Non merita quello che tu provi per lei. Quella ha più a che fare con I ragazzi del liceo… ho sentito dire che si incontra con un ragazzo del terzo anno.*" I did not exactly have a concrete image of the kind of person she was beyond the classroom, but Mimmo added a dimension I was ready to accept. According to him, she was not worth the effort because she had a selfish streak, and that rumors had her dating a junior in high school. I was good knowing that Stella was popular with older guys; she had the maturity that made me feel still like a kid around her.

Carminuccio countered with his own theory. *Mimmo, tu lo sai che il padre di Stella è il direttore locale del Partito Comunista e sono certo che Stella condivide lo stesso parere del padre. Si sa che possiede una grande antipatia per le cose Americane. Stella si è fatta sentire delle volte parlare di, non so, questa rivoluzione comunista mondiale … ma io veramente preferisco l'America e la cultura del Rock and Roll.* Mimmo fired back: *Ma tutti lo sanno in classe che il suo nome completo è Stella Rosa … è probabile anche che intendeva chiamarla Stella Rossa addirittura! Il padre è uno di quei comunisti fanatici che si aspetta questa enorme rivoluzione anche in Italia.* I understood the whole Communist thing from the lessons back at Mount Carmel Elementary, and knowing that Stella's father was the head of the local chapter of the Communist Party, had me instantly demonizing her whole family. The boys sided with America refuting the notion of a worldwide Communist revolution. Mimmo even revealed that Stella's (Star) full name was Stella Rosa (Pink Star) and that he thought her idiotic father intended to go all the way and name her Stella Rossa (Red Star) to fully pay tribute to the Russian Communist Party. The nuns and priests back in the Bronx did a great job planting images about the Godless communists, and those lessons had carved a strict notion of the evils associated with the hammer, the sickle, and the red star. The animated images in our social studies books drove home the theme with Soviet uniformed soldiers dragging people away from churches and into concentration camps. The fact that Stella seemed to approve of her father's politics had me questioning my

MERECÀ

affections for someone who did not care for America. I never thought anyone could dislike the country that we had been taught to idolize, convinced that the entire world loved us and our way of life. Why else did so many immigrants want to make it to America? Our young minds had been filled with honorable and unselfish American deeds that defeated the bad guy Nazis and Fascists, dropped the bomb on the evil Japanese Empire, championed democracy, and gave us seven channels of television programming ... not to mention Elvis, Superman, Rock and Roll, JFK and the Peace Corps, Hollywood, blue jeans, the New York Yankees and skyscrapers. It never crossed my mind that iconic, good-guy America could ever generate disapproval from anywhere on the globe. It took Stella's grit and her steadfast views to cause me to question my unconditional allegiance to the perfect social blueprint. Could there be something wrong with America?

Months of play were needed before I could compete at the foosball table, so I gave way after getting slaughtered each time. Sitting and watching with a satisfying scoop of *stracciatella* (chocolate chip) gelato was all I needed to smooth over my deflated ego. I knew I could always get back at the guys on the basketball court, so the losing streak was quickly set aside. As the funds ran out, and we gathered our books, stacked like pyramids and held in place by long, hooked rubber bands the width of *pappardelle* pasta, we spied Stella across the *rettifilo* seated on a bench holding some guy's hand. Mimmo would not let the opportunity slip by, so he practically pushed us across the street into her path. The look of exasperation on her raw, pinkish face gave the impression that, not only was she ready to do battle, as her eyebrows met just above her nose, but that she had no intention of losing. "*Ciao Stella Rossa*", accenting the word *Rossa* purposely distorting her name, "C*ome mai ancora qui? Non ti cerca tuo padre?"* Mimmo let loose with his sharpest cynicism when he made an issue of her name, questioned why she was still around after school, and that her father must surely be on the hunt for her. She accepted the challenge, giving it right back. "*Scemo, il nome e' Stella Rosa. Ma tu che cazzo vai trovenn'...? Chell che faccio io non sono interessi tuoi ... truovete na via ...*" There was that word *cazzo*. I knew it was colloquial for *dick*, but when used in a phrase it sounded more like *fuck*. So, using that translation, Stella spoke more like one of the girls back in the schoolyard on Crotona Avenue. *What the **fuck** do you want*-had been the most common phrase when confronting a bullying intrusion. And *fuck* came out on high volume, making certain it rose above the lesser words. A powerful, boastfully spoken *fuck* had the desired effect of announcing a serious threat or a determined act of self-defense, and that the person using it had every intention of committing to the fight. Once you introduced *fuck* into the argument, it only escalated, and no one backed off until someone was down on the ground.

Stella fit the definition perfectly. She was in the fight, finishing off her remark insisting that he leave. She shot up from the bench, inviting us to walk away. Mimmo stiffened like a Roman statue and stood his ground: *"Ma tuo padre lo sa che ti metti con uno del liceo? Quel ragazzo lo sa che pericolo corre se si trovasse a passare di qua tuo padre? Un direttore del Partito Comunista non può permettersi na figlia puttana.* Stella stood stunned, unable to react, while Carminuccio scolded Mimmo for going too far. "*Mimmo, ma sei veramente un incosciente ... nun nge vulevano ste parole, e perché tutta sta'rabbia*? I was aware that Mimmo had labeled Stella in the harshest way by using the word *puttana*, and that an important man like her father could not afford a daughter with a reputation. Carminuccio's reaction was what I had come to expect of him. I had a clear, old fashioned image of what a whore looked like, and Stella did not fit it at all. I sided against Mimmo, echoing Carminuccio's curiosity about why so much anger. I could have been the jilted guy using the opportunity to malign her in support of some jealous pinch, but I had already endorsed Stella's affinity for older guys, putting her out of my league.

There may have been an expectation of some sympathetic reaction for her from the guy sitting on the bench, but he decided to stay out of it. I guessed he had a less than amorous attraction to the middle school debutante. She was well developed, and despite her attempts to tone down her attributes, her stiff, bloated breasts drew the attention she craved from older males. The plump lips puckered up when she ate, spoke, or smiled … it seemed that any facial expression added more volume to them. The dominant green in her eyes overshadowed the smaller brown spots, and it was that tincture that lit up neon in the sunlight, abducting your attention and refusing to let you go. Her theatrical brashness was a show to behold. The loud controlled anger, the expressive facial contortions, the piercing pupils, and the wiry strands of indigo colored hair that kept whipping across her face, were all props in the production. The comparisons to the roles played by Sofia Loren and Anna Magnani, were inevitable. My brother and I had spent lazy Italian American Sunday afternoons in the years before the birth of our sister, at the Tremont Cinema on Webster Avenue, slouched on lifeless theater seats bookended by our parents, expected to sit quiet and motionless watching the latest black and white neo-realism gems from the motherland. *I Ladri di Biciclette*, *La Strada* and *La Dolce Vita* were the most memorable because they kept me from staring at the ceiling or back at the projector's lamp wondering each time how that bright, round light could turn into the images on that giant screen. It was enough to keep me from disturbing Mom and Pop when the movies were not to my liking.

The Bicycle Thief had me living in the shoes of the young Bruno who despairs over his father's misfortunes, but never loses hope. The trials of *Zampanò* were enough to keep me engaged with *La Strada*, and my mother's attempts to steer me away from watching certain parts of *La Dolce Vita*, hardly covering both eyes with her stubby fingers, only ramped up my curiosity.

Stella and company provided all the intensity needed to bring the neorealism to life. I could hardly have imagined, as the fast-moving subtitles tortured my eyes and my brain, that one day I would come face to face with those characters. The world on the big screen was suddenly all around me, alive and acting out its passions. All Sarno was a stage, and people blissfully went about their lives unaware that in my eyes each was a seasoned actor. Life could not have intrigued me more. As each new day unfolded, so too did the next episode in that colorful opera.

MERECÀ

Stella used all that pent-up guile to silence Mimmo when her small pile of books went flying from her hands using his chest as a bullseye and knocking him awkwardly off balance. He had little time to recover, when she sabotaged him with an open right-hand slap to his defenseless left cheek. Unable to juggle them successfully, the books scattered along the street with scooters and the three wheeled *Aparelle* swerving to avoid shredding them. His face had no chance of withstanding the trauma, soon flaunting spotty scarlet bruises. As Stella attempted a second helping of female fight with her left hand, her swing missed the untouched right cheek but caught his nose. The blood poured almost immediately from one nostril adding a scintilla of serious pain to his battlefield look. I grabbed him by the arm and guided him to one of the other benches. He was too defeated to help himself, so he followed directions and plopped his wounded frame on that cold surface. A few heavy tears plunged from his eyes onto the cobblestone, as Carminuccio trotted back from the gas station waving a small stack of paper towels. The embarrassment, more the cause for the tears than the pain, painted another shade of red all over his face and ears. The comically pathetic image of the big guy sitting there like a sad, tattered teddy bear had me adjusting my thinking about girls. Stella had used a lethal combination of stinging words and physical assault difficult to associate with a young female, and I resolved to never become another Mimmo style victim of a woman's rage. We owned the bench for a while as we concerned ourselves with our friend's recovery. We sat on either side of him, vaguely discussing the event, trying unsuccessfully to lighten the severity. Despite his sympathy, Carminuccio could not hold back as he delivered a short, stinging monologue on male stupidity. "*Una battaglia inutile e proprio stupida. Ti sei 'mbacciato di fatti che non ti riguardavano. Chell'che t'ha fatto Stella te lo sei meritato ... ti si creat'nu guaio pecchè quella è una ragazza che non te lo fa dimenticare.*" He took Stella's side in her actions maintaining that he deserved it. He also reminded the despondent bully that he had indeed picked a losing battle, and that Stella was not the type to easily forget the transgression.

MERECÀ

We helped him to his feet and walked him home. Nothing was spoken during the short trip to the more elegant side of town where many of the old money families had built their homes. Mimmo's parents were both doctors, and the pressure to follow them into the profession had a ball and chain effect on him. He was an obedient son who gave into his fears, submissively guided into adulthood, rather than urged to choose his own destiny. We left him at the large, ornate, ivy covered gate. There were two tall palm trees just beyond the threshold that stood guard on the path that led to a small, but elegant palazzo that dated to the early nineteenth century. The big guy thanked us, trying to mask his humiliation. Carminuccio finally pulled me away from the drama and onto the road that led to our side of town called *San Sebastiano.* The neighborhood was named after the local church that stood across from my *portone.* On Sundays, the small church filled mostly with kerchiefed women of all ages. The front pews were informally reserved for the elderly and the wives of local big shots. Young mothers filled the back pews cradling their babies, ready to slip out the door if they were unable to quiet the child. Men made up a small portion of the worshippers, most opting for the weekly soccer matches or that game of cards, lounged on café' chairs, puffing on unfiltered cigarettes. They crowded the sidewalks, forcing pedestrians to detour onto the street, and only losing contact with their card play to fixate on the seesaw motion of a standout female buttocks stuffed into a tight Sunday skirt. Once again, the slight jerking of the head, in sync with twitching eyebrows substituted conveniently for words. A quick upward nod of the head, first to get the attention of his fellow players, followed by a second nod launched in the direction of the strolling ass, and suddenly four sets of eyes became fixated on that mass of see-sawing female hormones. Only seconds were needed to complete the male ritual which concluded with facial expressions of approval and praise, but still no words. The game would quietly pick up where it left off, and life flipped to the next page.

    When Carminuccio spoke of Mimmo, he did so apologetically. He had invested much in advocating for Italian civility, and Mimmo's insensitivities towards Stella had become difficult to explain. I eased his anxiety pointing out that my feelings about life in Sarno had not been dampened by Mimmo, and that I did not consider him a brute because of his actions. "*Carmimù* (I had picked up on how many called him by the truncated Neapolitan version of his name in direct conversation. I felt friendly enough to try it out), *Io so che Mimmo ha sbagliato, però lui non è veramente una persona brutta*". He smiled and seemed relieved. "*Mercà, tu sai che non è il nostro carattere di trattare una donna in quel modo ... anche qualcuno un pochino storta come Stella ha diritto di essere rispettata. Poi, in verità mi sembra che Mimmo reagisca in quel modo per mancanza di maturità ... è un ragazzo che vuole essere uomo, e capisce che una ragazza come Stella non potrà mai innamorarsi di uno come lui, e quindi la sua rabbia.*" I picked up on the notion of respect for women, but I missed the meaning of the word "*storta*". "*Cosa significa storta?*" I asked. "*Sai, quando una persona non è di forma giusta ... come quando una persona ha le gambe storte, oppure gli occhi storti*". He likened Stella to a distortion, like crooked legs and crooked eyes ... not exactly evil or a bad person, just someone a bit off center. "*Storto*" became another of those idioms that critiqued the grey areas of Italian life so well. I made good use of it in the months to come finding it worked so well when pointing out a person's shortcomings without offending ... the word fell well short of being distasteful. He went on to describe Mimmo as an immature boy attempting manhood, understanding that a girl like Stella could never have feelings for one like him, thus his stinging anger towards her.

    We strolled into the *giardino* past Mom and nonna mechanically shucking peas, peeling potatoes and talking up a small storm about the state of things. We sat on the short, crumbling wall under the towering calypso tree. The winters were mild, so the calypso never completely shed all its leaves. It was a lazy, mild afternoon with the hibernating sun acting more like a confused ball of fire in a mid-July sky. Carminuccio loved the peaceful *giardino* and the way it carried us off into a neutral place where we could imagine our teenage utopias. His poetic attachment to life staggered me out of my elementary existence,

MERECÀ

forcing me to give it a fuller meaning. *"Gianni, sai che mi dispiace molto per Mimmo. Non mi sembra una persona che trovi mai pace. I genitori sono molto difficili con lui e si aspettano solo perfezione. Non so, come se per lui la vita è una lotta continua, anziché un'avventura piacevole. Lasciamo perdere ... sai che in questo posto mi sento pieno di serenità, ma anche pieno di energia come questo calipso che ha le radici ben piantate, ma con tantissimi rami che puntano verso destini diversi".* In his philosophy there was always room to forgive or explain away another's actions. Condemnation only surfaced when the act was pure evil. He felt a deep sorrow for the war Mimmo waged within himself, never finding peace enough to enjoy more honest experiences in life. As interest in Mimmo waned, he turned his attention to the *giardino* as the soft, playful breeze teased the hunched winter branches lamenting the loss of some of its inhabitants. He invited nature's serene energy to drench his senses as he compared himself to the calypso: sturdy and deep rooted-ambitiously projecting its branches towards different destinies. I never considered a tree to have that much character, but the imagery summoned by his explanation had given it a cryptic life ... and I allowed myself to believe that I could hear it whisper its wisdom, asking me to pay attention. Life now had many paths, and like those branches, I learned that those choices stemmed from each of us, solitary and distinct, directing us to jumpstart a more acute awareness of our own power to define ourselves. This was a complete departure from the single, narrow option the streets of the Bronx offered.

    There would be many consequential stops on this Italian journey, governed mostly by Carminuccio's ripened instincts that played a fateful role of inching me away from the parochial constraints of an American neighborhood, and toward a more emancipated existence. This divergence allayed the fears and apprehensions of defining my American life beyond the borders of Little Italy, replacing them with an enthusiastic empathy for the more authentic Italy with no ethnic boundaries. Life had granted this opportunity to travel a different road, one lined with the vestiges of a long history forged in marble and stone, of the spoils of Popes, emperors, and empires; of wars and conquerors; of resurrections, and renaissances. Along the way it meant mastering the expressions on the sun-dried, leathery faces of a vintage and wise agrarian people, because being Italian was all about people, and ultimately it required one to adopt a cultural compass as practical as the arrow shaped black and white signs that guided travelers to the next town. I was to wonder no longer about the person I would have been had I been born in Italy, and the opportunity to live an altered life was becoming a sustainable enterprise.

MERECÀ

CHAPTER 7
PRIMO NATALE

Winter in Sarno was more like a New York autumn. By February there was still little hope of seeing snow. In school, talk of snow only got me a smile and a collective reaction with Mimmo as the spokesperson. *"Mercà, non ci pensare che qui non si vede neve da cent'anni. Non è che ci troviamo al nord, nelle Alpi, a Milano, anzi a Bolzano dove nevica tutto l'anno"*. Stella rolled her eyes and shook her head eager to make a correction. *"Mamma, che esagerazione! Ma comm' fai a dire che fa a neve tutto l'anno? Second te allora a Bolzano nu iesce mai o sole? Nu cresce mai nu fiore? L'estate n'arriva manc pe nu iurno?"* Raffaele, who chose mostly to keep his thoughts to himself, found a small crack in the heated dialogue to slip in his humble reaction. *"Secondo me fa a neve sempe, ma poi esce o sole e se scpegne. Poi dopo duie o tre iurn' fa nat a vota a neve. Se capisce che a neve c'a fatt' sa da scpegne pe fa spazio p'a neve ca da fa'... si no, tutta sta neve add'o mettene?"* It was more of the same, enjoyable theater with Mimmo making a point about snow being a complete rarity in Sarno. The town was not nestled in the Alps where it snowed year-round. Stella then exposed his exaggeration, claiming it couldn't snow the entire year even in the alpine town of Bolzano, that the snow had to give way to the summer and the sun at some point. The expected innocence of Raffaele was a joy to behold as he described Bolzano as a place where it always snowed, but where a timely appearance of the sun would melt it away to make room for the next snowfall otherwise the alpine city wouldn't know where to put all that snow. It was a testimony to the insular nature of young lives guessing at the how the outside world worked even within their own country ... the occasional school trip to a museum in Naples or Greek ruins at Paestum were, for many, the furthest they ever ventured from Sarno. The differences between north and south were stark, and Bolzano, more German than Italian, was an imaginary world away.

MERECÀ

It was late December with Christmas approaching. Mom did her best to decorate the apartment American style. Sarno could not match the consumer holiday appeal back in the states, but it basked in centuries old traditions that had all to do with connecting spiritually with others rather than exchanging wrapped gifts. Pop cut down a small evergreen and we strung up as many silvery and gold items from around the house. Nonna joined in tying her heirlooms to the tree with strands of ribbon. We asked around town about popcorn, but despite our best efforts at drawings and descriptions, and since there was no Italian translation, we got a shrug of the shoulders and a defeated, *"mi dispiace"* (I'm sorry) or *"bo"(pronounced bow)*, the local slang for "*I have no clue*". Friends and relatives made their time-honored pilgrimages to the homes of close relatives with gift baskets (*panari*) filled with produce from their own farms. Homemade fruit preserves, dried meats like prosciutto and sopressata, and small burlap sacks filled with hazelnuts and walnuts were common contents. The holiday pastry ensembles were usually the only purchased items that stocked the rest of the baskets with *Mostaccioli, Cornetti al Cioccolato, Brioche, Paste a Mondorle,* (almond cookies), and all types of biscotti which, along with the artistically packaged Panettoni, made the most memorable impression on a youthful palate. The sweets were meant to last through the Christmas week, but hardly survived the hunger inducing jitters of a night of *Tombola (Italian Bingo).* The competitiveness rivaled that of the weekly Bingo gatherings at the senior citizen center on Southern Boulevard. On Thursday nights we could hear the distorted, crackling microphone sound of the master of ceremonies calling out the numbers, along with the euphoric screeching of winners smothering the exasperated sighs of the losers.

Tombola was serious business. Before long, the tenants in our building had become family. Sharing time, coffee, and food had become a regular routine. The apartment of Don Antonio and his wife Lucia had become the gathering place for most social celebrations. It was a ritual for Lucia to bake cakes and biscotti to mark birthdays and dates dedicated to saints. The Catholic calendar in her living room clearly listed a saint for each day of the year, and where she penciled in reminders to send *gli auguri,* (good wishes) to all acquaintances with that name. With what seemed more than three hundred sixty-five saints, each day of the year gave cause to celebrate, and they carried as much weight as birthdays. That Christmas Eve night we all readied ourselves to do Tombola battle at the table of Don Antonio.

    Each card cost ten lire, and with twenty-five people crowded around a dining table built for twelve, the atmosphere became intense. The pots were divided into *ambo, terno, quaterna, quintina and tombola* (two, three, four and five numbers, increasing in booty with the grand prize being *tombola!).* My first Christmas Eve Tombola started in the early evening as daylight gave way to a chilly, glassy, star-speckled darkness lasting till midnight when it came time to join the orderly procession of adults and children on the short uphill hike to midnight Mass at the church of San Sebastiano. It was one of two holy days when the number of men sitting in the pews equaled the number of women. Christ's birth was a serious event, not a birthday celebration, but a solemn, VIP event. Don Nunzio, the head priest, had turned every woman in attendance into the Blessed Virgin with his oratorical sermon. With the severity of a judge dishing out a sentence to a penitent criminal, he chastised them, demanding that they aspire to the same level of holiness, to live life as Mary did, and to raise their children in the image of Christ. The tiny church had no heat, so people buttoned up and huddled, as Don Nunzio's words added to the shivers. The stone walls and marble floors surrounded us with a constant chill that kept our toes numb and the tips of our noses pink and moist. The good priest wore a stern expression, moving deliberately between altar and tabernacle as he prepped for Communion. He punctuated the ceremony with several head scans of the audience committing the faces to memory. He would use that information in the coming days to make a point of those who showed. The women were quick to have him check them off his mental roster. Favors were not easy to come by for those who made only occasional appearances, so making sure your presence

MERECÀ

was noted paid benefits as needed. In the two decades following the war, priests and churches still performed a list of services that would eventually move to government bureaucracies.

Tombola jackpots could reach two hundred lire which turned into a small fortune in a teen's pocket. So, winning that last pot of cash could make a kid a happy consumer for at least a week. Christmas Day was more about exchanging good cheer than it was about gifts. Life continued as most days with coffee shops and pastry shops opening their doors to the gathering locals. The fancier clothes and the festive packaging of foods gave the day that special, uncommon flair. There had been talk of *Babbo Natale* (Father Christmas) bringing toys and gifts for children, but the practice had yet to take a more uniform hold on Italians … only a few practiced it. American soldiers had introduced Santa during the war, but children remained attached to *La Befana,* the old woman who brought gifts to children on the 5th of January, the eve of the Epiphany. We had a tough time with the old woman thing, so Mom kept Santa alive at least for another year.

After dinner, Carminuccio kept our appointment to meet our friends on the *rettifilo*. We each grabbed another pastry, talking and plotting in between bites. As we glided along the cobblestones down Via Umberto, we spoke of Christmas in nostalgic tones, sensing the dying hours to the most glorious day of the year. The first to greet us was Mimmo as rounded the statue of Mariano Abignente. I noticed for the first time that the *rettifilo* had a more formal name: *Via Giovanni Amendola.* I asked about the name prompting a short response about a journalist who was assassinated because he was a critic of Mussolini. In the coming months, as I became more curious about my parents' past, I kept my father busy with questions about his own youth. The more he revealed, the more improbable it all seemed in comparison to my clinical existence. His war years were marked by death, days and nights sequestered in caves during the Allied bombardments, small portion pasta meals, and frequent trips to the cemetery to bury German soldiers or relatives. The bombs cut short my father's education, allowing him only a third-grade diploma. It was a slight handicap overcome by diligently hovering over the pages of his favorite daily *Il Mattino* in Sarno and *Il Progresso Italo-Americano News* back in New York. He sat stoically at the post-dinner table with the oversized, news filled daily sprawled across its width end to end; at times having to elevate the droopy extremities to read even the smallest of articles. No news was insignificant enough to pass over, so he would skip a day buying a fresh paper if there was still more to read. Once he mastered the pronunciation of the more difficult words, he understood their meanings. The spelling may not have been familiar, but the sound was. I would continue to watch my father self-educate as the years rolled on. Any final exam would have easily earned him a college degree.

Mimmo appeared jovial and eager to round us up. There had been some minor recurring animosities between him and Stella, but neither would miss out on the opportunity to spend a few precious hours together outside the classroom. There existed an inexplicable need to allow affection for others to have a life of its own-and my Italian friends possessed the ability to separate kindness from malice and have one prevail over the other on the appropriate occasion. Mimmo's actions and words were a common revelation of how humanism could stifle bad feelings. It was another trait they practiced unpretentiously, baffling an American kid used to holding grudges. The appearance of the others at the far end of the rettifilo brought on a titillating anticipation at the thought of soon becoming one large group. I longed for and treasured those times that brought us together unencumbered by obligations. A sweet sense of casual freedom would own us, keeping any past bitterness at an innocuous distance. No force could usurp our need to just feel good in each other's company.

We walked the length of Via Amedola laughing, gossiping, exchanging partners, walking arm in arm. For one glorious day, social barriers were ignored in favor of discovering the depths of our friendships. As I recovered from a laughing fit at something

MERECÀ

Mimmo said, Stella maneuvered to my side and slipped her arm into mine. Had it been just another day, it probably wouldn't have happened, but it was Christmas and, as that silly, easy kind of love permeated the chilly air hovering over our small town, it seemed that all forms of tenderness were possible. Stella's embrace caught me by surprise with no chance to interpret it. After a few paces, I relaxed myself into a hormonal high. Stella was easily the most beautiful girl ever to cross my path, as well the most unapproachable. Yet, there she stood, holding on tightly, still casting comments in the direction of the others, while signaling that she intended to extend her stay.

"Merecà, sono stata un po' impertinente con te da quando sei arrivato e spero che tu possa perdonarmi." The slight shock of Stella asking for forgiveness for her insolence towards me since my arrival had me stumbling over my limited Italian, hardly able to speak the words I had taken a few seconds to formulate. *"Non bisogna, non hai fatto niente male con me."* The grammar and choice of words were a bit choppy, but I made it clear there was no need for apologies since I felt no wrongdoing towards me. She forcefully disagreed, punishing her own insensitivity. *"Non è vero. Mi sento così colpevole. Sono stata insensibile e mi vergogno."* She continued to explain that her initial dislikes had nothing to do with me. She further expressed that she had been conditioned by to view anything American as corrupt capitalism that favors the rich over the poor. She placed herself and most of her fellow citizens in an Italian version of the blue-collar wage earner, making a case for how little they earned in comparison to the people who ran the country and corporations. She made the Italian money gesture of rubbing the tips of three fingers together lowering her hand to her knees to indicate how much people like her father earned, to then raise it to over her head to give me an idea of where the rich stood. *"Ti confesso che quando sei per prima arrivato, eri per me proprio quell'Americano di cui parla mio padre. Ma poi quando ho incontrato la tua famiglia, in particolare tua mamma con i suoi racconti da immigrante, siete tutti entrati in un'altra luce ... vi vedevo più chiaro, più veri. Insomma, ho capito che tuoi genitori*

MERECÀ

sono stati fra quelli che hanno fuggito la povertà del nostro paese nel dopoguerra per le opportunità dell'America e che per loro non è stato facile arrivare stranieri in una terra che non parlava la loro lingua ... mamma, ho pensato che paura doverti spiegare a stranieri che non ti capiscono e forse nemmeno ne avessero fiducia. Figurati che quando viaggiamo in certi luoghi italiani, come al nord vicino Milano dove vivono I miei cugini, mi sento addirittura straniera. Sai, anche se si dice che parliamo tutti la stessa lingua, mi sono accorta che nelle zone del nord, parlo italiano, ma fanno fatica a capirmi. E poi io li guardo stupita e penso: ma forse questi non sono italiani veri, sono forse tedeschi oppure francesi. Poi mi allontano confusa e ringrazio Dio che almeno noi del sud siamo veramente italiani, che parliamo la lingua, mangiamo pasta e pizza e sventoliamo la bandiera. Perdonami, sto parlando troppo-è il mio carattere. Mia madre mi dice sempre di mordermi la lingua". She petered out as she stuck out her tongue and gently bit down on it several times to make sure I understood that her mother is forever telling her to bite it because she talks too much. Her short conversations with my mother had opened her eyes to a less biased understanding of who we were. Mom had exposed the immigrant side of being American. Stella had come to sympathize with the chances some had taken to move to a country where people spoke a different language and where perhaps the newly arrived were not completely trusted. She likened it to when she traveled to the north near Milano to visit relatives. She related her own feelings of alienation explaining that she no longer felt to be in Italy, and that the northerners were more German or French. She thought of the fears and the discomfort of living among those who did not view her as one of them. She could have spoken for hours without losing my attention. Her hypnotic delivery kept me in a trance with my mind split between listening to every word and delighting in her fierce expression. I had dared to think that perhaps she had grown some sympathies for the type of Americans we were, and that we had much more in common. She had to clear her conscience, thus the bench warming session. I didn't mind-I enjoyed her company, and the chance to gaze into her eyes and explore her face more completely without her sounding off and castigating me for showing too much interest. When I recalled her attachment to older guys, it was easy to crawl back into my reality and my place. She placed her hand on mine, smiled, planted a pillowy kiss on both cheeks, sealing the friendship and kickstarting a new relationship. It was an opening and, taking away that one best feeling from the encounter, was good and welcomed. I replayed the kisses over and over in the coming weeks.

Mimmo and Carminuccio had kept an eye on what was happening. They anticipated questioning me like two eager journalists that had fallen upon a juicy headline. I hesitated a bit, teasing their need to know more. Mimmo was full of adolescent questions about infatuations, lovers, secret encounters, and letters. *"Gianni, mi sembra che Stella voglia essere la tua ragazza ... so che non mi sbaglio da come ti parlava, come ti guardava negli occhi, come ha preso la tua mano nella sua, e poi quei baci inaspettati come due innamorati. Scommetto che se non ci fossero tanta gente in giro, ci sarebbe stato un bacio sulle labbra, Che improbabilità a pensare che non ti ha mostrato mai niente più che antipatia. Se hai bisogno di un postino che vi scambia lettere d'amore, io ci sto".* Carminuccio took a more cautious approach reminding me that Stella was a difficult female, mature beyond her years who needed the company of high school guys. In short, do not get your hopes up, she will make you shed tears. *"Gianni, ricordati che Stella è una ragazza difficile, molto più matura dei suoi anni con affezioni per ragazzi del liceo. Lascia perdere, che quella ti fa piangere".* I could forgive their misinterpretations because of how things appeared, so I explained the truth behind her change of heart. They remained a bit stunned but accepting. Their exhortations, however, did little to dissuade me from considering the possibilities. Her expressions, her beauty, her girlhood, and her strength of character were infectious; probably more than she would herself acknowledge. Stella was not the typical beauty queen who flaunted her assets. She had an odd mix of urban and peasant allure, much like the strong female character in a Sofia Loren movie. My boyish heart had been hijacked by Italian romanticism, allowed to wonder off to consider the pleasures of intimacy, of perhaps composing a string of love letters or scripting a collection of poems, genuine and well versed because of a powerful affection ... words that flowed easily, lines that came into existence spontaneously... the offspring of one's feelings. Courtship could blunt a teen's hormones and sideline thoughts of sex. For a budding teen, the act of courting had become a pleasurable occupation that could captivate sentimentality and corral and tame anxieties. In the lyrics of Italian songs, in the magazine articles, the short stories, in the poems and sonnets of my literature class, *amare o fare l'amore* (to love or to make love) implied a more complete delirium that started with taking notice of the individual, dwelling on her character, first in quiet thoughts, then in expressive language. The flirtation was to be prolonged indefinitely, holding out for dovetailing fingers, a possible first kiss, or a body warming embrace. Our *professore* of Italian literature introduced me to Dante's spasms for a woman named Beatrice. In his enchanting lecture, Dante expresses an impossible affliction which forces him to keep his love secretive. Any overt expression is discouraged, he must keep his distance, only imaging them together in his writings. The many compositions dedicated to her, exposed Dante's passions and how well he kept them in check. I could not get those stories out of my head ... how could he love a woman so deeply and still avoid contact of any kind? I thought of Stella and how difficult it had been for those few minutes to sit so close to her, with my hand in hers, to refrain from planting a tender kiss on her flushed, inviting lips. I never lost my heavy melancholy for Dante who had to endure writing about Beatrice in life and beyond her death as a ghost guiding him on his journey into Paradise in his *Divine Comedy*. I may have had a hard time believing that a mortal could embark on a journey through Hell, Purgatory and Paradise while alive, but I hardly doubted the powers that motivated his odyssey.

  Italian Christmases extended pleasurably into the first week of January because of the Epiphany. Carminuccio made sure we used the time exploring the latest album releases from England,

America, and Italy. The British had invaded just about every country with their music, and the focus was on the bands. There was something wondrous about four guys in leather bell bottoms, psychedelic shirts and long hair, projecting their guitars like phallic symbols targeting thousands of seduced girls in the audience. At the local record shop-*Casa del Disco*-my friend turned me on to the *Moody Blues*, then the *Doors*, the *Kinks*, and other future iconic names. I confessed I enjoyed the English-speaking bands, but that I had a soft spot for Italian bands like *I Pooh, Equipe 84, I Camaleonti, Collage,* and for a couple of guys named *Franco IV e Franco I* (Simon and Garfunkel Italian style) who's song **Ho Scritto T'Amo Sulla Sabbia** became branded in my entire being. It was the most iconic summer beach song that played continuously in the jukeboxes of the pavilions all along the Amalfi Coast. One of those tunes that stays with you into adulthood, impossible to forget the lyrics. It was easy to connect the music to the culture and how it complimented everything else Italian. They may not have had an international following, but their unique sounds added to the complete Italian experience-especially for foreigners. It was no wonder that German, British and American tourists kept playing Italian songs at the jukeboxes. Many also purchased copies to take home. I loaded up on several popular tunes that played daily on radio stations and from loudspeakers at the outdoor market (*mercato*). The 45's began to stack up on my turntable and the sounds filled much of my solitary time. It was easy to associate the music with Stella. Stories of loves won and lost, abandoned courtships, boyfriends leaving for military duty, and slurpy descriptions of the perfect woman dominated the lyrics. It was easy and appealing to lose oneself in that verbal whirlwind, becoming the hero and wanting to believe that it was all about me. Commiserating with the poor, heartsick lover in the song could come off as tragic initially only to learn, as the song neared its closing, that there was still a thread of hope that the obstacles could be overcome, and there would a-happy ever after-ending. The lyrics were four-minute soap operas that came to life when those sweet melodies were added. Imagining myself and Stella in those musical sonnets would rock me to sleep on many of those chilly nights. It was one thing to be a budding teenager in love, but it was quite cathartic to be one in love in Italy.

MERECÀ

CHAPTER 8
IL GIARDINO

  It had invitingly become a place of refuge for an American kid who needed the space and the time to understand the changes in his young life. The acre of land abutting our new home we simply called *il giardino (the garden)*, extended rectangular and deep, populated mostly with coarse and fuzzy leafed hazelnut trees shaded by towering, patrician walnuts. The open spaces were filled by honey hemorrhaging fig and aromatic orange trees to create a density in which one could smuggle away and embark on journeys to wherever the imagination allowed. At the far-right corner lay an abandoned, inverted, cone shaped water basin about twenty feet wide with inlaid brick steps that ran its circumference allowing one to climb in and out at any point. It was now filled with all sorts of weeds and seedlings reaching for the canopy and any slight exposure to the sun. Eucalyptus branches hung over the width of the pool caressing it, bowing gently in the soft breeze as if a giant plume bent on cooling off the ghosts of bygone bathers. Nonna explained that the eucalyptus had been purposely planted when the *giardino* was still a part of the land owned by the Count of Sarno. She added that the fallen leaves floated delicately, releasing a scented oil that over time created a spa-like effect. Aristocratic wives and daughters believed the water to be salutary and rejuvenating. It all made sense when splitting one of the leaves in two-it released an unmistakable essence. My thoughts turned suspiciously to the Vicks rub that Mom spread unsparingly on our chests when we were all stuffed up. The encounter with the nature of the scent, and recalling the word eucalyptus on the packaging, provided a clear understanding of the origin of the ingredient.

Often, I circled along the edge, imagining Greek goddesses and sirens frolicking, splashing about, laughing, and exchanging compliments in their ancient tongue; transplanted images that stayed with me from our daily readings of Homer's Odyssey. My sweet journeys into the past would soon be interrupted by the noisy

MERECÀ

rustling of an impertinent lizard staring up at me sideways, wondering if I qualified as a predator. These constant companions would remain expertly motionless, reconnoiter their surroundings, to then dash off if the coast were clear. The grey ones camouflaged conveniently in the crevices of volcanic rocks, while their green colored cousins blended nervously into the ground foliage. My early attempts at capturing one of them would have me standing baffled, holding only its severed tail while the main body disappeared safely into one of the many hiding places along the venerable, but weathered stone wall that separated the giardino from the Count's property. After stacking several large, uneven stones along the wall's base, I grew tall enough to peer into our neighbor's elegant, manicured grounds with marble fountains, classical statues, giant flowering urns, and royal palm trees that rose to the same height as the imposing eighteenth century Baroque palazzo. That spot became a daily destination in the hope of catching a glimpse of the mysterious family that lived there. I learned that the last Count to hold the title had it stripped from him after the war, rumored to have been an ardent supporter of Mussolini's Fascist government. He had survived the war, but not the wrath of the partisans bent on punishing those accused of Fascist sympathies. The stigma had forced the family into seclusion, ostracized by the local population, even threatened with death by communist fanatics. Carminuccio explained that much of the old family wealth had been used up maintaining the estate, but that local papers had carried a story about the family petitioning for a return of the title and assets that had been confiscated by the Allies towards the end of the war. "*Il Vecchio morì qualche anno fa. Il figlio, il nuovo Conte, si chiama Damiano e la moglie mi sembra Clara. Hanno solo una figlia Elisa. La figlia si vede solo ogni tanto quando esce con la nonna a fare la spesa. È snella, capelli biondi con fili castani, naso a puntino con labbra piene. L'ho vista solo un paio di volte. Ha una insegnante privata e perciò non si vede mai a scuola, e questo mi sembra addirittura triste per una ragazza la nostra età. Mia zia li conosce bene perché' fa servizio da domestica; sai, pulisce e cucina. Una volta avevano quattro domestiche, ma oggi giorno c'è solo mia zia. Non sono mica poveri, ma le grandi ricchezze sono cose del passato.* He gave a short history of the family with names and the facts he had learned from his aunt who worked there as a housekeeper and cook. There may once have been four, but now his aunt was the sole employee. The part that stood out for me was the mention of their daughter Elisa. I had never seen her during my many forays, perhaps because the section of their land abutting the wall was shielded in tall overgrown laurel trees that ran the length of the wall creating a tight canopy, allowing only slithers of light to penetrate on sunny days. The area beneath the canopy was a hollow corridor where no vegetation grew. Irregular openings in the foliage allowed for limited views. Carminuccio sadly recounted that the daughter was home schooled, to be seen only sporadically in town on short shopping excursions with her grandmother. He described her as petite, with long blonde hair laced with brown threads, a pointed nose, and plump lips. "*Non proprio la bellezza di Stella, ma bella abbastanza da essere simpatica. Poi, non la conosco abbastanza da giudicare, ma potrebbe avere un carattere piacevole.*" Not the same beauty as Stella, according to him, but beautiful enough to be appealing. He admitted to not knowing her well enough but considered that she may have a certain charm. He paused for a few seconds to contemplate how she probably yearned to be in a classroom with others her age, to make friends, to mingle with people... indeed, to live life. *"Non so come fa a non frequentare la scuola con noi, a farsi amici, a trovarsi fra la gente ... insomma, a vivere.* He still considered them upper class but was convinced that the big money was a thing of the past. His words stayed with me for days, and I invented scenes of daily aristocratic lives based on movies viewed or stories read. The palazzo had a ghostly appearance with outer walls stained in large, odd shaped, rust-colored blotches sliced into patterns of different sizes by dirty rainwater. Those waters sourced at the edge of the rooftop where the stone parapet, wrapped in sheets of bronze, encircled the top of the palazzo. The floor to ceiling windows on the uppermost level gave it four satanic eyes as they opened to narrow stone terraces covered in moss and ivy. Each terrace had a stone center piece gargoyle at its base with a savage face and exposed fangs, forewarning strangers to approach at one's own risk. In the distant right corner stood a small glass cupola. I imagined a chapel or an observatory with a long, retracting telescope. The building kept me in its grips for days, wondering how magnificent the interior might be with cavernous rooms, tall ceilings, and endless hallways where words ricocheted off walls. I pictured imposing medieval suits of armor flanking giant fireplaces, and romanticized portraits of past title holders and family members. With the Bronx offering no such experiences, I let my imagination run wild.

It was early May of that first spring when I dropped my books on the kitchen floor after school, frustrated by the inability to find news of the baseball season back in the states. I had asked several store owners if they would oblige me with a copy of any American newspaper from their vendors, but to no avail. Nonna asked about my unusual nasty mood, but my confession only garnered a confused look when I attempted an explanation of the game of baseball and my passion for the Yankees. She blessed me with her usual charm, accepting that it was all especially important to me, after which she shrugged complacently, leaned back into her chair, and continued to sort out the beans that lay scattered in her apron prepping them for the pot of boiling water hissing away on the stove. I smiled at the awkward clash of two distant generations and cultures, understanding how improbable it would be for her to fully sympathize despite the sincere concern. With thoughts of the new season, the Yankee roster and how the first games had gone, I picked up my diary and started out for the giardino. I had settled most times on a spot under the eucalyptus, shaded and silent. Several large, flat boulders had been arranged into a comfortable platform in decades past and, as its new occupant, it was where I spent hours filling in empty pages with short vignettes about school, my friends, love and girlfriends, life in Sarno and my untamed emotions. I set aside some pages for sketches of the nature that befriended me: lizards of all sizes and color combinations, the plump figs that hung precariously from sturdy branches oozing small globs of their sweet, nutty elixir sheltered by large, paw-like leaves; walnuts emerging from their green, prickly cocoons, and tiny hazelnuts peeking shyly from their spiked bonnets. That afternoon my senses floated poetically, caressed by gentle, sporadic breezes while the whispering foliage attempted to lullaby me to sleep.

The narcotic trance was suddenly shattered by a playful female voice from just beyond the wall. It pulled my attention towards it. Once I was able to lift myself above the wall, climbing clumsily onto the stone stairway I had hastily erected, my eyes were met instantly by those of a young girl who had fixated on my spot, spying the disturbance. She took a step back, gazed up at me startled, quickly making her discomfort known. *"Mamma, che paura! E tu chi sei?"* Startled, she demanded to know my identity. *"Sono Gianni, I live here, I mean, abito qui."* In my panic, I uttered a few words in English, followed by a quick Italian translation. *"Oh my, but are you English? Have you come from England?"* My thoughts blurred, unable to decipher the probability of her asking me a question in perfect English. I stumbled through my answer, hoping to prolong the dialogue. *"No, I'm from America, I speak English but not like you ... I mean, I speak American English, you know the kind we speak in New York."* She gave it a quick reflection, showing a similar interest in keeping the discussion alive. *"I have been to New York, I love New York ... yes, Times Square, Fifth Avenue, the Empire State Building, Broadway... I suppose you must know these places well."* Caught off guard, my first instinct was to construct an easy lie or two, but I could not find the artistry in a short time to be convincing. I had never been to any of those places, so to admit to it was difficult. How could I have lived in New York for fourteen years and not be able to match notes with a girl who had grown up in Sarno? I was taken by her own honesty, so I confessed. *"Well, I lived in the Bronx, and although it is part of New York, it isn't close enough for me to go to all the places you visited. It's out of the way, far from Manhattan, you know, most people never even heard of it"* Her diction added a layer of polish and grandeur beyond my world. She could have shown some disbelief or made a killer comment or two focusing on our differences, but she simply giggled and asked me in her Italian accent laced British English, to climb over the wall onto her side. *"My dear Gianni, are you able to bring yourself to my side of the wall? I do understand ... I read that New York is quite large. When we were there this past summer, our friends did take us to the Bronx to see a baseball game, I believe it was hardly a fifteen-minute drive. You must know the Yankees, surely! Did I pronounce it correctly? My father has always been interested in the game ever since he watched American soldiers play on a campo in Naples during the war. The soldier also gave him a gift, you know the big ... how is it called ... the guantone."* I scratched my way down her side of the wall, which was deeper and less creviced, finally letting go and landing on one foot, stumbling towards her all in one motion. I avoided embarrassment by regaining my balance without tumbling onto my butt. *"The guantone is the glove, your father was given a baseball glove as a gift ... that is so cool. Does he still have it? I brought one with me from America. You really went to Yankee stadium? You saw the Yankees?" By the way, what is your name?* I wanted to deflect attention away from my exaggeration on the location of the Bronx. I wondered if she was the girl Carminuccio had spoken of while I was being forced to admit to the additional sad fact that I had only been to the stadium once. *"Elisa, mi chiamo Elisa, everyone calls me Eli (pronounced Ehlee), and yes, Gianni ... I did go with our American friends, but I wanted to leave straight away ... non ci capivo niente e c'era troppo casino, do you understand Italian?"* She found the game complicated and the noise and confusion annoying. *"I have loved the Yankees all my life. If you live in the Bronx, the Yankees mean everything; I don't think the Bronx would even exist without the Yankees."* A smile connected her cheeks as she rolled her eyes. *"Gianni, that is perfectly silly, and I greatly admire your passion ... la tua passione. My papà always tells me that we must have a passion, or we are not alive. I have many passions, but my greatest are music and football."* Surprised, I asked how she could find football appealing. Her answer made the question seem out of place. *"But why do ask so confused about football because I am a girl? I love calcio, my team is the one called Juventus from the city of Torino. I feel for Juventus as you feel for the Yankees."* I had confused American football with soccer. She explained that the British call soccer football. I found it funny, but I understood the slight connection thinking that the term was more accurate for soccer than it was for our version, since most of the play was done by kicking the ball. *"I'm sorry, I didn't mean to ..." "Non c'è bisogno di scusarsi-please, no need to apologize. Most people think I should not show so much interest in a man's sport. I say bugger to that!* As soon as those words slipped out, she covered her mouth with both her hands, turning back to make sure no other person had heard them. *"Why did you cover your mouth?" "I said-bugger-I'm not supposed to say that word." "Why? What does it mean?"* She searched for an adequate explanation. *"Well, it is the same as saying shit."* I chuckled at her pronunciation of a word we used freely on the streets of the Bronx. She gave the word an elegant spin, depriving it of its nastier character. Her speech had become captivating to the point that I loved just listening to her. Her English took me back to the Beatles movie, *A Hard Day's Night.* It was the last Saturday of that last summer in the Bronx when we followed the girls to the Savoy Movie House on Hughes Avenue. The feature cost us an astronomical fifty cents which left no money for the popcorn and Coke. It was also my last date with Debbie. Elisa took no offense to my reaction sensing it was more of a compliment. *"Do you enjoy listening to me talk?" "Yes, I do. I've never heard shit pronounced like that."* She caught my Bronx pronunciation, accusing me of substituting the "t" with a "d". I denied it, so she laid out a lesson in elocution. *"Dear Gianni, repeat after me: shit".* She prolonged the hard "t" sound. I followed with my version: *"shit".* She jumped at the opportunity to make her point. *"See, you left out the 't' and it sounds like a 'd'. You just said 'shid', not 'shit'. Try again."* "Shid." "No, it's shittt." She kept adding more and more 't's', and despite my willingness to follow the lesson, my strong 't' sounded more like an artificial appendage. It was her turn to chuckle at the liberated use of the word, exaggerating the way one would to over-appease an attentive audience.

MERECÀ

Her English was born of the full summers spent at a boarding school in a London suburb. The Italian accent, combined with the British English, created a melodic fluency that could have been considered an art form. Class differences were unknown in my Bronx neighborhood, they only came to life on the television screen. Elisa's life and her expressions introduced me to those real distinctions for the first time. If I felt less than her, it was more of an uneasy imposition I placed on myself. She never set our budding friendship on unequal footing, as she played down talk of her history, her home and the summers spent in England. She preferred to cloak it, but her pedigree was obvious enough to cast an occasional shadow ... still, she found the humility to nurture us along. *"Gianni, raccontami la tua storia-perché' ti trovi qui a Sarno? Tell me please, why you are here in Sarno?"* I would have normally shied away, but with her I felt a to tell my story. Her habit of speaking in both languages was funny but inviting. *"My parents were both born here, and they left for America after they were married. Me, my brother, and sister were all born in New York ... we are Americans. Everything was fine and then my grandfather died and my nonna got sick. We sold everything we had in the Bronx and came here to live."* *"But don't you want to go back to your country?"* A few months back I would have given her a resounding-yes, but now my words were filled with hesitation. *"When we first arrived, all I wanted to do was to get back on the ship. Now I feel different ... now I wonder about my new life and being Italian. I like Sarno, I like my friends. My best friend is Carminuccio."* My comments about school increased her curiosity. *"What grade are you? My parents refuse to send me to your school, the public school. I have a private tutor much like a governess in England. I often wonder what it would be like to go to a real school."* She was introducing me to English words I had never come across. I confessed I did not know what a governess was. *"I'm finishing eighth grade. What does a governess do?"* *"I already passed the eighth grade and will finish my ninth soon. Of course, I cannot imagine you would have many governesses in the Bronx."* She hesitated. *"Sorry, I didn't mean that as an insult, it's just that I always believed it to be a British thing."* I took no offense to the accurate characterization. *"A governess is concerned with a child's complete education. I have never had one, but many of my friends in London do. It is usually a well-educated single lady who can teach anything from the sciences to how to dress for certain occasions. Here I simply have a tutor who teaches all the same things you probably learn in school... you know, history, mathematics, literature, and the arts, and sometimes astrology ... we do have a telescope in our observatory, and I very much enjoy learning about the stars, planets and the universe."* Her knowledge of things seemed deeper, with a natural excitement. I came to accept it much the way we reacted to those who had better report cards. *"So, you're fifteen years old? I have never looked through a telescope-can you really see the planets?" "Yes, I will be fifteen next month. You can see the planets and much more. I am told that the universe is infinite, that it has no beginning and no end. Can you imagine not ever reaching the end of something? Like being in a tunnel that goes on and on with no exit."*

    It hit me that she was just short of a year older, causing a slight flutter. Her words once again had the power to take me to places unknown. I began to think of our lives and earth as miniscule and almost insignificant within her explanation of the vastness of the space around us. This was the case with most of the conversations with my Italian friends. Carminuccio, and even Stella, had a way of forcing my mind to think beyond its limits. They provided the stimulus to philosophize about life as something more than just the conventional, of so much more than just survival. I was suddenly bewitched with thoughts of who we were, where did we come from, were we alone in the universe and, as Eli put it: what is the purpose of life? Within my more tribal Bronx setting there was never anything about life that needed questioning. One accepted an existence that came to be defined by the neighborhood, ethnicity, the Catholic Church, and the limited, suspicious exposure to life beyond the borders of Little Italy. Television was our only window on a world that eluded us into our adulthood. Many were born and died on the same block, often in the same apartment. If all we asked of being alive was to be able to make it as comfortable as possible from day to day with the fewest disruptions, then life had all the definition it needed. It was all good and blissful.

Sarno was not allowed this easy way out. There was no way it could avoid the greater influences just beyond its city limits. It was wedded to everything that was Italy and the Mediterranean ... there was no escaping it. Those educated to these facts had the tools to think of their lives as continuous and boundless involvements, and not simply an existence. I was reminded of the passion that motivated even the simplest experiences like a sublime plate of pasta, the round trip *passeggiata* along the *rettifilo*, the first sip of a steamy cappuccino, or the pleasure in greeting others with a heartfelt -*buongiorno*-. That simple passion was the premise for the more powerful ones that burrowed deeper into the explanations of life, asking one to consider a multitude of questions with no concrete answers. In that, one discovered the beauty of the interminable search, and it was the search that kept my Italians intrigued. Elisa was no exception, and I understood that she had the power to only hypothesize about answers. I snapped back to life asking: *"But isn't everything created by God?"* I could only latch onto the Catholic playbook that reduced all things to the will of God. It was easy to apply a teaching that was an absolute- no need to question its validity, it was non-negotiable, and the ultimate reason why everything turned out the way it did. "*Gianni, diciamo per caso che Dio non esiste. Come facciamo allora a spiegare noi, la terra, l'universo? Devi ammettere a tutte le altre possibilità. So che è facile attribuire tutto alla volontà di Dio, ma forse ci sono altre spiegazioni. Anche se non è evidente, dobbiamo darle qualche considerazione. Do you understand? What if God does not exist? How then do we explain everything? Is there another explanation? Should we not consider other possibilities even if they are not so evident? These are topics I have discussed with my tutor when we look up at the stars. It is also discussed in my classes at school in England.*" It was apparent that science had equal footing with religion in her view. I was only in the early stages of processing those considerations.

MERECÀ

We had moved to a corner of the property housing a small fountain and a bench. We sat in full view of the palazzo. I wondered if her parents had caught a glimpse of us. No sooner had I worked through that possibility that I notice a tall, slender woman walking briskly towards us. My first reaction was to stand and make my way back to the wall, but her inviting voice held me in my place. *"Ciao Eli, ti sto cercando da quasi mezz'ora. Allora, come si chiama questo ragazzo così simpatico?" "Mamma, parliamo in inglese. Si chiama Gianni, nativo americano, da New York. He has moved here to Sarno with his family. Theirs is the land on the other side of the wall. We met, started talking and I asked him to come to our side."* Her mother was an elegant woman, dressed stylishly, with necklaces and bracelets that jingled with each movement. *"Well, Gianni, welcome to our town. I do hope you will not compare it to New York ... you will be sorely disappointed. Eli, we are having dinner shortly, and we are hosting some of papà's friends. Be sure to join us soon."* The brief encounter was enough to add to my new understanding of class distinctions. Elisa had kept it to a minimum, but her mom gave it new energy and a concrete image. *"Mamma would it be fine for Gianni to leave through the front gate rather than have to climb over the wall?" "Yes, of course. You may show him out."* We lingered a few minutes more while her mother returned to the palazzo. *"My mother can appear to be a bit severe at times. She becomes that way when we are expecting company." "She actually seems nice. She reminds me of some movie stars ... not sure which one, but she could definitely be a famous actress."* My new friend wrapped her arm around mine and led me across the courtyard to the front gate. The closer we got to the palazzo, the less it appeared a distant monument and more a real home. I noticed the crest above the entrance with a cross surrounded by small stars and the word *Marabbecca* on a sash enveloping the cross. Eli explained the palazzo was named after a mythological monster who scared children away from drowning in wells. Her father took an affection to the name used by his grandfather in bedtime stories. Its origin was in Sicily where her paternal ancestors were born. (The word palazzo usually meant building, but when it had a crest, a pedigree, and a name, it resembled more a British country mansion). Cars were just then parking on the half-moon driveway in front of the huge portico with her mom and dad about to greet the occupants. Elisa kissed me softly on both cheeks and invited me back for the following afternoon. I stood there, stunned, unable to return any salutation except for a very weak-*ciao*-. I followed her every move as she turned and joined her mother and the guests, waving as she disappeared into the chandeliered foyer.

    In two short days, I had been shaken out of my skin by two girls with a total of four kisses to a face that refused to wash them away. I walked the few blocks home in a romantic daze of puppy love crushes, and as I glided through the portone, I was happy to see Carminuccio searching for me in the giardino. When he and Nonna approached asking why they were unable to find me, I narrated my improbable encounter with Elisa which put a smile on nonna's face, as she made her way into the kitchen. Carminuccio gave me an inquisitive look, finally accepting an invitation to stay for dinner. My friend suspiciously picked up on my aura, leading me first into the giardino to relieve his curiosity. *"Gianni, ma è proprio vero? Ti sei incontrato con la figlia del conte?"* I took a quick look in the direction of the wall and thought how different an afternoon it had been, replaying scenes filled with Elisa's words and expressions. *"Si, proprio Elisa. Sono andato al suo lato e abbiamo parlato e adesso siamo amici."* I admitted to my encounter with Elisa on her side, our conversations and how we had become friends. There was so much more I wanted to narrate, but I struggled to find the Italian. My expression, however, gave me away when Carminuccio looked into my eyes for a few silent seconds, then with a smile reaching into his dimples asked more probing questions. *"E allora? Come ti è sembrata: bella? simpatica? Ti sei innamorato?"* His need to know if she came across as pretty, likeable, and if I had fallen in love could have been a bit annoying, but he guessed correctly that I wanted to reveal more. *"Sai, è molto simpatica e siamo solo amici. Mi ha chiesto di ritornare domani. Lei parla perfetto inglese! Va a Londra in estate per la scuola inglese.* He was taken by the fact that she spoke English. *"E questo è una gran bella cosa ... avete questo in comune, tanto da capirvi senza problemi ... e i genitori?* He commented that the English was a good thing since there would be no misunderstandings. He also wondered about her parents. *"È vero, capisco tutto quando lei parla anche se è un'inglese dei Beatles, capisci? La sua mamma, molto elegante"* I agreed that we could freely communicate despite her Beatles English and that I had met her mother. He asked me to explain the English thing, surprised that there would be differences between England and America. I described it as a matter of pronunciation and much less as one dealing with words.

Later that night, with the familiar street rhythms of my Southern Italian world about to rock me to sleep, thoughts of Elisa conspired to keep me awake. I wished away the differences in class, blissful that they would be of no consequence in our friendship, but I struggled with the possibility that I would be looked down upon by her family and circle of friends. In my New York reality, class and wealth lived in clearly separate neighborhoods and suburban towns. Despite physical distances of mere city blocks or a few miles beyond the city limits, contact was rare. I recalled episodes of those occasional Sunday excursions in my father's Fiat into the elite towns of Westchester County just beyond the Bronx border. Mom was always taken by the size and beauty of the homes and manicured lawns, my father showed proletarian resentment while we sat indifferent in the back seat wondering if there was a Carvel ice cream store nearby. I resolved not to let Stella's nobility bother me, and that I could deal with any rejections by leaning up against the pillars of my blue-collar values. I thought of my grandparents and parents as being just as noble without the aristocratic titles and clothing, but I was not certain that Elisa would share the same opinion. Her spunk and the English had me hoping the friendship could endure, but in a world in which I was hopelessly without experience, outcomes were unpredictable.

MERECÀ

CHAPTER 9
PRIMO BACIO

Carminuccio couldn't help himself with the news of Elisa, *la figlia del Conte-the Count's daughter.* The story had spread quickly. At school I was pelted with questions about someone who may have been the closest thing to a local mysterious celebrity. Raffaele was the first paparazzo to probe. *"Merecà, ma è vero, ti si 'ncontrat'ca figlia 'ro Conte? Chell' nun se vede mai pe'miezz Sarno. Nun a fann'asci'quas'mai. E comm'te par, bella, brutta, se po'sapè?* He mouthed off about the rumors of her cloistered life, hardly seen in town and wondering if she was pretty or ugly. Stella sat at her desk seemingly disinterested. Her fidgeting however, betrayed her envy, and within seconds, she delivered her own conclusions: *"Comm'po' essere bella si chell'nun se vede mai? Significa che è brutt'se sta sempe chiusa 'rint na casa. Se capisc'ca nun esce pe nun se fa vedè!* Her use of the Sarnese dialect never failed to reveal her discomfort with topics that stressed her. Deflecting her concern, she determined Elisa to be a pariah who hid in her mansion to avoid exposing her ugliness. A bit cruel I thought, so I felt the need to defend my new friend's honor in my best Italian. *"Non è vero! Elisa è molto bella e simpatica ... non giudicare perché' non conoscete lei."* I showed some anger for the first time as I insisted on not judging a person they did not know. Mimmo backed me up by attacking his favorite target. *"Dai Stella, chejè? Mi sembra na poc'e gelosia. Tu na conosci nemmeno e l'hai condannata ... e addittura brutta? ... e forse ti è già antipatica? ... ma che coraggio!* He called out her jealousy for a girl she had never met, and who, in Stella's words, must certainly be unattractive. He even anticipated her finding Elisa a possible contender for attention, guessing that would annoy her. Stella had spent the last few months learning how to ignore her nemesis, so when Mimmo was done criticizing, she turned away and announced her new policy in a slow, deliberate tone. *"Cretino, quann'tu parli, io come se'rrecchie nun e tenesse ... hai*

MERECÀ

capito? Sono una sorda completa ... non sento niente ... e le tue parole se perdono ndo'vient. Te fai semp'cchiu scemo; tu può parlà pur pe n'ora e dopo tutto stu tiempe se mi domandono: 'ma Mimmo ca'ditto?' Io rispondo 'mbo?... na'gio sentuto o'cazz'e niente.' E così io ti riduco in un fantasma ca nun se ved' e nun se sent'." Mimmo had to deal once again with an unchecked anger that reduced his words to kernels of dust. After calling him an idiot, she claimed to have no ears attached to her head whenever he spoke and that by ignoring him completely, she had reduced him to a ghost: mute and invisible. The theatrics again brought a smile to my face, loving every bit of it. By now my bold classmate had learned to dodge her flak and to walk away with few wounds. That was how the Mimmo-Stella feud would play out the remainder of my *Guido Baccelli* days. The faces, expressions, words, and body language I would eventually take home to America, would fill me with a heartfelt nostalgia when the cold, indifferent nature of my Bronx streets was incapable of warming my heart.

In our world of familiar faces and daily routines, Elisa's star status sparked a growing interest in a person outside our group. They had all now become nonsensically meddlesome in search of information on the elusive young aristocrat. My reaction was to downplay her importance attempting to selfishly keep her to myself, thinking we had an elitist bond because of our English. Young Italians, especially in the south, had few inhibitors when it came to the examination of others. Curiosity, in all its natural instincts, drove them into the lives of neighbors and strangers alike with a playful, forgivable insistence. Americans would have felt violated by the intrusions, but to these sons and daughters of an ever-evolving culture of inclusion, no one's life was beyond exploration. I came to enjoy and accept that these probing natures had mostly positive outcomes, with the power to melt away apprehensions, foster an emancipated trust, and create honest, folksy friendships.

Stella was having a rough time with the topic of Elisa. She looked at me more than once, saying nothing. She may have wanted to ask a question or two, but wisely bit her tongue, since even one question would have validated Mimmo's words, and

Stella would have none of it. As the bell rang signaling the end of classes, the girls congregated on their side of the classroom, while the boys piled out. We were more than a block away when I turned back to notice that the girls were still inside. I brought it to Carminuccio's attention prompting him to make an eager about face. I followed, as did Mimmo and Raffaele. Halfway back we came upon the cackling flock in the courtyard, aware that Elisa was still the object of their infatuated symposium. Carminuccio insisted that we should not be surprised by the amount of time and energy the ladies were dedicating to an unknown. "*Gianni, sai che non mi sorprende affatto che le donne riescano a dedicare tutto sto tiemp' parlando di qualcuno che ancora non conoscono. Mi stupisce addirittura ... molto strano.* He dwelt on his not being surprised at the amount of time women could dedicate to things unknown, finding it strange. Stella was still there, marginalized, content in paying attention, not fully a participant. It was a sight to behold-Stella perched on the outside as one of the quieter girls, interested, but incapable of blending in. She elicited a boyish compassion in me seeing her weakened by her own strength. I had always thought of her as the dominant female capable of projecting her power at will, forcing others back on their heels. Yet, in that moment she appeared so out of character: frail and bewildered.

    The girls finally joined us, and we all marched up the *rettifilo*. The chatter hardly died down as the topic shifted to celebrating Mimmo's birthday that coming Saturday. In class he had handed out invitations to attend a party at his home. Everyone eagerly accepted, as I tried to imagine what an Italian birthday party would be like. I expected most of the same rituals as our American versions with some hesitations considering how different Christmas had been. At the top of the *rettifilo* we all spilled into the piazza breaking up into smaller groups each pointed in the direction that led to their part of town. As Carminuccio and I headed toward San Sebastiano, I paused and asked about Stella's neighborhood. He quickly suggested that we turn back and follow the girls. It was too tempting a detour, so we tailed the girls from a safe distance until we came upon a sloping street that wound its way up towards the town cemetery. At the

MERECÀ

fork we steered away from the tombstones and towards a parcel with rows of pre-war public housing. Just beyond the first row we spied Stella entering the second building on the left. We walked into what was a lot of dirty, treeless streets, mangled light poles, and walls still sadly disfigured with wartime graffiti. In the distance a handful of kids did their best to punish a half-inflated soccer ball as they kicked up clouds of choke inducing dust on a sun parched dirt field. The cadaverous buildings, some still cratered by the war, stood defeated and depressed, succumbing to the grotesque scars, the inverted triangular stains of dried dirt created by rainfall duped into thinking it was cleansing the rooftops, and the splintered shutters that had shed their shine when the first bombs fell. Giant overflowing garbage bins played host to dozens of flies, while an emaciated, colorless cat scavenged for whatever scraps it could uncover. Between the buildings, long clothes lines laden with the day's wash swayed rhythmically to the will of the warm breeze, granting the only color contrast to the dull, drab surroundings.
An oversized, sun scarred flag of the Italian Communist Party, tied tightly to the outside of the rusted railings of a corner terrace on the top floor, threatened all other political views.   Carmiunuccio knew, as he looked up, that it was Stella's apartment. As I took in the image, it became clear that the banner was nothing more than the full image of the hammer and sickle of the Soviet flag covering the green, white, and red of the Italian flag so that only the bottom third could be seen. The sight of the red and yellow flag brought on my Cold War fears. I turned sad at the thought that the Italian flag was playing backup to the much more prominent Soviet one. I could only conclude that Stella's father wanted Italy to be part of another country. As Carminuccio pointed up at the terrace, he reminded me of her father's affiliation with the party. *"Ricordi che il padre, Mario, è direttore del partito qui a Sarno. Ogni primo maggio quella bandiera sventola durante le celebrazioni della Festa dei Lavoratori su e giù il rettifilo e poi per tutto Sarno. Molti lo conoscono e dicono che è molto fanatico. Non si vede spesso, ma si fa sentire quando si tratta di politica. Parla di rivoluzione e di un giorno vedere l'Italia un paese completamente comunista.*

MERECÀ

Per me sono chiacchere perché gli italiani sono troppo cattolici per accettare una vita senza chiese e preti, come dicono I russi. Credo che Mimmo abbia ragione quando dice che il padre avrebbe deciso di chiamare sua figlia addirittura Stella 'Rossa' se fosse stato ancora più scemo." He spoke of Stella's father's fanaticism, foolishly believing that Italian Catholics would allow a Soviet style revolution with no churches and priests. He noted how that same flag could be seen being carried zealously during the May Day (Italy's version of Labor Day) celebrations each year throughout the town. He found common ground with Mimmo when they both believed it would have been completely idiotic had he named his daughter Red Star (Stella Rossa). My feelings were forced out of their safe zone and into the very real and present world of European politics. The Cold War paranoias of the Soviets, communists and the Berlin Wall were light years away from the streets of the Bronx. The closest we came to a similar reckoning was the fun boys had spying the girls' underwear as we dropped to the floor and under our desks at Sister Mary Joseph's command in third grade during nuclear war drills. Still, the comparison was weak since the Italians stood on the front lines of the ideological battle between Democracy and Communism. As we turned away, a man's voice caught our attention. Carminuccio looked back tapping me on the shoulder. "*Guarda, quello è suo padre. Ti sembra strano? È un uomo piccolo, non alto, snello e con baffoni troppo grandi per la sua faccia. Per me, ridicolo credere che una persona simile possa decidere per tutti noi come vivere. Gianni, io adoro l'America, la musica, la cultura, i blue jeans, e sono certo che gli Americani non permetterebbero mai una vittoria comunista in Italia ... così dice mio padre.*" It was her father on the terrace. He described him as smallish, skinny with a mustache too big for his face. A strange character, he whispered, more of a joke, and one that would not be permitted to decide for others how to live their lives. Once again, he sang the praises of my native country, in love with the music, the culture, the jeans; convinced that the Americans would never allow Italy to fall into the hands of the communists. I wanted to believe his words with all my heart, but the sight of the Soviet flag, the catalyst for so many fears of subjugation, nuclear war, and complete annihilation of the world, left me with a sickening throb. I had to work at separating Stella from what her father represented. My mood had changed enough to earn Carminuccio's concern. *"Gianni, cosa senti, mica lo prendi sul serio a quel cretino? Non merita un pensiero in più. Fa sempre brutta figura quando scende in piazza a protestare le decisioni del governo o ultimamente la guerra nel Vietnam. Si mette a strillare come uno impazzito e non ci sono mai più di una decina di persone che lo ascoltano. Basta dire che è fanatico e lo dimostra ogni giorno. Infatti, lui e mio padre furono studenti nella stessa classe proprio alla Baccelli, e che anche in quei giorni dimostrava le stesse tendenze contro la società. Non so se mi capisci, ma fu una persona che non associava.* He urged to let him go and to not take him so seriously. He also described the pathetic way he would attempt to lead protests of the government and the Vietnam War, with his extremist speeches to smallish crowds. Even Carminuccio's father, who had gone to school with him at Baccelli, described him as awkward and a loaner. I refused to believe that Stella would voluntarily adopt radical views of the world-she was a fighter, but lacked the cynicism to demonize anyone, and separating her from her father was worth the task. I shared my opinion with my friend as we walked home. *"Stella non è come il padre. Lei sembra più gentile e vede la vita come noi. Non importa la politica, vuole essere giovane e vivere felice ... io credo."* I was looking for approval when I described her different from her father, and that she viewed life more like us away from the politics, more into living a happy life. We were in agreement. *"Sai che molti di noi giovani ci siamo allontanati dalla cattiveria della politica proprio per questo motivo. A volte penso che senza la politica, la religione, e la povertà, si potrebbero eliminare le differenze e vivere così tranquilli."* He claimed that many young people had distanced themselves from the nastiness of politics, and that without politics, religion and poverty, differences would be eliminated, and people could live in peace. It may have been utopian, but there was an undeniable appeal to his wishes. I gave it some time, nudging me into what seemed radical thinking on a much more pleasant level. Doing away with politics and poverty were easy enough to imagine, but the thought of a world with no religions seemed so impossible. We were surrounded by churches, Catholic schools, nuns, priests, Jesus on the cross, and a calendar with a different saint for each day … I thought, how could all that just disappear?

    On the way home we stopped for a gelato. We sat at one of the small sidewalk bistro tables. The weather spoke of an early summer, and it showed in the clothing the women had begun to wear. While most went about in lighter dresses and skirts, some had begun to show a more liberated side strutting about in jeans. I gave it little thought, but my friend took notice. *"Guarda, Gianni ... le donne incominciano a indossare i jeans, che meraviglia! Si sono finalmente stancate dello stesso stile, e a me piace molto questo nuovo fascino femminile".* Women in jeans were to him a novelty and he was happy to see that some had given up on the usual style. *"Chissà se Stella e le altre indosseranno questi blue jeans. Vedi quella, li porta così stretti ... e da dietro non si fatica a immaginare il suo corpo nudo".* He wondered if Stella and the other girls would soon be wearing them. He then took quick notice of one of the ladies walking by in tight jeans commenting on the fact that the view of her butt made it easier to imagine her naked. *"Quando le donne insistono a farsi belle così, è come stare in un museo circondato da tanti capolavori ... che bel mondo in cui viviamo, diciamo la verità".* His inclination kicked in again, praising women for their beauty, likening them to masterpieces in a museum, and crediting them for the wonderous world we lived in. His poetic praise jostled my roots once again, and now women in blue jeans, which were common in my Bronx world, had become living works of art. I shook my head wanting to discredit his views, but it was futile. He was so right, but he had no clue that, what was to him a natural appraisal, was to me another revelation, another awakening.

    On the last stretch of road to my *portone,* we spoke about Mimmo's party, and how much we looked forward to it. He also thought it was an opportunity to see the inside of his house. I was curious. *"Perché tu vuoi vedere dentro la casa sua?"* I asked him why he was eager to see the inside of Mimmo's house.

MERECÀ

"Veramente è solo perché quando si entra nella casa delle persone si può avere un quadro completo della loro vita. Per me ha niente a che fare con ricchezze ... mi piace conoscere le persone in un modo più intimo... mi sbaglio? He answered that it had to do with getting a full picture of the lives of others, and that it had nothing to with riches, but rather to know people more intimately. He asked if this was misguided. By then I had become accustomed to that level of intrusion, and I no longer found fault in it. I also had been curious about Mimmo's classical building, so I shared some of his feelings.

We were coming to the end of my first school year, and Carminuccio made note of the progress with my Italian. *"Sai merecà, il tuo italiano ha fatto molti passi ... fra poco parlerai proprio come uno di noi ... bravo, ti faccio i complimenti!* He pointed out that soon I would be speaking as one of them, and in doing so, he complimented me. His words brought a smile to my face. My goal had become to learn the language as completely as my abilities would allow; I wanted to speak freely, with no hesitations searching for words, so his evaluation felt as good as making the Honor Roll at Mount Carmel.

That last Saturday in May, Mimmo's birthday, Mom and I went shopping for some new clothes and a gift. She granted me the freedom to choose my new wardrobe, which I put to a frenzied use, wanting to replace my more adolescent American style. I loaded up on what I thought would have me fit in with the Italians. Carminuccio met me at around five that evening, and we made our way to the party. We were greeted by most of the others from class as well as by Mimmo's elegant parents. All sorts of foods and pastries covered a long, slender table, with bottles of soft drinks standing at attention on a smaller table nestled in the corner of the ornate parlor. Chairs had been set up on the perimeter, but they went mostly unused. Everyone was too excited about being at the standout social event of our young lives to waste the time sitting. There were no cliques, no exclusive group huddled together passing judgment on the others. We all moved around greeting and talking, fully enjoying the unique opportunity to mingle as most had never done. Later in the evening, his parents had moved onto

the back terrace opting for the company of other adults. Mimmo took it as a cue to start his turntable already stacked with the latest hits. He was bent on giving the gathering more of an American Bandstand feel-he wanted us to dance. British, American, and Italian songs played. The Beatles, The Rolling Stones, The Hollies, Herman's Hermits, The Temptations, The Animals were some of the Anglo artists in Mimmo's collection. Bobby Solo, Gianni Morandi, Equipe 84, Adriano Celentano, Caterina Caselli, and a British band that sang Italian versions of English language hits called the Rokes... odd name, I thought, until I heard the Italian pronunciation which came out as the Rocks with a rolling -r-. It sounded cool to them, so I let it go. Mimmo's size did not keep him from being the best dancer on the floor. We stood there in silent amazement, entertained by his moves ... they were borderline professional. The amount of practice he put into it, solitary in his room on countless days paid off. Stella kept repeating the words: "*ma no, ma no, non è possible!*", as she jaw-droppingly fixed on the big guy putting on a show. As daylight started to fade, Mimmo and one of the girls lit candles, shut the lights, and slipped Bobby Solo's song, *Una Lacrima Sul Viso* onto the turntable and lowered the volume. He announced it was time to pick a partner for the slow dance. "*Please, everyone, take a partner for this dance romantica ... dai, scegli un compagno e si balla.*"
Before I could scamper off to steal away one of the chairs, Stella pulled me to the middle of the room. She placed my hands around her waist and locked her fingers around the back of my neck. I hardly moved, except to keep myself from stumbling over my feet, when she took the lead urging me to follow her steps, assuring it was not difficult. "*Fai come faccio io, seguimi non è difficile.*" There was no escape, so I settled in becoming the object of her experiment. Mimmo and Carminuccio inevitably looked on with their penetrating stares, smiling and whispering encouragements to stay the course, to keep at it. My hands refused to tighten their grip, reminding myself it was Stella's waist. When her head landed softly on my shoulder, I ignored my nervousness hoping the song would play on forever. We were hardly moving, just swaying, unable to catch up to the song's rhythm, when she looked up and

planted her lips on mine, closing her eyes. I had no idea how long to stay with it, so I waited for her to decide. A few seconds in, she pulled away for a quick moment, and came back for a replay. The second time around, I could hear the whispers getting louder as others joined in to grab a glimpse of the teen spectacle. For those magical moments, I erased everyone from the room. I set free my senses to absorb the full force of her lips against mine giving birth to one of those teenage first timers not quickly forgotten. It was clear she was the experienced one. Unable to initiate a third kiss on my part, she returned her cheek to my shoulder, my hands relaxed around her waist enough to sense the warmth of her body. I had to remind myself to let go as the song ended. No more was needed for an eighth grader to fall in love, so I thought myself in some kind of love, unable to separate realty from fantasy. I refused to struggle with it since I was content, for the first time, to live the act in its uniqueness, sheltering it from intrusions.

  The closing minutes of the evening had us singing the birthday song in Italian, with me pathetically lip synching the words I had yet to learn. Gifts were opened, Mimmo dished out his sincere thanks, we showed our appreciation to his parents for the wonderful display, and we bid everyone a *buona sera.* Stella walked out first, accompanied by most of the girls … their chatter filling the hall that led to the front door. Once in the courtyard, they stopped and waited for me and Carminuccio to catch up. She had a few last words. *"Volevo salutarti, Gianni. Domani è domenica, forse ci vediamo sul rettifilo. Carminu', accompagnalo tu, facciamo na passeggiata tutti insieme, vengono anche le altre. Allora, ciao' a domani".* She granted us a date for the following day, Sunday, to stroll along the *rettifilo* with her and the other girls, asking Carminuccio to join as well. With that, the girls continued arm in arm, briskly making their way home. The boys wandered off in the opposite direction. Not long into our stride, my companion stealthily projected his need to evaluate the evening with glancing eyes, delaying his speech. I forced him to do it several times before admitting that I too wanted to talk, asking him why he was looking at me that way, and what was on his mind. *"Allora, che cosa vuoi sapere, perché tu mi guardi così?"*

MERECÀ

"Gianni, non ti sembra piacevolmente strano quello che ti è successo stasera? Ti sei baciato con la ragazza più difficile di tutto Sarno, e forse anche la più bella ... io ancora non ci posso credere. A pensare che quella non ti dava nessuna confidenza. Non è che Stella si permette di essere baciata da chiunque." The not so routine kiss had him flustered, unable to understand Stella's change of heart towards me, noting that I had kissed probably the most difficult and prettiest girl in Sarno ... one who didn't allow herself to be kissed by just anyone. *"Forse perché' sei così diverso, non uno di noi, capisci? Certo, che se una bella ragazza americana dovesse trovarsi come te, naufragata a Sarno, mi sarebbe molto simpatica. Lascia perdere, come ti è apparsa Stella, sincera o ti prende in giro?"* As he searched for answers, he touched on the possibility that being different, not one of the natives, had finally turned her interest in me, hypothesizing that if a pretty American girl had landed in Sarno under similar circumstances, he would have found her likeable. There was no satisfying his inquisitiveness because I had no answers for my own. I knew that I had enjoyed it, feeling all the anticipated tingles, the palpitations, the sweaty palms, but I had no clue of her motivation and whether she experienced the same. *"Carminu', tu credi che Stella sente lo stesso che io?"* I engaged my friend's wisdom asking if there was any emotion in her actions. *"Caro Gianni, cosa ti posso dire? Per quanto la conosco io, direi che sente ben poco, può essere solo la sua curiosità ... ma poi si capisce che la gente cambia, matura, e forse Stella è arrivata a quel punto. Insomma, per adesso resta un mistero che si potrebbe svelare nei prossimi giorni."* He followed up with a sincere analysis. His instincts told him that there was no substance, simply her curiosity at play. He paused, then trailed that thought with a correction that people do change, they mature and that perhaps Stella had reached that point. Exasperated, he finally settled on it being a mystery that could unravel in the coming days. As much as I wanted to give it more energy and go the full boyfriend, girlfriend route, I heeded his caution, and scaled back my enthusiasm. I too was maturing, and at a quickening pace. With Italian culture subtly imposing its will, laying back passively,

waiting for things to happen was no longer the norm-the topic of females and sentiments was to be taken seriously.

Standing in front of my *portone*, I had to deal with one more of Carminuccio's convenient pangs that just could not wait. *"Permetti di chiederti, ma è stato il tuo primo vero bacio quello con Stella? Non voglio dire il primo bacio addirittura, ma il tuo primo amoroso? No so se mi spiego ..."* I made like I did not understand, just to turn him a bit uneasy. He wanted to know if it was my first "real" kiss. He dodged the insult putting it that way, although there was no angst in owning up to it. *"Si, mio primo bacio come innamorato. Un bacio con sentimento, si. Va bene, sei contento?"* It was my first real kiss, not an adolescent *make out* kiss, I admitted. Then I put him on edge, asking sarcastically if he was happy. *"E no, Gianni, non offenderti ... perdonami se sono stato insolente ... non so cosa dire."* He took it a bit hard, making a sincere attempt to correct it by asking forgiveness. I let it fester for a while, finally easing his tizzy with a devious smile, dropping the act, assuring he could never offend me. *"Sai che scherzo con te ... tu non puoi mai offendere me."* With those words, the palm of his right hand coddled my left cheek and neck the way soccer players do in displays of good sportsmanship. The gesture was an emotion onto itself, the sensation of a truer and more pious friendship, exposing me to that remarkable spark of altruistic perfection that lays dormant until wrenched from us when our humanity demands it. Carminuccio had been raised in a culture that coaxes that altruism to awaken at the earliest age, and with age, it becomes a common practice offered to others cleanly, with no liability.

That night, I carried off to bed a sack full of teenage emotions doing battle, each trying to win me over. Falling asleep took hours, perhaps because I did not want the day to end. No amount of time spent dwelling on that immediate past could ease the turbulence, so I employed the best of my Bronx wisdom to detach and shut it all down as if it had not happened. I refused to anticipate the Sunday invitation, the gathering on the *rettifilo*, and how things would play out. I supported my own urges to know and feel more, but I feared crossing lines. I spent most of Sunday morning sitting at the kitchen table across from nonna. Between sips of *caffelatte*, I stared up at her until she sensed my unusual behavior, asking if I was fine. I answered hesitantly that all was well which made her want to know more. I wanted someone older to talk to, but I knew Pop shied away from questions about intimacy, and Mom would dismiss it as youthful folly. I had gone to nonna for advice in the past when it came to relatives and neighbors. She had always taken the time to listen and dish out some old school wisdom, so I brought up the topic of girls … I got an earful. *"Figlio mio, tu si tropp'giovane! Chist' non so' pensier pe te. E femmene ti fanno chianje' e po' se spacc'o cor… lascia sta, nun nge' pensà. Tu sai che papà tuo non ha saput nisciuna femmina, sul' a mammeta e tenev' già vint'ann! Nu jurno tu ti truov na bella signorina, ve vulite bene e ve spusate e restate insieme tutt'a vita."* I listened, eager for a balanced argument. I expected the -you are too young-lecture-, of how it wasn't time for these thoughts, but I was taken by her one-sided caution on how women will make you cry and break your heart. She told me to let it go, and that my dad had known only my mother, and he was twenty when that happened. She assured me that one day I would meet a beautiful lady, be in love, get married and live out our lives together. It may have all been predictable, but listening to her delicate way of putting it, sent a reassuring flutter through my veins that all would work out. She had a way of tenderly moving me from paralysis to decisions with her melodic speech in sync with all the facial drama. There had been some frustration in those moments of difficult assimilation for her young grandchildren, so she slipped in lessons camouflaged as blessings, and corrections in behavior came with easy instructions.

    The last few sips of coffee were always the best, littered with mushy pieces of *taralli*. I scooped them up, and with a small mouthful, I grabbed my diary and headed for the giardino. It was another perfect spring day with a slight breeze, rays of sun peeking out over the Appenines, and the scent of freshly plowed dirt. My pages eagerly anticipating my words, I made for my favorite spot under the eucalyptus, after a quick mounting of my rocky staircase to check on Elisa. I had not seen her in more than a week, wondering if she had already left for London. With no sight of her as I poked my brows over the wall, I plopped myself comfortably on my stone platform, pen in hand, ready to spill my thoughts and feelings onto the blank pages. The words flowed like an energized tributary traveling unhindered over stones and pebbles, softening its passage as it flowed downstream, picking up speed, splashing and spraying about, drenching, and baptizing its habitat. I wrote feverishly. I feared interruptions, and my hand labored at keeping up with my thoughts. As I paused to read over the pages, Elisa's voice called out several times to catch my attention. *"Gianni, are you there? Hello… are you there?"* I forced my diary into my jacket pocket, and I quickly brushed up against the wall to show my face. *"Elisa, hi, I'm here."* Ciao Gianni, can you come over?" I climbed over without answering. *"Hi, I kept looking over the wall, but it has been a week …"* She nervously interrupted. *"Gianni, I must confess I should have said something. We had to travel to Rome for my father's affairs. We spent the entire week in a hotel room because they kept postponing his meetings."* She agonized as she unburdened herself. *"You see, after the war my father's title was taken away and he was prohibited from administering his lands for a period of twenty years. The municipalities in those areas were given authority to use the lands for social projects like building schools, if needed. He was allowed only this land and this house. With his petition he was declaring that the twenty years had passed and that he should be able to reclaim his property."* My sense of property rights may have been a bit clumsy, but I had an American understanding or ownership. *"I don't understand how a government can do that to people … I cannot imagine us losing the giardino that way.* She hesitated, but then gave in to the urge to tell the entire story. *"This part is difficult … during the years that Mussolini was in power, my father's family owned a textile factory here in Sarno and in several other towns. He had won contracts to make military uniforms for the fascist government. Mussolini even visited the factories, and the story was carried by the local papers with photos and articles. At the end of the war, the locals turned against everyone associated with the fascists. My father was never involved in the politics. He was not even a member of the party, and most of the people in Sarno had a good relationship with my family. The partisans were a small band of communists who used their propaganda to keep my father tied to fascism. They forced the Americans to treat him as a wartime criminal, and he was placed under house arrest. In 1945, a republic was declared, and the twenty-year ruling went into effect. The people of Sarno had no bad feelings towards my family, but the local district office of the Communist Party kept up the pressure to keep my father from his proper position. My mother tells me that in those years, after the Americans left Sarno, armed partisans would drive up to our house on motorcycles and write ugly graffiti on our outer wall. Several times rocks shattered the windows. The worse incident was when my dad discovered an unexploded bomb on our doorstep. They had to send for British soldiers stationed in Naples to remove it. Whenever my mother and grandmother went out to shop, they would be followed, and nasty words were spoken to them. Once my mother was confronted and pushed to the ground. They reported it to the police, but they did nothing."* The story added a layer of disorder associated with war. Beyond the battlefield, when the guns fell silent, I was learning that there was collateral pain endured because some were bent on not allowing the past to die. There may have been a general feeling that Italy was emerging from the darkness, but it was also clear that not all were invited to join in. I would have asked why her father did not just stop making the uniforms, but I quickly concluded that someone had to make them-soldiers needed uniforms. Eli was in the thick of it, learning about and living her family's past, while coming to grips with the reality of her own life. *"Now I understand why I must live as I do. I thought my life was normal until I learned of my parents' past. The private tutor, the trips to London to private schools, the lack of friends here in Sarno, are all painful ways to protect me. How sad it makes me to think that I could be living and enjoying my life as you do. Gianni, I so envy you."* She checked her desperation, but she could not hold back the tears. Thin streams flowed down her flush cheeks, some collecting on her top lip, others parachuting to the ground mingling with the dew on a fallen laurel leaf. I had no clue on how to offer her any meaningful sympathy, being so detached from all the bad politics in her life. Still, I felt I had to do something. My instinct to wrap her vulnerability in my arms worked. She accepted the invitation, knowing she could stay if she wanted. Knowing words would have been useless, I said nothing. I could feel her comfort as I pressed my forehead to hers. A very masculine impulse of wanting to take care of her overcame me. I had no other way of explaining it, except that I would have considered anything heroic to rid her of her sadness. As she composed herself, she looked up and paid homage to my efforts with a bold, but short kiss on my lips. Pulling away she searched for a reaction, then quickly apologized. *"Perdonami, Gianni ... non intendevo imporre ... please forgive me, it wasn't my intention to impose."* Flustered, I wanted to assure her it was acceptable. *"I really didn't mind, you know. I haven't said much, but I feel bad for what you're going through. Can I kiss you back?"* It dawned on me after asking, that she could say no ... then what? When she accepted with a soft-yes-, the anxiety lessened. We both closed our eyes and our lips met haphazardly. With a slight adjustment we were practicing it as intended. As our lips retreated, the dryness kept them clung creating a sticky sensation that sent electrical shivers up my spine. She then ran her fingers calmly along my lips. I stood frozen, incapable of identifying the feeling. Youth had conspired to deny me the ability to fully appreciate her touch.

"Why did you touch my lips? I asked calmly. *"You may think me foolish, but it is the first time I wanted to kiss a boy, and I do want to remember everything about it. I had been kissed by a boy once in London, but I didn't care for it. Touching your lips will help me make it a beautiful memory. Do you think it silly?"* I was taken by her honesty in revealing the virgin kiss. *"I don't think any of this is silly. I feel the same, I also want to remember it."* She was instantly delighted with her next words. *"Carissimo Gianni, ma allora è stato anche per te un primo bacio? Was this a first kiss for you as well?"* I refused to panic and came clean with the truth. *"No, it's my second."* I feared her disappointment. *"That's quite all right, you know, I should expect that your life is different and that there would be more opportunities."* She wanted to know

more. "*It was actually just yesterday at a birthday party. Most of my friends from my class were there. This girl, her name is Stella, we kissed while dancing. I was surprised since I thought she didn't exactly like me. I'm not sure what happened, but it just happened, I can't explain it.*" My stumbling had her resenting her intrusion, so she steered us in a different direction. "*Well, all I can say is that she must be very pretty and a spectacularly fine person. Now, tell me, how is it being in a class full of students, and what is like being out with your friends?*" I knew I would never want to be tutored at home, and that being in a class with others was always a pleasure even on bad days, but I played down my description. "*It's fine ... I like the kids in my class. I get along with them, even the girls. I like all my teachers except our math teacher, he is mean to the ones who struggle. When he calls them up to do a problem on the board, he yells at them if they get it wrong. He made one of the girls cry ... I felt so bad for her.*" I gave her more of the bad stuff than the good, since there was probably no chance of her ever being one of us. Painting a rosy picture would have only left her yearning for something she couldn't have. "*Come now, Gianni, there must be more bloody excitement than that. I would imagine much laughter, joking, outings for ice cream, strolling together arm in arm, carefree living, simply enjoying each other's company ... I suppose.*" As her remark faded, so too did her smile. She had gathered that her version was the one that carried more truth, and I could do nothing but validate it with a pitiful look on my face. "*We do have fun when we hang around in town. We play biliardino, you know, the table soccer game. Sometimes basketball on the courts at the high school, and there is a pool table in the café' across from our school; we get to play after school sometimes when there aren't any adults. My favorite is when we are all together on the rettifilo. We just walk around, checking out who is there. I know it doesn't sound like much, but I think is has more to do with just being with each other ... that's' what I like the most.*" She tuned in, imagining herself doing the same. "*I love biliardino! I always play when I am in London. My situation is different there. Vorrei tanto incontrare I tuoi amici-You know, I would love to meet your friends ... Gianni, mi sento così sola ... I feel so lonely at times. I*

MERECÀ

dream of just walking out of my home and roaming the streets of Sarno, greeting people, listening to their stories, shopping with friends, eating pizza ... I suppose it would be wonderful ... I so do not enjoy being different." My thoughts ran a bit wild when I proposed an improbable ploy. *"I just thought of something, but then again ... it would be just crazy."* She clutched my arm, imploring me to tell more. *"You mustn't stop. Please, Gianni ... what are your thoughts?"* *"My friends are all meeting later today in piazza Municipio in front of the statue of Mariano Abignente. My friend Carminuccio will meet me at around five here at my house. I was thinking if you could get away for a few hours, you could climb the wall and walk with us. I can come over and help-I have a small ladder that would work. I told you it was crazy, but if you really want to change things, then maybe you could find a way.* She moved over to the bench, sat, and set her mind to work. *"Gianni, I do have an idea. Each evening I spend hours alone reading, writing in my diary, and painting. In good weather I usually spend that time here in the garden. Most times I am left completely alone, no one cares to bother me. Mother and father spend their Sunday evenings reading in the study and having cocktails. Even if found out, the most I would receive is a scolding and a warning ... have had those before. No need to convince me further, and there will be no use for the ladder. There is a hidden entrance to the garden at the far end of the property close to the road frontage, beyond the main entrance. It is a narrow gate covered in ivy; my grandmother uses it when she goes shopping. When you pass the front portico, keep walking to the end of the outer wall, you will come upon it. What time shall we meet?"* *"I can be there at five with Carminuccio."* In a fit of happiness, she kissed me one more time, and ran off.

    That evening Carminuccio showed up on time. I rushed out to meet him to relate the plan. He showed enthusiasm, and together we rushed to the meeting point. The gate was exactly where Elisa had mentioned. We approached hesitantly when our fabled friend jumped out imploring us to move quickly. We turned the first corner out of sight of the palazzo when she slowed to a stroll asking to be introduced. *"This is my best friend Carminuccio ... I* mean Carmine." I was not sure which form of the name to use. *"Well, piacere fare la sua conoscenza, mi chiamo Elisa."* She started in English, then made a quick shift to Italian introducing herself in a very formal way, to which she received a cordial welcome and a request to keep it informal. Shedding the stiffer formalities of her world brought a friendly smile to her face. *"Ciao, Elisa, molto piacere, ti dispiace darci del tu?" "Si, scusa, allora, diamoci del tu. Gianni, Carmine is very agreeable, and I can see why you are good friends."* We walked three across with Elisa sandwiched between us. She innocently ignored our attempt to jumpstart a conversation, choosing to scan the scenes that unfolded in front of her. She anticipated coming upon our group with a muted eagerness she kept under control ... not knowing what to expect. We were a bit early, so we stopped at the *gelateria*, lingering there until Mimmo's fluttering hand and big smile greeted us from a across the *rettifilo*. His surprise was expected when we introduced Elisa enjoying her *gelato alla nocciola (hazelnut)*. *"Ciao' Elisa, ma sei di Sarno?* We failed to add that she was the count's daughter, so he asked if she was from Sarno. Elisa eagerly responded she was, while asking his name. *"Si, sono proprio di Sarno, e lei come si chiama?"* Carminuccio then made his clarification exposing her identity, which turned Mimmo into an inquisitive sack of jellybeans. *"Piacere, Mimmo. Ma sei veramente lei, la figlia del conte? Che piacere! Proprio la figlia del conte? Finalmente ci conosciamo ... sai che di lei ne abbiamo parlato a lungo per la curiosità."* His skepticism of being in the company of the count's daughter became comical, bringing a sweet, welcoming smile to Elisa. He didn't shy away from admitting that she was a constant topic of conversation. The interest in her was intriguing, but Eli insisted she was just another girl. *"Caro Mimmo, come mai questa curiosità? Come vedi sono una ragazza chiunque."* Mimmo's slight smirk prefaced his remark. *"Elisa, non offendo, ma tu sei altro che chiunque. Si vede che sei gentile e non affatto presuntuosa, ma avere un titolo aristocratico è qualcosa da non trascurare."* Elisa was ready to deal with Mimmo's insistence that she was more than just another girl, and one with an aristocratic title that shouldn't be ignored.

MERECÀ

"Forse hai ragione, ma almeno per la durata di questo giorno, nel caso ci incontrassimo di nuovo nel futuro, mi faresti il grande favore di trattarmi come una chiunque, te lo chiedo dal cuore." She turned to me with her English version. *"Gianni, please help this along, and implore the others to treat me as one of the many, as just another of the girls. I so would like to lose the title when in the company of your friends. I will not deny who I am, but perhaps we can ignore it, at least for a day ... I suppose.* I understood her need to be viewed as just one of many, but there was a chance that the differences would somehow taint the meeting, at least at first. *"Eli, I know they will be excited at first, but it won't take long for them to treat you like me. I did feel different in the beginning, and then after a few months I felt more like I fit in."* Mimmo had picked up on Eli's angst. *"Elisa, perdonami, non volevo crearti alcun affanno. Intendevo solo farti capire che i nostri amici avranno qualche interesse perché' non ti conoscono così bene, e quindi ci sarà qualche parola e sguardo in più. Comunque, si vede che sei simpatica e per niente vanitosa, e per questo che presto ti faranno una bella accoglienza."* Mimmo's softer side showed up, assuring her that beyond some initial prying, she would be greeted favorably considering her pleasantness and lack of conceit. Carminuccio glanced over and signaled that he was not so sure about Mimmo's easy explanation. Stella came to mind immediately. In my naïve world, I had ignored the possible conflict she could cause. The agonizing started for me when the kisses came to mind. I wondered if the topic could be avoided, and if Stella had intentions of carrying on with what had transpired at the party. Certainly, Eli would recognize her name, but I could not guess her reaction since there was much of her still unknown to me. The innocent invitation to Eli suddenly had the potential of a total backfire depending on Stella's reaction. As the main square came into view, most of our classmates lounged seated on the marble wall surrounding the statue of Sarno's sixteenth century hero. Stella was there in all her splendor, fashionably dressed, with a very visible cosmetic boost to her beauty. She seemed still older, and the sophisticated urban look had me gazing with unchecked attention. Mimmo again took the lead moving a few steps ahead

with the task of introducing the stranger joining the group. *"Ciao' ragazzi, vi presento Elisa Tuttavilla, figlia del conte e amica del nostro Gianni."* The reactions were swift. The air filled with whispers, facial contortions, and hand signals. Those awkward few moments quickly evaporated as Stella's brazen character kicked in. She walked over to Eli, wrapped her arm around hers, and led the way down the *rettifilo*. The rest followed completely baffled except Mimmo. *"Guarda quella! Chi poteva crederci. Però, se la conosco bene, Stella ne approfitta per imporre la sua amicizia tanto da diminuire l'importanza di Elisa. Ma ti sembra giusto?"* His reaction was classical Mimmo. He accused Stella of monopolizing Elisa to diminish her importance. I was not quite sure what he meant until Carminuccio added his interpretation. *"Secondo me, Elisa sa comportarsi con una come Stella. Non credo che la figlia del conte si lasci prendere per scema."* He was convinced that Eli was not the gullible type and would not let herself be governed by the likes of Stella.

Some tailed off into smaller groups, until we were just a handful seeking out Stella and Elisa. Near the opposite end of the *rettifilo,* across from the high school, we finally caught up to the girls relaxing on one of the benches. They reduced their chat to a murmur once we closed in. Stella abandoned her conversation to give us an opportunity to join in again expressing her surprise at the amount of time it took us to reach them. *"Finalmente! E ci voleva tanto per trovarci?"* Eli was happy to see us. *"Ciao', Mimmo, Carminuccio e caro Gianni. Io e Stella siamo diventate amiche intime in questo breve tempo. Mi sento così libera, così innamorata della vita. Gianni, can you believe my good fortune in meeting you? How brilliant! I have become such good friends with Stella, and all of you have made me feel so free, so in love with life."* Mimmo had been eager to engage with Eli, wanting to know more about her. *"Elisa, parlaci di te, della tua vita, di come mai non sei nella nostra scuola ... certamente se non ti dispiace parlarne."* Stella got a few words in before Elisa could respond to Mimmo's questions. *"Ma guarda che cretino. Mo' fai tuttte ste mosse da gentiluomo perché ci sta Elisa? Questo con le ragazze della nostra classe, e specialmente con me, ha fatto sempre la*

MERECÀ

parte di uno stronzo." She called out Mimmo for appearing gentlemanly in Elisa's presence when in fact he treated the girls in the class with a certain disdain. At first Eli appeared saddened, but soon relaxed her serious look after I reassured her that the hostility between them was old news. *"It's not that serious. They do this all the time. We mostly ignore them."* The smile returned to her glowing face, and we settled in to give her a chance to blend. *"Caro Gianni, Stella e gli altri sono tutti simpaticissimi. Finalmente sto scoprendo la mia città. Figurati che ho vissuto qui una vita senza veramente conoscere la sua bellezza."* Mimmo interrupted by asking her to speak in both languages. He found it appealing and considered it a big help in firming up his English. Eli pleasantly agreed. *"Okay, so my dear Gianni, Stella and the others are all very agreeable. Finally, I am exploring my town. To think that I have lived a life here without knowing its beauty."* Mimmo tied in again, this time in his English. *"Elisa, I am happy for you to find your city and for you to like your city. I hope you to be with us many times."* Even Stella had begun to relax her attitude and found his words charming. *"Bravo Mimmo! In breve, parlerai addirittura com'o'merecà. Elisa, che ne pensi? Hai capito bene quello che ha detto?"* She congratulated his English and asked Elisa her opinion on the quality of his words. *"He has spoken very well. I easily understood all he said, and I very much enjoyed his cute accent, how sweet. Ha parlato molto bene, ho capito tutto, e mi è particolarmente piaciuto il suo accento ... che carino!"* Mimmo's baby face turned blood red, as had become the custom. It got a hearty giggle from Eli which caused all of us to join in, including Mimmo. Eli then delivered a brief autobiography as Mimmo had requested. She hadn't been in the habit of talking about her private life, but she now felt the need. She spoke of being born in Sarno, and of her pride now that she had met all of us. Politics forced her to miss out on a normal life, and of how annoying it had been living secluded. Then she became candid about her father's problems after the war, losing his lands, his title, of the struggle to regain them and his reputation, and of being falsely labeled a fascist. *"Non mi è mai capitato di offrire una storia personale ad un gruppo di amici, ma sento la voglia di farlo.*

Sono nata proprio qui a Sarno, e ne sono orgogliosa ancora di più da quando ci siamo incontrati. Mi è mancata una vita normale a questo punto per ragioni di politica. Figuratevi che noia chiusa ogni giorno in casa, senza amici, costretta a lezioni private. La vita dei miei genitori è stata molto difficile in Italia. Nel dopoguerra mio padre ha sofferto per i lavori fatti dalla sua ditta per il governo fascista. Lui non è stato mai un fascista, ma le false accuse furono abbastanza da distruggere il suo buon nome."

    Our conversations lasted well into the evening with many words sacrificed to the incessant interruptions of wanting to be heard-no one was content in just listening. We continued to stroll, with the guys offering the girls ice cream and the yellow *lupini* beans loaded into paper cones. We nibbled on the slippery legumes with some missing the mark as we tried torpedoing them into each other's mouths. We had reached the peak of our silliness that night, and it had us all caught up in an unimaginable teen euphoria … pure friendship, pure innocence, and pure love. When I often thought back on that day, I understood that it was the only time we were collectively immersed in the purity of youth, sheltered from the contaminants of adulthood.

    As the clock in the main square looked down approvingly on our impromptu celebration of life, it did its best to slow time to an agreeable pace … we could have carried on forever. When the eight o'clock hour struck a sad chord, we accepted that our soirée had to end. We volunteered first to accompany Stella home. She nervously refused, despite Eli's insistence. The two girls became one in a lingering hug, each reminding the other of appointments they had scheduled, and phone numbers exchanged. For a second time, I had witnessed Stella's more humble side. She had contradicted her own nature by choosing to bestow her softness on two individuals who shared no history with her. She showed me an unexpected kindness in asking forgiveness for her perceived rudeness, and she had sincerely accepted Eli as a friend, despite Mimmo's suspicions that she did it for the selfish reason of neutralizing any advantage Eli could have had over her. There was no reason for me to see it that way, so I felt a certain pride in not regretting the invitation.

MERECÀ

We took the same path back to Marabbecca with each of us expressing a strong satisfaction in how the day had unfolded. Eli was living the greatest thrill having navigated her entrance into a society in which she had been permitted little interaction. She had abandoned the fears her parents harbored since the end of the war, believing that the world had changed for the better and no longer found reason to condemn their past. *"Sai Gianni, and my dear Carminuccio, non capisco perché miei genitori non possono abbandonare le paure del passato. Credo che il mondo si stia cambiando per il meglio. Sono anni dalla fine della guerra, abbiamo una repubblica senza dittatura, e vedo intorno che la gente si gode la vita. Stella e gli altri sembrano così felici, liberi, e pieni di speranze per il futuro-e mi affido al loro spirito, e condivido la stessa anima. Se mi sbaglio in questo parere, fatemi capire perché."* She delivered a knockout punch to our provincial existence by exposing us to her world, beyond the confines of Sarno, beyond the borders of Italy and into a world on the verge of a greater humanity. She dwelt on the reasons why her parents insisted on living the fears of the past when the world had moved on from the darkness of the war and dictatorship. She saw Stella and the others as happy, free, and full of hope for the future. She wanted to become one with them in sharing the same spirit, the same soulful existence. Finally, she asked if her view was wrong, and to explain why. Carminuccio and I were instantly of the same mind, so there was no way we would burst her bubble. Perhaps we did not agree with the innocent utopia she imagined, having experiences on a different scale, but we admired her vision and her need to nurture it. Carminuccio attempted to create some balance. *"Elisa, ciò che dici tu è veramente bellissimo, ma il mondo non è arrivato ancora a quel punto, e forse non ci arriverà mai. Però tu hai ragione nella speranza che i tuoi genitori potranno darti il coraggio e l'augurio di crearti una vita nuova senza quelle paure di cui parli. Certo, non è affatto piacevole vivere giorno in giorno con tutte ste' paure. Ci sono davvero tante cose belle nella vita e tu hai ogni diritto di provarle."* She took his words to heart understanding that perhaps the world had yet to reach the level of compassion she envisioned. He was gentle in expressing his hope that her parents would be able to come out from the past and allow her to live free of all the fears, and that she had every right to enjoy the best of life. She latched on to the emotional conflict, accepting that perhaps the world still had some evil to inflict, but she was adamant that she could not give up on hope, the only weapon she had. *"Si, forse hai ragione che questo mondo voglia ancora scaricarci addosso qualcosa diabolico, e forse sono ancora troppo giovane da poter capire, ma non voglio abbandonare la speranza, credetemi ragazzi, è l'unica arma che possiedo."*

    We dropped her off at the same gate, wanting desperately to stay together. None of us had grown tired, as we clung to the freshness of our encounter. We received a kiss each on one cheek and a warm caress on the other from our female protégé, actions that crystallized our affections. Our time together would become an irresistible craving as she nudged us from our routines. We watched Eli make her way across the garden and into one of the back doors to the palazzo. We were curious, but we would have to wait till the next day to find out if there had been any repercussions for the unsanctioned outing. *"Gianni, cosa pensi, è riuscita a rientrare senza farsi vedere?"* Carminuccio could only speculate on whether she got back in without being seen, asking me for my opinion. *"La casa è grande e forse i genitori non fanno attenzione, e poi lei mi sa evitare le regole"* I alluded to the size of the house thinking that her parents would be distracted, adding that she seemed the type capable of dodging rules and reprimands. We caught a glimpse of her in one of the upper floor windows as she waved and blew kisses. We gave back what we received as we slowly moved past Marabbecca and onto Via Umberto. Carminuccio gave an enthusiastic account of our time with Eli. *"Sai Gianni, mi è proprio simpaticissima, e si è subito sentita così comoda fra di noi-come se fosse stata un'amica già da tempo. Con poca fatica ha ricevuto l'affetto di tutti, anche Stella. Figurati, ma che sorpresa quando Stella si è fatta avanti offrendo un'amicizia sincera verso una ragazza che poco conosceva, e che credevamo l'avrebbe presa con antipatia. È un lato di Stella che poco si vede ... proprio strano, ma piacevole."* He praised her for being very likeable and capable of having people appreciate her, even Stella. He expressed his surprise at the sincere friendship Stella offered Eli, despite not knowing her well. He happily admitted our fears of Stella creating bad feelings towards the young aristocrat never materialized, exposing a seldom seen side to Stella. In a few short words I aligned my feelings to his, convinced he had explained it perfectly for us both. We looked forward to the coming days as he bid me a *buona notte* in front of my *portone*.

    That night I entered a few pages into my diary highlighting the unraveling disbelief that all went as well as it did. I would have questioned Stella's intentions, but there was little reason to do so. I wondered about the suspiciously natural friendship between Stella and Elisa, but there again I found an acceptable answer in the power of their characters, and the cultural tendency to foster acceptance. Even Stella was powerless to fight off her own nature, and Eli got the best of it. The two were from different worlds, and it could have been the catalyst that cultivated the interest each had for the other.

    I was unable to shake off the confusion about the "kisses". Was I allowed to consider either of the girls any more intimately than just friends? We had acted out as a group that evening, with neither of the girls giving me much personal attention. I brushed it aside, understanding that intimacy was not something that was easily advertised in public in Sarno. Yet, I probed for answers or, in the least, to play out the possibilities. I also imagined myself a boyfriend to one of the girls. Stella's softer side, mostly overshadowed by her tougher, more belligerent side, was spiritual in nature for its rarity and, having experienced it, one could only ask for more. Eli appeared more mature and refined, consistently gracious, and seemingly incapable of any vulgarity. Ignoring her pedigree, however, was not working. There was too much depth to her upbringing to consider her an equal. Convinced that upgrading my Italian was one way of bridging that gap, I nudged my parents into sending me off to a tutor twice a week. The commitment worked well enough to have me closer to literate by the start of my second year in Sarno.

MERECÀ

Sarno girls insisted on friendship before anything else and, as I grew into my solid teenage years, I came to accept that intimacy could be an unexpected, impromptu occurrence, and that any disruption of that female invented rulebook, would have any one male suffer the indignity of being described as incapable of understanding women, expecting to hear *"questo le donne non le conosce affatto"*... " *this one doesn't understand women at all ..."* It would seem innocuous enough to be labeled as such, and a minor insult easily set aside, but for teenage Italian males, discounting the covenant between the sexes was indefensible.

CHAPTER 10
ELISA E STELLA

September of 1968, we entered high school. The Liceo Classico (best translated as Classical or Libral Arts High School) *Giovanni Amendola*, located on the outskirts of town, was a noticeable upgrade from *Baccelli*. The classrooms were larger with single person desks, and the newer building showed none of the traumas of the war. High school life was meant to last five years with a heart stopping battery of tests administered at the end of the school year both in written and oral formats. The three possible outcomes included: *Promosso* (graduated to the next grade), *Bocciato* (left back-repeat the year), and *Rimandato a Settembre* (the equivalent of summer school with a retake of the tests in September). A cloud of serious academics seeped into every inch of the *liceo* as we encountered our *professori* and upper year students. The constant chatter in classrooms and throughout the hallways, of classwork, testing, chapter readings, and projects, demanded that we abandon the more frivolous nature of middle school. In an odd way, the transition into my Italian high school added a noticeable layer of maturity to our characters. I was never sure at the time if the place imposed the standard or did something happen to us at the end of that summer. I understood the imposition to be or act older, so I followed and adapted in the wake of those who were better at it.

That summer had spent itself in late August on beaches along the Amalfi Coast, while the girls in Sarno had spent much of their time taking care of younger siblings while their parents worked jobs or ran their farms. We did get to spend some time with them in the evening hours along the *rettifilo* mostly on the weekends and during the *Ferragosto* week. By the end of the month their giddy, girlish interactions had been replaced with an older quality. The difference was noticeable in the cosmetics that colored their faces, and the long-delayed conversion to the tight American blue jeans. The look had a deliberate sexiness that made it impossible for the still awkward boys to blend comfortably with the budding females. The girls had morphed into young women, while we naively held on to our quirky eight grade habits. The girl-shock had us rushing to condition ourselves into some form of matching male adulthood. We had no artificial ingredients to apply to our faces to add maturity, and no one item of clothing to elevate our manhood except to loosen a button or two on our shirts. The efforts had some desired effects, but no quick hormonal enhancements. Our take on girls maturing quicker than boys was that it had more to do with appearance, and little to do with character … with the girls proving many times over that we were right. Their deceit, however, worked, and it would forever be known that boys matured much slower than girls.

    Elisa had spent the summer once again in London. She returned in late August with a longing to rekindle our friendship. We spoke and sent signals beyond the wall, but I no longer needed to hurdle over it to meet up. I was invited to enter the grounds through the front portico, having won over her parents as a safe friend. Carminuccio and Stella were eventually introduced, having survived the complicity in producing Eli's sneaky night out on the town. The four of us began spending more time together as the days pushed us deeper into our peak teen years. Carminuccio began writing his own music and performing it acoustically in the giardino. He had taken to the Italian singers Gianni Morandi and Bobby Solo. His rendition of Morandi's song *In Ginocchio Da Te*, and Solo's *Se Piangi, Se Ridi* had been practiced and performed to perfection. With guitar in tow, he played whenever the mood demanded our escape from the mundane. No venue in town was off limits, becoming a regular at the café on the *rettifilo* to an enchanted audience. The *lire* patrons dropped in a cup was a bonus, but never became the motivator. Our hair length started dipping onto our collars and halfway down our ears, and the bell bottom jeans made sure we never wore our shorts again. The summer months between middle school and high school made it seem like a whole year had passed and we welcomed the forced maturity. We had become a foursome with no pretense of anything more than canonized friendships-somewhere between idolized human beings and lovers. Ignoring the fragility that defined who we were to each other could have easily reinstated the formalities we so despised, so Eli insisted on selfishly protecting our liberated group existence by having us pledge to secrecy. The pledge unshackled us further, allowing for deeper discussions with few boundaries. It led us on a quest of self-discovery guided by a desire to peel away our adolescence and the protective mantels our parents had wrapped us in, to satisfy curiosities about ourselves. Our sessions would become frequent and impassioned, with few interruptions once we found a way around intrusions. We made this happen by seeking refuge in the *giardino* or in a remote corner on the grounds of Marabbecca. In the propitious absence of other meaningful entertainment, we became jesters, movie stars, poets, and confessors. Eli likened our excursion away from the mainstream to the experiences in Boccaccio's *Decameron*. I knew nothing of either the author or the book, but her lecture would preface my introduction later that year in my Italian Literature class (*Letteratura Italiana*). Her narration of ten friends hiding out in the Tuscan countryside, telling decadent stories to escape the horrors of the plague, had me bewitched. The thought of so much fragility and uncertainty among the young, so long ago, floated my heart across the centuries wishing for a way to have been their eleventh member. She had a romantic attachment to the classics, nourished with summer classes in London and stacks of books on European literature at home. She would often refer to passages to enhance her take on youth, dreams, the future, and love. It was never annoying or self-centered, and I found it as pleasant to learn from her as my *professori.* She had reached that pivot when life could not wait, when living her interpretations took on a sober urgency, as if our days were as numbered and unpredictable as in the lives of Boccaccio's characters. The suspicion that her grasp on her destiny was precarious at best, kept her indulging more completely in her gutsy passions. She appeared gripped by a debilitating fear that time would cast its selfish shadow and deny her a complete set of life's seasons. I wondered if she would continue to advocate for her bohemian tendencies, or would I return to Sarno one day to find she had abandoned her aspirations for the safety of her aristocratic privileges. Judging from the content of her short lectures, she had enough antipathy for the world of her parents to detour her onto paths where she could recreate herself. I could imagine no other prospect for Elisa Tuttavilla.

In those last days of summer, she and Stella became increasingly inseparable. They had struck a chord which neutralized any barrier that would have otherwise kept them from associating. The girls became consumed with each other's lives. The proverbial tracks meant to keep them apart were no match for the powers that galvanized their budding attachment. There was hardly a time when meeting up with one did not include the other. Eli had been given more freedom outside the grounds of her palazzo, and she spent most of that time with Stella, even visiting her neighborhood. Eli never passed judgment on her friend's less than proletarian life, she ignored her father's Communist attachments. On chance meetings in town, she endured his coldness and unkind receptions. Eli was not conditioned to fear men, so ignoring him came easily. When she stayed focused on Stella, she came to worship her friendship for the exposure it offered to the local life she had been denied. Stella was the portal through which she invited herself into the everyday life she had been forced to ignore.

Our first group gathering came to order in the shade of laurels where Eli and I had first met. It took a few weeks to organize, bringing us to edge of September. Stella lost no time in disclosing her anxieties about high school into a mixed bundle of questions and observations. She fumed about being only a few days away from a new experience, with no information to ease her through the process … a transition with no orientation. We all had apprehensions about fitting in while feeling a certain pride for having made it that far. For Stella it was more of an accomplishment considering that many girls from low income and farming families would be forced to end their education after middle school to take on household obligations in preparation of becoming young wives. Survival for many families had much to do with each playing their parts. *"Io sono piena di ansia per quello che deve avvenire fra pochi giorni. Stiamo per entrare al liceo senza nemmeno n'idea di quello che ci aspetta! Ho un nodo nella gola, e non so se sentirmi completamente ignorante, oppure coraggiosa per esserci arrivata."* Elisa wasted little time in setting her at ease with a fiery monologue that lit up her eyes and exposed her naked passion for things that turned her on. *"Stella, cara, ma perché' dai così poco valore al tuo carattere? Sei una donna scaltra e capace di tutto. Sei la mia Sofia Loren, la mia Anna Magnani; ma capisci che sei il risultato di una cultura antica e brillante? Si può dire figlia di antenati che hanno costruito la storia mediterranea. Ti invido con tutto il cuore! Bisognerebbe nascere di nuovo per essere più come te. Sai confrontare qualsiasi situazione, non hai paura di nessuno, sei al tuo agio in tutti gli angoli di questa città, e quando metterai piedi in quell'aula liceale, sarà un altro passo naturale per te, senza timori, e dove ti aspettano tanti successi."* Carminuccio and I remained stunned by the beautiful words Eli granted her friend. She praised Stella's powerful character, the quintessential tough southern Italian female, the product of an ancient and brilliant culture, a daughter of the Mediterranean world. She turned Stella into her Sofia Loren and Anna Magnani, alluding to the strong, righteous female film characters afraid of no one, and capable of forcing others to accept them. She declared her envy, admitting that she would have to be born again for the chance to be more like her. She assured her that high school would offer a venue where she could exercise her nature, without fears, and where success was a foregone conclusion. Eli had confessed her love of Stella's secretly emancipated spirit-the girl who could still define herself as she saw fit despite the harshness of the social norms denying her that ability. Stella's misunderstood brashness had become an invaluable asset to someone like Eli. I had to express the same appreciation, having experienced it from my earliest days in Sarno. Our friends insisted we speak in English as often as possible to give them exposure. *"You know, I felt the same about Stella when we first met. I was very shy around her because I feared her power. She put so many people in their place-especially Mimmo. I took a few shots from her as well, but it didn't keep me from liking her, a lot*

MERECÀ

... like a girlfriend. My first real kiss was with Stella at Mimmo's birthday party. I still have no clue why it happened, but I won't deny I enjoyed it. I thought about it over and over, for days. See, Stella is giving me that look like she understands." Eli giggled and agreed that she had an idea of what I had said. *"Stella did understand. She is awfully familiar with the word-kiss-, so I fear she quite caught on to your story. Stella, hai capito quello che ha detto Gianni di te? Hai capito la parola-kiss-?"* Eli turned to her to ask if she had picked up on the word. Without hesitation she summarized and then let her feelings known. *"Ho capito bene. Yes, I understand what Gianni say about me. Si, ci siamo baciati in casa di Mimmo, e ammetto anch'io che mi è piaciuto. Ho baciato altri ragazzi, ma avevo una grande curiosità di sentirmi baciata da uno straniero. Però, non offenderti Gianni, ma non è stato un bacio da farmi innamorare. Infatti, nessun ragazzo è mai riuscito a farmi innamorare."* She had a clear understanding of what I had said, and she backed up the kiss story by admitting to it. I was not offended when she underlined the fact that, like other guys she had kissed, it did not make her fall in love. Carminuccio had no intentions of letting the conversation peter out, asking how she would then know if a kiss was the kind to make her fall in love? He wanted to know how much passion must be present. *"Allora, Stella, che cosa devi sentire da un bacio per concludere che ti sei innamorata? A che punto devi arrivare, cioè, quanta passione ci deve essere?"* Stella closed her eyes, took a deep sigh, and described it in spirited detail. *"Innanzi tutto, ci deve essere un'attrazione che fa sudare le mani, che ti fa girare la testa come le farfalle che battono le ali pazzescamente senza destinazione, così anche tu non sai più dove vai. Poi, quando ti avvicini a questa persona, più respiri il suo spirito, e puoi sentirti il cuore che ti batte in ogni parte del corpo comm'a nu tamburello napoletano che te fa bollire il sangue. E quando quel brivido ti colpisce, e ti trovi a faccia a faccia, diventi debole e senti solo il dolce calore delle sue labbra. Innamorarsi significa perdere ogni senso in quel momento, e di non essere più alla guida della ragione, di crollare e arrendersi completamente. Solo così puoi assaggiare un amore vero e forte, anche se lo senti solo tu."* Her sermon on love was a

compelling jolt that sent us emotionally to a place we would have normally visited years later. She spoke about love in terms of sweaty palms, of an attraction that sent your mind off aimlessly like the frantic fluttering of butterflies searching for a destination. She described the ability to inhale the person's spirit, causing your heart to beat like a Neapolitan drum, bringing your blood to a boil. And when that seizure owns you, finding yourself face to face, you are weakened by the sweet radiance of the person's lips. She was determined to take it to another level when she spoke of being in love as losing your senses, abandoning all reason ... to surrender unconditionally. In her mind, it was the only way to experience true and powerful love, even if it was one sided.

It was thought provoking enough to listen to lectures in school about infatuated damsels, troubadours, and heartbroken poets, but to hear Stella, one of us, break it down so convincingly, was agonizing. I had to sullenly come to terms with the crudeness of my emotions, sadly acknowledging that I had been incapable of having thought of love in the same manner. Stella's was an adult rendition of how human emotions are born and then saturated with the essence of others. We all sat quietly, waiting for our brains to catch up and process. There would be no disagreements, no challenges-only stunned obedience.

Stella, as was her nature, was pushing the unconventional, an opening that would help coax us away from our innocence. Carminuccio joined in after pondering a side of her few had ever experienced. He welcomed her views but remained curious about the value in one-sided love. *"Stella, perdonami, ma non ho mai conosciuto questo lato del tuo carattere così profondo. Sono d'accordo con tutto ciò che dici, però non capisco che valore ha un amore a senso unico."* Eli was eager to participate in support of Stella's beliefs with references to the Renaissance greats who were forced to love women that were forbidden. One-way love affairs, as she called them, were individuals who lived with unrequited love that astonishes us even today. *"Sapete che I grandi del Rinascimento-Dante, Petrarca, Botticelli, furono innamorati di donne proibite? Tutti amori a senso unico, vissuti con passioni solitari che stupiscono ancora oggi. C'erano altri grandi amori tra*

MERECÀ

due maschi oppure due donne non solo proibiti, ma anche contro legge. Figuratevi che maledizione essere innamorato o innamorata di una persona dello stesso sesso senza mai poterlo dichiarare per paura di andare in prigione o condannati a morte! Non ho mai capito, e questo mi dà un grande dispiacere, come si fa ad assegnare limiti all'amore tra due persone. Non accetto che l'amore sentito da qualsiasi persona possa essere più vero, più sincero, addirittura più legale di un altro. L'amore è la cosa più personale, più che ci appartiene. Tocca a noi definirlo, non alla società, non alla chiesa, neppure dai nostri genitori." When she did not stop at mentioning the greats of the Renaissance, moving on to talk about other forms of prohibited love, my world took another hit. Her unapologetic introduction to homosexual love forced me to confront another of those taboos prejudicially imposed on our young minds by social forces bent on shielding us from behaviors taught to be sinful. She spoke freely about the cursed lives of those in love with others of the same sex, and of the laws prohibiting such behavior with the threat of imprisonment or even death. She found it unacceptable that one person's love could be any greater or lesser or any more legal than another. She judged love to be the most personal of possessions, and that we have unconditional power to define it without interference from society, the church, not even our parents.

For this American kid still wet behind the ears with Catholic holy water, Eli's serious exposure to sexuality had me confronting my crossroads: stay the course or retreat. I had yet to add my feelings to the topic, so Eli pressed me on it when she noticed my discomfort. *"My dear, dear Gianni, are you bothered by the topic? I should have been more considerate. We can let it go until another time, but I believe we must continue speaking of these things if we ever want a world that is more compassionate. Please do not abandon us."* I staggard through my response. *"No, I am fine ... I mean, I understand ... I am good with your words ... it is just that I ... I never ... you know."* Thankfully, she finished my thought for me. *"You never had to deal with homosexual love, that's it, right? I suppose you were taught that it is wrong, that it is sinful. Gianni, you must not let those opinions influence what is in your heart unless you want to honestly believe what has been told you. Could you sincerely think that any two people, no matter who they are, should reject love for each other because some rule or law prohibits it?"* Off balance, I had to question my beliefs, and I could no longer judge another's choices when it came to love. It all seemed suddenly so logical as Eli broke down the concept of pure freedom. Catholicism had taught me to recognize and respect only the limitations on freedoms ... we were aware of our sinful actions which left little room to exercise choices. America was a free country-we all knew that, but there were so many things that we could not do. I had never concerned myself with the protection of freedoms. Eli was teaching that to be free one needed to live it unencumbered and to demand that others respect it. She had placed love at the very top of the list of human needs, asking society not to interfere-how could I argue with that. I began thinking in terms of mutual respect to live and let live. Stella and Carminuccio received a translation, but it seemed they had already locked into the discourse having picked out the words they understood. I tried to appear modern and responsive to the topic, but Eli again noticed the battle in my head, so she pushed the envelope. *"Gianni, I know you are struggling with this, but you must come to understand and to accept. This is bloody easier in London-in this place taboos live on forever. Let me make you understand in the best way I can."* The words had barely slipped from her mouth when she turned to Stella, gently took her face into her hands, and kissed her passionately on the lips. Stella initially thought of pulling away, she had courage, but little of the eccentricity Eli had gained from her summers in England. Unable to resist, she relaxed her body and allowed the kiss to last long enough to make sure it was not understood to be a demonstration. Eli pulled away for a second, then enhanced the message when the kiss was repeated with even greater legitimacy. When it was over, they both stared us down waiting for some reaction-anything. We delivered nothing. Stunned into silence and brain dead, our thoughts could find no direction as the confusion siphoned away any chance that we could quickly homogenize and appear cool with it. Eli insisted on reading into what little we gave away. *"Carmine, Gianni, guadatemi! Look at me! Please tell us you understand."* She had taken an irretrievable chance, gambling on the strength of our friendships … she needed to know there was trauma that could be dealt with. Carminuccio spoke because he had some inkling, I, instead, was completely sterile. *"Allora, se non mi sbaglio, noi dobbiamo capire che voi due siete innamorate, cioè che vi amate come Eli aveva spiegato poco fa. Questo sarebbe un amore profondo fra due donne, così come si possono amare un uomo e una donna? Volete farci capire che non c'è differenza, anche se a me sembra strano? Gianni, ma a te sembra strano lo stesso? Ti fai capace di quello che vogliono farci capire?* Carminuccio delivered his reaction, recognizing that they were lovers, and that their love, between two women, was to be understood to be as valid as the love between a man and a woman. He was being asked to accept even if he admitted it all seemed strange. Then he dragged me into it. He wanted to know if I thought it strange as well, and if I had wrapped my head around it. My conflict was more intense. I was still struggling with a first teenage kiss, wondering what girls looked like naked, and exactly how intercourse worked. Now they wanted me to leapfrog all that coming-of-age stuff and deal with making sense of lesbian love. I tried to untangle my feelings in English. *"Eli, Stella, Carminuccio, all of you, this is the first time I ever heard of such a thing … I mean … I never thought that girls could or were meant to … you know, do the same things that a man and a woman do. I never saw a girl kiss another girl on the lips. I think I am confused, but I'm not sure. Besides, it is not like I never saw Stella with guys. She even seemed to have a much older boyfriend. You even kissed me once. That would make me think that she likes boys."* The frustration mounted, and I lost confidence, finding it difficult to bring together a string of worthy thoughts. I switched to Italian to make sure the three understood my anxiety. *"Non so cosa dire. Io voglio avere tutti voi come amici per sempre e così se Eli e Stella si vogliono bene come innamorati, io capisco. Però, io non voglio amare un ragazzo, voglio amare una ragazza. Io voglio bene a Carminuccio con tutto mio cuore, ma solo come amico"* Their friendship was important to me, so Stella and Eli's declaration found support in my heart. I was, however, adamant in announcing that I had no intentions of being in love with a guy, making it clear that my wishes were to fall in love with a girl. I pounced on Carminuccio by emphatically making an example of him as a male I loved very much as a friend. Stella giggled as she mumbled a few words. *"Gianni, sei così sciocco, però proprio simpatico. Non aver paura che stiamo cercando di cambiare il tuo parere sul tema dell'amore. Si è capito dal bacio che io e te abbiamo provato quella sera da Mimmo che fai il tifo per le donne. Questo è completamente naturale, e non è che io o Eli non provassimo qualcosa per maschi. Secondo Eli dovremmo considerare naturale qualsiasi amore condiviso fra due persone. Non so se sei pronto ad accettarlo ... cosa pensi?"* She thought me silly but cute. She assured me that no one was trying to change my mind on love, and that, my need to love a woman, was perfectly natural. She did not put off her feelings toward males, those were still a consideration which only heightened my bewilderment. Then she pushed me to ponder that perhaps any love exchanged between two people should always be considered natural. She asked if I was ready to accept that, while Eli sought to add more detail. *"Gianni, Stella and I have felt this way about each other for quite some time. Neither of us had the will or the courage to admit it, believing it too risky. Then one day, when Stella was visiting, we were together in my room, and it finally all came out. I suppose we could no longer deny our feelings. We freely spoke of our sentiments after our first kiss. It was a first for Stella, but she would have invited it earlier had she met the right female. We discussed how we both liked girls, and how bloody afraid we were of admitting to it. Stella could never be exposed, especially in a place like Sarno and with a father who would crucify her. I may have a better chance of sympathy with my family since I have an aunt, my mother's sister, who enjoys the company of men and women. No secret there-indeed, she is an eccentric who spends her days in the company of very strange people. I do hope that you and Carmine can keep this within our group. You know how devastating this could be to us both if found out. I must insist on the sanctity of our friendship to protect us."* I didn't admit being unaware of the meaning of -sanctity-, so I guessed it to be some

MERECÀ

sort of commitment one made to a deep friendship. I agreed to live up to it, and I asked Carminuccio to do the same.

The day came and went, evolving into a first true anomaly- as an Italian day unlike any lived thus far. The whirlwind stayed in my head as I retreated to my room, having barely touched my dinner. Mom asked about my mood when my pasta sat undisturbed in my plate. I said all was fine, and that I had been talking to Carminuccio about what to expect in high school. Her involvement may have been superfluous to the truth, but it was still a pleasure to listen to her words laden with the soothing maternal instincts that Sarno had inseminated early in her childhood. Then nonna, who had been sitting patiently sipping her daily small dose of wine she claimed had the same power as medicine, turned to mom and gave her impression in her raspy Neapolitan. *"Maria, chist' sa'nnamuat'. Se ved'nda l'uocchiu ca s'ha venduto o'cor."* I had made the mistake of hinting to nonna in an earlier conversation the topic of girls, and at the dinner table that night, it came back to haunt me. She blurted out that I was obviously in love, and that it was clear in my eyes that I had sold my heart. She probably meant to say that I had sold my heart to the devil, but she backed off the more extreme view despite having earlier expressed her disdain for females who had a hold on men. She had warned me to back down in the face of teenage love and that it could wait for an older age. I knew she meant well, but I guessed her generation had little experience with "gray" areas ... all was non-negotiable black or white. I denied the love thing but admitted to liking Eli very much. Mom saw through me making sure I knew she was good with my explanation.

In bed my thoughts wanted to run wild, but I opted for an orderly and inevitable sequel where I would have to set aside my feelings for both Stella and Eli. I recalled how sweetly involved I had been with both, holding onto the hope that one would help me earn my teenage love wings. All that now seemed obliterated and buried in the past. There was little room for resentment, given the honesty. The addictive bond with the girls was something I was not willing to part with-acceptance and allegiance were the only options.

MERECÀ

MERECÀ

CHAPTER 11
ESTATE (SUMMER)

Summers were always a welcomed salvation from the shorter, colder winter days whether you were on the 12 bus on the way to Orchard Beach in the Bronx, or on a *pulmino* (minibus) heading for the Amalfi Coast. In less than two hours each Saturday morning in July and August from the center of town, we were rolling out our blankets on the pebble strewn beach of Maiori. The small seaside village was our favorite choice with modest crowds, an almost secluded beach, and an abundance of local girls who worked their families' restaurants and small hotels. They could be seen cleaning, making beds, and delivering food and drinks in their summer skirts and colorful aprons. Flirtations were fun and expected giving us the perfect reason to never miss our appointment with the eight o'clock *pulmino*.

The beach towns had a character all their own. The timeless appeal of the pastel-colored houses rising into the cliffs, the Hit Parade tunes that played nonstop from the jukeboxes, and the aroma of freshly baked pastries like *cornetti, brioche* and *ciambelle*, spiritually beckoned locals and tourists to return like faithful swallows each year. That first Saturday in July, Mimmo had organized my introductory excursion collecting the two hundred lire for the round-trip tickets. If we allowed our attention to be governed by our beach fantasies, we could ignore the incubating heat of the *pulmino*. Opening the windows only allowed more hot air to slap us around. The bumpy trek took us through familiar local towns. Pagani, Nocera Inferiore, Cava dei Tirreni, Vietri sul Mare and Minori were the names of towns that posted along the local route avoiding the *autostrada* (highway) and the annoying tolls. I enjoyed the longer ride which showcased the regional world beyond Sarno. The energy that propelled human activity bewildered me early on-it's power could be felt in every task, job, interaction on the streets, the sounds of people talking, shouting, directing, blending with the rumble of donkey carts, the sputter of scooters, motorcycles and diesel engines creating a

MERECÀ

concerto of life that paralyzed and preoccupied the outsider with observation and absorption, incapable of diversion. Short storylines, colorful characters, and a host of wordless sub plots, offered their contributions to that living documentary. I thought Sarno offered enough social excitement until the Campania region put its heartbeat on display.

As we approached the exit for Maiori, the boys began chatting it up, anticipating the downhill run to the first pavilion. We hopped off and rushed to the counter to buy our passes and a tasty *cornetto* to get us in the mood. The beaches may have been public, but the concessions rented and run by locals offered more comforts and easier access to the jukebox and food. For a few lire more, one could also have a chaise set up with an umbrella. We wasted none of our limited funds on luxuries-our towels were all we needed, and once we had claimed our strip of pebbly real estate, we dashed for the water like newborn turtles. Youth fears little or nothing, so the water temperature played no part in how quickly we jumped in. Carminuccio always brought a small soccer ball which kept us active for hours with diving, water kicks, and splashing headers into imaginary goals. We paused only when our curiosity fell prey to the girls and women in untamed bikinis that needed constant tugging and adjusting to keep breasts from escaping. A rough wave could easily dislodge one, exposing the forbidden nipple. The girls were quickly reprimanded by eagle eyed mothers, then forced to sit out the rest of the afternoon plugged into their transistors or reading through the latest gossip in teen magazines.

The second Saturday in July, I came face to face with the latest Italian shock to my nervous American puritanism when my eyes fell upon a set of mature, topless breasts basking in the mid-morning sun. In my quiet panic, I started to slow my pace and, attempting to steady my gaze, I risked walking into others until Carminuccio grabbed me by the shirt and pulled me away, instructing me quickly in the subtleties of not starring at topless females. *"Merecà, che fai? Non ti devi fissare sulle donne nude."* He took me to the side, turned me away from the nudity and toward the sea and asked me to pay attention and not stare, while

MERECÀ

Mimmo and Raffaele chuckled, explaining to each other that I was to be forgiven for being American. *"Gianni, guardami. Alle donne nude è imbarazzante fissare lo sguardo. La nuda è una cosa naturale, una bellezza da mirare per pochi secondi discretamente. Dai un'occhiata e poi continui ai tuoi affari. Tu ti sei addirittura fermato e ti sei paralizzato-questo non è permesso. Comunque, è la tua prima volta e anche quella donna ti avrebbe perdonato."* He explained the embarrassment in staring down a nude, and that nudity was to be treated as nature ... something beautiful to be admired discreetly for a few seconds. He said one was to toss a glance and then move on, and that I should not have permitted myself to stop and stare. He noted it was my first time, and that even the topless lady would have forgiven me. I took the lesson in stride, deflecting my clumsiness with help from the boys. The following Saturday I peeked haphazardly at the lady exposing her naked soul (*la sua anima nuda*, as Mimmo explained it), while Carminuccio nudged me along beating a quick path to our regular spot. I would avoid the same mistake each summer until the delicate reaction to female nudity became my nature as well.

Summers were made of -yet to be realized- memories. My three summers on the Amalfi Coast were no exception, unaware of the life-long effects. Each generation is blessed with the images and sounds that define their teen lives. The movies that made us want to fall in love from 1968 to 1971 were *Doctor Zhivago,* an Italian hit *Nel Sole, To Sir With Love,* and the *Graduate.* Despite the dubbing or the subtitles, the themes remained undisturbed. The big Hollywood hits would arrive in Sarno typically a year after they were released. It was our habit to see the same movie more than once since the new releases played for several weeks at the Cinema Augusteo or the Cinema Moderno-the two movie houses in Sarno. Spending a disproportionate amount of our allowances on the giant screen color flicks was worth every lira to escape even the best our television sets could offer. T.V. movies from the forties and fifties in black and white, and horribly dubbed, were the standard, often leaving me no choice but to retreat to my bed to flip through my Italian comic books.

MERECÀ

The beach jukeboxes played the big hits all summer long. The songs, blending with the atmosphere, the Mediterranean sun, the food, and the girls, created the perfect soundtrack to our own motion picture. I may have been less inclined to engage with others, but my companions were all about meeting people, often attracting a growing group of other teens to our towels, fooling me into thinking that they had known each other all along. The goodwill extended to the foreigners. The boys owned a great curiosity of people from beyond Italy's borders. Money was always in short supply, but on those beaches, we lived life richly without a cabin rental, chaises, or fancy sunglasses.

During the *Ferragosto* week we got to spend more uninterrupted time lounging on those sands. The days leading up to the fifteenth of August made up the prime vacation period for most Italians. For many, work came to an abrupt stop, the large city populations emptied to the mountains or the beaches, while factories building new Fiats suffered from worker absenteeism. The word concerning the purchase of a new car cautioned not to buy one that had been built in the month of August to avoid getting stuck with a lemon. Ferragosto was just another Italian excuse to slow down the pace of life and shun the daily grind of making a living, receiving the same welcome as any other holiday, birthday, feast, or saint's day. My sympathies grew for the list of reasons Italians chose to set obligations aside and indulge in a tamed, hedonistic love affair with just living; understanding that the country offered a multitude of cravings impossible to ignore. I reasoned that Italians needed a healthy, long lifetime if they had any expectation of experiencing all that their homeland had to offer.

It was during that week in August 1969, in our second summer, that Mimmo ventured into the pavilion for some food and to choose his favorite jukebox Beatles songs when he latched on to some American kids visiting from New Jersey. They followed him back with the promise of meeting another kid from America. He introduced them by name and gave an account of all he had learned in the short time he befriended them. "*Ragazzi, questi sono dall'America qui in vacanza. Infatti, sono proprio dello stato di*

MERECÀ

New Jersey e di origine italiana. Hanno preso in affitto quella villa gigantesca che si incontra sulla strada prima dell'uscita. Quella con la piscina e il motoscafo. Mi dicono che sono due famiglie e contano dieci persone. Comunque, questo si chiama Carlo e questa è la sorella Stefania. Questi sono i loro cugini Anthony e Michelle. Ci credete, questa porta il nome del disco dei Beatles ... che meraviglia! E poi è così bella da poter essere proprio la faccia della canzone." Mimmo had to make the point that the girl's name was the title of a Beatles' song. *"Please, I must say your name is the same of the song from the Beatles-Michelle-. Do you hear the song? Is magnifica and you are beautiful like the music."* His bravado set the Americans a bit off balance, not quite used to the ease with which Italians offered praise, especially for beautiful women. Mimmo had already prompted me to say something in English, so I used the moment to clarify his heavily accented words. *"Hi, I'm John. These are my friends Mimmo, Raffaele and Carmine from my town Sarno. It's common for Italians to say something nice about people they meet. They notice the beauty in things and people, and they never shy away from speaking it out loud. I heard you guys are from New Jersey."* Michelle expressed her amazement at my situation. *"Hi, Mimmo mentioned that you moved here. Where are you from?" "The Bronx, little Italy." "I know that place, we've been there a few times to visit relatives and to have dinner ... the restaurants are amazing." "The food is almost as good as here. How long are you guys staying?"* Carlo happily answered my question with the hope of furthering the friendship. *"We will be here for two weeks. Maybe you can meet up with us back at the villa."* I turned to the Sarno crew who stood by quietly trailing our English, finding it difficult to understand for the speed with which we spoke. I let them in on Carlo's invitation. *"Ragazzi, Carlo ci invita a visitare loro alla villa dove restano per due settimane."* Each stiffened in disbelief, hesitantly accepting. Anthony then added substance by choosing a date for us with the promise of a great time. *"Can you guys make it this coming Saturday? We will be gone for two days visiting relatives in Calabria. We will be back on Friday. Just meet us at the villa around eleven. Our parents have been wanting us to meet some*

MERECÀ

teenagers here. The villa has eight bedrooms, so if you guys want to sleep over, bring some clothes; it will be great." Mimmo already sported a boyish smile having understood most of Anthony's words. He translated for the rest. "*Io poco ci credo, ma questo simpaticissimo ragazzo ci ha dato appuntamento per questo sabato di trascorrere una giornata, secondo me più che meravigliosa, nella loro villa. Se ci facciamo perdere quest'occasione, saremo i più fessi di tutt'a Campania.*" He then followed up with his own opinion that not accepting would make us the standout idiots of the region. I turned to the Americans and agreed that we would meet with them that Saturday. I wanted to be there as much as the others.

On the way home we imagined how the villa stay would work out. I reminded them that we were given the option of sleeping over, but we all shied away from committing. I knew it would be a longshot at best trying to convince my mother, so I set it aside hoping nothing would get in the way of us spending the day in the lap of luxury. Just the thought of diving into the large pool had me wishing the days to pass quickly. It would be my first ever dip. The closest we got to one in the Bronx was when the vandalized fire hydrant spewed gallons of frosty water creating a thin rushing stream that ran downhill from the top of my block to the bottom, emptying into the sewer. We stretched out flat on our stomachs and backs cooling us down in the midsummer heat. It was urban and minimalist, but on those hot and humid concrete summer days, it offered as satisfying an escape as those enjoyed by the members of the exclusive clubs along the Long Island Sound. I once saw one of the elegant, manicured grounds and caught a glimpse of the Olympic size swimming pool during an evening wedding reception. I imagined it populated with the regulars during the daytime, people out of my league. It was a lone experience, quickly forgotten to keep kids like me from thinking that we could ever belong. A convenient reality check that kept unnecessary depressions from disrupting our safe, segregated lives.

That Saturday we eagerly kept our appointment with the *pulmino* and the Americans. We got off at the usual stop down at the beach pavilion, then energetically trekked the road uphill towards the villa. As we slipped through the tall, ornate iron gates, we came upon two adult women chatting and looking up at the grapefruit size lemons dangling from a wooden trellis that covered the entire length of the walkway leading to the villa's doors. They approached us with huge smiles and welcoming glances. *"Ciao"*, said one of them. *"Vui site i ragazzi della spiaggia. Io songo la mamma di Antonio e Michelle. Questa è la mamma di Carlo e Stefania."* Her accented, choppy Neapolitan caught us a bit by surprise expecting an English greeting. She explained they were the mothers of the foursome we met on the beach. There was little about them that reminded us of our mothers. They wore fashionable summer dresses, and a Bloomingdale's display of the boldest jewelry that had me asking why so many bracelets on one wrist. The bulky sunglasses left only nose and mouth exposed, Jackie Kennedy hairstyles would have the locals mistaken them for celebrities, and wafting perfume overpowered the scent of the lemon groves. Mimmo had started the trend of calling our new young friends *"americani"*, so it stuck. The ladies walked us to the pool area where the *americani* invited us to join them. We dropped our bags, pulled off our shirts and sent our bodies flying into the chilly water. The child in me took the opportunity to live an experience I never had, and it instantly became a place I never wanted to leave. The soft pool water paid attention to me like a best friend, cheerfully adding quality to whatever I was thinking or feeling. Mimmo was spending his time in the willing company of Stephanie (*Stefania* to him). They seemed to have much in common, including size, so there was much sympathy being exchanged. I was happy for him-he had struggled with females, displaying much boorishness, even hostility, particularly with Stella. He used his evolving English with gusto, and since she was smitten with his pronunciation, she gave him the attention he craved. Her quiet, sheepish smile revealed the character that would become the perfect devotee of Mimmo's bubbly character. The dynamic was glorious to behold.

Raffaele had worked his way into the affections of the adults for his knowledge of things agrarian. Raffaele grew up on his grandfather's farm outside Sarno in the rich San Marzano valley.

MERECÀ

They kept him busy with questions about the summer fruits of the region, the best way to grow eggplant, zucchini, and beans, and the legendary San Marzano tomatoes. My friend possessed a kind and genuine sweetness, making him instantly likeable. He spread a good amount of his *"contadino"* charm that day, and soon they could not get enough of his body language and his Neapolitan. The mothers kept him busy repeating his words then giggling at their own distortions. We learned the adults were first generation born in America from immigrant parents all from the same town of *Afragola*, a suburb of Naples. They spoke a handful of words in proper Italian, with a more meaningful inventory in the local dialect. My Italian had improved enough to cause me a quiet chuckle or two listening to them speak.

After a buffet style lunch, we left the adults behind, and headed to the beach. The early evening hours had remained warm and less humid enticing us to take to the Mediterranean waters one more time before catching the last *pulmino* to Sarno. The jukebox played a string of tunes that would forever footnote my Italian summers. The sun was about to keep its appointment in the western sky, and the pizza oven had been fired up in anticipation of the hungry crowds that would soon fill the pavilion tables. The aroma of burning wood added to the mesmerizing allure of the late day hours of a Neapolitan August when life slowed to a crawl, and people were invited to amplify the joys of being alive. We stalled the *pulmino's* departure for as long as we could to extend some silly talk, to thank our hosts for their kindness, to dish out hugs and kisses, and to declare our promises to return. Mimmo and Stefania spent the remaining minutes together as fantasy lovers, with each projecting awkward affections, wondering how to script a meaningful separation. The big guy wanted desperately to plant a kiss on her lips, but with his blushing pink cheeks turning a hot red, he melted into a heap of jelly causing him to stumble toward her like a puppet learning to walk. Off balance, he finally decided that the only honorable exit was to retreat, unable to bring the day to a perfect conclusion. We all felt his embarrassment without raising his suspicions-it was an emotionally delicate moment that desperately cried out for normalcy. We would pull into Sarno just before ten, with almost two hours to help Mimmo gain back some of the self-confidence he had clumsily spilled on the pavilion terrace, and to compare notes. My first instinct was to get Mimmo to tell us more about Stefania, thinking him eager to unload his infatuations. He chose to stay silent, preferring to listen in on our conversations. I asked Raffaele about the mothers, and he enthusiastically delivered his tale. "*Si, una grande simpatia per nu tipo e'mamme che non potevo mai immaginare. Me sembravano più comm' sorelle anziché' mamme come le nostre a Sarno. Portavano vestiti più da giovani, e non ci hanno mostrato nisciuna preoccupazione, manc'na'poc e antipatia. Mia madre m'avess'fatt' tante raccomandazioni: dint'a piscina se more, mangiate sto pan' e po' aspiett' almen'n'ora per torna' nda l'acqua. Addò vai tutt' mbuss? Lievete stu custum e annietete cu sta tovaglia ca piglia nu raffreddore. Figuratevi che io alla spaiggia con mia madre ci sono stato solo una volta. Non so se le vostre mamme sono noiose accusi', ma me pare che le signore americane nu tengano gli stessi vizzi. Per me è stato proprio nu piacere enorme incontrare adulti calm'accusì che permettono e vivere senza 'ste scocciature.*" Poor Raffaele admired the American mothers so much, he gave his own mother poor grades. The more liberal attitude of the ladies from Jersey was a sweet revelation for him. They were mothers unlike the one he had known all his life who had made his one other trip to the beaches a memorably annoying one. He praised them for their hands-off attitude toward their own children and the pleasant way they hosted their visit. Carminuccio agreed with most of what he said, but he found room for some adjustment, reminding him that they were on vacation so the children were granted greater freedoms, but that upon returning to America, things would probably go back to normal. He added his opinion of the richness on display minus the buffoonery; that if they had been more high society, they would not have extended an invitation to us. "*Raffe', però l'argomento che fai è na poco sbilanciato. Fatti capace che quelli stanno in vacanza, e quindi danno quella libertà in più ai figli. Una volta in America, tutto ritorna a normale. Per me è stato lo stesso piacere per l'amicizia e la ricchezza senza buffonate. Credo che se fossero stati quelli di alta società, non ci avrebbero invitati a passare na juornata con loro."* Expressing positive opinions of the Americans had me rekindling my affections for things American. It was not lost on me that being able to afford that size villa for a couple of weeks with expenses for airline tickets, food, sightseeing, and shopping made them well off, maybe even rich.

Mimmo finally broke down, no longer finding the fortitude to keep his experience to himself. We knew he would eventually talk it up, for there were few instances when he was at a loss for words. Speech to Mimmo was like running to a marathoner. *"Ragazzi, non riesco a trattenermi. Devo dire che ho sentito per la prima volta il potere femminile di fare innamorare un uomo."* He admitted to not being able to keep it in, so he announced how for the first time he felt the power of a female to make a man fall in love. *"Stefania è una di quegli angeli che si presenta completamente naturale, senza pregiudizi, senza giudicare prima di conoscere bene una persona. Non sapete quanto mi dà coraggio che in questo mondo tutti possano trovare la propria felicità. E non pensate per un momento che sono diventato uno sciocco che si dà alle fantasie-so bene che non è una cosa che possa durare. Siamo troppo giovani, lei vive un mondo lontano, e la probabilità è che questa estate magica passerà e non ci incontreremo mai più. Ma la mia verità è che non mi aspettavo di vivere sogni, ma di darmi fiducia che nel mondo ci siano altre come Stefania, e che con un po' di fortuna, le nostre strade si incroceranno."* In a delicate, short span of a few minutes, Mimmo had exposed the aspirations of a boy making contact with his manhood, and I was taken by the sincerity and the hidden desperation. Stefania's friendship had become the stimulant to overcome the barriers that kept him from the same passions and affections that came easy to those with more fashionable assets. He expressed himself with maturity and class in pointing out he was following impractical dreams, and that Stefania would most likely be a one-time encounter. His greatest take away from the reality of the Jersey girl was that she was perhaps one of many, holding out the hope that his path would one day cross with another Stefania. Recalling earlier days, his hostility towards Stella was finally making sense.

MERECÀ

Mimmo's despondency had much to do with the hard-core conclusions he had dumped on himself. Unable to escape a reputation built around the harsh defense mechanisms he employed with the girls that were part of our lives in Sarno, he had consigned his life to a future that may have never delivered on the affection of a female. Stefania had erased all that. She granted him the opportunity to redefine himself, and to like himself more. Mimmo had taught an unexpected, but sobering lesson about the blind selfishness in the things we took for granted. For those of us who had easier, more fluid and accepting relationships with girls, being in Mimmo's shoes during that ride home, gave a better understanding of the dejection with which others lived. Italians were very much aware of things beautiful, and things not so beautiful. The standard was high, and I was made aware many times of how often descriptions of people involved reference to beauty. Stefania had genuinely beheld the beauty in Mimmo that Mimmo refused to see. It changed his life for the better and it enlightened the rest of us to seek beauty beyond the physical. We never did get in another day with the *Americani*. The bittersweet memories, however, were most powerful in Mimmo. He would remain in touch with Stefania for years to come.

MERECÀ

CHAPTER 12
AMORE PROIBITO
(LOVE FORBIDDEN)

The introduction to unconventional love became a lesson on subversion. The girls had no second thoughts of what they meant to each other. Consuming their affections meant finding ways to eliminate suspicions that would have created unwanted interference. They played up the girlfriend relationship by doing all the things that were expected of two best friend, teenage girls. Stella had become a steady at Marabbecca, spending countless hours with Eli in her large, comfortable room. The girls were left to themselves without interruptions; her parents were content in having her indoors with someone to keep her busy. Stella had conveniently arranged her school schedule to be able to leave at the end of her last class. Italian high school schedules were more like American college schedules. There was no meat day with timed periods. Classes were scattered throughout the day often with enough free time to plan for extracurricular activities. The girls played their records, performed lip synched versions of popular songs, flipped the pages of fashion magazines, experimented with make-up and perfumes, and wrote secret love letters. Most of the time was spent at Eli's home with occasional visits to Stella's tight two-bedroom unit when no one was home. The talk around town about Stella's mother Adela, was that she had been one of the most beautiful women Sarno had ever produced. That appeal was still evident despite the toll her husband's dead end, fiery politics took on the family, the borderline poverty, and the tedious work as a seamstress. First time I met her I understood Stella's beauty. Her husband, Mario, was mostly known as *-signor direttore- mister director* of the local office of the Italian Communist Party by the handful of party faithful who came and went, attending short meetings, picking up leaflets for distribution, dropping off and collecting party mail, and

MERECÀ

sharing pasta meals cooked by Stella and her mother almost daily. Her father insisted that the family had to play a part in advancing the cause of the party-nothing was more important. He had indoctrinated his wife and partly motivated a still young Stella, who had recently begun to question her father's fanaticism as she entered her teen years. She understood her role as a daughter in a southern Italian household, but her rebellious side had sparked a budding independence. Eli had become the catalyst that drove Stella to reimagine her life. The more time they spent together, the more she questioned her father's teachings.

Carminuccio and I shared the same reaction. We agreed that the passions the girls were living had helped them overcome the annoyance of prohibitions. Italian girls, no matter their class, were shackled with cultural expectations that forced them to forfeit personal visions for antiquated female roles. Eli had to live up to her aristocratic breeding, while Stella had to carry her load in the daily, mundane workings of her bourgeois life. Their affection for each other was not outright rebellion, but rather a choice to live as they desired, invisible to the world that would judge them harshly. In many ways it was easier to nurture intimacies with a female than it could ever be with males.

It was Eli's insight that guided the affair, blunting their love pangs with strategies to allay speculations, restraining their impulses until they could be alone. Taming Stella was no easy task, so their conversations dwelt on managing their crush. A typical stay at Marabbecca would have the girls spend some time in the company of Eli's parents in silly, condescending chatter until a more pressing issue called the adults away, allowing the girls to escape to Eli's room. The bedroom became their safe house where the most delicate physical exchanges took place and where their emotions generated thoughts of a fantastical future.

"*Finalmente! Non vedevo l'ora che I miei genitori avessero altri impegni. Non sai quanta gioia mi dà rifugiarci in questa camera, su questo letto, nelle tue braccia. Stella, a volte penso che tutto questo sia solo una stupida fantasia, che il nostro amore vive una falsità. So che sono sciocca quando mi sento così, ma non riesco a capire se questo mondo possa mai accettare ciò che siamo.*" Eli used her philosophy with greater compulsion, and she expressed it best when they could dodge her parents to engage in more intimate talk. Once in her room, the girls were free to scale back the limitations to practice their extraordinary love. On Eli's bed they frivolously commented on the things they loved the most about the other, ran their fingers along the contours of their lips, and touched each other delicately, creating the arousals they both craved. They were happiest when they could mold their ideal world covertly, guided exclusively by their desires. Inevitably, hesitations crept in as they lost the power to keep the affair juvenile. As it ripened, Eli, plagued by maturity, first made her concerns known when she questioned the truth, wondering out loud about the possible falsehood of their kind of love. She blamed her insecurities on social acceptance, not nature. Would the world ever approve, and did it matter? Stella had more reasons to derail her feelings. Hesitations for her had more to do with defying the only nature known to her: that hard core, mainstream life blissfully oblivious to alternative lifestyles simply because they did not make sense and could be easily dismissed as being practiced by a handful of radicals. Sarno was not some evil kingdom pushing a set of uniform norms. For the most part, it was a place blissfully stuck in a comfortable existence, and generations had fallen in line with those practices. I thought of their type of conformity as a way of life aligned with survival. Listening to my nonna's stories about the past, it was easy to conclude that not defying that social formula provided for a comfortable life, even it wasn't the happiest. The consequences for Stella had to do with those traditional norms. Discovery would bring harsh judgment, not so much to condemn the physical act, but to frown upon the union as being foolish, out of place in a small, indoctrinated town unaccustomed to modifying the fundamentals. *"Elisa, ti rendi conto che per me c'è molto più da perdere? Se tu non sei sicura dei tuoi sentimenti, se non sei convinta che tutto questo sia vero, cosa ti aspetti da me? Mi fai perdere il potere di tirare avanti. Io non voglio vivere la vita di mia madre, non posso immaginarmi una donna schiava alle convinzioni di un uomo come mio padre. La verità è che mio padre mi fa schifo, lo odio. Non sai quanti schiaffi ho ricevuto da bambina quando le cose non andavano a suo piacere. Mia madre ha sofferto tanta umiliazione le volte che la prendeva a pugni e calci sul balcone. Devo trovarmi un'altra strada, forse in un posto lontanissimo da Sarno. Nel tuo mondo ci sono più possibilità di essere accettata, di esprimerti come vuoi, con poca difficoltà. Eli, ascolta, io non ci riesco senza il tuo saper fare e il tuo amore."* Stella's emotional flareup had nothing to do with social acceptance, her battle would involve only personal upheaval. How could a girl like her be in love with one of her own sex? She expressed her antipathy for Eli's selfish take on her own anxieties about the relationship. While she acknowledged the importance of social acceptance, Stella knew that topic had more to do with class and geography. She pointed out how much easier it would be for Eli to find the acceptance in her more liberated world, where the nature of one's sexuality had already been amplified to included newer definitions. Stella relied on Eli's direction and strength to empower herself. Any display of weakness made huge dents in her own capacity to accept herself. She had to stay the course to avoid her mother's life of servitude to a man like her father, whom she confessed hating for the beatings she received from when she was a little girl, and for the humiliation her mother endured each time he punched and kicked her in full view on the balcony. In dealing with personal circumstances, Stella had closed the one-year gap in age. In matters of love and sexuality, she could only claim virginity. Having understood the disparity, Eli responded lovingly to Stella's fears by asking forgiveness, admitting she should have known better, giving her the impetus to offer still greater love for her candor. *"Sei così sincera, e per questo che ti amo ancora di più. Perdonami, dovevo essere più consapevole delle tue condizioni-sono stata incosciente-non è che ci conosciamo da poco. Lasciamo stare, insegnami a parlare Napoletano. Non mi è stato mai permesso di parlare il dialetto, ma lo trovo molto simpatico e così naturale. Insomma, come si dice in Sarnese o Napoletano-mi viene la voglia di baciarti?"* When Eli changed the subject wanting Stella to teach her to speak in dialect, the mood became playful. She asked to have the words-I have the urge to kiss you-translated.

MERECÀ

"*Si dice così: Me ven u'vulio e te vasà*". Eli's amateurish attempt at speaking Neapolitan turned the girls silly and weak with laughter. Stella insisted on a more southern accent, but all Eli could manage was to exaggerate the pronunciation which brought Stella to tears with laughing stomach pangs as she fell exhausted onto the bed. Recovering, she asked for a way of describing a clumsy person. "*Come si descrive una persona goffa? Ho una amica a Londra che sbaglia quasi tutto in un modo comico e simpatico*". "*Ecco, il dialetto ha una parola perfetta, molto adatta per una persona del genere. Si dice- è na 'nzallanuta-.*" Stella had the perfect word, and Eli thought it ridiculously cute. She tried several times to speak it, but got tongue tied each time. Exhausted from the laughter, she cuddled up ... Stella's swollen lips were too much to resist. "*Come mi dici baciami?*" Stella thought about it for a second after Eli asked her to say kiss me in Neapolitan. She responded with just one word. "*Vaseme*". The word sparked that instant of seriousness just before the tingles take over. "*E allora ... vaseme*". Their tender teenage intimacy played out like a symphony of musical movements with each touch, each kiss striking a new chord. They explored and charted destinations on their bodies that instigated singular sensations, journeying to those places time and again, committing the routes to memory. As Eli rolled to one side of the bed, she curiously asked to translate-you are a miracle, and not a day goes by that I don't want you with me. "*Come si dice-sei un miracolo, e non passa un giorno che non ti voglio con me-?*" Stella gazed deeply into her eyes, pulled her face close, swept her lips over hers creating the wetness they both desired. "*Si dice accusi': Si nu miracolo, e nu pass nu iurno che non te voglio cumigo.*" The Neapolitan from Stella's lips only made her more irresistible, magnifying for Eli all the natural, untamed beauty she came to identify with her lover. That afternoon became a time and a place onto itself, just as Eli had described it. Being in love for her meant being in love with the purity of the moment, with no interference from promises, from things that were and things yet to come. Stella was slowly coming to accept that their relationship could turn out to be a lonely crush smothered by circumstances.

MERECÀ

High school kept us busy with note taking during long, theatrical lectures, research papers, slide presentations on Italy's artistic heritage, and satisfying readings and interpretations on the best of Italian literature. Eli was still being schooled at home, with the addition of a British tutor, friend of the family on sabbatical in Sorrento. Carminuccio had me spending most of our afternoons together completing assignments and studying for tests. My Italian had improved enough to communicate with greater ease, and with vocabulary enough to give my expression more color. Mimmo was writing a letter a week to Stefania in New Jersey, while pulling the highest grades in our class, and Raffaele had taken on a part time job working as an orderly at the local hospital in the Episcopio district. The money he earned helped his family move to a nicer home on the outskirts of town, and it allowed for newer clothes. The added income, while making a material impact, caused no lessening of his humble character. Stella kept up her good daughter act at home only because it bought her time with Eli. By the new year, the girls were seeing enough of each other to ignite some suspicions in Stella's father. *Signor direttore* already harbored certain antipathies for Eli's family and their history. He had been one of the Communist Party foot soldiers after the war bent on harassing the rich and those who had associated with Mussolini's government. The 1946 referendum abolished the monarchy and gave Italy a constitutional republic. The communists organized politically, but their motivations were still dangerously aligned with rogue partisans and the Soviets. Stella's father had been radicalized enough to advocate for the overthrow of the government by Italy's own Russian style revolution. In his view, with American influence there was no defeating the capitalist tendencies of the new republic without a revolution … the Americans had to leave.

Eli's family could not escape their past and what they still represented to a man like *signor direttore*. Early in 1969, he conspired with several of his associates to spy on his own daughter, convinced she was being influenced by Eli to turn against his ideals. His instincts were accurate, and he conveniently used the information to keep the girls apart. Stella could only spend time with Eli entirely on the sneak, sometimes skipping classes for clandestine trips to Marabbecca. She would enter through the ivy-covered gate and the back door. Eli's lessons were done by two each afternoon. This gave them little more than an hour alone with enough time for Stella to make it home at the expected time. She had no clue she was being followed by her father's spies. No appointment went unnoticed. He had, however, no intentions of confronting her. He was still consumed with the destruction of the aristocracy, and the trips to Eli's palazzo made it easier for him to learn as much as possible about the routine lives of the Tuttavilla family. The girls had begun to feel the discomfort as Stella was forced to adjust to her father's pressures. No conflict emerged between the girls, and the offbeat appointments were kept with the same enthusiasm.

    Eli asked me to meet with her after school on the Thursday before Easter Sunday. Her tutors had both departed for the holiday, and we had the long weekend starting with Good Friday, extending into *Pasquetta,* the Monday after Easter which was the ultimate do-nothing day for Italians, with stores and restaurants shuttered, and families lounging out the hours with no intention of burning any calories. She greeted me at the front gate, and we quickly moved into the rear of the grounds to our favorite bench under the laurels. Her smile faded as she replaced it with a serious look that reflected her panic. *"Gianni, please forgive me, but I want you to know that I selfishly invited you here to ask questions about Stella. You must see her often in school, and perhaps you can help me with things I do not understand. We have been meeting here on days when she can leave school early. Twice per week she has a last period study class which she skips willingly so that we can be together. This week we were to meet on Tuesday and Wednesday, but she never showed. Her father has become stricter, forbidding her to visit me. I have called several times and each time her mother answers the phone to advise that Stella is too busy with chores. Is there anything you have noticed? Is there any news you can give me?"* I had much to say. I told her how Carminuccio and I had spent time with Stella after school at the café across from the Municipio. How she seemed unsettled, struggling to find herself.

MERECÀ

Our questions about the relationship finally broke through the silence, after which she unleashed a torrent of feelings and doubts as her eyes bubbled up with tears. She worried that her parents had either found out or drawn conclusions about them. She could not explain the abrupt change except to think that somehow, they knew, and they would eventually confront her. If that were to happen, she could hardly imagine the misery and torture. We noticed how fear had replaced her strength. In her speech she was a child again, hostage to adult judgement. I spoke of how her doubts were consuming her. "*Eli, she is convinced her parents know about you two. She is full of fear. These were her words*: '*Tutto sta cambiando così in fretta che non riesco a scappare questa paura che mi consuma. Miei genitori forse hanno scoperto qualcosa. Ne sono certa perché' mi proibiscono di visitare Marabbecca.*'". Everything was changing so rapidly. She was certain her parents knew because she was prohibited from visiting Marabbecca. "*Eli,* we *would have agreed with all she said, except for the fact that her parents had not reacted the way I thought. According to Mimmo, her father's beatings are a neighborhood topic. Her mother had worn a bruise or two on her face, and Stella was forced to cover up black and blues on her arms. We then tried to help by explaining that her parents most likely did not want her influenced by you and your family. If I understand the politics, you should be disliked for who you are.*" She took a moment to react. "*I can only hope you are right. If her father knows the truth, it is only a matter of time before he tries to destroy her. I wonder if he will target me as well. I fear my parents will become involved and must relive all the disappointments of the past when they are so close to regaining their status. I need to see her. I give her my love so easily, so freely; there are no hesitations, no wondering if it is real, no question of whether I am fooling myself or being fooled, and no fear of being hurt. Gianni, I have been so inconsiderate. I Think back on our kiss, and I beg your forgiveness for insisting on it. It was a moment of pure affection. You own a special place in my heart, it was my way of showing it.*" She ran her fingers through her long, silky hair, caressing the ends of a few strands, and nervously bit her lower lip before continuing. "*I love the boy*

in you, and how it makes me wish for a boyfriend to make my life what it is perhaps meant to be. Then I fall into Stella's arms, and I know that only a woman can complete me. I do not expect you to fully understand, but I do hope you can accept." I had begun the process of embracing the novelty of their relationship because the girls were dear to me, but understanding it came with more difficulty when too much of what I had been taught got in way. My world of man and woman had never gone questioned. Relatives and friends lived as heterosexuals, at least superficially, eliminating any chance we would be exposed to alternatives. Catholic upbringing frowned on any deviancy from the norm-we were aware of the immorality of certain behaviors, and then they were avoided as topics for discussion. *"Eli, I have no reason to doubt your feelings for Stella, but I don't quite understand them, even when I try hard to imagine what it is like to feel the things you do. I never had a reason to consider any other relationship between two people. If what I learned in the past is all wrong, then I need to figure out why, and the way you explain it does help. I have to stop thinking of you as two girls, and just as two people. I know that when I like a girl, and I have the urge to kiss her, it seems so right-so proper, as you say ... and stop apologizing for the kiss. I only regret that it may never happen as boyfriend and girlfriend."* The smile she gave when she was in control of a situation quickly owned her face and I had to pull away twice to reject her offer to kiss again. Her words allowed me my doubts. *"Okay, I understand, I'm sorry, and you are right in feeling this way. I must tell you, however, this time around it had more to do with love, and not an attempt to reward you."*
I was just coming to terms with all that was happening when Eli decided to amplify the confusion. *"But this would seem like cheating on Stella. I thought you were completely in love with her ... you just mentioned how only a woman could complete you. What does that mean? To me it means you need a woman to do what men do ... I mean, Stella is a woman, and she gives you what a man normally gives a girl ... do you know what I mean? Shit, I don't even know what I mean. This is getting so weird."* She tried to fix me. *"Carissimo Gianni, the only way to set you right is to*

MERECÀ

speak more frankly. The time has come, and while I didn't believe you could handle more of this, I now understand that to avoid it any longer would be evil." She wrapped my arm around hers and cuddled up. "*You are right in reminding me of how brilliant Stella is in my life, of how easy it is to love the beautiful woman in her. You may still find this difficult, but she fulfills my indescribable attraction to the perfections of a female. To me, a woman's softness, her clean beauty, the graceful nature of her body is so much more than a man can offer. Gianni, do not be offended, please, but imagine multiplying by one hundred the sensations you get when you think of being with a woman you adore ... that is what one woman can feel and give to another. In a man, instead, I seek his strength, the creature in him, the temptation to please him, and the power I possess to control his emotions towards me. Think back on the effect my first kiss had on you. I knew I wanted to kiss you partly because I needed to set myself straight about boys, but I also knew that it would send you off into a frenzy. You see, I confess that I must satisfy my curiosities about both sexes. I cannot go through life wondering about the nature of things, I need to experience them. I may be in love with Stella, but I do find you attractive as a male.*" She paused to catch up with her thoughts. She had sparked her convictions, and every inch of her was on fire. "*I believe that only two women can truly become one being, while a man and a woman will always remain individuals even when they unite in love, sex, or marriage. The differences were meant to be, and the expectations are practically unrealistic. This is not to say that what a man and woman experience is not special. I believe it is, but it becomes that way because of the amount of time a couple spends together. They become lovingly complacent with the life they have had in each other's company. It is a beautiful thing to behold; my parents are the perfect example of how it can work. My grandmother once told me that when a man and a woman spend many years together, they eventually become like brother and sister. I suppose she meant that they have a need to still be together, but that need has become one of companionship rather than lovers. I may be unfair, but I cannot imagine it happening between two women in love. I believe two women have a better chance of remaining lovers throughout their lives."* I had questions. *"But why is that so important? My parents do act like friends, but why is it necessary for them to still be lovers?"* She looked at me in disbelief. *"My dear, dear friend-what could be more important? If two start out as lovers, they must remain lovers. There can be no greater purpose.* I had to shut my eyes for a moment to think it through-this was deep stuff, and as much as I wanted to give in and agree, my logic kept pulling me back. *"So, we are supposed to only have one lover during our entire lives? What if we choose one and later, we find out it was a mistake?"* She pounced on the loophole. *"There are no mistakes. If you take a lover, and it does not work out, well then it may fall apart, but the only thing you ever were to each other was lovers. The point is to be lovers, not spouses, not engaged, not boyfriend-girlfriend ... just lovers, pure and simple. I would think that the very first attraction between two people hot for each other is looking forward to being lovers-that's what brings them together, and that needs to survive all the intrusions in life ... you know, family, children, choosing a home, paying bills, and I am convinced that two women in love would be best at remaining lovers. They know what the other expects and living up to it is hardly a burden. You can see I'm infatuated with the concept of lovers."* She doubled down, castigating traditional relationships, describing them as damaged. *"To me, traditional marriage will become obsolete. There's this very real notion that marriage became an institution imposed on people by the church and governments. There's nothing natural about it. Why should some priest or official have the power to validate my relationship? I should be the one to consider myself married to another. Besides, the expectations between a man and woman are much too complicated and, I would say, very selfish. They readily break down and are not easily mended. I have witnessed this in my own parents and many friends and relatives, and I endeavor not to live those lives."* There was little I could say to match her power trip. I had not experienced the same, but then, there was little I knew about my parents' personal lives. The occasional scuffle between Mom and Pop lasted only minutes, was usually over something silly like too much salt in the pasta, type of upgrades to our home, or why Pop disliked accepting invitations to dine at the homes of friends and relatives. The disagreements were easily repaired, with the normal pace of life hardly impacted. It was that fluidity and predictability to our lives that kept me blissfully unaware of the disarray in the lives of others.

Eli had me on the ropes again, forcing me to poke my head outside my shell to experience what seemed to me as dysfunctions. It would take years into the future before society started treating those "dysfunctions" with more compassion and acceptance. I was living the earliest days of that revolution, filled with dangers and stinging consequences, especially for women. Stella had made Eli aware of how she was haunted by the expectations placed on her, forced to live her days cautiously, secretly responding to her own needs, always a mistake away from the calamity of being found out. I was not completely appeased. "*I definitely understand and accept your feelings for Stella ... she is easy to love. I wonder if you expect you and Stella, or you and any other woman to live a normal life. Am I crazy for thinking that people will always have something to say if they know the truth?*" She perked up like a kid organizing a schoolyard game for which she knew all the rules. "*Yes, Gianni, yes ... in London there is a neighborhood called Soho, and it is a place where people like me can live without having to worry about being judged. My London friends and I find the energy there irresistible! It amazes me to know so many loving and peaceful people, and I can properly imagine myself living amongst them.*" The single-minded response turned my attention to Stella. "*That is fine and good for you, but you know Stella doesn't have that choice. There is no way she can feel good about the two of you if she learns that you can escape to your Soho while she is forced to keep fooling others and herself being stuck in Sarno. I am sorry, but I would not tell her about Soho. I know Stella well enough, and she will pull away to protect her reputation and act like nothing ever happened between you two. She will know there is no future for her in being a lesbian, and no matter how much she wants that kind of relationship, she will deny herself, she is strong enough to do that. Being labeled would kill her, and if you had never made it possible for her to be in love with a woman, she would have buried that feeling, and that would have at least saved her from herself. You know, girls like Stella do not have many choices, and from what I have seen, they learn to live with the rules placed on them. You have options that can save you. If you lead her too far from her reality with no way to completely escape it, she will not be able to fix it, and the consequences will be rough."*

For all the ability Eli had to process her progressive world, she lacked a deeper understanding of how necessarily conventional the lives of girls in a place like Sarno were. The years she was kept hidden away in her compound had denied her a connection to life outside her walls. One of those lives belonged to Stella, and Eli had failed to give it a deeper understanding. Despite embarking on her new life, Stella could not allow herself the luxury of completely abandoning the life she was born into. Eli's belief that her lover had the power to choose and keep the life she wanted was a mistake and straying from the truth could brutishly expose them.

CHAPTER 13
MANCANZA DI EQUILIBRIO
(LOSS OF BALANCE)

Even Sarno could not escape the turbulence in the spring of 1969. In high school, contemporary issues came into the classroom on the front pages of daily newspapers like *Corriere Della Sera* and *La Stampa*. Our professor di Scienza Politica (Political Science), started class each day reviewing the headlines on the front pages. He walked in with several papers covering a range of political views. We all enjoyed the exercise which yanked us out of our safety nets into a stressed-out world. The endless war in Vietnam, the Soyuz and Apollo space race, campus protests, police in riot gear beating up on young people in major cities, race riots, My Lai massacre, Boeing 747, Yasser Arafat, coups, assassinations … all topics that filled those pages. The presentations were stark and disturbing, and they stayed with us for days. The universe outside Sarno had begun to close in on us. That same loss of balance on the world stage crept into our lives, determined to change us. I could feel our innocence slipping away as we were confronted with controversies that could have waited until we were older. Eli became impatient with the demands that stifled Stella enough to shut down her emotions. Her experience with less social apathy had her believing that nothing was impossible, and that even teenagers should be empowered to run their own lives. It drove a wedge between her and Stella, which Stella was incapable of understanding, nor was she in a position to fix it.

Carminuccio asked me to hang around after school the last Friday in May. We played a quick game of *biliardino* at the café', but he lacked the usual competitive enthusiasm. We then grabbed two bottles of San Pellegrino and dragged a couple of chairs to an empty table. He normally spoke freely, but the serious look of a student who had just failed a final exam and the long pauses, caused some concern. I asked him what was wrong, why wasn't he talking. *"Che c'è? Perché non parli?"* He mumbled a few indecipherable words before coming back more coherently. *"Merecà, non so. Mi sento così appesantito da questo mondo che ci scarica addosso tante novità, come la relazione tra Elisa e Stella. Non mi aspettavo di dover capire un amore tra due donne così deciso, così naturale. Eppure, a parte la stranezza, conoscendole intimamente, spero per loro una vita normale, anche se sembra improbabile. Secondo me c'è poca speranza, specialmente per Stella, di essere accettate. E questo mi dà un grande dolore perché tutti meritiamo di essere felici e di scegliere la vita che si desidera. Tutto sta cambiando da come siamo cresciuti, da quello che ci hanno insegnato a casa, a scuola e nelle chiese."* His monologue was filled with anxieties about how his world had been hijacked by the changes attempting to sweep aside conformist attitudes with liberation movements. We had mostly a hazy understanding of the forces that were marching in the streets of big cities, making their demands. Our sympathies were with the young people, but for one like Carminuccio, the fear of being uprooted so violently away from the life he had nurtured was causing him to question the girls. He considered it another revolutionary ripple that was rocking the steady, stable course handed down by family, school, and church. Despite thinking it a longshot, especially for Stella, he still wished them a normal life-even if normal had come to include the strange. He was pained by the thought that they would not find happiness. I played the part of the grounded friend, in control of his feelings wanting to calm his storm. I agreed it would be a rough stretch for Stella but flipped it a bit by offering an explanation that gave the girls the power to choose a path to a life they wanted, even if it was strewn with booby traps. *"Le cose per Eli forse andranno migliore, ma per Stella ci può essere una tempesta si capisce, ma tu devi accettare che per loro scegliere la vita che vogliono porta tante difficoltà. Credo sono pronte a confrontare quel futuro se loro accettano quella strada piena di trappole."* After falling into a momentary trance, he questioned the genesis of their sexuality. *"Gianni, tu credi che si nasce così, come le ragazze, oppure è un sentimento che cresce man mano? Ci ho pensato a lungo, ma non credo ci sia risposta ragionevole. Se le donne nascono donne, e gli uomini nascono uomini, si intende che è la nostra natura. Adesso vogliono farci capire che le nostre nature non sono quelle vere. Vedi la mia confusione?"* I stumbled through an answer. *"Adesso le cose diventano più serie, mi sembra di stare nella classe di filosofia. Non ho mai pensato alla nostra natura in questo modo. Se le ragazze sono nate così, significa che è una parte della natura umana che non abbiamo mai conosciuto. Se, invece, questi sentimenti sono venuti durante la vita, sono scelte che possono fare. Io credo che il mondo non debba avere il potere di negare loro."* His dilemma of whether a person is born with certain tendencies or they are learned was thought provoking, and there was no way I could engage without thinking it through. He questioned the very essence of human nature ... were not women born women and men born men? If so, he concluded that it was our true nature. He was suspicious of the attempt to change that truth while admitting to his confusion. I tempered his feelings a bit using my improved Italian to present a more moderate view justifying both the birth and the acquired theories. Hoping to make sense of things, I claimed that if the females were born with a nature to be in love with another woman, then it must be a legitimate nature we had never known. If, instead, those feelings are acquired through the years, then they have every right to their choices, and that the world had no power to negate them.

    We became anxious, wondering whether we were satisfied with any of our explanations. Thrown off balance, we wanted to expand our comfort zone to naturalize what we thought was unnatural. The demand to change our way of thinking now extended necessarily to anyone advocating that lifestyle. *"Merecà, accettando ciò che sono le ragazze significa accettare ogni tipo di relazione? Se dovessimo incontrare due ragazzi che si vogliono amare ..."* He let out an exasperated sigh before finalizing his thought. *"Potrebbero mai aspettarsi lo stesso livello di simpatia che abbiamo per le ragazze?"* He feared having to show the same level of acceptance if we were to encounter two boys in love. The hidden message in his words was that he was not ready to take that step. I lacked a solid opinion, but he silently waited for something from me, so I offered. *"Se restiamo per sempre a Sarno, forse non incontreremo mai due ragazzi così. Allora, non preoccuparti per adesso. E poi se è la loro scelta, perché dovrebbe dare te fastidio?* I sarcastically proposed that he would hardly encounter two guys in love if we never left Sarno. I also asked why he would be so troubled if it were to happen. He threw up his hands in a slight fit. *"Come fai a farmi questo ragionamento? Non è una cosa che posso immaginare, e quel poco che mi passa per la mente, mi fa un po' schifo a dire la verità. Avrei creduto che fosse lo stesso per te."* Pissed off, he scolded me for asking the question. The thought of two guys together turned him off, and that he expected the same reaction from me. Again, it was hard to form an opinion since I had developed no images. *"Io a queste cose non ci penso, e quindi non so cosa dire. Certamente, non è per me, ma se due ragazzi sentono quel tipo di amore, io non voglio giudicare.* I defended my position declaring that I had not given it much thought. I admitted it was not my cup of tea, but I refused to pass judgment.

  We floated in that limbo for months, sensing that things had changed irretrievably. Stella cautiously scaled back her enthusiasm for the secret meetings but ramped up her love for Eli in passionate letters for which I became the courier. I shared in some of the content which Eli read to me in fits of despair. *"Gianni, how is it possible that the world is not ready to accept us? Are these the words of a destitute, of a social reject who has no soul of her own, no humanity?* She pulled the letter from the wrinkled envelope and started reading. **Mia cara Elisa, sono passati per me giorni pieni di dolore da quando non ci vediamo. Con il tuo amore, il tuo affetto, con il tuo calore potevo affrontare qualsiasi ostacolo. Adesso invece, non riesco a reggermi da sola. Mi sento completamente indebolita. Le ore meravigliose avvolta nelle tue braccia, dolci sospiri, il sapore delle nostre labbra e la nostra pelle ... ormai sono fantasmi del passato, vittimi di un mondo crudele. Capisco che il nostro è un amore che chiede troppo agli altri, ma tu mi dici che non possiamo permetterci di rallentare il passo, che dobbiamo insistere in una società che deve ammettere anche noi che siamo**

diverse. Io sono sempre d'accordo e questo tu lo sai. Però, la mia strada sarà molto più dura, ed ho paura, ho veramente tanta paura.
Stella's words were filled with the fever of a young woman struggling with identity, dampening her passions, yearning for the one thing that would have made her mundane life tolerable. She spoke of how she missed Elisa's company, her love, affections, and the sweet perfume of her body ... of the strength she gained from their time together. She turned depressed at the thought of feeling weakened, unable to stand alone. Her nostalgia recalled the precious moments spent in her arms, the sweet sighs, the taste of their lips and skin ... now only phantoms of the past, victims of a cruel world. She sobers up to the thought that their love will put many on edge. Still, she chooses to carry on incited by Elisa's rebellious spirit that insisted on a society that must accept their differences. She signs on to the crusade warning that hers will be a much more difficult path. She ends her letter shaded with a heavy, unmistakable fear.

"*Eli, those are words written with tears. I feel my heart blown to pieces for her. You do understand why she has so much fear, don't you? It is the kind of fear you or I have never experienced. She must consider that her father can destroy her life, or at least force her to live one she would continue to hate. He will stop at nothing to have her obey what he wants for her. She is not free to make any decisions, so she is forced to lie and sneak around, and that only makes it worse should she ever get caught.*" She had to finally deal with Stella's sad reality. "*Gianni, you are so right. I have been so blinded by her perfections, and how much I want her in my life. I feel as if the only solution is to break it off for her own good. It would be a completely evil act, but what other choice is there? What would you do?*" Her stiff question forced me out of my skin to imagine myself in her place. "*You may have to practice what Dante had with Beatrice. He knew he couldn't have her, but he refused to stop loving her. You can love Stella from a distance. You will experience the same pain, the same emptiness, but at least you will have the possibility later to be together. I mean, the world is changing, people of all different lifestyles are making demands,*

and they are being heard. Dante would have been perfectly comfortable with that. His world would never have allowed him that opportunity." She reflected. Her quiet, sullen smile betraying some weakness. *"I'm so uncertain of myself. I do want to do what is right for Stella, but I cannot imagine giving up so much when time will never allow us to relive these days. What if all the lovers in history pissed away the days of their youth to surrender to stifling rules? We would never know true love, true passions, the intimate tales of those courageous enough to be defiant. Those are all my heroes, and I want to keep that flame lit. Gianni, we mustn't abandon the fight."* I insisted on Stella's behalf. *"Eli, your heroes will become Stella's demons if you do not back off. Stella has no fight, her battles are more about getting by, tolerating who she is, and avoiding the life her parents and this town expect of her. I'm not sure she will ever be able to take the chances you talk about. Make up your mind, but you can't be selfish about it."*
She fiddled with the cross at the end of her long, beaded necklace, and sat for a moment. We hugged, she caressed my cheek, took me by the hand and we walked towards the Magnolia tree in the middle of the garden surrounded by neatly manicured hedges. We paused beneath the massive branches heavy with pink and white flowers. She insisted on a fleshy kiss which only deepened my despair of having this sublime creature in my arms wishing it could have lasted a teenage lifetime.

MERECÀ

CHAPTER 14
QUANDO IL DIAVOLO TI ACCAREZZA...
(WHEN THE DEVIL CARESSES YOU...)

Letter writing had become the only option for the girls, except for Thursdays when Stella was able to leave school early to keep her appointment in Eli's room. She knew she was still being spied on but remained defiant because the hour or so she spent in Eli's embrace was the only pleasure left to her. It was hardly enough to offset her boredoms, but it gave her the little she needed to feed her dreams. Signor *direttore* did nothing to interfere with his daughter's short interludes. Stella, however, was puzzled by his sudden hands-off attitude. She feared approaching him, so she took it up with her mother. She learned that he was having a slight change of heart regarding the aristocrats on the other side of town, and that Stella could learn more about her father's social battles once she was exposed to the true nature of privilege. Her mother insisted that he meant no harm by keeping Stella from her friend, except to shelter her from the ills associated with the upper classes. When Stella asked what she meant by the ills, her mother echoed her husband's teachings in a stern voice. *"Quelli non sono gente comm'a nnuie. Non 'nzanna gudagna' o'mangia' tutt i iurn. So' famiglie antiche ... che sono nati ch' e sacch chiene."* She pointed out that they were not like them. She used an old Neapolitan saying that described the difference between those who had plenty, and those who had to earn the food on their tables each day; that they were old money families born with their pockets full. Stella hesitated because she had refused to make the distinction, she held no resentments. Eli was just someone she had fallen in love with, not a member of a social caste. For her part, Eli had eagerly set aside any privileges, even praising Stella's more proletarian character. The time spent in her room had nothing to do with parading and describing possessions. The few items Stella found interesting were lovingly gifted to her.

The summer of 1969 brought more social unrest. In Italy, radical communists were organizing with new leaders and centralized headquarters for the dissemination of propaganda. The movement had gained enough members to spread their influence even to small towns like Sarno. While Stella's father had been an adherent to that part of the party aligned with the Soviets, committed to change through political activism, the radicals had begun to gain his attention. His frequent complaint was that things were moving too slowly, and that some sort of revolution in the streets was needed to speed things up. He never had a plan, and he possessed no progressive agenda or leadership skills. He towed the party line remaining a disgruntled anti-social mostly because he had been unable to find a place for himself in the evolving capitalist system. The few times he had been employed, he was let go for absenteeism or disagreements with company heads. The family lived in a subsidized welfare unit, and they received a monthly government cash stipend, a form of unemployment benefit, while his wife earned a small wage as a seamstress, and stitching leather gloves for the black market. Life was subsistence at best, so Stella babysat the neighbor's child, a single mother with an evening job. The few lire she earned were used to satisfy her urge for the chocolate snacks she craved. She saved the rest hoping to build a war chest that would take her away from Sarno one day. Her summer had become unbearable in the hot and dusty fifth story apartment. The heat and the humidity took hold of the town in June increasing in intensity throughout July and August. The amount of activity generated by her father's politics added to the agony. Signor *direttore* had become consumed with the extremist propaganda taking hold of the party. He had begun to side with those calling for kidnappings, bombings, and assassinations as the only way of advancing the revolution and doing away with the old order. Stella had noticed some new faces who were not locals spending hours in secretive meetings with her father. She was discouraged from interacting with them. He warned her not to speak a word to them or ask any questions. They stayed most of the summer, eating and working at the apartment. They slept in a rented room in a town an hour away. Stella found that to be

MERECÀ

unusual given that rentals in Sarno were abundant, and common among the emigrants returning from seasonal work in northern Europe to spend the winter months home. These unfamiliar faces spoke a different Italian, one that reminded her of the kind used on television news programs. She recognized the northern accents, and figured they were from Milano or perhaps one of the regions north of Rome. They spoke only with her father, never exchanging a word with any other member of the family-only cold, silent stares. They both had shabby beards, one wore eyeglasses, the other smoked a pack or more a day. They arrived at exactly eight each morning, ate breakfast and lunch, and left exactly at three right after making several phone calls. They never left the apartment during the day. Only two of her father's trusted party soldiers were invited to the meetings. They were also sworn to secrecy and whenever other members showed up, they were never made aware of the two mysterious men.

     The workload for mother and daughter now catering to five adult men allowed for only time enough to compose a letter to Eli before falling exhausted onto her bed. The days dragged slowly, hot, and humid ... the arrival of Eli's letters offered a way out of her depression. She read them over and over, inhaling each word, creating just the right dosage of hope. The occasional trek to the mercato with her mother's shopping list got her away from the *palazzine (the local name given to the low-income housing projects)* for a while. Once she turned the corner out of sight, she dashed off to the other side of town to spy Marabbecca, pacing the front portico for some sign of life. There were more servants than normal, and the palazzo was undergoing a good amount of updating and refurbishing. She would learn that the count had been restored to his aristocratic title, his properties returned, and liens lifted from his bank accounts. A tribunal had determined that he committed no war crimes, with no evidence he had participated in criminal Fascist activities. With Eli away in London, the secret gate she used to sneak in had been locked with a thick chain and a medieval looking lock which conveniently disappeared once her girl came home.

MERECÀ

During one of her visits, she eyed a servant hanging clothes to dry, and with a few hand gestures and a quiet shout, she was able to get her attention. *"Scusate, per favore, potete dirmi quando ritorna Elisa, sono un'amica."* She asked about Eli's return, and received a sympathetic response. *"Signorina, veramente non è sicuro, ma ho sentito dire che forse ritornano presto quest'anno, intorno alla festa di Ferragosto."* Her words cautiously raised her spirits. She was told that there were rumors of them returning earlier, mid-August, around the time of the *Ferragosto* festivities. The news sent sharp tingles darting through her pores, returning a long-lost smile to her face as she imagined soon being wrapped up in Eli's arms. As she approached the *rettifilo,* she ran into me and Carminuccio walking in the opposite direction. We had ventured to Stella's neighborhood hoping to make contact, having lost any sight of her since the end of freshman year. I had left several messages by phone with no return calls. Her mother answered each time with the same words: *"Stella e' occupata, mi dispiace."* Stella is busy, I am sorry. Our friend approached us sporting a radiant smile adding brilliance to her beauty. We were completely elated to see her, stumbling over ourselves, rushing towards her for hugs and kisses. At one point we all embraced awkwardly like kindergarten children. We took a small table at the café to catch up. She nervously revealed what she had learned about Eli and *Ferragosto*, laboring to avoid the giddy, pathetic appearance of a lovesick schoolgirl. *"Non sapete quanto piacere mi dà incontrarvi! I vostri bellissimi visi mi portano via dalla malinconia che mi riempie i giorni."* Her enthusiasm spilled over at seeing us, noting that our beautiful faces had carried her away from the melancholy that filled her days. Carminuccio was curious about Eli. *"Allora, ci aspettiamo il ritorno di Elisa per Ferragosto? Non vedo l'ora. È un carattere che veramente ti può mancare. Non siamo completi senza la sua fiamma."* He asked if Eli's return for mid-August would work out. He described the socialite as someone easy to miss, and that we were incomplete without her spark. Stella was eager to keep Eli in the conversation for as long as possible; she kept steering us in that direction. *"Ci siamo scritte una dozzina di lettere da quando è partita. Tutte lettere sincere e piene d'amore.*

MERECÀ

Non so come spiegare quello che sto trascorrendo, e la fatica di convincermi chi sono. Sapete che tutta la vita ho sempre creduto che dovessi innamorarmi di un ragazzo, sposarci, fare dei figli, e vivere felici per tutta la vita. Non avevo mai nessun dubbio. Trovavo difficile che due persone potessero restare insieme una vita sempre innamorati. Pensavo ai miei nonni e genitori che sembrano abbiano vissuti tanti anni insieme, ma mai innamorati. Non vedevo in loro quella stessa intensità che sento per Elisa. Forse pensate che sono sciocchezze di gioventù, sentimenti privi di maturità." She spoke softly about the dozen or so letters she had received from Eli, all sincere and filled with love. She was not sure how to explain her mood, of the confusion in trying to come to grips with herself; of how difficult it was to shed what she had been taught, of having to fall for a man, marry, have children, and expected to live happily ever after … never doubting that destiny. Now she questioned whether it was possible for two people to stay together a lifetime never truly in love. She hadn't witnessed the same intense love in her grandparents and parents that she felt for Eli. She wondered if we thought her to be living silly teen impulses … childish, immature feelings.

Sitting across from the bewitching Stella made it impossible not to fall in love with all of her. I had no use for words. Our senses had aged, puppy love had grown up moving our passions from childish tingles into the world of adult desires. Wanting to experience your first kiss marked one threshold but wanting the entire person because everything about her turns you on, had become a sudden, powerful fascination. Carminuccio had more experience with that compulsion, and he cautioned that it needed to be controlled. Failure to do so, will have women find you annoying, even threatening, he would say. The cultural concept had seeped in, and in that moment, I came to my senses, keeping my feelings in check. The jukebox had been playing the song *Acqua Azzurra, Acqua Chiara* by a breakout artist named Lucio Battisti. Closer to us in age, Lucio was easily becoming the Italian spokesperson for our generation. His lyrics had a Bob Dylan feel to them, and the connection was sincere and soulful. From that day on, I associated that song with the image of Stella sitting there, Mediterranean, perfectly smooth cappuccino colored skin, big green eyes, and lips as plump as the little cherry tomatoes my grandmother tossed into salads, eloquently summoning one to admire another Italian work of art. Seconds later, Mimmo emerged from the bookstore across the *rettifilo,* darting towards our table with an excited energy. We all stood up looking for another chair when he unexpectedly smothered Stella in a giant bear hug. His words were not typical Mimmo. "*Ragazzi, Stella, quanto siete belli! Mi mancate da settimane, sono così contento di vedervi! Stella, sei proprio elegante, guardati, una donna, non più una ragazza. Non riesco a contenere la mia gioia ... cosa posso offrire, un gelato, un cafè? Su, fatemi la cortesia di ordinare qualcosa.*" Mimmo was so elated he was full of compliments, especially for Stella. He commented on her transformation from girl to woman. This was a radical, mature departure from the usual interaction with her. Stella welcomed it with a genuine, but somewhat confused smile. He offered to buy and, being all in desperate need of another espresso, we willingly accepted. The changes in us were noticeable. On an Italian social landscape, it was inevitable. All the institutions instigated to have us grow up quicker than was expected. Besides school, family, and friends, even cafés, restaurants, the arts, fountains spewing water in town squares, and gathering areas around statues of famous historic figures all endowed a sense of association that transcended age. In all places, among all the people, we were delicately urged to come of age. As the conversations dissolved into laughter, lightening our spirits, and the beauty in their mannerisms owning the moments, I knew that I would never get my fill of my graceful and charismatic Italian companions.

    Eli had convinced her parents to shorten her stay in London. She dropped one of her summer classes which gave her more time to mix in with the counter-culture crowd where flirtations were common, and where the numerous parties became fertile grounds for all types of hook ups. Despite the opportunities to satisfy any itch for companionship, Eli remained nostalgic for her Stella. The more time she spent with her favorite crowds, the more she missed the small-town paramour. Each letter from Sarno

MERECÀ

increased her anxiety. Stella's letters were filled with passionate lines, recounting the sweet hours in Eli's bedroom. As the melancholy took hold of her, she became more conditioned to the non-conformist, liberation movements which forged the sophisticated and informed demagogue she would become, ready to abandon every caution upon her return to Sarno.

    She landed in Italy in early August of 1969 ripened by the urban progressivism that shaped her London life. There was no way she would have left that part of her in England and had no intention of shedding it ... even if Sarno wasn't ready. She surprisingly showed up at my front door, and with her usual flair, joined me and Carminuccio for the lunch my grandmother had prepared. Nonna had a soft spot for Elisa and enjoyed her spunk. For her part, Eli loved hanging around, watching nonna cook, and learning as much from her about local women and the past as she was able to recall. After lunch, we were chasing Eli down Via Umberto I, and onto the grounds of Marabbecca. She stopped only when we were under the laurels. Her eagerness to talk about her London stay did not keep her from granting us unending hugs and power kisses on our mouths and her trademark Italian comments with English translations. *"Non so come spiegare quanto sono contenta di vedervi. You have no clue how happy I am to see you. Mi mancate fortemente, e mi sento sollevata da una nuvola e trasportata in questo posto pieno di benessere, pace e amore. I missed you intensely, and I feel as if I have been transported on a cloud to this place where all is full of goodness, peace, and love. Come siete belli! You're so beautiful! Carmine, sei proprio maturato, guardati, sei un uomo! Gianni, your Carminuccio seems so mature, such a man, and I am so impressed by your appearance, you have truly become Italian!"* My hairstyle, clothes, and demeanor had taken up with the Italian versions, and it showed. She pulled us into her orbit so easily ... we offered no resistance. With each trip to London, she returned refreshed, updated, and itching to spread the new social gospel. Absorbing her liberalism came easy. The promises of a world nurturing equality, peace, love, and the prospect of living the life you choose without judgment, was no longer a vague philosophy. Her stories

of what was happening beyond the English Channel were real, and according to her, people were already living those changes. With Stella on my mind, my enthusiasm became subdued. Carminuccio picked up on my mood and turned it into a needed conversation with Eli. "*Elisa, sono tutte belle notizie, ma ti rendi conto che forse Sarno non è allo stesso livello di Londra? So che non mi sbaglio se ti dico che questa città non è capace di assorbire questo nuovo mondo. Forse lo sarà nei prossimi anni, ma per ora ci sono troppi ostacoli."* His warning could have come from any of the town's teenagers. "*Eli, are you aware that maybe Sarno is not at the same level as London? I'm not wrong when I tell you this town is not able to absorb this new world. It may come to pass in the next few years, but for now there are too many obstacles."* I knew he was right, but I held onto the hope that Stella could escape her sad life, and that Eli was her best chance. If only their relationship could endure a year or two more, they would be old enough to create another life for themselves. It may have been a naïve conclusion, but there was a certain desperation that became magnified in a person like Stella. Her pathetic circumstance, and the prospect of nothing more than a repeat of the mess her parents were living, had me advocating for the impossible. "*Carminu' forse tu hai ragione, ma pensare che Stella non avesse via d'uscita se non per Elisa, dobbiamo credere in un futuro migliore anche con i pericoli. Credo che una come Stella farebbe questa scelta. Lei è un carattere unica, piena di coraggio e deve essere felice."*
Carminuccio had a good argument, but I insisted that a capable and grounded person like Stella deserved better, and to be happy even if it meant taking some chances. It was all easy talk for us, but Eli took it a step further, showing her budding feminist frustration and anger with Carminuccio. "*Carmine, se tutti la pensassero come te, l'unica scelta nella vita sarebbe la delusione, la depressione, una vita senza sangue, e io questo non l'accetto! Avvolte ti credo una persona senza coraggio, senza spina. Per voi maschi tutto è molto più facile. Adesso capisco perché' mia nonna mi diceva sempre-beato chi nasce maschio-. Per voi la vita è molto più soddisfacente. Da bambini e da giovani avete vostre madri che vi fanno la schiavitù, e poi vi sposate e tutto va avanti come se niente*

fosse perché sono le vostre mogli che poi prendono il posto delle mamme. Credevo che tu avessi avuto più simpatia per ragazze come noi, ma vedo che poco cambia in questi piccoli paesi perduti al tempo e che preferiscono di rimanere sconosciuti, di modo che tutto andasse avanti senza guizzi.
Che strano modo di vivere: un futuro prevedibile per le donne, senza il potere di cambiarlo per qualcosa migliore. Gianni, per favore, dimmi che tu non la pensi così! Aiutami a credere che gli uomini moderni abbiano il fegato di promuovere la dignità delle donne."
Her frustrations finally reached a boiling point, and any male in her path was fair game. Carminuccio was the first to bite the poison pill, so she unloaded on him. In her rampaging chastisement, the focus became the sad lives that many women lived in a male dominated world. Her lesbian inspired feminism ruled the moment, and all we could do was to avoid counter arguments that would have exposed any insensitivity. I was in quiet agreement having witnessed enough comparisons between Southern Italian and American women to understand the hold tradition had on what was expected of females in Sarno. My mother had elements of that allegiance, but her years in New York had balanced it with a sense of independence … product of a demanding American landscape where jobs were abundant, and immigrant women willing worked for the added income that created wealth. A job gave many women a paycheck and a measured freedom from their men. Mom always worked, and managed money in concert with my father. Eli characterized Sarno as backward, a town preferring to defend the status quo that kept the lives of women predictable with little opportunity to trade up to something better. Finally, she implored me to provide evidence that I did not lean in that direction, but rather was man enough to promote the dignity of women. I gave the only answer I could. *"You know me well enough by now. If I had it in me to be unconcerned, then I would have rejected who you are. You have your strong opinions, but your demands on a place like this are a bit much. My father always tells me that revolutions are severe, temporary, and they never accomplish long term changes. Sarno is not a place where revolutions begin or end.*

MERECÀ

It is a place that can absorb change if it comes slowly; it practically needs to sneak its way in." Carminuccio had understood and agreed with much of what I had said. Eli stood her ground. *"Gianni, amore mio, non è che Sarno si trovasse in qualche angolo oscuro del pianeta, senza luce, senza intelligenza. It is not as if Sarno finds itself in some dark corner of the planet, with no light, no intelligence. Da Sarno si arriva a Roma in macchina in tre ore. From here you can get to Rome in three hours by auto. Sono salita su un aereo a Londra e in poco più di due ore siamo decollati a Roma. I arrived in Rome from London by plane in about two hours. Il mondo diventa sempre più piccolo e questo benedetto paese deve adattarsi. The world keeps growing smaller and this bloody town needs to adapt. I make no secret with you two of my feelings for Stella ... I cannot simply walk away as if she and I never happened. We did, and it is real, and wonderous, and full of life. So, if you are asking me to respect antiquated rules that will deny our humanity, I will sorely disappoint you. Our moment is now, our lives are now, and even if this has no future, I refuse to squander the present ... just as Carmine once told you about his relationship with Teresa, his girl from the clothing store. Was it not he who spoke of love and affection as feelings that need to be consumed in the present, and to leave the future to its own impulses? He took it upon himself to carry on with Teresa with no commitment whatsoever, and no damage to his conscience. My conscience is clear, Stella's conscience is clear, those rules apply to us as well."* Eli sobered us up with a stern monologue. She smothered our cautions with a determined argument and enviable conclusions ... we could only hope that time would prove her right.

      The following day we were able to get word to Stella that Eli was back. She used the shopping excuse to keep an appointment we had set up for them. In Eli's room they were once again pining lovers ready to pick up where they left off. Their love making had morphed into an adult affair. The time apart inspired the fury that pushed and twisted their bodies to the edges of the mattress. In those moments, Stella wasted away to Eli's supple fingers in search of regions longing for their touch, and to the

MERECÀ

recklessness of her feverish lips showing no mercy. The girl from the *palazzine* had been anesthetized, ripped from her womb into a newer and uncontaminated existence.

 Her energies expired, she held on tightly to Eli's hand, applying gentle strokes to her shoulder and breast. *"Elisa, non lasciarmi qui in questo incubo, portami con te ... non importa dove andiamo, non posso restare a Sarno. Tu vivi un'altra vita, e puoi scappare ogni estate per Londra. Se tu sapessi quanto detesto la mia vita, la mia sfortuna. Tu forse mi dirai che drammatizzo troppo, ma la mia verità non la conosci. Nun ngia faccio cchiu a fa sta vita schifosa tutt'i iurn. Non sono padrona di me stessa, e forse non lo sarò mai se resto qui. Con te invece, mi sento viva, e capisco bene chi sono, convinta di quello che voglio. La cosa più bella è che perdo qualsiasi paura, sento il coraggio di affrontare questa nuova vita con un cuore pieno. Io ti amo fortemente. Ho sempre capito cosa poteva essere innamorarsi di qualcuno, e non ho mai scaricato i miei affetti su chiunque, aspettando la persona giusta".* She fumbled through her last words *"poi ci sei capitata tu nella mia vita ... then you stumbled into my life ... "*, as the tears spiraled down her feverish cheeks, onto her upper lip, finally emptying into the watery discharge escaping her nose. Eli wiped away as many of the runaway droplets as she could hijack, clutching her lover closer to her bosom, combing out her tangled, indigo locks with her fingers, searching for the words to reassure her. *"Stella, io non ti lascio, ti prometto. Mi hai donato tutto di te, e non penso ad altro che mostrarti che ne sono degna. Capisco la grandezza del tuo amore, e che merita di un amore uguale. Saremo insieme, e troveremo il modo di costruirci la vita che sogniamo ... guardami ... guardami, io ti amo, mio corpo sarà per sempre il tuo rifugio."*

Stella spilled her guts onto Eli's conscience. She implored her to take her away from Sarno, from a life she detested. She turned to her Neapolitan to make the point that she could no longer go on living her disgusting day to day life, not hers to own. She knew she may never have the power to choose for herself, but that with Eli, she felt alive, understood who she was, convinced of what she wanted. She added an upbeat note about losing her fears and gaining the courage to confront her new life with a brimming heart. She described her intense love for Eli, and that she had always understood the power of falling in love, never emptying her emotions onto any person, but choosing to wait for the right one ... and then Eli came into her life. With a clear head, Eli promised not to leave her, and recognizing how Stella had given all of herself. She tells her she wants to prove herself worthy, acknowledging the magnitude of her love, and that it deserved to be equaled. She assures her weakened lover they will be together, and they will find a way to build the life they dream of. Demanding that Stella look at her, Eli declares her love and offers her body as a place of refuge.

    That afternoon Stella returned home with most of her emotions repaired. As she entered, her mother signaled that her father was waiting to speak with her. In a makeshift office, sectioned off from his bedroom with a thick curtain, she stood by his desk trying hard to recall the last time he asked to talk to her. He pushed aside a stack of papers, and some envelopes, and with an uncharacteristically humble tone, he asked about her. "*Figlia, dimmi, come vanno le cose? Tua madre mi dice che vai molto bene a scuola. Come stanno i tuoi amici ... l'Americano e la figlia del conte. Vi parlate ancora?* He asked about me and Eli, if we were all still friends and if we had kept in touch. Stella, who had never been invited into a father-daughter conversation, suddenly found herself confused and unsure of what to say. She had been aware of his spies, and that her trips to Marabbecca could no longer have been secrets. What he did not suspect was the extent of the girls' relationship. Stella had to take a chance with the truth, nervously hoping he thought of them merely as friends. She knew that if he had known of their affair, he would have confronted her violently. "*Veramente, siamo amiche e lei mi invita spesso a trovarla. A me piace trascorrere tempo nel suo giardino, scambiando storie e notizie, non c'è niente di male.*" She focused on their friendship, on how she enjoyed time spent in her garden, purposely avoiding talk of Eli's room. Of stories and gossip, nothing out of the ordinary. She waited for his delayed reaction. "*Sai, forse ho sbagliato a scoraggiare la tua amicizia. Penso che invece per te ci*

MERECÀ

fosse molto da imparare, di come vivono quelli più fortunati di noi. Tu forse hai un parere diverso, ma secondo me, molti come i signori Tuttavilla non meritano le loro ricchezze. Se avremo modo di parlare più spesso, forse potrò convincerti dei meriti di un sistema comunista, come ho fatto con tua madre e molti altri di questa città." He made his best case for what he stood for and his crusade. He admitted that perhaps he had been wrong to discourage her friendships, and that contact with Eli's family would be a good lesson on how the other side lives, and of how they did not deserve their riches. He hoped they would have chances to speak more often to convince her of the merits of a communist system, as he had done with his wife and others in town. Stella bit her tongue, deciding to just listen. She granted him a fake smile. He took it as a sign of obedience, and gathered her into his arms, caressing her face, leaving her with some instructions. *"Senti, ci sono questi due signori che vanno e vengono nella nostra casa. Sono dirigenti nazionali del partito e hanno scelto me di promuovere il nostro movimento non solo a Sarno, ma in altre provincie del sud. Sono veramente simpatici. Uno, il più anziano, si chiama Carlo, e l'altro, giovane aggiunto universitario, si chiama Amadeo. Io e Carlo abbiamo degli affari fuori paese. Partiremo questo pomeriggio e si ritorna domani tardi. Dai una mano a tua madre, mi raccomando."* He told her about the two men who were there to help him set up more field offices throughout the south. He described them as friendly, the older gentleman named Carlo, the younger, a college adjunct named Amadeo. He and Carlo would be out of town for a couple of days. He reminded her to lend a hand around the house. Stella remained stunned at her father's tenderness. All she could think about was an old proverb her grandmother taught her. She kept repeating the words in her head, to get them right. *"Quando il diavolo ti accarezza, vuole la tua anima." When the devil caresses you, your soul he wants.* Despite sensing that the fatherly choreography had been fabricated, the motive escaped her. She likened his actions to the caution instilled in her by her grandmother, especially when it came to men. These were situations that called into play her fiercest instincts, and the toughness returned to govern her actions.

    Later that afternoon, her father and Carlo left for a remote area of the region of Basilicata far to the south of Sarno. The region was a forgotten stretch of mountainous terrain dotted with small, sleepy, medieval towns sparsely populated. The distances between the towns were bridged with dirt and pebble roads that climbed steeply into those hills with no guardrails. Most turned to mud and potholes during storms. The front pages of the local papers ran frequent reports of cars and trucks that had run off the roads, falling hundreds of feet into the valleys below.

    Stella and her mother spent the following day washing clothes, cleaning the apartment, and dropping off the neighbor's child at the summer school camp early that morning. Around noon her mother left for an appointment to take measurements for a wedding dress she was hired to make. The forty-minute walk was mostly uphill to an address near the hospital in Episcopio, not far from her mother's home. Stella kept to her work, happy to be alone thinking about the time she had spent with Eli. Good feelings and chills helped her tolerate the insipid workload. As she shuffled through the rooms, she noticed that Amadeo, who had been working alone in her father's office, had fallen asleep on the small day bed. She innocently approached the desk to empty the trash basket only to notice the messy load of documents and an unfolded map of Basilicata. A route was outlined in red pencil from Sarno to a town called Roccaforte. Above the name of the town, there was a handwritten notation with the words: *Paese quasi abbandonato, popolazione solo una centinaia. Casa dieci chilometri fuori paese in Via Castellina, funzionale con quattro letti, cantina, e latrina, circondata da venti ettari.* (Town semi abandoned , population about one hundred. House about ten kilometers outside town on Castellina Street, functional with four beds, cellar, and outhouse, surrounded by twenty acres). At the bottom of the page there was some sort of a schedule written with days of the week and hours. On a second page were instructions to sell the car that was being used by Carlo and Amadeo in a town at least an hour from Sarno, and to use the money to buy a new car in a different town. A delivery schedule had been devised to ferry supplies to Roccaforte through several different routes all to be completed at night. She never emptied the basket, left the room quietly, and jostled the information in her head for a while, convinced they were the plans her father had spoken about. The part she questioned was why an abandoned town? Why a place where the population was zero? All she could do was to guess at what it all meant.

When Amadeo shook off his nap, he spied Stella changing the bed sheets in her bedroom. As he approached, he startled her, and quickly apologized. She offered the usual-*buongiorno*-and went about her business, anxiously wondering if he had noticed her in the office. He asked questions about her age and school year, commenting on how much older she appeared, complimenting her southern beauty, and her dark, shiny hair as he lit a Marlboro cigarette. Ironic, she thought, that Italian communists favored American cigarettes. His northern accent forced her to listen more attentively to make out the words. *"Sembri molto più adulta dei tuoi anni. Hanno ragione quando dicono che le ragazze del sud sono le più belle d'Italia. Non ho mai visto capelli così neri e lucenti."* She felt the discomfort of his flirtation, attempting to deflect it with small talk. *"Nel nostro paese non è di usanza parlare alle ragazze in questo modo, ma grazie lo stesso. Tu sei del nord, si sente nell'accento."* She thanked him for praising her attributes while making a point that it was not an accepted behavior in her town. Then she questioned his northern origins, noting the strong accent. He found her curiosity appealing. *"Si, sono nato e ho vissuto a Belluno ai piedi delle Alpi. L'anno scorso mi sono trasferito permanente a Bologna per completare l'anno d'insegnamento all'Università."* He noted his birth and life in the alpine city of Belluno, that he had recently moved permanently to the city of Bologna to finish his teaching assignment, and that he was sure of receiving his diploma. She carried on, encouraged by the direction of the conversation, concluding he had not seen her in the office. *"Mi dispiace per te tutto questo lavoro e ansia. Ma se hai da fare a Bologna, perché' ti trovi qui a Sarno?"* She sympathized with the amount of work and the anxiety of completing his degree, but when she questioned him on why he was in Sarno when he should have been in Bologna, he became uneasy and, unable to contain his displeasure, came within inches of her face, lashing out at her. *"Io mi trovo qui per ragioni molto più importanti della mia laurea! Sono iscritto al partito con il dovere di diffondere la voce comunista per creare un'Italia migliore. Non badare a queste cose almeno che avessi intenzioni di seguire gli esempi di tuo padre."* She pulled away angered by his arrogant tirade, rudely insisting he was in Sarno to promote the voice of the communist party to create a better Italy, and that she should not involve herself unless she planned to follow in her father's shoes. Emboldened by Eli's return, and recalling some of her own southern heat, she put Amadeo in his place. *"Nun te permettere mai cchiù e fa ste mosse da scemo. Io manc'te conosco, e nun te scurdà che stai in casa mia come ospite! Aviss'ave' na poc' cchiù rispett, imbecile! Me fai saje o'sang ncap! Lievete'a miezz ca teng i servizi ra fa."* In her best dialect, she belittled his idiotic actions, showing no restraint and no fear, she warned him never to cross that line again. He was reminded that he was a guest in her house, and that he should show more respect. She described her anger with a Neapolitan phrase likening it to-blood rushing to her head-. Finally, she tells him to step aside because she has work to do. He stood there half stunned and half enjoying it. He found her dialect entertaining, and her feminine grit surprising, having never witnessed the same in northern women. It was the reaction that most outsiders had to women from the Naples area. These women shared a common willingness to stand their ground in confrontations, setting aside any refinements. The counterattack would be immediate, heavy, loud, rough, and decisive. Stella had all this, and in her case, a little more.

In the following weeks leading up to Christmas of 1969, her father continued to dish out tenderness towards her in bits and pieces. Stella's weekly trips to be with Eli continued uninterrupted. Andrea grew fonder of Stella, despite her apathy. His many attempts at flirtations were met with indifference, and when he sensed she was ready to go off on him again, he backed off, reengaging in his work. There were more trips ferrying supplies to Roccaforte, more printing of leaflets, and her father continued to

MERECÀ

give sidewalk speeches which few people attended. The second week in December, Amadeo offered to accompany Stella on one of her shopping trips. She insisted he stay and left without him. A few blocks away she noticed he was trailing her. When she stopped to look back, he begged to join her. Instead, she confronted him with harsh words explaining they shouldn't be seen together. He was not a familiar face, and rumors would cause her nothing but problems. She also made a point that her father would fiercely object. He tried calming her down mentioning that he had already spoken to *signore direttore* about his affections, and that he was good with it. She thought it a convenient lie and promised to take it up with her father. She went off to complete her purchases, while Amadeo admired her work from a distance, taking in the aura of the outdoor *mercato*. It was a mild Saturday, and it was packed with shoppers loading up on the usual holiday foods.

I waited for Carminuccio outside my *portone*, and together we met up with Eli to go shopping for new records at the on the *rettifilo*. As we blended with the crowds, Eli came to a full stop spying Stella engaged in an argument with Amadeo. He had walked over to her in a further attempt to gain her confidence. She, instead, became even more enraged; at one point becoming loud enough to attract the attention of others. Eli grabbed us both by our jackets and pulled us toward the noise. When she finally closed in on Stella, standing beside her, she yanked her away from the confrontation with Amadeo. When Amadeo resented the intrusion, Eli pushed into him inserting herself between the two combatants. Showing no tolerance for Amadeo's continued verbal assault, now becoming more threatening, she leaned back against Stella and, facing Amadeo, she unleashed a heavy-handed slap across his stubbled left cheek with the palm of her right hand. The loud pop startled her as much as the crowd, as she stared at him paralyzed, waiting for a reaction. The northerner backed away, and wisely made his way back. As things calmed down, and people lost interest, Eli asked the obvious. *"Stella, se ti sei ripresa, puoi spiegarmi chi è quel cretino?"* If you have recovered, can you tell me who that idiot was? We shared the same curiosity, as Carminuccio noted that he was not a local. Picking up on his accent, and he too took him to be from the north, wondering if he was some relative. *"Dall'accento sembra essere uno del nord ... un parente?* She told them what she knew ... that they were two colleagues, members of the party working in her home preparing to open an office in Basilicata, but that they were strange characters. *"No, è un collega di mio padre. Sono due uomini del partito, quello si chiama Amadeo e l'altro Carlo. Stanno per aprire un ufficio in Basilicata e preparano tutto il necessario in casa nostra. Sono tipi strani.*

Eli showed interest in Amadeo wondering if it was some attempt on the part of Stella's parents to set her up with some acquaintance from the north. She knew they had relatives there, and perhaps they were also involved in the workings of the party. Her mind ran wild with conspiracies meant to keep her focused on an early marriage, emigration to the north where jobs were more abundant, and where young couples had a better chance at making a reasonable living. She was aware of the many women from the south that followed that exact path, and her lover qualified completely. Amadeo was reasonably appealing, and she thought the argument could have been a result of Stella's confusion ... was she a lesbian in love with Eli, or was she a typical southern female living on the edge, wanting to escape her environment, knowing that marriage to an established man might be her best chance? She also reasoned that girls like Stella did not have many options, if any. Would she opt for the sure thing, or would she continue to pursue her heart, and the difficult road to an unconventional life? Eli pondered all these storylines, wanting desperately to deliver on her promises. She also knew it was a battle she could easily lose. In the coming days she prepared herself for a future without Stella.

  Carminuccio decided to walk Stella home, while Eli and I made our way back to Marabbecca. She took me by the arm, as she always did, cuddled up as the temperatures dropped, and refused to turn jovial. I had not experienced her often enough in that sad, pensive mood, so I probed. *"What's going through that head of yours? It is not often I see you like this."* She pulled to a stop. *"I suppose you may think me a perfect nutter, but I believe Amadeo was sent here from Milano or somewhere up north to court Stella.*

MERECÀ

She is being set up for a relationship that will get her to leave Sarno for the north. I can't fathom the thought of her either being forced into it or deciding on her own that she just can't keep living our truth." "What the heck is a nutter?" She giggled ... *"how silly of me, a nutter is someone crazy. I guess you yanks use nuts instead."* The occasional British idiom would pop into her speech which made it a game to figure out what she was saying. *"Fine, I'm good with nutter-it fits. Most of my female cousins are also making plans to find a convenient marriage to get out of Sarno. They don't hate this town, but they have to accept the reality and the limitations. Many of them who married young ended up in New York. My parents helped them get there. If you walked the streets of Sarno and spent some time in the homes of these girls, you would understand why they choose to leave. Stella would be living the same life as her mother which she obviously hates. If the chances of you and her being together won't happen for several years, and she knows that you can end up in London permanently, then what other choice would she have? The way Stella was treating Amadeo revealed her true feelings. She was in his face for involving himself in her life-he figured he gets the young, beautiful wife by making a deal with her father. No way that would work for her, even if she had never met you. She would have treated him better if she really wanted an easy way out.* As I tried to say more, she cut me off. *"I know why they were arguing! She was so confused about her feelings, that she had to back him off from coming on to her. I can't imagine him having any doubts about her. He is agreeable, but she is too beautiful to ignore, she's too beautiful for any man. Once a man wants a woman, especially in these small towns, he sinks his claws into her. No one can fall in love with Stella and not want to possess her ... there are so many times when I need to stop myself from feeling that way about her. I know that would destroy our love. I've seen it happen even with my mother. Despite my father being a well-balanced, enlightened man, he has withered my mother's love for him because he smothers her, possess her, rather than just allow her to be the person she was meant to be. She fell out of love with my dad years ago, and that's when she had an affair in London with an old friend; she had dated him during her university years. He loved my mother intensely, the story goes, but her father would have none of it. She remained bitter when they moved back to Rome where she was introduced to my father. Amadeo is here for Stella. His task, with her parents' blessings, is to strike up a relationship and have her commit to a life with him wherever it is he lives. This is their way to safely unload a female burden. My heart would crumble into countless pieces if that were to happen. Caro Gianni, I am so distraught over this. If only we could hold on for a couple more years, we could surely leave this place."* I knew Stella didn't have a few years to play with. Most of the girls in Sarno didn't have that luxury. Marrying young, having children, and letting the male worry about earning a paycheck, was a custom that had grown old. There was little chance she would get through high school without a husband waiting for her as a graduation present.

    Eli invited me up to her room. I was skeptical at first, but I couldn't hold back the curiosity. There was still a mysterious, less known side to her. I imagined her bedroom to be a living diary, the pages of which were filled with her intriguing life. We scurried up the back staircase into her micro world. There were still vestiges of her adolescent past with ceramic dolls and small stuffed animals sitting abandoned on mahogany shelves, flanked by childhood books in English and Italian. Her poster bed had not kept pace with her age, having failed to grow up still dressed in pink and white bedding with decorative lacy pillowcases, the kind you don't sleep on. The part of the huge room that had come of age had a wall decorated with posters of the Beatles, Twiggy, The Who, and The Moody Blues. I asked about the bands. She had been to the Moody Blues and The Who concert in Cambridge, England in 1967, and fell instantly in love with their music. Her record collection rivaled Carminuccio's.

There were photos of her London friends, schoolmates in fancy uniforms, in a bikini on a friend's yacht off the coast of Corfu', standing in front of iconic landmarks like the Tower of London and Buckingham Palace, and one of her at the 1966 World Cup Final at Wembley Stadium. The spirit that motivated all she was about was abundantly evident in every pose. The short biography

MERECÀ

in images needed no words. She had lived a life most of us could only wonder about. As I dwelt on the photos, getting up close, I came face to face with the Eli who didn't seem to fit in Sarno. I had only known the one hidden away inside Marabbecca, but the girl in the bedroom scrapbook was a whole new person, and it took some work to blend the two. I didn't want the new Eli without the old Eli, despite not faulting her for the life she had been granted. The old version was difficult to process since she had never flaunted her privileges. She did take notice of my reaction to her room. *"Gianni, are you taken by what you see? Is this what you expected?"* I had to be truthful. *"Not exactly, no ... but I'm not surprised. You have a second life outside this town, and I can see that you live it the way you should. What amazes me is that you can leave all that behind when you are with us. I'm proud of you ... I really am."* She was relieved by my comments. We sat on her bed, listened to her music, and spoke about what was going on in London and the rest of the world. She described it as young people creating a revolution of love, peace, and tolerance, and that we all needed to participate. Her words sent me off into a trance, imagining such a world, despite thinking that only Heaven could pull it off. I didn't trust human beings to keep to it, to rid themselves of anger, prejudices, and greed. My political science professor had dealt with the topic in class, saying we were still too primitive to rise to that level; that humans would need hundreds of years of evolution to reach that point if they could get there at all. He said evolution doesn't always mean that things improve. I shared that thought with Eli, and she agreed, but she was adamant that we didn't have to wait for evolution, that with new laws and education we can speed up the process. People needed to be guided in that direction, and young people could get us there. Nothing could derail her search for *Shangri-la*, and somehow Stella had to be part of it. It was incredibly courageous to think so rebelliously outside the box. We were expected to live conventionally within the social boundaries dictated by a succession of generations, now Eli was making a case for a whole new set of norms. I just didn't see how it could happen. *"Do you really think there could be so perfect a world? You realize that only one bad apple could mess it* up? I mean, we could even try it with a small group of people, say about ten. All could start off well with each person acting the same towards each other. But then some time goes by, and conflicts begin to come up, and people start taking sides and getting angry. You could have two girls in love with the same guy or two guys arguing over food. How do you fix that without screwing up the experiment? Now imagine a whole city, a nation or even the whole world. I think the reason we have all the problems we do in the world is because people just weren't made to get along, but to actually compete. My professor taught that our instinct is to compete for resources because we want to survive, we will do anything to avoid dying out. If that's the case, can people be trusted?" She pondered for a moment or two. "Well then, that may be when evolution takes control. I'm more interested in planting the seeds for such a world. Over time people will buy into it. I suppose you may be right to consider that not all individuals can be trusted to abide by a code of love, peace, and tolerance, but the world needs to move in that direction. If there are more of us than them, then the good will win out. Now stop playing devil's advocate and tell me what you think is going on with Stella. Is it possible that she will give up on me?* Stella was a topic I never shied away from. *"No way Stella would give you up if that choice was completely hers to make. I mean, in this town many girls seem to be set up for marriage. It happens more in the farming areas where the girls marry young because school is hardly an option. The parents chose the man, and in most cases the girls give in just to get away from their family. Stella is a perfect example. Amadeo may be the man chosen for her. He is from the north, and she has relatives near Milano. Maybe her destiny is to be a wife to a guy like him in the north where they can find work. If you think about it, what future does she have here? My mother married my dad in Sarno, and within a month they were on a ship to New York. I'm not being mean, but you have your escape from here if the two of you don't work out ... she has nowhere to run. If Amadeo is a sure thing, then I would say that Stella may consider it. Age wise she is ready to get married to a man, but she is too young to take a chance with you. Still, this has nothing to do with the way she feels* *about you; she will never love Amadeo."* I gave her much to think about. She hugged her stuffed penguin a little tighter, fell into my arms and we both slumped onto her bed. I held her softly as her words turned to whispers and she melted away into her quiet world. I studied each twitch, each breath, and the artistry of her face while she slept. Left undisturbed, she made me the beneficiary of unfathomable minutes. It wasn't a deliberate, planned lesson, but everything Italian had tacitly taught me to appreciate the aesthetic in all of life. I thought, it was as natural for Eli to feel that same appreciation for Stella as I did for Eli. That perhaps the path to falling in love had nothing to do with male or female but was a purely human stimulus. As I caressed her hair, she nudged closer and gave up a responsive, sleepy smile. In that infallible moment, I allowed no interference from flesh or infatuation. Coming to, she impatiently sketched out her fantasy. *"Gianni, I had the most wonderful dream. Stella and I had moved to London to take up in a large flat. We ran our own café in Soho. I can't explain how happy we were. We had friends of all sorts, from all walks of life sharing stories. Music filled the air, and the streets came alive with minstrels, clowns, and entertainers of all types spreading love and happiness. Do you think it silly to have such dreams?"* Her dreams were a step from reality given her energies to see things through. *"You have every good reason to think it can all be real. I can't imagine destiny would want to get in the way of all that happiness. It's sad to think that Stella could have the same dreams but awake to believe them impossible."* She perked up delivering her usual strong opinion. *"I want to change that for her. I want to believe the impossible belongs to us, to do as we please. My dear man, you realize our souls have become one. You have granted me the best of friendships that perhaps I haven't earned. I must share this with you ... I have known just by the sullen looks on your face, and the way you tremble at holding back your feelings when we are together, that you would want us to fall deeply in love. I am so sorry for my selfishness in thinking that we could spend moments like these and expect you not to want to feel my lips or touch my breast. Your willpower astounds but does not surprise me."* With that she stood up on her knees, unbuttoned her blouse exposing a

MERECÀ

thin, lacy bra that, once unhinged, fell unblushingly onto her lap. My body knew what it wanted, but my mind had no clue. I went into lockdown and did nothing. Grasping the dilemma, Eli raised my hand to her breast and held it, releasing it only when she sensed my willingness to maneuver on my own. Her arousal produced strong, fierce, almost breathless kisses, as she fused her lips to mine turning them into lumps of trembling jelly. I sidelined any sense of morality. I would have trouble with my decision later, but for the moment there was no escaping the very selfish need to satisfy an instigating teenage fascination. As my timidity eased, I ran the palm of my hand over her firm, vertical nipples. She pulled away from my lips, stood erect on her knees, lowered her eyelids, and consumed with intensity the sensation of skin on skin. She swayed and moaned, leaning backwards, touching herself, projecting her breasts upwards, stretching … every aroused pore an invitation to be touched. The tempestuousness of her orgasm, rife with spasms and convulsions was nothing less than stunning to witness. I did little, but my exhaustion matched hers. Her head slipped onto my chest sliding down to my lap. I got the shivers like when someone strokes a feather along the back of your neck. I wanted to move, but she dug in tighter. She placed her hand over my crotch, and I lost it. The erect stick figure in my underwear had nowhere to run, no escape plan to employ as the very unexpected caught me so off guard. At that age, the most immediate and wounded transition from boyhood to adulthood is the demoralizing and debilitating uncontrolled ejaculation. It's too early for manhood to intervene smoothly, so you surrender to the embarrassment. You replay the episode over and over, recalling how impossible it was to hide the stain seeping through the pocket side of your pants or to coax your protrusion into returning to a more relaxed position. Next, you implore both mind and body to form the necessary alliance to keep your weaknesses caged to make certain it never happens again … a repetition is out of the question.
Eli eased me through it with hardly a reference to my awkward condition. Thankfully, she had her own bathroom which I put to good use as soon as she allowed me to unclench her fist. I stayed

long enough afterwards waiting for the spot to dry. We laughed it off as something we would both remember with measured fondness. She backtracked a bit to learn of my reaction.

"Carissimo, what is it they call you ... merecà? I guess that means americano. Well then, merecà, tell me, were our actions purely selfish and sinful or shall we blame our instincts? That is, only if you feel we did something wrong. If, instead, you believe it to have been a purely natural, human inclination, then I beseech you to treasure it, as I will. So, if your nickname is so conveniently merecà, what name shall you bestow upon me?" My first thought would have been one of regret, but our generation had adopted a *carpe diem* approach to life. Seizing the moment had become an opportune excuse to favor our pleasures and fantasies, and to ignore the repercussions. My time with Eli was far from the extreme, and despite its newness, I found a way to let her know I was good with us. *"First off, I have the perfect nickname for you, sciuscella. I believe you may have never come across one, they grow wild on the hillsides of Sarno. Not sure if it is a fruit or a vegetable, let's just say it has no definition ... much like you- difficult to put into a category. It is tough and hard on the outside, but soft and sweet on the inside. My cousin Tullio led me to the trees where the sciuscelle hang upside down like sleeping bats. He instructed to pluck one, take a bite, chew, and suck out all the juices, then spit out the hard stuff. It does taste a lot like honey. It's not to gross you out, but I think the name fits. Look, I'm coming around to your way of thinking. What happened today is something I wanted as much as you, so I have no regrets, and I know it takes nothing away from you and Stella. You mentioned once that boys are just a curiosity for you."* She reacted to the solemn look on my face. *"You will never be just a curiosity for me. We have been so intimate, and you have been so good at friendship, accepting me for who I am and supporting my love for Stella. You could have felt slighted, angry in a boyish way, guided by immaturity I suppose. Instead, here you are by my side, still passionate about what we mean to each other ... and I love you immensely for that."*

She walked me out into the courtyard holding my hand when she eased up, wrapped her arm around mine, and guided us onto the stone bench across from the fountain. We lounged a while, catching up on school talk. My sophomore year was about to begin, while Eli had already completed her requirements for an Italian high school diploma. Most of her home schooling in 1969 and 1970 would focus on obtaining her British diploma. Her parents were good with her first selection for college at the Sapienza University in Rome. The choice would keep Eli within a train ride of Sarno. The plan would bring her home on weekends and holidays, and hopefully into Stella's arms. Her parents' properties had been restored by an Italian court. That included the apartments in Rome, so she seriously lobbied for La Sapienza. A London college had always been her choice, but Stella changed all that. She could also expect more privacy when her parents were off to London on business. She had a place to live while in college, and she even wondered how joyous it would be if we could all meet up in Rome. *"I know I'm a tad wishful, but how glorious would it be if you, Carminuccio and my lovely could come to Rome. Nothing would make me happier, nothing could more brilliant. Imagine all of us dipping our feet in the fountain in Piazza Navona, strolling fancy free down the Via Condotti and onto Piazza di Spagna, and perhaps a tour of the Vatican. I could be your guide, and in the evening, I know of spectacular places to eat in Trastevere and cafes with the best coffee and pastries. I'm being silly again, please forgive me ... life excites me especially with such excellent friends. I want to live and feel every pleasure, every sensation, every wonderful human moment. Gianni, I have so much love for you, Carminuccio and my Stella ... I'm bursting with happiness. If only things could be as we envision them."* She paused as she floated back down to earth. *"I think it best that I stop talking. Come, let me walk you down to the gate."* I was about to leave when Carminuccio, who had dropped off Stella after detouring onto the *rettifilo* for a gelato and an opportunity to catch up on her life, called out to me from a block away. I waited and together we walked up to my *portone* after watching Eli disappear into the back entrance. He said nothing on the way, but once inside he spoke freely about Stella. *"Merecà, credo che le cose per Stella non vadano bene. Lei non voleva ammettere troppo davanti a*

MERECÀ

Elisa, ma è vero che il padre ha deciso che il suo destino sarà lontano al nord con quel tizio Amadeo. Non solo, ma secondo la madre, Amadeo ha già preso in affitto un appartamento per loro e le aspetta anche un posto in una ditta, iscrizione al sindacato e al partito, figurati! Mi fa uno schifo enorme a pensare che una ragazza come lei farebbe questa brutta fine. Ovviamente non c'è nessun amore tra lei e Amadeo, infatti lo odia. Amadeo parte domani per Milano, e ritornerà fra un anno per mettersi d'accordo con il padre per un matrimonio civile al municipio. Il padre, curiosamente, la sta trattando con tanto affetto, secondo lei, però, un affetto falso, privo di sincerità, come se fosse il diavolo di cui ne parlava la nonna. Questi sono fatti che Elisa ad un certo punto deve sapere, sei d'accordo?" He shared that things were not going well for Stella. Her father had planned out her future with Amadeo somewhere in northern Italy. An apartment had already been secured and she had been promised a job in some factory, and membership in the local union and communist party. Amadeo was to return sometime late the following year to marry her in a civil ceremony. She spoke of how unusually kind her father had been to her-a kindness she described as fake and insincere, likening him to the devil her grandmother had warned her about. I agreed that soon Eli would have to know what was happening. I doubted there was much we could do, but Stella had it in her to put up a fight that could end badly. I reminded him that she was determined to avoid her mother's life at all costs, that it wasn't an idle threat, and that she would act on her feelings.
We could have distanced ourselves, but the girls had become an obsession for both of us. These weren't fleeting friendships that melted away as soon as adulthood forced us to turn the page to the next chapter in our lives. We came to define what we meant to each other as ghostly, not of this world. It was a poetic journey out of the common and into the extraordinary, for we had evolved into an abstraction, a new life with four inseparable components losing ourselves in our compassions, dreams, urges, and ultimately our mortality. Eli had pressured us to accept a finite life, and to then own it. Between birth and death, she said we had an obligation as living, breathing humans to come to terms with our true selves; it

was the only way to validate our existence. Stella had bought into Eli's philosophy completely, her hopes resting on her lover's words. I dreaded the thought of the two not realizing their wishes, but it was Stella that we feared for more. She was vulnerable, and the most to suffer should all of us disappear from her life.

MERECÀ

CHAPTER 15
IL DESTINO NON PRENDE CURA DEI TUOI DESIDERI
(DESTINY CARES NOTHING OF YOUR PLANS)

Eli spent Christmas 1969 in Rome celebrating the season and the reinstatement of her father's title which was to take effect in the new year. The following day she and her family returned to Sarno to host a holiday gathering for British dignitaries serving with NATO at their base in Naples. They had sent for their families to vacation in Sorrento the week between Christmas and New Year. In the group were two of Eli's female London classmates. Stella had spent the holy day once again at her grandmother's house where the Christmas spirit was very much alive. Her parents had stopped celebrating the religious day years ago. As indoctrinated communists, they rejected religion as a cult practiced by the weak. Her father had over the years taught his daughter that there was no god, so Stella had drifted into her grandmother's arms against her father's will preferring religion, enjoying her Sunday masses. *Nonna* Nicolina was a hardnosed lady who had written off her son-in-law as a heathen, sheltering her granddaughter from what she described as the corrosive, sinful life practiced by her father.

The two weeks leading up to the Epiphany were filled with festivities at Marabbecca with Eli playing hostess to her British girlfriends. The mild weather made for frequent strolls about town, down the rettifilo to enjoy cappuccini and pasties at the recently opened Bar Michelangelo-a modern and posh alternative to the drab places we normally frequented. The Sunday after Christmas, Carminuccio had me meet him and Mimmo on the rettifilo to make our way up to the *palazzine.* Stella had promised to meet us halfway with the excuse of visiting her nonna. Not far from our old middle school Baccelli, we came upon her waving and greeting us with a cheek-to-cheek smile that complimented the glow of her frosted face. It was a cold day by Sarno standards, but no more than chilly if we had been walking the streets of the Bronx. She

MERECÀ

was even happy to see Mimmo, greeting him with the customary two kisses and a heartfelt hug. Me and Carminuccio got the hug, but when she cradled our faces in the palms of her hands, her lips landed on ours with the kind of ferocity reserved for a soldier's homecoming. We pranced down the rettifilo with the municipal building to our backs pulling up to the café entrance haphazardly, laughing, chatting and just being loud. Inside we were greeted by a surprised Eli and the London girls. Stella turned suddenly tense as her giddy mood gave way to a quiet, sober gaze. Eli rushed from her chair to welcome us, soon diverting most of her attention toward Stella. The girl from the *palazzine* gave a frigid response as she rejected Eli's invitation for us to join her table. Eli picked up on the nasty mood and slowly rejoined her company. I looked over at Carminuccio who shook his head to leave it alone while whispering *"ti spiego"*, I'll explain. I wanted to avoid intruding on Eli's group, so I stayed behind to catch up on my friend's intuition. While Mimmo and Stella grabbed a table, we walked over to the counter faking an interest in the pastries. "*Merecà forse non te ne sei accorto, ma quando siamo entrati ho notato subito, come pure Stella, che Elisa e quella con i capelli rossi, quasi arancioni, avevano le mani intrecciate scambiandosi, non so cosa, ma sembravano due innamorate.*" It seemed that he and Stella noticed Eli and her red-haired friend holding hands and acting like lovers. I had missed it, so I remained skeptical. "*Forse ti sbagli. Sai che Eli porta tanta affezione verso gli amici che sembra innamorata di tutti ... è il suo carattere unico. Si fa volere bene da tutti i tipi, e sono certo che a Londra, dove le cose sono assai più libere, vive amori che a noi sembrano troppo intimi. Stella non deve sentirsi abbandonata. Secondo me dovrebbe incontrare le ragazze inglesi e poi si sentirà molto più comoda. A parte tutto questo, io devo confessarti un episodio che è successo tra me e Elisa. Però, non voglio che tu mi giudichi e non voglio perdere la tua amicizia. Io e lei siamo stati nella sua camera da letto. Parlavamo di tante cose, discorsi piacevoli, ridendo, ascoltando musica. Poi, ci siamo persi in un momento intimo e lei si è spogliata togliendosi il reggipetto. Non sapevo come reagire, così lei ha preso la mia mano portandola al suo petto. Si toccava tutta e si muoveva come presa da un incantesimo. Calmandosi dopo alcuni minuti, è caduta stanca su di me toccandomi ... tu sai, lì. Forse potresti immaginare il resto ... veramente non so come spiegarlo."*

I hadn't noticed what was going on between Eli and her friend, so my reaction included an excuse for Eli. I mentioned how friendly and loving she is and how she invites the affections of all different types of people. It makes her unique, different in her own way, sometimes going beyond the usual. I insisted that Stella would change her feelings once she had a chance to befriend the British girls. Since I shared so much of my personal life with Carminuccio, I couldn't keep hidden the short affair with Eli. I gave as much comfortable detail as I could, asking him to imagine the rest. He was stunned but covered it up with a hesitant smile.

"Povero amico mio! Capisco bene il tuo affanno. Considerando il carattere della nostra Elisa, io non ti do nessuna colpa. Hai reagito bene e hai assaggiato la vita che si è presentata così, spontanea in quel momento prezioso. E se ti preoccupi per Stella, non è stato un tradimento se lei accetta la verità di Elisa, la quale non può vivere incatenata ... il suo non è un destino nel lontano futuro-il suo destino lo vive minuto per minuto, e questo Stella lo deve capire per meritare il suo amore. Quello che hai provato con Elisa è stato un capitolo che Eli ha scelto di vivere in quel momento, non perdendosi quella voglia. E tu, seguendo l'esempio, ti sei portato via una fantasia. Non è che poi le fantasie dovrebbero rimanere fantasie."

He was sincere and kind in his reaction, placing no fault in either of us. He reminded me of how she could live life unshackled within and outside of common norms-choices she made freely. He didn't see it as cheating on Stella, but rather a part of Eli that Stella should come to understand if she wanted to keep loving her. He chalked it up to Eli's character that insisted on living daily, individual destinies, not waiting for one to happen in the distant future, and that I had followed her example and seized the moment-that I had chosen to live that one-time fate and own one of my fantasies. He insisted that fantasies weren't meant to remain fantasies. I conveniently rushed to agree despite still not feeling completely at ease with a perfectly good argument. As was the

MERECÀ

case with Carminuccio, he went where I hoped he wouldn't go, asking about what I felt when she touched me and if I had reached orgasm noting that I probably still had my pants on. With that last thought, he took it to the next sad conclusion from the pathetic look on my face. *"Dimmi, quando ti toccava, che sensazioni hai sentito? Sei arrivato all'orgasmo? Perdonami se chiedo troppo, poi mica ti sei tolto il pantalone ... Aspetta, da quella faccia che mi fai ..."* I cut him off choosing to finish the thought my way. I admitted to his predictable version peppered with silly looks on his face and sarcastic remarks, chastised him for laughing and called him an idiot in our dialect. *"Si, proprio come la stai pensando, va bene, hai indovinato tutto .... E adesso ridi? Ma comm' si scemo!"* He had to know it all, asking what I did with my wet pants, observing that I couldn't exchange it for a piece of her clothing unless I was prone to trying on one of her skirts. *"Ma poi come hai fatto con i pantaloni bagnati, non è che potevi scambiarli per un abito suo, almeno che qualche gonna ti stava bene."* I laughed it off, called him *cretino* (jerk) and placed an order for *cappuccini* and *cornetti*. Back at the table Mimmo updated us on Stella. She had abandoned him to take on Eli. After a heated exchange, the two took the argument outside, across the *rettifilo* and into an empty portone. We stood on our side of the street deciding whether to get involved. Stella never gave us a chance when her anger and her tears pushed her away from Eli and up the rettifilo to make her way home. Carminuccio took off after her. I waited for Eli who was already crossing back towards us. I had questions, but she cut me off. *"Gianni, please can we take this up later? We can meet at my place. Come, let me introduce you to my London friends."* I looked at Mimmo who insisted that we join them and be gracious about it. With *cappuccini* and *cornetti* in hand we joined their table. Eli introduced us to Chloe and Margaret, also juniors and her dorm mates during the summer sessions at the William and Mary School for Girls. Their fashionable clothes, and the way they held their cigarettes, helped them appear older. It bothered me a bit, but Mimmo wasn't fazed and engaged immediately insisting on speaking English.

MERECÀ

"*My name is Mimmo. Happy to meet with you. Please be welcome to our city, Sarno. It is not so beautiful like your Londra, but we are very friendly, and we love ... Merecà come si dice stranieri?*-(I translated *stranieri* to foreigners for him) ... *yes, we love foreigners.*"
The girls were delighted with his introduction, and Chloe found him instantly irresistible. "*Oh my, I am in love with his accent! Mimmo, you musn't stop speaking. Italians speaking English is absolutely charming.*" She turned to me to ask about my name. "*I believed your name to be John, but he called you something else.*"
"He called me -merecà- which is the local dialect for americano. I received the nickname when I first moved here. I kinda like it, it sets me apart."
"*Eli told us of the sweet way in which you met. You are neighbors who met by chance, and now she can't stop talking about you. We had already learned about you in London. She considers you the best of friends. You must be special indeed to have this very fussy girl shower you with praise. Eli, dearest, you are so right, he is perfectly yummy. Margaret, what do you think?*"
"*I so agree, he is utterly lovely, and in a feminine way.*" Mimmo, who understood, cracked a smile asking me if she thought I was girlish. "*Ma se ho capito bene, lei ti crede addirittura femminile?*" Eli clarified the feminine remark. "*Gianni, Margaret is saying that you have a gentile character. Don't be offended if we believe that men should be less masculine. Men wrongly think they need to play up their manhood to appeal to women. We find the gentile side, which we often describe as feminine, to be more engaging. Please, take it as a compliment.*"
"*I'm fine, it doesn't bother me.*"Mimmo showed a greater understanding. "*Merecà, l'immagine è di un uomo come I rock stars. Uomini pieni di passioni nella loro musica, capelli lunghi, faccie morbide, a volte truccate, labbra piene, corpi snelli privi di muscoli, abiti unisex. Pensi, per esempio, a Jim Morrison, Paul McCartney oppure Mick Jagger. Insomma, uomini che incorporano il meglio delle donne, senza perdere il loro vero sesso ... non so se mi spiego.*" Mimmo cleared it up nicely when he lectured me on the male images that had become appealing to

women. He used rock star examples describing their passionate music, long hair, soft faces, at time using make up, skinny, non-muscular bodies, unisex clothing. Of men who incorporated the best of women without giving up their sex. He was right. I had never questioned the notion of men being anything but men. I was again nudged beyond my conventions to consider a more effeminate manhood, and according to Margaret, and perhaps even Eli, I fell neatly into that category.

The image of Eli and Stella as lovers came to mind as I listened to Mimmo. I thought that in some cases women sought the kinder, more gentle human interaction in another woman rather than deal with a man. In Stella's case it made much sense when I factored in her father and the men he associated with. She had repeated her desire not to live her mother's life, and of the abuses she endured. Amadeo was thought to be nothing less than a younger version of her father, and he was the destiny she so desperately wanted to avoid. Eli was her greatest hope, and she clung to it with the expected grit.

  At the table, Eli finally took up the topic of Stella out in the open. The London girls had known about the relationship, but Mimmo had no clue. *"Gianni, you must help me convince her she shouldn't feel slighted in any way. She witnessed a flirtation or two between me and the girls, but it is common practice for us. I didn't intend any distress, but she hardly gave me a chance to explain. Her anger was misplaced."*

"I would call it disappointment. Her life is full of disappointments, and I think that's the way she deals with things that hurt her. Stella isn't like you and the girls, and you know that. If she had the same background, I think she would understand. She has no clue what you, Chloe and Margaret mean to each other and how you can separate actions from emotions. In this place actions mean much. People judge what you do first, then what you say. If you kiss someone on the lips, the message is clear unless they know you well enough not to make a big deal of it. You kissed Margaret on the lips, and Stella saw it for what it was. The most I can do is try to get her to understand that it is a common way to show affection. You have done it with me and Carminuccio, so I'm good with it. I

still think you should introduce her to the girls, I'm sure she will like them." Chloe felt the need to ease us a bit more. *"Brilliantly said, John! I know we can explain if she is willing to listen. I'm dying to become friends; I have heard so much about her. I must admit she is daringly beautiful, so I finally get to approve of Eli's choice."* Mimmo had been listening, attentively stringing together English words he understood to decipher the conversation. He couldn't hide his confusion while he searched for a way to ask his question, so Eli did it for him, impatiently upset that she had to explain. *"E va bene, Mimmo. Io e Stella ci amiamo, siamo amanti. Cerco di alleggerire la tua confusione. Ti spiego, ma sappia che me ne frega poco di quello che pensi!"* Unable to keep her feelings in check, she revealed her love for Stella, sarcastically appeasing his confusion. She was willing to continue explaining, but she cautioned that she didn't care a scratch for what he thought. Mimmo, however, was intuitively picking his moment to alleviate her anxieties. *"Elisa, tu non mi conosci bene abbastanza per sapere che, come te e Stella, ho sofferto la mia inquietudine credendomi diverso dagli altri. Come vedi sono molto più alto del normale, peso almeno trenta kili più di Gianni, piedi larghi e grandi, e pelle color latte. Credi che io non abbia dovuto lavorare molto più del normale per essere accettato? Allora, se pensi che io non avessi simpatia e la sincerità di capirvi, ti sbagli fortemente."* Mimmo was powerful and convincing in his response. He opened up about his own bouts with acceptance, sounding off about being too tall, his weight, his large feet, and his milky skin. He challenged Eli to believe that he would be unsympathetic to her condition. Her lips twitched, she got up from her chair and produced an intense embrace despite her arms reaching only halfway around Mimmo's massive chest. The act reawakened the pink blotches that quickly coated his cheeks. The big guy was super sensitive to a female's touch, making no secret of how much he yearned for it. The reaction was precious-and the girls took fond notice of it.

  Carminuccio had finally convinced Stella to return to the café. They entered to our grateful surprise. Eli instantly took her by the arm with an invitation to join the group. Chloe and Margaret

MERECÀ

greeted her with smiles and double kisses. She looked at me and I nodded approval at her decision to return. The day had grown warmer with a blinding sunshine that turned the winter day into a springtime afternoon. As the café filled with patrons, Eli suggested we could rid ourselves of the crowds by retreating to Marabbecca. We walked briskly through town with Eli and Stella arm in arm, and us boys being shared by Chloe and Margaret. As we turned into the driveway, the group size caught her mother's attention through one of the front windows. She pleasantly detoured us inside into the guest room with a large, ornate fireplace. The room was furnished with two soft pillowed sofas, and four large lounging chairs. We sat enjoying the heat from the burning logs. Minutes later one of the maids dropped in with a tray of *aranciate* (orange sodas) and slices of *panettone*. Eli asked her mom for some privacy which was granted with a smile. We were treated to our first visit inside the massive palazzo, and it did not disappoint. Once we settled in, Eli sat next to Stella, cozying up to her, wrapping her arm around hers with dovetailing fingers. Chloe was determined to keep the earlier conversation alive. "*Eli, I believe Stella is still owed an explanation. We must have words we could employ to best describe our friendships. We have shattered barriers that still exist here in Sarno, it makes it difficult not to get the reaction Stella first had to our intimacies.*"
"*I suppose we can talk more about it; my dear Stella has every sensitivity to things beautiful. Stella, cerchiamo di farti capire che l'intimità tra me e le ragazze è segno di un amore idealistico della nostra generazione. Un amore di forte amicizia che non si occupa delle regole, delle reazioni, e dei pregiudizi, e quindi lo dimostriamo tutto a modo nostro. Non è un amore fisico, romantico come il nostro. Invece, è un amore di poca serietà, ma pieno di passioni pazzeschi, giovanili. Quando penso a noi invece, voglio possederti completamente, voglio che noi diventassimo una sola persona ... non so se mi spiego bene.*"
"*Si, capisco tutto. Perdonami se sono stata sciocca a credere che fosse così facile perdere l'affetto di una persona amata.*"
Eli spoke of the idealistic love she shared with the girls from London. She called it a strong *friendship love* that had an

expression all its own with no fear of rules, reactions, or prejudices; a love expressed as they saw fit. The more frivolous, juvenile, kind of crazy and impromptu relationship the London girls practiced, proved to be no threat to their more romantic, physical, and erotic love; it was enough to draw Stella away from her jealousies and hesitations. She asked forgiveness for her silliness, confessing she didn't think it would have been that easy to lose the affections of someone deeply loved. Eli caressed her face, kissed her gently, and tightened her grip. I fixed on the image of the two lovers thinking back to when they first met. In that quick glance I appreciated my inability to detect that initial spark, hardly suspecting love at first sight between two girls. It must have been immediate and irretrievable … a force that needed an avenue of expression, even if covert. Stella would have kept it a guarded secret given the stigma, but Eli wanted to shout it out. Declaring their affections to me and Carminuccio was the most Stella could tolerate. Now that Mimmo knew, she remained edgy, but had begun to accept that exposure was inevitable. She favored a slower pace so that she could retain control. Still, the girl from the housing projects appeared vulnerable to the choices she would make. Eli and the girls had less to fear; they could easily retreat to more welcoming people and places.

  The London girls, diming any sense of superiority or snobbishness, had taken a liking to us and Sarno. The town and its culture were a conservative counterbalance to their London experiences. Stella was the perfect example of the humble, blissful nature of a life removed from the fermenting urban centers of reform and liberation. Chloe expressed it best as our fondness grew for the British ladies. *"Please don't take this the wrong way, but there is a primeval beauty to Stella which is beyond brilliant. Eli, I understand your bloody attraction. One is overcome with an irresistible urge to explore her completely, to unravel her secrets, to strip her down to admire her perfect nakedness … have no fear my Italian friend, I have no plans to steal her away."*
"*You would hardly succeed. It would be a useless attempt.*" Stella understood they were talking about her, so she turned to Eli for a translation. "*Chloe si scusa se non si fa capire bene, ma per lei tu*

MERECÀ

rappresenti una bellezza primitiva, si può dire classica, brillante, ed è per questo che lei capisce la mia attrazione. Dice che chiunque troverebbe irresistibile il desiderio di scoprirti completamente, di svelare tutti i tuoi segreti, di spogliarti tutta per ammirare la tua perfetta nudità. Mi avverte che non dovrei aver paura che non ha alcuna intenzione di portati via da me." Stella offered a modest smile, and a bashful response as her other hand joined the one holding Eli's.

"Magari fossi tutto quello. La tua amica crede troppo di me, sono una ragazza comune, di periferia. C'è poco di elegante. Le sue parole intime, anche erotiche, di desideri, di segreti e perfezione mi fanno veramente intimidire, non mi sono mai pensata in quel modo. Chloe, non offenderti, potresti tentare di prendere il posto di Eli, ma ti assicuro che non ci riusciresti." She scaled back all the accolades, describing herself as a common, suburban girl, not very elegant. Chloe's intimate, erotic descriptions made her uneasy, admitting she had never thought of herself in that way. Finally, she sarcastically warned Chloe that she could try to replace Eli, but that it would end in failure. We spent another hour or so in that cavernous room, glowing in the rays of the fireplace. Our conversations continued to challenge the ordinary. We had set aside all the taboos on sex, religion, and love, opening the door to the new liberation philosophies that kept us intrigued and engaged. The paradox didn't escape us boys who sat across from four remarkable women sharing their most penetrating passions that had little to do with males. Carminuccio would constantly remind me that he labored in having to stop himself from falling in love with anyone of them. I was forced to agree since I found the temptation equally irresistible.

    That evening, Chloe and Margaret bid us affectionate, heartfelt farewells. They were due to return to Sorrento the following day to complete their vacation. They left a humble impression on me, as they sincerely embraced us as we were, and not pompously casting us aside as insignificant. Carminuccio and Mimmo walked Stella home, while Eli offered her company for my short journey up Via Umberto. She treated me like a barometer in gauging her interactions. My reactions and opinions weighed

MERECÀ

heavily even if she could have easily ignored them. *"Gianni, you didn't speak much inside. Tell me, tell me what goes through your mind ... what thoughts can you share?"*
"I said little because I was too interested in listening. I so enjoyed the conversations, the way in which we were able to talk about even the deep topics without conflicts. I really enjoyed Chloe and Margaret, of how free they are to speak their minds. I admit that I felt a few pinches at some of the stuff they mentioned-not used to the intimate details, but in the end, it all made sense."
"That's fine, but I am more interested in what's in your soul and your heart. I know that when you are quiet, your mind is off composing a narrative. I beg you not to keep that composition to yourself, please share."
She had maneuvered me once again into one of her corners, but this time I had the gut to come on strong enough to lose it a bit.
"Fine, I was good with keeping this to myself, but I'll tell you what you want to know. I thought about how difficult it was for me to sit opposite four beautiful women, listen to your sweet voices, admire the shape of your breasts, Chloe's legs in her dark stockings, Margaret's red, full lips, Stella's silky hair and the way she pushes it back with both hands exposing her neck, and finally, the way you make me feel each time I look at you or the tingles that own my body each time you wrap yourself around my arm, to then have to let it go and deny any more of you. Do you have any idea how difficult this is for a romantic, but in control sixteen-year-old? There, I said it. I think that what gets lost in all of this is the sad way you and the girls expect us to just shut down our masculinity. I know that me, Carminuccio and now even Mimmo, have understood what you mean to each other and that your destinies are supposed to be with another woman, but when Carminuccio secretly tells me that he is having a tough time not falling in love with any of you, I have to agree and feel the same anxiety. I don't want to make a big deal about this, we want you and Stella to be happy and we love how courageous you two are, so it's up to us to deal with our own feelings. Look, I haven't been able to stop thinking about the time you and I spent in your room. Everything that happened were all first timers for me, so you can probably

MERECÀ

understand how easy it is to want more of it, especially considering that in your case it's about the heart as well as the body."
She came to an abrupt stop, as I left her a few paces behind. She stared me down with the look of someone who had missed all the signs, knowing she shouldn't have. I turned into the portone and waited. A minute or so passed when she slowly caught up.
"So, I suppose you have been and still are in love with me?"
I hesitated. I had mouthed off, but I wasn't prepared for the obvious.
"Oh God, I mean what do you want me to say? Yes ... I'm not sure that's what you want to hear. Let it go. I shouldn't have said anything."
"It's cold, can we drop into the café across the way?"
We slipped into the Café Bar Totò just across from the portone. She kept her hands warm cradling a steamy cappuccino, while I opted for a creamy espresso.
"My dear Americano, I should be flogged! You are so spot on; I have been so blinded by selfishness. We have treated you boys as spectators. Non so cosa dire, I don't know what to say." She paused. *"Gianni, love me, but don't love me. I'm sorry, that was confusing and insensitive."*
"No, actually it wasn't. I understand what you are saying, and I'm okay with it. I only hope I can keep that love alive for someone much like you. You know, I never had a reason to think of life as being unfair, but now I see that often it is, and I'm learning to cope. I'm glad we were able to talk about this; I have wanted to tell you for so long. I just didn't think it had any place in our friendship, and I didn't want bad feelings."
"No bad feelings, only good ones. Amore, I so look forward to our next encounter. We will lay on my bed, talk, listen to Lucio Battisti, look into each other's eyes, and make our own kind of love. Sarà il nostro tempo prezioso, il nostro canto, la nostra storia-it will be our precious time, our song, our story. Gianni, we shall live the life that may only last moments, a life that allows no interference from other lives ... a heartbeat unto itself. Haven't you ever wished for the chance to explore all of you, to know yourself so completely as to be able to fall in love with all the beauty that surrounds us? It's

what I hope for when I think of Stella. Two women in love with their reality, without the limitations of traditional roles ... it would not alter who I am, it would make me more of it. Gianni, I don't want to be a man's wife. You may not understand now, perhaps one day it may make sense to you." Her words made time stand still. The days, months, and years all disappeared, life itself switched up on me in search of a new meaning. The continuum of living as we had known it, one long sequential timeline of the human experience had suddenly become compartmentalized. She had turned one life into countless smaller, shorter lives. Tradition was all I had known, and it may have remained that way into a much older age had I not landed in Sarno. I wanted to be shocked, but with Eli, the improbable drowned in her philosophy, dissolving any abnormalities. She courageously exposed a life choice that for her had been normal all along.

"*Somehow, I just can't picture you married to a man. It's hard to explain, but you have a kind of nature of your own, it's what defines who you are, and I admit a man would just get in the way... even someone like me because I wouldn't be able to share you with the rest of the world, unless you taught me how. For me things may end up looking more like the traditional stuff you talk about. I want to fall in love with a woman, I want to have a life with a woman who adores me, to feel all the same sensations you feel with Stella. I love you, but I also want to be loved in the same way. I understand why that can't happen with you, and it doesn't hurt.*" She took my hands, held on tight, smiled and gave me more of her adorable wisdom. "*You realize that all that has happened thus far today will instantly become history? I think about that often because it keeps me sober about the value of time. One of my professors in London once started a class with a short lecture on a stark reality. He said that if there were one billion people alive on the earth in the year 1800, they are now all dead. Imagine, one billion people born, lived, died. He was making a point on the unstoppable forward movement of time. It made me wonder how many of those individuals truly lived the life they wanted, and if they owned their destinies. I ventured to guess not many, and I was determined not to be one of them.*" Eli had become one of life's

MERECÀ

blessings. She opened my eyes and my heart to a humanity that could have otherwise escaped me. She altered my trajectory, forcing me to choose a path that was well lit, with markers that reminded me it was all about the people, about individual fulfillment and the role others played in helping it along. It had already been a force in Italian culture, but now it was casting a wider net, and the tremor that accompanies social evolution was knocking at the door.

    In late August of 1970, Amadeo returned to Sarno with a renewed drive to claim Stella's hand, and a promotion to deputy secretary of the Communist Party for the region of Lombardy. He took a room on the outskirts of town, meeting frequently with Stella's father. Expanding the party's influence into the southern regions was still a priority, and Amadeo brought with him new instructions and a sizeable budget to get the task done, starting with Basilicata. That first night he was invited to diner in his honor at a restaurant reserved for the occasion. Other party dignitaries from the Campania region were in attendance as was Stella and her family. She feigned feeling ill but gave in when her fathered threatened to keep her locked up at home. She couldn't handle not seeing Eli. Their relationship had grown deeper with a sense that they could plan a life away from Sarno for Stella's sake. We were all turning seventeen while Eli had already celebrated her eighteenth birthday. The age was upon us when many of Sarno's young adults were planning to escape the poor promises of southern Italy in search of careers and jobs in the north, in Europe's industrial belt, or in America. Some, like Mimmo, had enough resources to keep them at home with better prospects for local employment through family connections. Others would continue working on their father's farms in a labor intensive, but comfortable living. Stella's future was being planned by her father and Amadeo. She was forced to tolerate her circumstance for the time being because she wanted desperately to finish high school. We were about to enter our junior year, and Stella had performed exceptionally well placing in the top ten percentile. I witnessed her brilliance in classes, especially in literature. She freely memorized her favorite poems, read passages from texts with dramatic effect, and composed works of her own which she inserted into letters written to Eli. Literature was her great, personal flight from life's disappointments. It buttressed her notions of being in love and granted her a refuge when her days became intolerable. Thoughts of Eli, their love making, their contrived dreams of constructing a perfect future, provided all the hope she needed. In her minimalist world, her mind became her greatest asset.

Amadeo was spending much of his time into the fall months setting up the party office in the city of Matera, about a thirty-minute drive from Roccaforte, the first town they had considered as a southern headquarter. Increased revenues afforded access to major urban centers and greater exposure into the political mainstream. Roccaforte had grown less populated and more remote. The town housed what seemed to be one last generation since its young had moved away in search of work, probably never to return. The abandoned country property scouted about five kilometers outside the town had been a cheap temptation for rehabilitation, but the owner had died in the war, and there were no relatives to claim it. Amadeo would keep the property in mind as a country retreat for ranking party officials-much like a Russian *dacha*. Stella avoided contact with Amadeo as much as possible, dodging any confrontation. She had been factored out of discussions about her and was convinced that party deputy would soon introduce the topic of marriage. His preoccupation with his work gave her precious time to think through a strategy to defeat the proposal. She worked on every possible approach short of exposing herself as a lesbian but promised herself she would if nothing else worked. She thought of appealing to Amadeo's more cosmopolitan heritage to have him respect the wishes of a woman and abandon the effort to make her his bride. This would all have to wait till Christmas when he was due back in Sarno. In the meantime, she turned to her mother hoping for some support. Getting her to counter her husband's decisions would be a long shot, but Stella was bent on exhausting every option to avoid outright rebellion.

"*Mamma, non so se fu la tua decisione di sposare papà, ma ti prego di capire che io non posso sposare Amadeo. Sono sicura che*

MERECÀ

non potro' mai amarlo. Nun nge teng' manc' na poc e affezione; a verità è che me fa proprio schifo. Comm' faccio a vulè bene a n'omm che nun pozz' stummecà? Aiutami mamma, ti prego."
She confronted her mother with the truth that she couldn't stand the man and could never love him. She begged for her help in saving her from Amadeo who disgusted her. Her mother showed no sympathy in a flurry of Italian and dialect, instructing her on the uselessness of love.
"Pienz' e te mettere a cap'a ppost! Chest'so fesserie. L'ammore nun esiste. A cosa cchiù importante è che chill' te mette a ppost' cu' na casa, nu stipendio, cu'nu futur senza preocupazion'. She took her daughter's shoulders into her hands shaking her violently. *"Guardeme, sono na schiava e nun valgo duie soldi. Amadeo nun è comm' a tuo padre, è assai cchiu' gentile, ten na bella faccia e poc a poc chill' te fa 'nammurà cu na vita nuova. Te port' luntan da Sarno a fa na vita migliore, na vita da signora. Nun te permettere e fa qualche scemenza. L'anno prossimo a chist'u tiemp ti fai capace e poi capisci che dopo sposata, a tuo marito lo devi solo rispettare anche se non lo vuoi bene. Nun te perdere sta fortuna."*
Her lesson was stark and depressing. There was no room for romance, love didn't exist-it was nothing but a foolish impulse to be set aside. She praised the advantages of leaving Sarno to a home in Milan, married to man, unlike her father, more gentile, with a paycheck who will give her an upscale existence, and disavow her mother's life of slavery. She cautioned not to mess it up. A year from now she guaranteed her daughter would be settled and accept that it was the best choice and that after marriage she needed only to respect her husband even if there was no love.
The formula that had condemned countless women in previous generations was an option Stella detested. Her mother's words intensified her angst, making her more determined than ever to avoid that fate. Her thoughts turned to Eli for comfort as she retired to her room. She was too angry to cry.

The Christmas week 1970 kept us disjointed. We didn't see much of each other. Carminuccio and his father had several gigs booked in Salerno and Naples to play for Christmas and New Year's parties in local hotels. Mimmo and his family would be away at their yearly medical conference and skiing the Alps in Cortina. Raffaele took on more hours at the hospital covering for workers who had put in for vacation time. Eli had several days with the London girls and her usual appointment with Stella. Two days before Christmas Amadeo returned to Sarno. In true communist fashion, Stella's home saw no Christmas celebrations, no decorations. Nonna Nicolina intervened each year, to her son in law's strong displeasure, with gifts and treats. Her appearance at their door on Christmas caused heated arguments between husband and wife. He blamed her for tolerating her mother's intrusions. Nonna Nicolina did as she pleased. She had no fear of the communist, and no sympathy for her daughter whom she accused of being weak and an enabler, unwilling to confront her husband. Stella often spoke of the abuse her mother had endured for years to the point she had become numb to it. She described her as a zombie, a mannequin who could no longer feel any emotions, and completely submissive.

   Amadeo settled in for the winter. He had planned his trip to Basilicata with a long layover in Sarno to get better acquainted with Stella. She had become a deal, a business transaction, an investment in furthering her father's career. His ambitions went unchecked, everything was negotiable. He would unload her to become Amadeo's concern, selfishly clearing his conscience despite knowing that she would hate her life in Milan. The Milanese communist had become powerful enough to grant his future father-in-law greater local authority, maybe regional director one day. Amadeo's intentions were to showcase his reputation and offer the promise of a stable material life which he assumed would be enticing to any southern female on the edge of poverty. He was a pragmatic party operative who was fine with draining free expression out of life and replacing it with a fanatical communist blueprint. There was nothing "Italian" about the world he envisioned, so Stella was a bad fit. The man had little to offer in appearance and character which persuaded him to abandon any attempt to win her over romantically-he was aware of his handicap. Her beauty was the stimulant, and the idea of a trophy wife to show off at communist party gatherings, he reasoned, would make him a standout. The almost twenty-year age difference was never an issue for him and her father, but in her eyes, it not only made him too old, but she pitied him for even considering her.

The girls were able to spend one of the days after Christmas together. They chanced a meeting at the Bar Michelangelo to add some pomp to their holiday. They acted as girlfriends would, and since it was customary for girls to walk arm in arm and huddle close, their actions raised no eyebrows. The meeting provided an opportunity for Stella to come clean on Amadeo. Again, she was turning to Eli for answers, even a rescue plan. She waited for a reaction, but when Eli hesitated, fumbling about for a coherent thought, Stella got serious.

"*Devi capire che I miei genitori fanno sul serio con questo benedetto Amadeo. Sono convinti che sposandolo sarà il miglior futuro. Vedi come la pensano? Per loro, mettendomi a posto in qualche appartamento a Milano a cucinare, lavare panni e fare figli è vivere una vita ideale per una donna. Sai che insistono a farmi partire con lui alla fine di quest'estate prossima e senza potare a termine il liceo, decisi che gli studi per una donna non hanno valore. Cosa mi dici? Mi guardi, ma non parli.*" She explained her parents' conviction that marrying him would be her best chance at a stable future; that living in Milan cooking, washing clothes and having children would be an ideal life for a woman. She cautioned that they wanted her married and to depart with him at the end of the coming summer, without completing high school in the belief there was little value to woman receiving an education.

Eli betrayed some frustration in her response. "*Dai, smettila con le accuse! Sai che se non parlo cerco di dare ordine alla mia confusione. Sento un dolore profondo ascoltando le tue parole. Non posso immaginarti incatenata da un uomo, chiunque sia, e poi costretta ad abbandonare tutti i tuoi sogni, il tuo proprio destino. A pensare che non ci fosse via d'uscita, porta ancora più tristezza. E se rifiuti?*"

Eli asked her to temper her accusations, noting that she is silent when she is giving order to her confusion. She was deeply troubled listening to her words, rejecting the thought of Stella being shackled by any man, forced to abandon her dreams, her chosen destiny. To think that there was no escape brought more sorrow. What if Stella refused to comply?

When she turned to her dialect to make a point, it meant she was losing it a bit. *"Ma dici sul serio? È certo che rifiuto! Comm' putisse mai pensa' che io fosse accusì ignorante e iettà na vita intera appriess' a n'omm' comm' a chill? Se insistono me faccie piglia' pe pazza, me portono dint'a nu manicomio che sto meglio là."* She sarcastically asked if Eli was serious, declaring that she certainly would refuse to go. She questioned how she could even consider that she would be so ignorant as to piss away her life with a man like him. If her parents insisted, she would react as one insane, and even if she ended up in an asylum, she would be better off there.

"Stella, abbassa la voce che ci sentono. Ho solo chiesto per sapere che reazione ci fosse da parte dei tuoi genitori. Sai che mi fai venire i brividi quando parli in dialetto. Ti trovo sempre più simpatica ... me fai murì ... ho detto bene?"

Once again Eli had to ask her to calm down and lower her voice in the crowded café. She defended her question about not complying, only to know how her parents would react. Telling her she gets the chills and finds her more irresistible when she speaks her dialect forced a slight smile on Stella's face. When Eli herself produced a few words in her distorted Neapolitan, Stella broke down some more. When Stella tried being serious again, she could hardly finish a thought without breaking into spastic giggles.

"Quando rifiuto, devo solo andarmene da quella casa. Vado da mia nonna. Lei odia mio padre e pensa poco di sua figlia. A diciotto anni sarò adulta e scelgo la strada che voglio fare. E se tu lasci Sarno per sempre, dovrò inventarmi una vita nuova. In un modo o l'altro troverò qualche pace e gioia nella mia vita con una donna." Stella's words, saturated in a selfish bravado, was an attempt to prop herself up in designing her own future. Her refusal to marry Amadeo would force her out of her home to shelter with her grandmother who hated her father and thought little of her own daughter. As an eighteen-year-old adult she would choose her own path. After a deep sigh, she envisioned Eli leaving Sarno for good,

giving her cause to reinvent her life. She finally declared that in one way or another she would find peace and joy with a woman. Stella played her hand with direct words that weighed heavily on Eli. It added a layer of reality that triggered unhappy thoughts of living apart, of not adding more pages to their story.

Classes started up again the Monday after the Epiphany. It was a welcomed return to a routine that kept us busy and in closer touch with the entire cast of characters I had come to love. We reconnected with much fanfare, hugs, kisses, summaries of holiday events, and with an odd insistence on squeezing out any novelties or bits of gossip. True to his word, Mimmo had been mum on Eli and Stella. The girls needed the comfort of knowing that they wouldn't become the objects of talk, speculation or judgment. As much as they wanted to scream it out to the world, their better sense had them scale things back in anticipation of an older, more independent age when they could live as they pleased or move to a place like London with a friendlier population. Stella hinted that she would make the move across the Channel, willing to take that chance rather than remain in Sarno or be forced to move to Milan. Eli understood and had considered the possibility.

In February of 1971 we were halfway through our junior year. Eli was preparing for her British General Certificate of Education exams, as she called them. They were scheduled for the end of May in London. Mimmo had graciously invited any of us to his home to work on assignments. We had also started the practice of working together in the afternoons in the small, but well-equipped school library. We would start our research there, gather as many resources as we could find, and then take the task to Mimmo's to polish it up. The group usually included me, Carminuccio, Raffaele, Stella, Chiara and Elena, originals from our eight-grade class, and Eli whom we eagerly invited to participate. The most memorable meeting was on a cold March afternoon when our assignment was to read, and group analyze the fifth Canto in Dante's Inferno. Once completed, we would all sign our names to the product. The Canto took us to the second circle of Hell. In it, Dante introduced us to the souls of the lustful, condemned to eternal punishment for forfeiting reason to unchecked passion. Their punishment was to be tossed about for eternity in the stormy, blackened clouds of a raging tornado. The two characters that stood out for Dante and for us were Paolo and Francesca, two tragic lovers, contemporaries of Dante, involved in an adulterous affair ... both eventually murdered by Francesca's husband who was also Paolo's brother. The author showed little sympathy for the other souls he meets on his journey through the circle, except for these two lovers. As we absorbed the reading, Eli pointed out how the tough language employed in describing the sinners softens noticeably when Dante comes upon Paolo and Francesca, imploring the reader to feel his attachment and his pity that perhaps the lovers were judged too harshly. The power in the narrative for Stella was the triumph of love over adversity. It struck a note with her as she found common ground with her struggle to overcome the obstacles that would deny her a relationship with Eli. Her profound contemporary view on the medieval lovers was a pleasure to behold in a mix of Italian and dialect.

"Per me i due innamorati rappresentano un amore che non si arrende, anche quando ci sono ostacoli enormi, anche confrontando la morte ... l'amore che sfida tutto per sopravvivere, per me è la massima espressione umana. Se pensate che le anime di Paolo e Francesca, intrappolate in quella bufera per eternità senza nu minuto di riposo, proibiti di toccarsi, né di scambiare due parole, sentendo forse la stessa grande passione da vivi, lo stesso amore profondissimo, con nessuna possibilità di consumarlo. Mimmo, la tua lettura poetica m'ha commosso tanto che m'hai fatto chiangnere. Io nu putess' mai supporta' nu dolore accusi' assoluto. Sono passati secoli, ma è come se Paolo e Francesca fossero qui con noi, così eterna è la loro tragedia che si sente ancora oggi." Her eyes filled with tears as she glanced over at Eli, who understood the connection with the lost souls. I watched as the two silently exchanged a volume of emotions. I was first overcome with the intensity of Dante's encounter, and then with the legitimacy of Stella's words, certain that she wondered if they were on the path to sin and tragedy. For her, the souls represented a love with no surrender in the face of enormous obstacles, even when confronting death. She praised the love that challenges all as

the greatest human expression. She asked us to think of Paolo and Francesca trapped in that whirlwind for eternity, prohibited from touching, from speaking, feeling the same great passion as when they were flesh, the same profound love, forever unable to consummate it. She thanked Mimmo for his poetic reading, which moved her to tears. In her native dialect she expressed the impossibility of enduring such an absolute agony, and she noted that despite the passing of so many centuries, it was as if Paolo and Francesca were there with us, testament to the timeless nature of the tragedy.

    It was the way we would spend many of our afternoons. We started with topics related to our schoolwork only to go off on many tangents-extensions of our insatiable curiosities. Mimmo was the best of moderators. With magazine and newspaper articles in hand we touched on topics from sexual and gay liberation to the legitimacy of the Vietnam War, to the abortion debates, to rock and roll lyrics, to Catholicism and contraception, and inevitably to our lives beyond graduation. I had set my goals on graduating in Italy, but at home there was talk of returning to America. Life in Sarno was pleasant enough but making a living either employed or in a business of your own was difficult. My parents had become American citizens. That didn't help when applying for local jobs in short supply, or starting up a trade when it meant greasing the palms of the many hands that controlled licensing, certificates, leases and loans. When my parents ran up against these rooted habits, they became disenchanted, forfeiting any enthusiasm. They much preferred dealing with the bureaucracies in the states than to subject themselves to a system that functioned outside of legitimate government agencies, mafia style. Mimmo would always castigate those agencies for being inefficient, enabling and tolerating peripheral players such as the Camorra. Since they had left Italy as a young couple, Mom and Pop had no experience with the exclusive culture of -it's who you know. That soured their feelings for the motherland, while giving them a renewed appreciation for their adoptive land. Mom would always caution me to love Italy less intensely. She warned that if I stayed till adulthood, I would run into the same hurdles. I didn't disagree, but

MERECÀ

I wasn't done with my Italian life just yet. I wanted to get through high school with my friends. In my heart I felt that graduation would be the end of one life and the beginning of another whether I stayed or returned to New York.

It was at the end of one of our sessions at Mimmo's that Eli and Stella decided it was time to confront Amadeo. The plan was for Stella to speak with him in the hope of appealing to any sense of decency he may have to drop his negotiations with her father to take Stella away as his bride. Her parents had repeatedly deflected their daughter's pleas, so going directly to Amadeo was an option she needed to explore. Amadeo had backed off a bit while he was involved in doing the party's work. He had been to the apartment for meetings with her father and dinner. He used the occasions to engage Stella in conversations, even driving her to her nonna Nicolina's house on rainy days. Stella remained courteous, but cold and indifferent to any of his advances. Eli had reminded her not to overreact, to tone down the drama and remain as neutral as possible, and to save her strength and fury for the moment she will need it the most.

The girls asked me and Carminuccio to tag along. Stella knew that the guesthouse-*Stanze da Luisa*-in which Amadeo had a rented room, was located about three kilometers outside town. He was due to leave for Matera the second week in April, just after Easter. That gave Stella some time to work him, to try to get him to understand. The leisurely trek to the guesthouse took about an hour with each of us talking up our support for her decision to meet with him. From a distance we could see the sign. As we approached, we noted the entrance to the property took us down a long, one lane dirt road to a small courtyard with a stone cottage. The three of us waited in the courtyard as Stella walked into the small office. There she asked about Amadeo to which the owner, signora Luisa, responded that he had returned a few hours earlier, that he was presently with some woman, and that it may not be the best time to disturb him, asking if she understood her meaning. "*Signorina, è tornato due ore fa, ma adesso sta con una donna. Stavo tornando dal mercato quando l'ho vista entrare nella sua camera. Forse non è il caso di disturbarlo, non so se intendi. Comunque, la camera*

MERECÀ

numero sette si trova al secondo piano e si entra dalla scalinata che porta alla terrazza." She told her room number seven was on the second floor and could be accessed up the outdoor staircase leading to the terrace. We watched Stella make it to the terrace and disappear into a short hallway. She could hear chatter through the door that was slightly open. She recognized Amadeo's voice and detected a faint, familiar female voice. Instead of knocking, she pushed the door just enough to peek through the opening. The woman standing near the bed, half naked with her back to the door, dropped her bra to the floor and turned sideways to face Amadeo who was seated on the bed. Stella then had to endure the sight and sound of her mother's sensual purr as the man slid his tongue across her nipples. As his hands moved up her skirt, Stella panic and moved away from the room back down the hallway. The shuffling of her feet startled Amadeo who paused to shut the door. She now understood the reasons why her mother praised the man's kindness in trying to get her to marry him. Mom was speaking from experience.

Stella waited behind a wall on the terrace wondering if he had come out to investigate. As she scurried down the staircase, she motioned to us to leave, to make our way down the dirt road. We moved away from the courtyard back toward the entrance to the property. She quickly made up the distance between us. We pounded out a retreat back to Sarno. She was visibly angry, in a frenzy, refusing to speak. Eli kept asking, receiving no response, no reaction. Carminuccio gave me one of his hand signals to say nothing. The silence amplified every crackle beneath our shoes along the stone and gravel sidewalk as Stella increased her pace, moving ahead of us until she reached a bus stop bench. She sat, we stood staring at her. Finally, she looked up and screaming her first words. *"Non ci posso credere. Non è possibile, non ci posso credere!"* She startled us claiming she couldn't believe what she had seen-that it was impossible. Eli, thinking there had been a nasty encounter with Amadeo, needed to know, asking what had happened, what did he say.

"Stella, dimmi cosa è successo. Cosa ti ha detto?"

MERECÀ

"*Non ho parlato con Amadeo, non ho parlato con nessuno. La porta era aperta appena abbastanza e ho visto mia madre nuda con la faccia di quel disgraziato sepolto nel suo petto. Pensate che questo è l'orario quando la puttana di mia madre dovrebbe trovarsi da mia nonna. Chissà quante volte ha fatto questa strada. Adesso capisco perché cercava di convincermi che Amadeo fosse un uomo gentile, e non come mio padre. Mi parlava delle sue esperienze!*"

We could only be in total shock, there was no other possible reaction. She told us what she saw. Carminuccio wasn't completely convinced, mentioning that perhaps it wasn't her. He urged her to walk back to the guesthouse to make sure since she had only gotten a side view of the woman and through a small opening. We walked back into the courtyard and waited out of sight. I hoped she was wrong. Her mother's infidelity with the man they wanted her to marry may have been a good enough excuse to get her out of going to Milan, but it added another layer of bitterness to a life that had already asked her to endure too much. Not more than thirty minutes later the woman that emerged from the short hallway, scurrying down the staircase fixing her blouse and hair and slipping on her sweater confirmed what she had witnessed. Stella couldn't look while the rest of us watched as her mother scurried away in the opposite direction. Carminuccio noted that she was taking the back-road home through Episcopio to make that stop at her mother's, covering her tracks. When she was safely out of sight, we returned to the main road. We made it back to Sarno in a daze. We stayed with Stella back to the *palazzine*. As we turned up the hill approaching the housing complex, her mother called out to us from behind. Stella panicked, while Eli did her best to keep her composed. Carminuccio whispered his advice to stay calm. "*Stella, non è il momento di fare scena, controllati.*" He told her it wasn't the moment to make a scene, to control herself. Our friend nodded and took a deep breath. We waited for her mother who greeted us with a half-smile and a *ciao* asking if we were her school friends and our names. "*Stella, chist' sono i compagni di scuola? Famm' capi' chi sono, comm se chiammane?*"
Carminuccio stepped in to make the introductions when he noticed

MERECÀ

Stella faltering. "*Signora, io mi chiamo Carmine, questo è Gianni e questa è Elisa.*" She knew who we were. "*Allora, chist' è Gianni o' merecà, e questa è la figlia del conte ... Elisa. Finalmente nge simm' cuntrate. Ve vuless' invita' sopra, ma aggio 'fatt' na poc' tarde, stavo da mia madre, e devo ancora cucina'. Forse un'altra volta? Dai Stella, andiamo, è tardi.*" She called me out as the American and Elisa as the count's daughter. She would have invited us up, but admitted to getting home late from her mother's, and still having to cook. We got a raincheck and Stella was told to follow her home. There was nothing pleasant in the encounter. I had grown accustomed to affectionate, over the top greetings from the parents of my friends. Aside from her classical beauty, the woman was cold, detached, not very motherly, and condescending to me and Eli. In an Italian world where people exchanged strong emotions even in simple encounters, signora Adela left me sadly dispassionate.

The three of us remained in our spots as we watched mother and daughter walk away and into the crumbling building. I leaned backwards against a short, jagged wall, my face failing to hide the melancholy that weighed me down. In that moment I could only think of the battle that lay ahead for Stella if she called up the courage to confront her mother with what she had witnessed at the guest house. Carminuccio and Eli shared the same feelings, both hoping that Stella would choose her actions wisely.

We walked Carminuccio home. On the way, we caught a glimpse of Teresa as she stood by the entrance to her store. Eli had always been curious about her. Carminuccio waved as she blew him a kiss. Her mother's image just beyond the beaded curtain kept us from stopping. To Eli she was another beautiful teenage girl victimized by circumstance. "*Teresa è bellissima, però sento una malinconia per le sue circostanze. Un'altra ragazza di paese costretta fare una vita senza scelte. Non so se vi siete resi conto delle situazioni depresse per noi donne. Molte di noi non abbiamo il potere di costruire una vita propria. Pensate per esempio, se donne come Teresa avessero modo di scoprire le loro capacità di diventare chissà chi. Io immagino Teresa un'archeologa studiando e lavorando in Egitto, una dottoressa pediatrica, oppure ufficiale*

MERECÀ

nella marina militare ... e poi se si parla in questo modo, gli uomini e anche le madri si fanno una risata e dicono di lasciar perdere che sono solo sciocchezze. È un delitto dell'umanità che mi fa impazzire. Il mondo ci giudica dal nostro sesso e non da persone. Ci troviamo negli anni settanta ma le donne fanno una vita quasi primitiva."

Teresa's image sent Eli off on one of her protests targeting the conditions of women. She saw Teresa as this beautiful female full of promise, sadly hampered by her circumstances, unable to make choices. She asked us to consider the depressed state of women and to think that each could become whatever they choose if they had that power. She imagined Teresa an archeologist studying and working in Egypt, a pediatric doctor, or perhaps a naval officer. She fretted that these thoughts were frowned upon and ridiculed by men and mothers, dismissing them as silly stuff. These were human tragedies that drove her nuts. She complained that they were being judged by their sex and not as persons, and that in the 1970's women were still living primitive lives. Neither one of us owned a way of expressing our agreement, stuck in our masculinity, knowing we had no solutions. She stared us down oozing with sarcasm. *"Non avete niente da dire? Si capisce, siete uomini."* You have nothing to say? It figures, you are men.

We dropped off Carminuccio and made our way back onto Via Umberto. We stopped at my house and strolled into the giardino. Down by the old swimming hole I showed her where I sat the very first time I heard her voice. I picked up where she had left off with her comments adding some jagged words. *"You know, I thought your comment on us being men was very unfair and insensitive. You can't lump us in with all men. We are not our fathers and grandfathers; we deserve a little more credit than what you gave us ... that was poorly done."* Masquerading her shock, she chose to ignore my words at first. *"Is this the rock you were sitting on? That must be the spot along the wall where you climbed over."* I said nothing. She sat on the rock and looked up at the eucalyptus. *"This tree is beautiful; this spot has a magical feel to it. I understand why you spend so much time here. Fine! I was bloody rude, you're right. I was starting to take you two for granted,*

MERECÀ

thinking that just because you accept us as we are, the rest of the town does as well when I know that to be far from the truth."
"Forget it, more importantly, I'm worried about Stella. When I think about her choices, I realize there isn't one that would work out right for her. There isn't much any of us can do for her either. I know what you mean when you say that this is a time in history when the world we live in just isn't ready for you two"
"I'm probably the only one that could make a difference in her life, but Gianni, I'm not yet able to act on it. There's still so much I have to get right in my own life. If only we could have lived as untroubled teenagers without all the heartache. Do you see how evil it is to deny Stella her nature, to be worried about a marriage, to start a new life in a place far from her home with a man no less? These are things we shouldn't be burdened with. In the best of worlds, she would be able to announce her affection for me and be done with it. I know, I'm hallucinating but I will not give up on what I know is right." I took a seat next to her, she leaned up against me for warmth, rubbing her arms, administering to her short tremors. I embraced the moment, aching to inhale every bit of her. This time around it was me who tempted a kiss. In that moment, the potion that bled from her lips, the scent of her skin, and the pulse of her racing heart were desires no deserving man or woman would have wanted to resist. I needed a dose of her delirium, and she responded. Secure that I was not to fall in love with her, she relinquished, granting me the intimacies that only she was capable of. We had our generational calamities, and like so many before ours, we possessed the frame of mind to live them. We focused on the fragility of our existence, which at that time was real to us, and as much as we would have preferred none of the turmoil, we gave it the seriousness we could mobilize.

   The week before Easter, Stella chose her day and time carefully. Her plan was to keep her mother's infidelity quiet, for the time being. She left for school that Monday morning as usual, arousing no suspicions. She detoured onto the road that took her past the cemetery and back to the cottage and Amadeo's rented room. She was determined to appeal her case and ask that he reconsider his proposal. She would accuse him of the affair with

MERECÀ

her mother if he attempted to deflect her demand. The morning was overcast with a powdery drizzle. She kept a steady pace sticking to the narrow sidewalk for about half the distance when she was forced onto the road as the sidewalk came to a rough and grainy end. Several times the tires of the passing cars sprinkled her legs with rainwater until she finally turned onto the cottage property. She kept to the grassy strips that lined the muddy dirt road. Encountering no one, she climbed the stairs to room seven. After a second knock, he answered. He struggled to get his shirt on as he pulled open the door, finally giving up as he realized who it was. Stella didn't hesitate.

"*Buongiorno, posso entrare?*" Good Morning, can I come in?
"*Si, certo.*" Yes, of course. He looked her up and down, confused at her condition.

"*Amadeo, non mi è stato facile venire qui oggi. Ho cercato di parlare con i miei genitori, ma non mi danno ascolto. Hanno deciso di controllare il mio destino anche se non ho alcuna intensione di permetterlo. È per questo che mi trovo qui. Se tu sei disposto ad accettare il mio desiderio di non sposarti, di non vivere a Milano e di non essere associata con il partito comunista, possiamo cercare una soluzione insieme.*"

"Amadeo, it hasn't been easy coming here today. I tried talking with my parents, but they won't listen. They have decided to take control of my life even if I won't allow it. This is why I am here. If you are ready to accept my desire not to marry you, not to live in Milan, and not to be associated with the communist party, we can find a solution together".

She attempted her appeal to what she thought would be a more enlightened sympathy for women. Amadeo, however, had a history of appeasing his ego, and women helped with that goal. His membership in the party had less to do with support for a political philosophy than it being the mechanism that would turn him into a somebody. He had worked his way up since 1955 as a twenty-year-old, and he was on the verge of moving into the ranks of those closest to the general secretary of the party. He used all of his supposed fame in his response."

MERECÀ

"Non sei nemmeno capace di capire che sono il tuo passaggio ad una vita migliore, lontano da questo paese di niente. Forse è la tua età che ti rende testarda, ma tuo padre è d'accordo che il tuo futuro sarà con me, signora di un dirigente del partito. Avremo una casa, una vita comoda con lavoro e stipendi, e figli con la possibilità di una vita piena e soddisfacente in un'Italia nuova, comunista, con uguaglianza per tutti. Ho trentacinque anni, ho dedicato gli ultimi quindici anni della mia vita a stabilirmi, a crearmi un titolo, e ora tocca a te completare la mia identità. Ti farà bene essere mia moglie, partiremo per Milano, e saremo felici. Ci sarà un grande profitto per tuo padre avendo investito la figlia in un modo intelligente ... Stella, renditi conto che non hai un valore individuale, fai parte di uno schema universale, siamo ingranaggi in questa industria umana."

He may have been less imposing, but the idea of a young and beautiful Stella complimenting the success he had already experienced, was too much of a temptation that kept sending him over the edge, blindly convinced it was the best path for both. His determination turned him brutish, and his words became clinical and revolting.

"You're not even capable of understanding that I'm your passage to a better life, far away from this nothing town. Perhaps it's your age that turns you stubborn, but your father agrees that your future will be with me, the wife of a party official. We will have a home, a comfortable life with jobs and income, and with children who will have the possibility of a full and satisfying life in a new Italy, communist, with equality for all. I'm thirty-five, having dedicated the last fifteen years of my life to establish myself, earning a title, and now you must play your part in completing me. You will become my wife, we will leave for Milano, and we will be happy. There will be much profit in all this for your father having invested his daughter so intelligently ... Stella, you must understand that you have no individual value, you are part of a universal plan, we are cogs in this human industry."

Stella couldn't believe her ears. With her blood coming to a boil, the girl from the *palazzine* employed her pedigree once again, this

time her attitude came armed with the stinging truth about her mother.
"*Va bene, conosco la strada che devo fare. Ascoltami, ascoltami bene. Io non sarò mai tua moglie. Scelgo io il mio destino, dove voglio vivere e con chi. Me ne frega dei tuoi schemi, di questo tuo mondo di uguaglianza, perché' tu non mi considerai mai il tuo uguale, sarò sempre una donna schiava ad un uomo come lo era mia nonna, e come lo è mia madre. Adesso ti faccio capire in un altro modo. Non posso mai amarti. Infatti, non potrò mai amare un uomo. Meglio che tu lo sappia-sono innamorata di una donna, e quindi non potrai mai considerarmi un dei tuoi "ingranaggi" in quell'universo che descrivi. Mi fai addirittura pena sapere che desideri un mondo così crudele, senza anima ... privo di libertà di seguire i propri sogni. Giorni fa, alcuni dei miei amici mi hanno accompagnata, dandomi coraggio di venirti a cercarti. Avevo deciso di fare allora quello che mi trovo di fare oggi, e cioè di supplicarti di lasciar perdere questa tua fissazione con questo matrimonio. Vedo invece che nemmeno tu hai intensioni di liberarmi da questo catenaccio. Mentre loro mi aspettavano fuori nel cortile, io mi sono trovata davanti alla tua camera. Con la porta aperta, ho visto te e mia madre nudi con la tua faccia da cretino sepolto nel suo petto ... a puttana cu nu figli' e puttana! Mi sbaglio? Guardami! No, non mi sbaglio perché' adesso sai che quello che ti racconto è tutto vero. Immagini se io lo spiegassi proprio così a mio padre! Ti avverto di non negarlo perché i miei amici erano tutti lì a vedere mia madre lasciare la tua camera. Abbandoni i tuoi patti con mio padre, torna a Milano, Bologna ... torna da dove cazzo vieni, altrimenti faccio crollare tutto. Faccio una scena per tutto Sarno. Tutti verranno a sapere che il direttore cornuto di mio padre ha una moglie puttana, adultera con un altro dirigente del partito. Tutti ti conosceranno, tutti sapranno il tuo nome. Amadeo, io non scherzo, non sai quanto mi fa schifo fare la fine che descrivi, e non lo permetterò mai. Pensi bene alla tua decisione.*"
"Fine, I know what needs to be done. Listen to me, listen closely. I will never be your wife. I will choose my own destiny, where I want to live and with whom. I don't give a shit for your plans, of your

MERECÀ

world of equality, because you will never consider me your equal, I will always be a woman slave to some man the way it had been for my grandmother and is for my mother. Understand that I will never love you. In fact, I could never love any man. You may as well know-I'm in love with a woman, so you will never be able to consider me one of your cogs in that universe you talk about. I feel sorry for you knowing that you would want a world so cruel, with no soul ... without freedom to follow our dreams. A few days ago, some of my friends came with me, encouraging me to come talk to you. I had decided then to do what I am doing now, that is, to beg you to abandon your infatuation with this marriage. I see that you have no intentions of freeing me from these chains. While my friends waited for me in the courtyard, I found myself in front of your room. With the door open, I saw you and my mother naked, with that idiot face buried in her breast ... the whore with the son of a whore! Am I wrong? Look at me! Am I wrong? I warn you not to deny it because all my friends were there watching as my mother left your room. Walk away from your agreement with my father, go back to Milano, Bologna or wherever the fuck you come from, otherwise I will make this all blow up in your face. I will make a scene all over Sarno. Everyone will learn that my father, the cuckhold director, has a whore for a wife, adulteress with another party leader. Everyone will know you, they will all know your name. Amadeo, I'm not playing games, you have no idea how revolting it would be for me to end up as you plan, and I will never allow it. Give your decision some serious thought." His reaction could not be contained.

"Hai il coraggio di chiamarmi un figlio di puttana quando tu te la fai con una donna. E che titolo dovrei darti io? Dimmi, è quella figlia del conte, di nome Elisa?" "You have some nerve calling me a son of a whore when you are making it with a woman, and what title should I give you? Tell me, is it the count's daughter, Elisa I believe?" Stella didn't hesitate-she spoke with conviction-her words saturated with disgust.

"Si, proprio Elisa! È molto più donna lei che sei uomo tu. Mi sa amare e io la amo. Questi non sono sentimenti da ragazza, sono una donna e ho già vissuto una vita di intimità vera con un'altra

donna ... si, una donna! Fatti capace che tu non risulti affatto nella mia vita, uomini come te mi fanno schifo!" With his opened hand raised above his head, he came face to face with Stella ready to do some damage to her tender cheek. She stood her ground, made eye contact, and stiffened her face ready to take the blow. He stared her down, his rage fueling his heavy breathing. As his blind rage took hold of his judgment, the palm of his hand struck her with enough force to send her stumbling and falling over the footboard and onto his bed. He hovered over her holding down her arms as she struggled to free herself. He smothered her mouth, muffling her screams. He pleaded with her to stop, agreeing to let her go. He asked her to leave, to return home. *"Stella, per favore smettila di gridare. Ti lascio andare. Vattene, torna a casa."* He couldn't afford a scene in a town where he was an unknown. He moved away from the bed to the opposite side of the room to calm his nerves. She kept watch, noticing the tremors in his hand as he lit a cigarette. He turned his back to her, afraid of reigniting the feud. Stella pulled herself together, and as she stood by the door, she assured him that she would say nothing to her parents until he had time to think things over, vowing not to report his cowardly assault, and that she accepted the pain with pleasure if it meant him leaving for good. She gave him two days to decide with a meeting set at 3 p.m. at the Bar Michelangelo on Wednesday, hoping it would be their last encounter. *"Non ho intenzioni di parlare con i miei e non ti denuncio per lo schiaffo da vigliacco. Anzi, soffro con piacere quel dolore se ti fa allontanare per sempre. Pensaci bene alla mia richiesta-ti do due giorni per decidere. Quindi, Bar Michelangelo in Piazza Municipio alle quindici, mercoledì ... e spero che sarà il nostro ultimo incontro."* She left quietly with no regrets, and with a deep sense of satisfaction. As she had warned, in waiting for his decision, she would say nothing about her mother's infidelity.

    The following day, Tuesday, unaware of her daughter's ultimatum to Amadeo, Adela kept to her new schedule, and detoured towards the cottage. He had thought of canceling but had no safe way of reaching her. The landlady had grown suspicious of the female visits to Amadeo's room. When Adela arrived that

MERECÀ

Tuesday morning, she noted that her stays were frequent, always early morning, and lasted several hours. She feigned some task in the courtyard to get a closer look at her face. They suspiciously exchanged a *buongiorno* as Adela made her way up the staircase. Amadeo had already showered and dressed. He greeted her coldly with a somber look that tore into her. There was no hesitation in her voice.
"*Che c'è, perché' questa faccia?* What's wrong, why the face?
"*Siediti, c'è molto da discutere. Ieri si è presentata tua figlia. A quanto pare, era venuta qui la settimana scorsa cercando di convincermi di abbandonare il matrimonio. Invece, quando è arrivata alla porta ci ha spiati nudi e sai ... impegnati, e precisamente con la mia faccia nel tuo petto... insomma, ha visto abbastanza, se non tutto*" With his anxiety mounting, he continued. "*A fare la cosa ancora più seria, c'erano i suoi amici di scuola e ti hanno visto lasciare la camera. Poi ieri è tornata di nuovo per avvisarmi che se non lascio perdere il fatto del matrimonio farà scoppiare tutto. Il primo a sapere i nostri fatti sarà tuo marito.*" He asked her to sit since there was much to discuss. He told her about Stella's first visit when she spied them naked and involved. He was convinced she had seen enough, if not all, that her friends from school were there and did see her leave the room. There was more. "*Ecco, mi tocca informarti che sua figlia ha confessato di essere una lesbica, almeno che tu già lo sappia. Mi ha confessato tutto. Secondo lei, non potrebbe mai amare un uomo. È innamorata di quella ragazza, la figlia del conte ... Elisa. Senti, tua figlia ha già diciassette anni, già una donna. Io direi che, ascoltandola, la loro relazione è molto seria. Per me c'è da considerare tuo marito, il partito, la mia reputazione e il mio futuro. La settimana prossima torno in Basilicata per completare i nostri affari, dopodiché parto per Milano. Ormai non vale la pena seguire il mio desiderio con tua figlia. In altre circostanze mi avrebbe fatto piacere avere una moglie giovane e bella al mio fianco. Il partito è molto a favore di integrare ed impegnarsi con le popolazioni del Mezzogiorno.*" "I must tell you that your daughter has confessed to being a lesbian. According to her she could never love a man. She is in love with

that girl, the count's daughter, Elisa. Your daughter is seventeen, already a woman. Listening to her, the relationship is very serious. I need to consider your husband, the party, my reputation, and my future. Next week I'm going back to Basilicata to finish up my work, after which I'm returning to Milan. It's no longer worth the effort to follow my wishes with your daughter. If circumstances were different, I would have been happy to have a young and beautiful woman by my side. The party is big on integrating with southerners. (Mezzogiorno is a reference to southern Italy)"

The misery that owned Adela's life like an unchecked disease, had found an antidote in Amadeo's bed. She tried to check her hysteria but failed at the thought of losing the only diversion that allowed her to rediscover her passions, her body, her sexuality, and all the sensations she had surrendered years ago. She clung to his waist, too stunned to cry. She used her best Italian and most dramatic Neapolitan in making her case for him to stay. *"Non puoi lasciarmi, mi uccido, me pigli'o' veleno, meglio morta. Amadeo, nun pozz sta senza te. Si diventato un grande amore ... si, sono proprio innamorata di te. Non te l'aggio mai ritt perche' sapev ca nun era cosa pe na femmena sposata, ma adesso non importa più niente, voglio stare con te, solo te! Ti giuro che non ho mai provato nessuno amore in vita mia, nemmeno mio marito. Poi si arrivat' tu e tutto è cambiato. Vengo cu tig, puorteme lontan da qua ... nun pozz'fa cchiù sta vita. Puorteme cutig si no me faccio piglià per pazza. Amadeo, sono una donna disperata e sono capace di tutto."* "You can't leave me, I'll kill myself, I'll take poison, better off dead. Amadeo, I can't be without you. You've become my great love, yes, I'm very much in love with you. I never said it because I didn't think a married woman should admit to it, but now nothing matters, I want to be with you, only you! I swear I have never been in love before, not even my husband. Then you came into my life, and everything changed. I want to come with you, take me far from this place ... I can no longer tolerate this life. Take me with you or they'll label me crazy. Amadeo, I'm a desperate woman capable of anything."

The northerner had misplayed his hand with the despondent southerner. *"Ma sei veramente impazzita? Capisci quello che dici?*

MERECÀ

Sei una donna sposata con una figlia. Quello che abbiamo vissuto non è stato amore. Una donna come te non può permettere di innamorarsi di un altro uomo così facilmente. Abbiamo provato un'attrazione fisica, sessuale e abbiamo reagito da adulti, e non spinti da qualche mania giovanile. Adela, ritorna ai tuoi sensi, questo non è un romanzo, non siamo due nuovi amanti, pronti all'imbarco di una vita insieme. Fatti capace-hai più di quarant'anni e io ne ho trentacinque, sarebbe una sciocchezza enorme credere di inventarci una vita nuova ... infatti, è una stronzata completa! Non voglio più parlarne." "You have truly gone mad! Are you aware of what you are saying? You're a married woman with a daughter. What we had was not love. A woman like you can't allow herself to fall in love so easily with another man. It was a physical attraction, sexual, and we reacted as adults, and not driven by some youthful fixation. Adela, regain your senses, this is not some romance, we are not two new lovers ready to set off on a life together. Get a hold of yourself, you're over forty and I'm thirty-five, it would be a complete folly to think we could start a new life ... in fact, it's complete bullshit! I can't discuss this any longer."

She would have none of his argument. *"Ti sbagli, dimmi che non credi a quello che dici. Sai che tutti mi credono la donna più bella del paese e sono ancora giovane e posso ancora darti figli. Amadeo, non buttarmi via così. Abbiamo fatto l'amore e non hai sentito nemmeno nu tantill'e affetto per me? Io te facc' cuntente, ti giuro! Saccio cucinare, lavare, sta'ccort'a na casa, e tu lo sai che sono assai appassionata del partito. Stella è ancora na criatura e non sa apprezzare un uomo come te. E poi m'aggia preoccupa' pur se Stella decide di dire tutto al padre, e lui ci crederà. Pe me salvà, io do a colpa a te, che tu m'hai fatt' perdere a cap'. Chill' me mette dint' a nu manicomio o me portano morta ndo cimitero, e per te nun nge addò scappare. Mio marito non ha paura dell'ergastolo. Amadeo, ti giuro che io nun te faccio fuggi', aggia veni' per forza cutig.*

She became frantic at the thought of being left behind, of falling victim to her husband should Stella decide to tell him. Amadeo understood he was now dealing with a liability, a woman who would never detach cleanly. He became flushed with regrets and sickening conclusions in which he saw himself losing everything he had earned the hard way. She warned that if Mario found out, she would play the victim of Amadeo's seduction. She knew her husband would either declare her insane or kill her, and there would no place for Amadeo to hide. She was certain that he wasn't afraid of spending the rest of his life in prison. Her ultimatum was that she had to leave with him. Amadeo felt stifled, the strict grip he had on his life chaotically slipping away. He shifted the discussion, asking about her daughter. "*E Stella?*" Adela already had a plan. "*Aspetto a venerdì sera quando Mario parte per un appuntamento a Napoli. Io sto perdendo i sensi. A pensare che mia figlia crede di essersi innamorata di una donna ... e poi proprio quella disgraziata figlia del conte. Figliema nun ne sapeva di queste cose ... chell' sa'nammurat delle richezze e non di Elisa. Nun c'ho mai pensat' pecche' credevo ca nun fosse na cosa natural', che foss'na cosa che facevan'sul i pazzi ... mio marito ha ragione che i ricchi non sono normali. A mia figlia ci penso io. Quella s'aggiusta si no le tir tutt'i capill'a cap.*" "I'll wait till Friday when Mario leaves for an appointment in Naples. I'm losing my senses. To think that my daughter believes she is in love with a woman ... and the count's bitch daughter no less. My daughter had no clue about all this ... she's fallen in love with the riches and not with Elisa. I never gave it any thought believing it was all so unnatural, things that only crazy people did ... my husband's right, the rich are not normal. I'll deal with my daughter. She'll straighten up or I'll pull her hair out." Amadeo wasn't completely convinced. "*Non sarà facile. Lei non apprezza affatto un futuro scelto da noi. Non intendiamo l'amore che lei sente per Elisa, non è un concetto comune per la nostra generazione. Per noi non è normale, ma per lei è naturale come la nascita di un bambino, la fame, e la morte. Tua figlia fa sul serio e non sarai capace di calcolare la reazione giusta. Porco Giuda, questo va a finire male! Io non ti permetto di mettere in pericolo tutto. Ho lavorato una vita intera per condurre al traguardo i miei obiettivi. Non puoi tenermi ostaggio alle tue fantasie. Fai quello che devi con tua figlia, lascia stare me ... non posso essere l'uomo che desideri. Non saremo contenti insieme."* "It won't be easy. She doesn't accept the future we have lined up for her. We have no understanding of the kind of love she feels for Elisa. For us it is not normal, but for her it's as natural as the birth of a baby, hunger, and death. Your daughter is serious, and you will react badly. Fuck, this won't end well! Adela, I won't allow you to let everything go to hell. I've worked an entire life catering to my goals. I won't let you make me a hostage to your fantasies. Do what you must with your daughter, forget me ... I can't be the man you want. We won't be happy together."

    A wave of desperation overcame her as she walked away from the cottage. Since Stella had factored herself out of contention, her mother inflated her chances of keeping Amadeo in her life. She would let that situation simmer a bit, while she turned her attention to her daughter. She knew she had to act quickly. She asked Amadeo to keep his meeting with Stella as planned on Wednesday at the café, but to ask for more days to decide about abandoning his proposal. The added time would give her a chance to plot. She planned to use Mario to deal with the lesbian revelation, knowing he would react with unchecked anger to the news of his daughter's relationship with Elisa. A lesbian daughter in a relationship with an aristocrat would send him off into a violent rage. Adela made her decision, constructed her strategy in her mind, and downplayed the evil in it to justify her need to escape her life. She would instigate Mario to his limits, claiming that his daughter's condition would destroy all he has worked for. His reputation would suffer irreparable harm, and the party would most likely replace him as director. Aware that his crude ego would overshadow his senses, she predicted his assault on Stella would rid her of her husband, possibly husband and daughter. Her sick calculations were a product of a woman pushed to her limits, and with nothing in her life worth salvaging, her unstable mind gambled to relieve the torture she was living.

    Wednesday morning Stella left for school at the usual hour. Adela used the time alone with Mario to put her plan in motion. She invited him to sit with her at the kitchen table to discuss over a cup of espresso. *"Mario, dobbiamo parlare di cose serie. Tua*

MERECÀ

figlia mi ha confessato tutto. Ha deciso che con Amadeo non ci vuole andare, non lo sposa. Io e te abbiamo pensato che fosse na cosa facile da accettare-sposare Amadeo, un dirigente del partito, andare a vivere a Milano a fare la vita di una signora. Cercavo na spiegazione, e Stella non parlava, non rispondeva. L'aggio guardata dint'a l'uocchio e ho detto-dimmi la verità, me pare che tien i segreti, ti sei innamorata di un altro? M'ha guardata cu na faccia seria comm se vuless chianjere. A chill'u punt' io ero convint ca nge stesse un altro ragazzo pe miezz e perciò nun se vulev'mettere cu Amadeo. Ma poi, le sue parole me sono arrivate comm'a na coltellata ndo stomaco. 'Mamma, so che tu non lo accetterai, ma io amo un'altra persona. Ti giuro, mi faccio le valigie e me ne vado, mi metto in camino e vado dove mi portano i piedi, ma so che qui non ci posso più stare. Sono innamorata di Elisa, la figlia del conte. Siamo lesbiche, cioè due donne innamorate.' Io non sapevo che dire, me so scesa a lingua, nun voleva uscire nemmeno na parola. Chest'so cose e pazz'! Comm è possibile che na femmena se mette e case cu nata femmena comm a duie 'nammurat, comm' a marito e moglie? Tu o'sai che è stata a zoccola ricca a fa girà a testa a Stella. E comm facimm' se o ven a sape' tutt'o paese? Io voleva sbattere ca cap mbacci'o muro pe me fa capì. Ho detto, Stella, cu ste sciocchezze tu rovini na famiglia. O'vuoi capì che pàrate perde tutto ... tutti suoi lavori, tutt'sti sacrifici ca fatto pe' tant'ann! Figlia mia, lascia perdere, quella te porta a na via sbagliata. Papà nun addà suffrì questa indignità, pienz'a iss, fatt'capace che iamm a finì malamente. Comm' putisse mai credere che tuo padre accettasse ca tu ti miett' cu gente che lui odia.". She had constructed her fictional version of Stella's coming out. The words were meant to instigate, to turn her husband inside out with rage. She wanted his full, deranged force directed at Stella. In her sad, unstable mind, her daughter's death at the hands of her husband was one of the possible outcomes. "Mario, we have serious things to discuss. You daughter has confessed everything. She has decided not to go off with Amadeo, there will be no wedding. You and I thought it would be an easy thing to accept-marry Amadeo, a party director, move to Milano to live the life of a respected woman. I asked for an explanation, but nothing-she had no words, no answers. I looked into her eyes and I said-tell me the truth, it seems you have secrets, are you in love with someone else? She looked at me with the saddest of faces on the verge of tears. In that moment I was convinced there was some other boy involved. Then, her words came at me like a stab wound to the gut. 'Mom, I know you'll never accept this, so I'm ready to leave, pack my bags and go wherever my feet will carry me, but I know I can't stay here. I'm in love with Elisa, the count's daughter. We are lesbians, two women in love.' I had no idea what to say, I swallowed my tongue, I couldn't get a word out. It was one of those crazy moments. I thought, could it be that two women come together like two lovers, like husband and wife? You know it was that rich bitch who messed her up. What will we do if the word gets out? I wanted to bang my head against the wall trying to understand." Mario remained paralyzed, dumbfounded by a mind that struggled to apply any of the customary logic. It was something so remote, so impossible to have ever given it any consideration. Yet, he knew he had to confront it. His first thoughts were to deal with Elisa as well as his daughter. Elisa and her kind were the social disease targeted so routinely in his communist dogma. Now he had the proof he needed to validate any retaliation, to put in motion the plot he had built around allowing Stella her friendship with the count's daughter. Mario now had his miserable reasons to punish a member of the class of people he despised, those he faulted for all the ills afflicting Italian society.

  That afternoon Stella and Amadeo kept their appointment at the café. Stella still wore the red bruise on her cheek which she refused to cover up for the occasion. Amadeo tried being cordial, even offering coffee or a drink. She refused and bluntly asked if he had made up his mind. Amadeo had no choice but to change his approach knowing how close he was to complete ruin if Mario found out. Recalling Adela's request, he asked for more time.
"*Stella, anche se sono d'accordo con le tue decisioni, dovresti darmi un altro giorno o due per mettere le cose giuste con tuo padre. Abbiamo parlato a lungo di questo fatto del matrimonio, mi dispiace per come sono andate le cose, e vorrei offrirgli una spiegazione senza svelare i fatti tuoi. Però, ricordiamoci che*

quello che hai assistito tra me e tua madre resta sepolto. Sai che quando per prima ci siamo incontrati ho semplicemente notato la tua bellezza, offrendo i complimenti ai tuoi genitori. È stato tuo padre, dopo un paio di settimane, a suggerire un rapporto tra me e te. Per lui e anche per tua madre, la distanza di anni fra di noi non fu un ostacolo. Allora, mi son messo in testa che fosse una possibilità e quindi la decisione fatta, ai danni tuoi, di mandarti via con me a vivere a Milano come mia moglie. Io ci stavo a quel punto anche se non ti offrivo un affetto sincero ... non sapevo come ... ti consideravo ancora una ragazza. Senti, mi sono rassegnato alla tua scelta di vita e ti lascio in pace a vivere come desideri. Dammi fino a venerdì per un nostro ultimo incontro e ti assicuro che ti farò un riassunto completo a tuo favore di come sono andate le cose." "Stella, although I agree with your decisions, you must give me a day or two more to put things right with your father. We have spoken at length on the topic of marriage, I'm sorry for the way things turned out, and I want to offer him an explanation without revealing your situation. However, let's agree that what happened between me and your mother must remain buried. You know, when we first met, I simply took notice of your beauty, and I offered my compliments to your parents. It was your father who first mentioned a possible relationship. For him and even your mother, the age gap between us was not an obstacle. Eventually, I began believing that it could work, and thus the decision, to your disadvantage, to send you off with me to Milan as my wife. I was good with it even if I didn't show much affection ... I didn't know how to ... I still considered you a girl. Listen, I'm good with how you want to live your life, and I will leave you in peace, as you wish. Give me till Friday for our last encounter and I will offer a summary to your liking of how things went."

   Amadeo had conveniently softened his attitude, and there was a hint of compassion in his feelings towards Stella. He was committed to freeing himself of the imbroglio he had created. Stella agreed to the Friday extension, promising once again to keep the affair quiet. Not long after their meeting, she was standing at the back entrance to Marabbecca with Eli. The mild weather gave them reason to stroll the grounds as Stella gave a complete account

MERECÀ

of her meeting with Amadeo. "*Abbiamo deciso che venerdì sarà nostro ultimo incontro e metteremo le cose a posto. Vuole offrire una spiegazione a mio padre della sua decisione di tornare a Milano senza di me. Il nostro patto è di custodire i miei segreti e quelli di mia madre. Eli, ho parlato di noi, gli ho detto la verità per farlo allontanare. Sono stanca di vivere con questa paura di essere veramente chi sono! Per me non c'è altra scelta. Devo affrontare anche il peggiore delle circostanze per guadagnarmi la libertà di amare come voglio. Non so che destino ci aspetta, ma se ci risulta una vita insieme, voglio che sia perfetta. Non potrò mai accontentarmi di meno. Ho vissuto fino adesso na vita schifosa, schiava alla povertà, alla politica, ai miei genitori, e a questo cazzo di paese. Ti rendi conto che l'unico divertimento è una passeggiata sul rettifilo, fare due chiacchere con amici, e comprarsi un gelato? Questo non è vivere. Amore, famm capì che m'aspett nu futuro migliore ... anche se non ci sarai tu ... guarda, mo mi viene a piangere comm'a na scema.*" "We decided to meet Friday for the last time to settle our differences. He wants to offer my father an explanation of why he'd be returning to Milan without me. Our pact is to keep each other's secret. Eli, I spoke about us, I told him the truth to get him to back away. I'm tired of living with the fear of being who I am! I have no other choice. I have to deal with even the worse of circumstances to earn the right to love the way I want. I have no clue what destiny awaits us, but if we were meant to be together, I want it to be perfect. I could never be happy with anything less. I've lived till now a slave to poverty, to politics, to my parents, and to this shithole town. You realize that the only pastime is to stroll down the *rettifilo,* bullshitting with friends, occasionally having an ice cream. Amore, tell me there's a better future for me even if it's without you …. look, now I'm going to cry like an idiot."

Once again Eli was thrown off balance by Stella's desperate truth. By 1971 standards the girls were approaching an age when they were expected to start taking marriage seriously. Southern women had been conditioned to settle down and start a family in their late teens. It was reasonable for Stella, then, to think of her lover as a long-term relationship. In the neighborhoods of

London, Eli openly lived who she was, but trying it out in a small town meant awakening the big mouth morality bullies who preached mostly undisturbed in the homes, the churches and on the streets of Sarno. There weren't many, but those that took it upon themselves to judge, were vocal zealots. She had to issue her caution. *"Stella, in quell'istante con Amadeo il tuo spirito non ne poteva più, e ti sono scappate quelle parole dalla tua bocca disturbando la nostra vita personale ... forse era meglio dire niente. Lui non mi sembra uno capace di mantenere la parola, e questo mi fa paura. Una frase maledetta può cambiare tutto."* "In that instant with Amadeo, your spirit just couldn't take it anymore and those words escaped from your mouth exposing our personal life ... it might have been better to say nothing. He doesn't seem capable of keeping his word and it scares me. One poorly chosen remark can change everything." Stella took a raucous Neapolitan offense to Eli's last words. *"Che stai dicenn, che se venessero a sapè chell'ca simm, tu si pront e m'abbandunà tutta? Che fai, te ne vai a Londra senza pensier?"* "What are you saying, that if they should find out what we are, you'd be ready to give me up? What will you do, take off for London giving it no thought?" Eli was beside herself. *"Come ti permetti queste parole? Dopo tutto che stiamo trascorrendo, con la nostra intimità, e con le nostre speranze, mi credi capace di buttare via tutto? E poi di trattarti in un modo così crudele?"* "How can you speak so foolishly? After all we have been through, our intimacy, and with our expectations, you believe me capable of trashing it all? And to treat you in such a cruel manner?"

Stella took a deep, exasperated breath. *"Perdonami, non posso occuparmi di proteggere i segreti. Per me non hanno più valore, e se questa vita di merda insiste a vestirmi di ignoranza, io scelgo invece di vivere nuda, di sbucciare questa crosta primitiva che mi tiene imprigionata come una bestia. A scuola ho parlato apertamente di chi sono, e i miei amici mi hanno accolta a braccia aperte. Credevo mi avrebbero presa per una stronza matta, ma hanno reagito con passione e senza pregiudizi. Mi sono meravigliata ... vedi, anche il nostro piccolo paese emerge dal buio."* "Forgive me, I no longer have it in me to protect my secrets.

MERECÀ

For me they mean nothing, and if this shit life wants to cloak me in ignorance, I choose instead to live naked, to peel away this primitive membrane that keeps me imprisoned like a beast. In school I have openly discussed who I am, without fear, and my friends received me with open arms. I thought they would label me a freak, but they reacted with compassion and without prejudice. I was amazed ... see, even our small town emerges from the darkness." She cradled Eli's hands against her bosom as the weight of her thoughts slowly lowered her eyelids, turning her voice sleepy. *"Eli, amore, tutto è cambiato per sempre, e forse tu saresti capace di apprezzarne la profondità, ma non possiamo negare le differenze tra di noi ... per adesso ci spostiamo su strade diverse. Sono pronta a dare il prossimo passo, e ti giuro è una decisone personale. Anche se sei stata tu ad aiutarmi a capire e accettare la mia realtà, è l'ora di affrontare i miei diavoli da sola."* "Eli, my love, for me all has changed forever and perhaps you may not be able to feel the intensity, but we can't ignore the differences between us .... for now, we are moving in different directions. I'm ready to take the next step, and I swear it's a personal decision. I know it was you who helped me to understand and accept myself as I am, but it's time to confront my demons alone." Eli cautioned her again to check her emotions and to be mindful that she was dealing not only with parents, but with two individuals who have bigoted views, with no chance of dishing out any sympathy, stressing that her father had too much to, having molded his life around a singular fixation, and that his reaction could be overwhelming. He would fanatically protect all he has earned.

Back home Stella could feel the tension building. A fuse had been laid, and it became a sit and watch game to see who would light it first. Her mother held the lesbian card and Stella held the adultery card. That Thursday morning, she left for school early to meet up with Eli at the Bar Michelangelo. They had already made a habit of quick breakfasts on the *rettifilo*. Spies had taken notice and reported the apparently innocuous encounters to Mario. He didn't have the time to analyze it deeper, so he did nothing with the information. The girls unfailingly acted like common high school friends in public, avoiding displays of lesbian flirtations that could have aroused suspicion. Adela had been told of her husband's plan to enlist his comrade from the north in dealing with Eli. It was extreme, risky and she welcomed the chance that it would all backfire in support of her own selfish designs.

Mario didn't hesitate. Following his daughter's departure, he dressed, grabbed his bag and made his way to Amadeo. The conversation was intense and uncomfortable. Amadeo had already made a choice to disengage, now he was about to be asked to further the party's cause by being complicit in targeting the young aristocrat. Mario arrived subjected to the scrutiny of landlady Luisa who was having bouts of suspicion with the activities in room seven. She looked up at the terrace as Amadeo came out to greet his colleague. He then called down to her to order two espressos. Moments later a knock on the door signaled the arrival of the coffee and Luisa's curious stares. The men sat at the small table in the miniscule room, haphazardly conversing while Amadeo prepared himself for what he thought would be an accusation involving Adela. He could think of no other reason why Mario would be there at such an early hour. He kept his nervousness in check as his mind created a succession of explanations hoping to wiggle his way out of a possible violent confrontation. As Mario spoke his first serious, hate filled words, he understood he was on the wrong track.

"Ho raccontato un fatto personale con dirigenti del partito a Bologna. So che tu hai deciso contro il matrimonio con mia figlia. Capisco bene le tue ragioni in fondo a quello che mi ha raccontato mia moglie. Stella è stata infettata da quella troia maledetta di Elisa, la figlia del conte. Si sono dichiarate lesbiche, decadenza che si associa con la vita puzzolente dei ricchi, dell'aristocrazia. Sono diventate amiche non so come, e avrei dovuto mettere fine a quelle assurdità mesi fa. Comunque, la mia noia si concentra su tutta la famiglia del conte e la sua storia fascista. Gli Americani hanno disgraziatamente restituito il suo titolo e patrimonio persi nel dopoguerra. Le inchieste contro di lui erano valide, c'era un grande rapporto con il governo di Mussolini. Le fabbriche del conte fornivano tute militari e abiti per funzionari del governo.

MERECÀ

Durante la guerra le fabbriche furono bombardate e distrutte, ma tuttora ha ricevuto fondi a tasso agevolato per costruire tutto nuovo con contratti Americani. Capisci che effetto fanno gli Americani? Si occupano solo dei capitalisti lasciando noi altri un popolo di schiavi. Non posso permettere la troia di un pupazzo del governo il potere di infestare la testa di mia figlia. Amadeo, sono in contatto con la fazione più radicale del partito che la pensano come me. Si organizzano tutt'ora a Reggio Emilia e capiscono che l'unico modo di sanare questa società corrotta è con il terrorismo e la lotta armata. La vecchia cultura deve essere cancellata completamente di modo che il proletariato ne possa inseminarne una nuova ... vedi, si incomincerà da capo, sarà l'anno zero per tutti. Chi non si arrende a questa rivoluzione, pagherà con la vita. Meglio eliminare quelli che insistono a vivere il passato." "I have been in touch with party directors in Bologna. I know you have decided against marrying my daughter. I'm aware of your reasons based on what my wife has told me. Stella has been infected by that harlot bitch Elisa, the count's daughter. They say they are lesbians, a decadence associated with the shit life of the rich, of the aristocracy. I'm not sure how they became friends, but I should have put a stop to the lunacy months ago. My problem is with the count's family and their association with the fascists. The Americans have shamelessly restored his title and property taken from him after the war. The charges against him were valid, there was a strong relationship with Mussolini's government. His factories produced military and government uniforms. During the war they were bombed and destroyed, but now he has received low interest loans to rebuild with American contracts. Do you understand the effect the Americans have? They concern themselves only with the capitalist and leave the rest of us a population of slaves. I can't grant the whore of a government puppet the power to corrupt my daughter's mind. Amadeo, I've been in touch with the most radical faction of the party which believe as I do. They are coming together in the town of Reggio Emilia and they are determined that the only way to fix this corrupt society is through terrorism and armed struggle. The old culture needs to be cancelled completely to allow the proletariat to seed a new one ... you see, we will start from scratch, it will be the year zero for everyone. Those who refuse to be indoctrinated will pay with their lives. Better to eliminate all those who insist on the status quo." Amadeo reacted with a subdued panic. The implications were severe, they turned him off, but he needed to fake his support.

"Mario, ma tu che cosa hai in mente? Cosa ti hanno suggerito quelli di Reggio? Ascoltami, io li conosco bene e si stanno preparando a questa lotta armata come dici tu, è una cosa molto seria. Ci saranno bombe, sequestri, e omicidi. Il gruppo è comandato dai più radicali del partito. Infatti, ci sono addirittura dirigenti che hanno denunciato il loro manifesto. Non so, direi di fare attenzione. Se vengono a Sarno, resteranno affinché avranno compiuto qualche delitto, un atto terroristico. Ti imbrogli in un mondo di pericolo e di piena rivoluzione e nessuno ti garantisce il successo, pensaci bene." "Mario, what are you thinking? What advice did those in Reggio give you? Listen to me-I know them well and they are preparing for this armed struggle as you put it, and it's serious. There will be bombings, kidnappings, and killings. The group is led by the most radical elements, and in fact there have been party directors who have denounced their doctrine. I'm not sure, I say proceed carefully. If they come to Sarno, they will refuse to leave until they have committed some crime, a terrorist act. You are involving yourself in a dangerous world of unchecked revolution and there is no guarantee of success, think it through." Mario grew slightly suspicious of the way Amadeo was expressing his concerns.

"Mi sorprendi parlando così. Sono stato io a chiedere aiuto di un sequestro. Si, adesso lo sai, proprio il sequestro della figlia del conte. Sarà non solo una vendetta personale, ma anche per le ingiustizie sociali. Ormai tu fai parte di questa storia, e sei costretto a partecipare. Saremo noi a progettare tutto: il giorno, l'ora, il posto. I nostri colleghi approveranno e saranno loro ad eseguire da professionisti. La destinazione sarà la proprietà abbandonata in Basilicata. Resterà li fin quando verrà pagato il riscatto. Se il fatto si prolunga, verrà trasferita in altri luoghi abbandonati al nord conosciuti al gruppo radicale. Solo così

possiamo avanzare la serietà del nostro movimento, di questa rivolta che farà crollare il vecchio mondo, il mondo che appartiene a quelli col potere e ai ricchi ... e ti giuro che non vedo l'ora." "Your words surprise me. It was I who asked for help with the kidnapping. So now you know, we are planning the kidnapping of the count's daughter. It will not only be a personal vendetta, but also one for the social injustices. You're now a part of this, and you are expected to participate. I mentioned you, and that we will be the ones to plan it out: the day, the time, the place. Our colleagues will approve our plans and it will be them to execute as professionals. We have already decided the destination will be the abandoned property in Basilicata. The girl will remain there until a ransom is paid. If things take too long, she will be transferred to other hideouts in the north known only to the radicals. It's the only way they can take our movement seriously, our rebellion that will make the old order crumble, the world that belongs to those in power and the rich ... and I swear to you I can't wait." Amadeo had to show complete adherence to the cause. He took one more chance to question the plan. He had to be careful not to downplay his allegiance.

"Va bene, sono d'accordo che la lotta ha merito, però mi infastidisce un po' l'idea di violentare persone per motivi personali che non vale a promuovere la nostra causa. Credevo di legittimare il nostro messaggio con la politica, usando la democrazia al nostro vantaggio. Se invece il partito sta cambiando strada, bisogna che ognuno di noi faccia la sua parte." "I agree that the struggle has merit, but the idea of using violence against people for personal reasons doesn't work to further our cause. I thought we were legitimizing our message through politics, using democracy to our advantage. But if the party has decided to change course, it means that each of us must do his part."

Amadeo had bought into the party platform as a young man because he was sure of a political path that could steer public policies and address the plight of the proletarian class. He had no intentions of adhering to a radical movement forming within the ranks on the extreme left. His knowledge of revolutions in history made him fearful of chaos, terrorism, and death. This was not his vision, but he knew that to stand his ground with Mario meant factoring himself out, and the radicals would use whatever means necessary to eliminate him as someone who knew too much. His name was out there, he had to play along. He needed to be absolute in eliminating any doubts that he was indoctrinated into the process.

"*Mario, intendo il tuo ragionamento che abbiamo speso già troppo tempo avanzando le nostre teorie senza molto successo. Credo che sia arrivata l'ora di cambiare strategia. Se riuscissimo a convincere la maggioranza del popolo che ha sofferto il peso del capitalismo, e che quel sistema è la causa di tutte le malattie umane senza perdere più tempo prezioso, allora io ci sto. Ho già speso una vita aspettando questo futuro migliore, questa promessa di uguaglianza.*"

"Mario, I understand your argument that we have already spent too much time furthering our theories but with little success. I believe then that the time has come to change strategies. If we were to convince most of the populace that they have suffered the burdens of capitalism, and that that system is the cause for all of humanity's ill without losing any more precious time, then I'm in. I have already spent a lifetime waiting for a better future, and that promise of equality." Mario had no hesitations, sensing now that Amadeo could be relied upon. "*Allora, io ritorno stasera dopo pranzo per elaborare. Abbiamo un paio di settimane per interessarci di tutti i movimenti di Elisa. A questo scopo può anche aiutarci mia figlia senza che lei lo sappia.*" "Fine, I'll return tonight after dinner to work things out. We have a couple of weeks to figure out all of Elisa's movements. To that end we can even get my daughter to help without her even knowing." That evening Mario made his way back to Amadeo's room to plan out Elisa's abduction. He had enough details to narrow down a place and time. The rest would be left to the professionals from Reggio who would know how to execute.

"*Le mie spie mi dicono che Elisa e Stella s'incontrano abbastanza spesso al bar Michelangelo o anche sul rettifilo doposcuola. Ogni mercoledì si radunano con altri studenti alla casa di un amico di scuola. Si chiama Mimmo, figlio del dottore Aiello. La loro casa si*

MERECÀ

trova nella zona di Sant'Alfonso. Verso le diciotto, Elisa torna alla sua abitazione-è una passeggiata di almeno mezzo kilometro. Lei e Stella camminano insieme fino all'incrocio di via Roma e via Lanzara e poi si lasciano. Da sola, Elisa passa per due vicoli stretti senza negozi e pochi abitanti. In uno di quelli, dove entra poca luce, in qualche passo oscuro si presenterà l'opportunità del sequestro. So che nostri colleghi ne saranno d'accordo. Che ne pensi?" "My spies tell me that Elisa and Stella meet up frequently at the Bar Michelangelo or on the *rettifilo* after school. Every Wednesday they get together with other students at a friend's house. His name is Mimmo, Doctor Aiello's son. Their house can be found in the Sant'Alfonso neighborhood. Around six o'clock Elisa makes her way back to her home-it will be about a half kilometer walk. She and Stella will stroll together until the intersection of Via Roma and Via Lanzara at which point, they go their separate ways. Alone, Elisa will walk through two narrow alleyways with no stores and few inhabitants. In one of those, where little light penetrates, in a dark stretch of road, we will have our best opportunity to carry out the kidnapping. I know our colleagues will agree. What are your thoughts?" Amadeo had to give the topic his full attention. He even participated in developing the blueprint of how the kidnapping would come off. Truth was, however, that at the time Mario had unwrapped his plan, he had already decided to leave for Milano after his last encounter with Stella. He had no intentions of making a victim of Elisa, and he had taken a liking to Stella, admiring her courage. He did, however, tell Mario what he wanted to hear. *"Si, conosco quella zona di Sarno. I vicoli sono davvero molto stretti, con abitazioni a buona distanza dai loro grandi portoni. A mio parere, sarà un posto ideale con poca gente e finestre che non si affacciano sulle strade. Se tutto si fa in pochi secondi, con furgone modificato, sicuramente non ci saranno testimoni. Possiamo anche passeggiarci alcune volte a quell'ora per essere sicuri, tanto il tempo c'è."* "Yes, I'm familiar with that section of Sarno. The alleyways are truly narrow, with homes deep inside their porticos. In my opinion, it would be an ideal location with few people around and no windows that open onto the street. If all is done in a few seconds, with a modified van, then I doubt there will be any witnesses. We can even do a trial run during that hour since we do have time."

"Va bene ... proviamo domani sera. Ci incontriamo sul rettifilo all'incrocio di Via Matteotti, davanti alla farmacia alle sedici."
"Fine, let's try tomorrow evening. We'll meet on the *rettifilo* at the intersection of Via Matteotti in front of the pharmacy at six."

As they parted ways, Amadeo's head filled with details that needed desperate attention. The following day, Good Friday, he was to keep his meeting with Stella first, then later that evening with Mario to trace what would be Elisa's route home. He wasn't sure if he had been forthcoming enough to be believed, and he feared retribution if Mario and his cronies thought otherwise. Stella would take up most of his energies that day-there was much to sort and difficult decisions to make in the timeliest manner. At three thirty that afternoon, Stella entered the Bar Michelangelo to find Amadeo waiting, seated at a small table for two. She approached and sat with a stiff resolve to see it through to the conclusion she hoped for. He greeted her warmly.

"Ciao, tutto bene? Come vanno le cose a scuola?" "Ciao, all well? How are things at school?"

"Bene, grazie. Sto per finire il terzo anno, poi gli esami, tanto da fare, un casino, sai." "Finishing my third year, then the exams, so much to do, a mess, you know."

"Posso offrire un cafè, non so, forse qualcosa altro?" "Can I offer a coffee, I don't know, maybe something else?"

"Un cafè, per favore." "A coffee, please."

"Cameriere, un café per la signorina." "Waiter, a coffee for the lady" Amadeo's tone hinted at a certain urgency-he had little time to play with.

"Stella, io avevo già deciso di abbandonare tutto qui a Sarno giorni fa. Dopo il nostro ultimo incontro, capii che per noi non poteva esserci un futuro, anzi addirittura un'assurdità crederci. Io parto per Milano questa sera, però prima di partire c'è un fatto urgente. Tuo padre sa di te ed Elisa. Secondo me è stata tua madre a parlarne. Fu colpa mia che avevo tradito il tuo segreto nella disperazione di cambiare il pensiero a tua madre di non

MERECÀ

allacciarsi a me. Mi vergogno ammettere il mio affare con signora Adela, erano momenti deboli sia per lei che per me e ci siamo cascati. Ti chiedo perdono. Sappia che è una donna disperata e che avrebbe abbandonato te e tuo padre per scappare via con me a Milano. Questo ha insistito lei, ma io ho seccamente rifiutato. Sembra essere motivata dalla rabbia di aver vissuto una vita senza amore, senza affetto, e schiava a tuo padre e la sua politica. Non me la prendo con lei se sentiva qualcosa più promettente nelle mie braccia. Sono stato uno sciocco a credere che fosse solo un'attrazione fisica. Secondo me, e non credo che io mi sbagli, lei sentiva una forte gelosia di te pensando che saresti stata tu a partire per una vita nuova con me. Ed è per questo che ha deciso di dire tutto a tuo padre. In un senso assurdo è come se lei ti avesse voluto del male. Mario è consumato dalla rabbia ma invece di prendersela con te, ha deciso di puntare tutto su Elisa. Per questo io e lui ci siamo incontrati ieri e mi ha parlato del suo discorso con radicali del partito al nord. Stanno progettando il sequestro di Elisa per motivi politici e di riscatto. Tuo padre però, lo fa anche per motivi personali contro Elisa e la sua famiglia ... possiede un odio forte per quella gente. Noi due dovevamo impegnarci di agevolare il lavoro dei professionisti una volta trovatosi a Sarno, con informazioni prevedendo i movimenti e abitudini di Elisa. Non c'è tempo abbastanza raccontarti tutti i dettagli, importante sapere che è una cosa seria e questi radicali non scherzano. Essi sono incaricati proprio con l'unico lavoro di mantenere i loro vittimi imprigionati finche' venga pagato il riscatto. Si spostano frequentemente senza traccia e con ciò, la possibilità che una come Elisa non riuscisse a sopravvivere. Questo fanatismo non mi va, ed è per questo che ho deciso di allontanarmi dai sentimenti di tuo padre e di ricostituirmi con quelli del partito che hanno denunciato il terrorismo e la violenza.

"Stella, I had already decided days ago to abandon everything here in Sarno. After our last encounter, I understood there would be no future for us, in fact it was absurd to believe in one. I'm leaving for Milano this evening, but before departing there's an urgent issue. Your father knows about you and Elisa. I believe it was your mother who informed him. It was my fault for revealing your secret in the desperate attempt to keep her from latching onto me. I'm ashamed for carrying on the affair with your mother, they were moments of weakness for her and for me, and we gave in. I beg your forgiveness. You must know that your mother is a desperate woman who would have abandoned you and your father to escape with me. This was her intention, but I flatly refused. She is motivated by the rage of having lived a loveless life, without affection, and a slave to your father and his politics. I can't fault her for believing in something better, but I was wrong to mislead her. I was an idiot for thinking it was merely a physical attraction. She developed a jealousy believing it would have been you to start a new life with me in Milano. It's what drove her to influence your father to come after you and Elisa. In a sick way it's as if she meant to do you harm. Mario is consumed with anger, but instead of taking it out on you, he has decided to go after Elisa. Because of this, he and I met yesterday, and he spoke to me of his discussion with the party radicals in the north. They are planning the kidnapping of Elisa for political reasons and for the ransom. Your father's motives, however, include a personal vendetta against Elisa and her family … he has a deep hatred of those people. Our task would have been to ease the work of the professionals once in Sarno by predicting Elisa's movements and habits. There isn't enough time to relate all the details, only that it is important to know that this is serious, and the radicals don't mess around. Their sole job is to keep their victims imprisoned until the ransom is paid. They are adept at moving about, frequently without a trace, with the chance that one like Elisa won't make it through alive."

    Stella became suddenly frail, weakened by the magnitude of his confession. Her young life still cherished the notion that people could never be evil enough to commit the destruction of others that Amadeo spoke of. The thought of Elisa being abused in such a manner violated the very real small-town morality that had characterized her upbringing. The world outside had added another radical encroachment on the provincial sensitivities of a place like Sarno. Stella was forced to balance the beauty and acceptance of her sexual awakening to the evil humans were capable of. Sarno may have held onto some feudal habits of its own, but there was nothing remotely matching those external extremes in the town's DNA. Without Elisa's intrusion, Stella would most likely have suppressed her lesbian awakening in favor of a more conventional life. She would have juggled the notion of marriage, probably defaulting to spinsterhood, and using her years in service to ageing parents. I would learn later, as my familiarity of Sarno's culture ripened, that women like Stella did indeed remain spinsters when faced with the impracticality of declaring themselves, adapting to more covert practices.

Amadeo's stark account on abduction, captivity, and the possibility of death, in this case one as young and innocent as Elisa, turned the unthinkable into a sick reality. Sarno and Stella were quickly being ushered out of their heirloom existence and into social upheavals, unforgivingly forcing changes on an undisturbed folklore. The girl had little choice but to make room for the improbable. She scampered out of the café in the direction of her neighborhood. She was ready to take the fight to her parents. A nauseating indignation governed her senses, and confrontation was all she could think about. Amadeo called out to her, following her for at least a block trying to get her to stop. When he realized he wouldn't be able to make up the distance, he retreated back to the *rettifilo*. His immediate chose to make his way to Marabbecca with the hope Elisa would be there. He predicted things would go badly for Stella, so Elisa needed to know.

That same afternoon after school, Carminuccio reminded me that we had been invited to hang out with Eli. She met us at the front entrance and took us into the kitchen where we loaded up on a few panini and *San Pellegrino* on our way out into the garden. The early spring day was invitingly warm with the scents of budding wildflowers riding on a soft breeze. We knew Stella was to meet with Amadeo-we all were anxious to know how things had gone. Less than an hour into our soiree, the new housemaid Delia notified Eli that there was a man in the lobby wishing to speak with her. Her parents were away in Rome, so she thought it may have been an acquaintance wanting to leave a message. When she learned it was Amadeo, she nervously asked him to follow her into the garden. He introduced himself to us and explained the reason for his visit. He left no stone unturned in his quick, organized summary. The staggering disclosures kept us a bit stymied at first, but as he urged her to react, Eli knew she had to make her way to the *palazzine*. *"Elisa, sarai l'unica capace di calmare la tua ragazza. Le cose andranno male per tutti in quell'appartamento. Stella sa troppo della madre e forse avrà già buttato tutto in faccia al padre."* " Elisa, you are the only one who can calm your girl down. Things will go badly for everyone in that apartment. Stella has too much on her mother and she may have already used it to attack her father."

We had no intentions of letting her go alone. The three of us took the quickest route to Stella's building while Amadeo trekked to the local police station to notify them of the kidnapping plot. He had developed a strong enough dislike for the tactics of the party radicals to disavow them. His apathy of revolutionary style violence and social chaos kept him grounded enough to advocate for peaceful, political change. The party had done too little to confront the radicals, and his growing appreciation for the courage being displayed by the young people of Sarno had given him the strength to become defiant even at the cost of his own life. The *carabinieri* (police) were skeptical at first, but the mention of the Reggio Emilia radicals was enough to raise the red flags since the declarations and the activities of the northern terrorist organization had already been exposed by Italian law enforcement. They now had Amadeo's statement and were interested in speaking with Mario and Adela.

  We arrived at the *palazzine* in time to witness a small group gathered in front of Stella's building, and others summoned to their balconies wondering about the commotion and the noise on the fifth floor. Eli became increasingly concerned, weaving her way to the entrance. We called out to her. She slowed her pace and waited for us to catch up. Carminuccio was tough on her. *"Eli, fermati e ascolta! Se ti presenti tu fra tutto questo fracasso, le cose andranno ancora peggio. Meglio se lasci fare a Stella."* "Eli, stop and listen! If you get involved in all the confusion, things will get worse. Better to let Stella deal with it."

MERECÀ

"*Carminu', ma sei sordo, non senti i suoi strilli? Sai che quello è capace di ucciderla! Per favore, lasciami passare.*"
"Carminu', are you deaf, can't you hear her screaming? You must know he is capable of killing her! Please, just get out of my way." She started screaming Stella's name when we refused her any space to get into the building.
"*Stella! ... Stella! Sono qui. Lascia stare tutto, scendi, io ti aspetto. Stella! Ascoltami, scendi, sono qui, Stellaaa!*" " Stella! ... Stella! I'm here. Let it go, come down, I'll wait for you. Stella! Listen to me, come down, I'm here, Stellaaa!" She gargled her words as tears flowed into her mouth. With her eyes fixed on the fifth-floor balcony, Stella finally made an appearance. "*Eli, dove sei? Non ti vedo, Eli, dove sei? Scappi via di qua! Vattene! Volevano sequestrarti, portarti via da me, dalla tua famiglia! Non lo permetterò mai, mi senti. Mai!*" "Eli, where are you? I don't see you, Eli, where are you. Get away from here, get away, go! They wanted to kidnap you, take you from me and your family. I'll never let it happen, you hear me. Never!" She then turned to her father to curse him out. "*Si n'omm e niente, fissato di essere uno grande, che delusione! N'omm e merda ... e non hai mai saputo amare e non ti fai amare, nemmeno da tua moglie che t'ha fatt' e corne con Amadeo! Si, tua moglie ha fatto l'amore con il tuo collega comunista, e non solo una volta. L'aggio visto io cu l'uocchi miei, nudi, hai capito, nudi, pelle a pelle, hai sentito? La faccia di Amadeo nel petto nudo di mia madre puttana! Si, proprio tua moglie che decise di dare quello che ti apparteneva ad un altro. Guardati, che faccia da cretino!*" "You're a nobody, you believe yourself to be someone important, you're so delusional! You're nothing but a shit, and you never knew how to love, nor do you allow yourself to be loved, not even by your wife who betrayed you with Amadeo! That's right, your wife made love to your communist buddy, and more than once. I saw them with my own eyes, naked, skin on skin, that's right skin on skin, you listening? Amadeo's face in the naked breast of my mother the slut! She gave what belonged to you to another. Look at you, nothing but an asshole loser!

MERECÀ

As the last words escaped her trembling lips, her father grabbed her by the hair pulling her back toward the kitchen. Stella wouldn't let go of the railing, she held on tighter as Mario gave into his anger using ever greater force. Stella stood her ground shrieking incoherently, enduring the obvious pain until her mother came out to unhinge her fingers from the railing. When she still refused to let go, Adela sunk her teeth into her left hand until she gave up her grip allowing Mario to finally stagger her back across the balcony and through the beaded curtain. Some of those who had gathered begged the family to calm down. The screaming continued, with Stella the loudest accusing her mother of the infidelity with Amadeo, shoving the information into her father's face increasing his rage, daring him to do her more harm.

A sudden lull in the fighting, an eerie silence, and a soft breeze flapping the sheer curtains in the direction of the balcony had us believing things had calmed down. I kept an eye on Eli who remained fixated on the fifth-floor balcony, consumed with the erupting madness. The trail of tears and the watery downpours from her nose kept her from talking. The pause in the confusion took my attention away from what was happening to Stella, when suddenly Eli jumped out of her skin screaming as she witnessed father and daughter come crashing through the doors back onto the balcony, with Stella's back moving toward the railing trying to stall her momentum. What soon became incredulously real was the blade that had pierced the center of Mario's left hand while Stella gripped the handle dripping with her father's blood, refusing to let go. As Mario pushed against her chest with his right hand, growling in pain, he freed himself when the force of his thrust sent Stella over the railing still holding the knife that had ripped away from Mario's palm.

In that instant, every movement, every sound, every voice became slow motion explosions that expired as quickly as Stella's life. Reality was no longer a consideration. The depressed buildings, the leafless trees, the dust covered pebbles, the faceless people, the stunned and powerless *carabinieri*, were all pitiful props surrounding Stella's lifeless body.

MERECÀ

I crawled like a dying corpse into the snapshot that unfolded in front of me, nauseatingly witnessing human essence degenerate into a pile of shit. I refused to justify the living that surrounded me, everyone was dead. I had been sheltered from personal extremes my entire young life both in the Bronx and in Sarno. That blissful existence went up in a puff of smoke kicked up by Stella's body the moment it created that sickening percussion as it punched the parched volcanic dirt.
Adela's maniacal shrieks echoed through the cavernous courtyard bouncing off the discolored walls of the buildings like those of female mourners in one of Sarno's churches. The older women in the crowd muttered their prayers, appealing to saints, the blessed virgin, and finally Christ himself for an explanation. The men backed away forging their own theories, then turning them into fictional versions of how the tragedy unfolded.
We kept vigil over the body as the Pronto Soccorso (EMS) made their way through the crowd. Carminuccio sat down next to Eli, sobbing dejectedly ... his disbelief shattered when the Pronto Soccorso pronounced Stella dead. I slipped into the twilight zone refusing to capitulate to the ... how could I possibly yield to what had just happened? Reality had become an irreconcilable monster, and as much as I wanted to avoid it, it stalked me like an insatiable predator. There was no more growing up to do ... the end of Stella's life had savagely torn away a piece of our own lives in a three second drop from that vulgar fifth floor balcony. The *carabinieri* attempted to pull Eli away, but she clung to her lover's body, violently pressing her lips against hers, inhaling her final breath. The only way to appease her anguish was to live Stella's death, deepening her own pain to match it, manipulating every broken bone, every drop of blood, flogging herself to deserve sweet Stella's last trickle of life.

MERECÀ

MERECÀ

CHAPTER 16
ADDIO
(FAREWELL)

The word spread quickly through the high school population. Mimmo was the first to mobilize, bringing together large numbers of students stunned by Stella's story. Even those who hadn't quite understood or accepted the girls, had come to terms with their poor judgement. Mimmo had become an effective advocate since the beginning of our junior year on the topic of marginalized teenagers, maligned for their sexuality, their appearance, or their poverty. The episodes were few, but in a place as sensitive to the welfare of others as Sarno, the words and actions of the most bigoted caused disproportionate pain. I spent most of Easter Sunday with Eli pacing the courtyard at Marabbecca, recalling episodes from our short history as friends, and entertaining her with stories of when I first met Stella in the eighth grade. Her body would lay in the morgue until an investigation had been completed. The Tuesday after Pasquetta a special assembly was called by the school headmaster to address Stella's death. The gathering was attended by teachers, staff, several priests, town officials including the mayor, and a woman advocate who had traveled from Naples to speak about her brother. Still dressed in black, frail, and all skin and bones, she possessed an uncanny fortitude and righteous determination in her raspy voice. She delivered an impassioned talk of how her wretched brother had been sentenced to the remote island of San Domino in the Adriatic Sea during the fascist era along with other gays who were rounded up, labeled as dangerous degenerates, and forcibly ostracized. She made the greatest impression of all when she spoke of her brother's ten years spent on the island, prohibited from leaving, not allowed visits from his family, and only learnings of his mother's death months later. She spoke of how kind, simple, and gentle he was, and of how he suffered from the lack of clean water, sanitary conditions, medical care, and food. When the allies liberated the south, she and her sister were finally able to ferry to the island to retrieve his body. She said he had died of a broken heart. Others that had survived spoke of how they had found happiness on the island living among their own, but that her brother was unable to find the same peace of mind because he couldn't accept being sent away for being different. The story struck a chord with the student body, opening more minds to the painful truth that so many are not given the same opportunities to live freely the life they desire. It was always easy to stimulate human compassion among the inhabitants of Sarno, but the story of San Domino amplified it further. Many of the students shook their heads in disbelief, some wiped away tears, others could be heard whispering *"non è giusto, non è giusto"* "it's not right, it's not right". It was an awakening that righted a wrong in a microcosm. I was fine with that, thinking that if one town after another could come to their senses, then changing sentiments and conditions could become universal. In death Stella had become the catalyst. She had befriended boys and men that provided comfort, but she had fallen in love with a woman that gave definition to her life, a life she was willing to expose and wager in defiance of all her fears ... I could believe in nothing more courageous.

  On Tuesday, the funeral became a showcase for Sarno's youth. Incited by Mimmo, several hundred showed up making a statement that resonated throughout the region. Local newspapers covered it and RAI television sent a crew. The procession covered all the main streets of the town ending in a slow climb up the *rettifilo* to the church of San Francesco. There had been no mention or acknowledgment of Stella being a lesbian by any of the priests, she was merely a local girl who had died tragically, paving the way for a traditional Catholic funeral. Six of us carried the coffin into the church while Eli, in a black veiled outfit, followed holding a silver cross that Stella had given her. The girl from the *palazzine* wouldn't compromise on her religion, she never thought of herself living in sin. She would say that God had to accept her as she was each time she defiantly walked into church on Sunday mornings. It was her understanding that her God was too good to pass harsh judgment on any of his children if they lived a righteous

MERECÀ

life, and that sins were an invention of the church. She loved attending Mass with her *nonna Nicolina*. She described her relationship with her maker best in Neapolitan. *"Dio ma d'accetta' così come sono. Si ma 'fatt issa significa che già o sapeva e me voleva accusi'. Si no, nun me facev part'e stu munn."* "God needs to accept me as I am. If he made me, then he must have known and he wanted me this way. Otherwise, he wouldn't have brought me into this world." It was lovely Stella grinding her philosophies into logic-a spectacle that inspired us to practice the same.

Adela attended the Mass and burial accompanied by two *carabinieri*. Mario remained sequestered on serious conspiracy to commit kidnapping charges regarding Eli, and manslaughter charges in the death of his daughter. The crowd was dominated by high school students. Adults were present in good numbers, but I wasn't certain if they were there out of mere respect or in support of a cause. The lack of religious orthodoxy on the part of the townspeople gave them a more liberated character. I would also learn that for many southern Italians of all ages, religion was practiced in the pews. Life outside the church doors was too personal to be judged with biblical verses. What was certain was that by the time Stella was buried, everyone knew who she was.

In church Mimmo gave a piercing, emotional tribute to our girl. *"Ho quello che mi resta di questa vita per piangere la morte di Stella. Oggi invece, preferisco celebrare la mia amica, mia sorella, la ragazza che sapeva amare ... la ragazza che ha vissuto la sua verità. Dotata di un coraggio che pochi di noi vantiamo, ci ha spinti ad elevare la nostra umanità, e di insistere a normalizzare e poi proteggere il nostro carattere personale. Lei ha fatto proprio quello: ha insistito nella sua scelta di amante e poi ha protetto quell'unione con la sua vita. In un mondo più cosciente, più maturo, Stella starebbe qui con noi passeggiando sul rettifilo, scherzando, ridendo, offrendo un gelato, innamorandosi, godendo la sua gioventù, come doveva essere suo diritto assoluto. Mi dispiace più per noi che siamo costretti, come forse lo meritiamo, di vivere senza Stella, di vivere col suo spirito, mancandoci il suo sorriso, la sua bellezza, il suo modo impeccabile di fare un ragionamento, e di vivere sapendo che c'è*

MERECÀ

qualcosa in noi, nella nostra comunità, che non funziona, che ci faccia esaminare la nostra coscienza di modo che questa tragedia Sarnese non avvenga mai più ... questo deve essere una promessa che facciamo a Stella" "I have what remains of my life to mourn Stella's death. Today however, I choose to celebrate my friend, my sister, the girl who knew how to love ... the girl who lived her truth. Possessing a courage few of us could match, she pushed us to elevate our humanity, insisting on normalizing and then defending our right to our own character. She did exactly that: she insisted in her choice of lover and then she protected that union with her life. In a more compassionate and mature world, Stella would still be with us strolling on the *rettifilo*, joking, laughing, sharing an ice cream, falling in love, and taking pleasure in her youth ... as it should have been her absolute right to do. I'm mostly sorry for all of us who are now ill-fated, as we perhaps deserve, to live without Stella, to live with her ghost, missing her smile, her beauty, her impeccable manner of carrying through an argument, and to live knowing that in us, in our community, there is something that doesn't work that would have us examine our consciences in such a way as to guarantee that this *Sarnese* tragedy never happens again. This is a promise we must make to Stella." My generation had mobilized its tears, frustration, and unleashed its repressed demand that our young lives could have been spared the morbid ordeal.

Stella's last *passeggiata* was to her resting place. We trekked nostalgically through the streets and the places we hung out that had once seen us happy, carefree and a universe away from unimaginable evils. The hearse kept a reluctant, morose pace through the cobblestone lanes lined with the somber faces of mourners and the inquisitive looks of the curious. Whatever the reason, it seemed the entire town had participated. As the procession neared the cemetery, we caught a glimpse of the wretched balcony beyond the flowering magnolias, the fall from which she took her last breath. The shredded Communist Party flag hung pathetically by a thread; it was the last thing Stella touched. The burial plot, dug in the newer section of the cemetery, would eventually be marked by a headstone, paid for by Eli's parents, as simple and genuine as Stella. The priest stayed away, refusing to administer a last sacrament ... Stella would have gone over his head to tenaciously plead her case directly with God ... and in my estimation, God would have relented.

The adults moved to the side as we gathered to bid her body farewell ... her still living spirit filling the spaces between us, loosening that fatalistic knot in our stomachs. I fell into a deep trance imagining how things would have turned out for Stella. I pictured her happy, fulfilled, in love with Eli, living in London, perhaps Rome, always beautiful, radiant, defending everyone's right to love as they pleased.

The sudden crackle of tossed dirt ricocheting off her casket brought me back, and as real time stubbornly replaced my daydreaming, pieces of me agonizingly limped into that hole, searching for signs of life, wishing to resurrect my dear friend ... unwilling to accept that death could ever own her. The adults walked away dejected, mumbling incoherently, unable to understand the role they played in Stella's death. They wanted to place guilt somehow within their ranks, but there was little consensus. I did admire their willingness to admit they should have known more, and how they spoke of the compassion they never had a chance to contribute. Eli cried the entire time, finally collapsing to her knees, laboring at catching her breath. I knelt to prop her up, keeping her from a total breakdown. She managed a few agonizing, disjointed words challenged by the flow of water from her eyes and nose. *"Gianni, I'm not sure I can survive this. I feel life is being drained from my body, I'm cold and numb. I'm alive, but I'm dead."* We kept a jealous vigil until we picked up on the signals coming from the groundskeepers that it was time to leave them to their work. I walked out with Eli glued to my arm. Carminuccio, Mimmo and the rest followed. Exiting the cemetery, guarded by black, perverse steel gates, the feeling was one of having turned our backs on a lonely soul, abandoned to a cold, alien world surrounded by dispassionate tombstones. We all suffered that moment intensely, brawling with a despondent desire to fall apart, lay your body down, and grieve forever.

MERECÀ

The passage back to our side of Sarno, to San Sebastiano was spent in silence ... conversations were difficult and seemed pointless. Mimmo veered off towards his home as we approached the end of the *rettifilo* onto Via Matteotti. We managed a small group hug with the promise we would reconnect in school. Minutes later, Eli's parents met us at the entrance to Marabbecca, expressing concern, asking us to stay for lunch. Carminuccio had other plans to meet up with Teresa. He kindly excused himself and made his way toward Via Umberto. Food seemed more like an unfriendly diversion, so Eli insisted on just spending some time in the garden. She asked me to stay. *"Gianni, would you mind staying a bit. I would like it if you would keep me company."* I was hoping she would include me-I wasn't sure I wanted to be alone. There was so much to process, so many emotions swirling about. *"Yes, I'll stay, don't want to go home yet."* We strolled past the courtyard arm in arm as she wiped away a rogue tear or two that had successfully dodged her tissue to reach her upper lip. The stone bench under the laurels had become our nesting place where we grew out of our adolescence to deal with a future that had finally caught up with us. *"I'm not sure I can stay in Sarno. You, Carminuccio, Mimmo and the others have kept me intrigued and in love with this town. Stella had added the ultimate magic, the greatest fantasy. Now I feel lost in some dark space, a place that has betrayed my happiness. Gianni, non so cosa credere, I have no clue what to believe ... I feel I'm telling lies, trying to convince myself that there is still a life here to live."*
"You're being way too harsh on yourself and Sarno. You witnessed almost the entire town come out to tell you they were sorry for the actions of only two people. You may want to condemn everyone for being blind to what Stella had to go through, and that maybe they chose to remain ignorant, but you can't expect the same level of tolerance you would have found in a place like London."
"She could have kept our secret. I was willing to live in the shadows. We were happy, we had each other, we had you and Carminuccio, we had all your classmates. Guardami (look at me), she was in my arms, on my bed, we made love, our words became poems, we shared dreams ... now she's lying in a grave. Like some

deranged soul, I kept asking her what are you doing in that casket, in that hole in the ground, covered in dirt? Do you understand how it's driving me mad?" Eli was destined to shed unscripted tears for months to come. The slightest reminder of anything Stella filled her eyes with droplets that emptied into wavy estuaries as they slid down her clean, dry cheeks. "I can't deny you the pain you are feeling. Her death has made it impossible for me to get back to the way things were. I feel that now my only choice is to keep to the plan even if the things that come my way are complete shit. I'm angry, but I don't want to be guided by that anger, and I desperately don't want to lose control. Eli, we have so much life ahead, and I doubt Stella would have wanted us to live it full of remorse and hatred. She was all about love, all about the wonder of others, and squeezing the most out of moments that counted ... the ones that made her magnificent and kept all of us in awe. Let's dream of things to come as Stella would have done. Nothing ever got in the way of hope ... she understood it to be her greatest asset. When all else got her down, she would say 'nge sempre la speranza.'(there's always hope)"
"You're right. Her "speranza" would have so much more power than yours or mine. Our speranza will travel a much easier route, with fewer obstacles ... you still have America to return to, I have London to escape to. My sweet Stella had cast aside her fears in the certainty that hope would deliver on its promise. Gianni, if we had never crossed paths, Stella would still be alive! These are the thoughts that linger about me, causing all sorts of ghostly doubts."
I wasn't happy with simply agreeing, I had to balance out her argument.
"Imagine if we lived constantly worried about the -what ifs-. We would never decide to do anything, afraid of hurting or being hurt. Stella was inevitable. We were drawn to her energy; we both knew we wanted her in our lives. Dante said: 'Beauty awakens the soul to act.' Stella's beauty was much deeper than her skin, it was all of her. So how could our souls not react? You realize it was difficult for me, it had to be a total impossibility for you. You did what was expected of a human being-you fell in love with one who was perfectly beautiful. Dante also said that the more perfect one is,

MERECÀ

the greater the pleasures and the pains. I can think of no greater pleasure than having loved Stella, and no greater pain than losing her. People go through an entire life avoiding pleasure and pain, choosing to live in some bubble, ignoring love ... refusing to take that chance." I paused, wondering whether I needed to choose my next words carefully. It was difficult being open and honest when feelings had been repressed for so long. *"I wasn't sure of myself. I too had to give up on my feelings. You asked me not to love you. You knew how I felt, but I had to respect that. But having known Stella's courage, I regret that my attempt was weak ... how many regrets can we keep living with?"*

"I feel I have been so insensitive with you, with Stella, with the good people of Sarno. My expectations have been selfish, I ask for too much. Stella had to chance all of her to find happiness with me. I chanced little, and yet I am suffering the greatest loss. I asked you to ignore your feelings while I gave you reasons to fall in love. I attempted to place blame on the ignorance in this town when the compassion they showed proved me to be so wrong. I have been foolish to think that most people would be hostile towards two women in love. Gianni, what's to become of us? There was a time when I believed the future was ours to mold. Now I fear it will be as unpredictable as the present, as if we play no part in what is to come."

"There is no way that you will ever give up on yourself and who you are. Eli, there's no turning back. You, me, Stella, Carminuccio, our generation has exposed too much of what we want out of life. Stella was tired of hiding, and we should follow in her footsteps. I'm not all about the kind of sick revolutions that Mario and the communists want, but I do think that change will happen, and it will be the kind of change that will help many people. Look at me-how different am I from who I was in the Bronx. It took these years in Sarno to open me up to the world beyond the neighborhood. Back in New York, I know I wouldn't have changed much, and I would have had a tough time accepting you. I wasn't the type to put you down, but I wouldn't have been much support. I'm no longer afraid of telling you that I love you, but I have no intentions beyond my words. I want to avoid not

MERECÀ

acting on my feelings ... this is the way I want to live from now on." She gave my sentiments some thought, smiled lovingly, embraced me with uncommon strength, and held on as if she knew our days together were fading. *"Tu sei incredibile, you know you are incredible. I suppose I'm doomed to live my regrets about you. If I could open all my heart to you, I would give of myself completely. My fear is that I wouldn't be able to grant you the greatest happiness you deserve. What I can give wouldn't be enough, and you should never settle. Merecà, I love you to death-te voglio nu bene da muri'."*

  On the way home, I fixated on Eli's use of the Neapolitan, understanding it was a sentimental tribute to Stella ... a phrase Stella bestowed on those she loved. The usual buzz of scooters and pedestrian chatter along Via Umberto, sounds that always reminded me of the purpose and vibrancy of life, had suddenly become irritating noise. Entering the *portone* finally provided a peaceful escape from the street. Nonna was alone in the kitchen sipping on a cup of tea. She offered to prepare some food, but I refused. She expressed some surprise, then probed to find out more of what she already knew. *"Parlame na poco e sta ragazza che è morta. Pecche' sta tragedia?"* "Speak to me of this girl who died. Why such a tragedy?" She had a delicate way of easing me into meaningful conversations. *"Nonna, Stella è morta per ignoranza."* I told her she died because of ignorance. She looked at me puzzled. I thought of being more direct and honest, but that wasn't happening. I doubted she could handle the truth about Stella and Eli, and I couldn't tolerate a useless lesson on prohibited affairs, so I tried changing the topic. Each time I thought she couldn't possibly tune into my way of thinking, she proved me wrong. *"Aggio saput' che se trattav e due ragazze innamorate, è vero? Sient', nun te credere che chest' foss'a prima vota che ndo' paese sa saput che doie femmene se vulevano bene. Anni fa nun se ne parlava e quasi sempre ievano a fini' dint a nu convento con le suore. Però non se moreva e nun me ricord mai na vota che na femmena avesse pers'a vita pe sta ragione. Stella e a figlia do'conte se vulevano bene e questo doveva essere fatti loro, e basta! Figlio mio, quann l'ammore è na cosa vera, è sempre na cosa giusta."* Nonna often proved generation gaps to be overrated. She was more enlightened than I gave her credit for and I always allowed her artful female wisdom access to my heart. She delicately gave her opinion. "I came to learn that it involved two girls in love, true? Listen, don't think that this is the first time in this town that there have been two women in love. Years ago, no one would talk about it and almost always they would be sent off to convents in the care of nuns. I can think of no time when a woman lost her life for that reason. Stella and the count's daughter were in love and that should have been their business, and nothing else! My son, when love is truthful, it is always right." Whenever storms raged inside of me, nonna found a way to calm the waters.

In our classes the mood had turned more upbeat as we approached the end of the school year. Summers in Italy were always a pure delight, and thoughts of sun, feasts, concerts, beaches and free time had us clinging to each other and making plans. Carminuccio and his dad were booked every weekend during July and August. The two-man band had grown to five with a regular following in the towns of the region. Mimmo was filled with hard to contain excitement having learned that Stefania was due back for the summer from New Jersey. They had written each other countless letters, leaving no emotion uncovered. Raffaele was happy taking on full time hours at the hospital where he had started secretly dating one of the nurses. They had to keep it covert since amorous relations between employees was frowned upon. I was happy that someone would get to experience his delightful kindness and passion for simple pleasures. Mom had broken the bittersweet news that we would be departing for New York the end of June. It was time to go home, as she put it. Pop was hoping we would choose to stay, but finances had become stretched, and America had been the most rewarding place to make a living. They also worried for the future of their three children, knowing that as American citizens, our best chances were back in the states. The strongest reasons coalesced to make it inevitable that it was time to recapture our American lives. The news was hard to swallow. There was too much for me to leave behind, and I knew I could never ready myself completely for the most difficult of separations.

MERECÀ

I felt the anxiety creeping into my days as I started thinking that there would be no easy, happy way to say goodbye, and no way of avoiding the pain that would depress our hearts. . I met Eli every Sunday after Easter to keep our appointment with Stella. The last Sunday in May we left early so we could be alone with her. Eli didn't enjoy the crowds that gathered at her grave, she claimed they had turned her into a curiosity. The number of flowers that covered the plot told me otherwise. I insisted that those who visited did so out of pure piety even if it did bring unwanted fame. Eli's relationship with Stella remained jealously personal even in death. She had been the girl from the *palazzine* to others, but she had been hers to love. The relationship she had dared to admit to, had become a possession she expected others to respect. After clearing the decayed flowers, Eli would wipe down the headstone that read: STELLA ROSA ARCANGELO 1954-1971 AMICA DI TANTI, AMANTE DI UNA (STELLA ROSA ARCANGELO 1954-1971 FRIEND TO MANY, LOVER TO ONE). Her way of sidestepping the sadness was to talk about the pleasure that was Stella. We sat on her marble grave and Eli would take a deep sigh, caress the surface of the shiny stone, and made me an audience of her anecdotes. *"Gianni, I remember when we sat on my bed, completely in love with each other's company, and I asked her to teach me Napoletano. Hers was impeccable, melodic, and theatrical ... I could listen to her for hours. When I tried, the pronunciation was too proper, and she would make fun of me. Then we would start laughing, but she would insist on trying again, but I couldn't even get a word out of my mouth because I couldn't stop laughing. Once I even drooled, and that got her laughing crazy. I can so picture her face, her amazing smile, her plump lips ... it was such a turn on."*

"What was it like making love?" It was too late to retract the question, my curiosity got the better of me, or perhaps it was just an excuse, and maybe I just had to know. It wasn't in Eli to hold back about Stella, and that day, in the presence of her spirit, Eli took the opportunity to exhume their deepest intimacies. *"Pure bewilderment because there are no words that could ever explain the feelings. My dear Gianni, ascolta, listen-all that is superior in the emotion and body of a women, found its greatest expression in my Stella. To make love to a willing creature who had never known the art of love making, whose body had matured years earlier with so many unfulfilled curiosities, shackled by cultural taboos, and self-imposed limits, was to suffer the purest and most perfect human temptation. Her submissive innocence in those moments was such to cause me to weep. Imagine the agony of love if you can, to feel the joyous pain of experiencing the inconceivable ... the absurdity of having it all. We captured that time together and glorified it. The scent of her body still hangs over me, the taste of her mouth still dwells on mine. Fantasies I never knew overcame me as I moved my fingers across her unblemished, creamy skin, probing each spot that kept us insanely delirious."*

She paused abruptly, startled at the thought that her words had resurrected a reality that was no longer, one that would never happen again. I tried to ease her through it. *"I could only hope that at some point in my life I could have the same with someone. Your time with an incredible woman will always be a priceless, beautiful memory. How many will ever be that lucky? I think you're feeling these things because it happened in Sarno. You couldn't have expected the same in London, there would have been too many choices. Sarno couldn't give you choices, but it did give you one rare gem. Considering what you found here, I think you should keep the love close to your heart rather than reliving this ordeal. Stella will always be with you and she will help you find your happiness again, and then you will need to live it jealously."* She buried her head in my chest, used my shirt to soak up her tears, and nodded that she was good with my words. *"Gianni, capisco-I understand. I only need to become more of the person you describe, but it won't happen anytime soon. I'm little more than a corpse, a mummy. I barely have any life left in me ... I cry constantly when I'm alone. My room has become a torture chamber."* The cemetery was the ultimate paradox; it was where I felt the most alive. It all came together there, confronting the greatest calamity with the greatest blessing.

Eli kissed the headstone, wiped away some dust from Stella's name, took me by the arm, smiled and led us away from the dead. We made it to San Sebastiano where she invited herself into the *giardino.* The dirt had been freshly plowed to cut away and bury the tall, coarse weeds. The perfumes of our southern Italian spring caressed us from every direction, helped along by the soft, tepid breeze. As we sat in our spot under the eucalyptus, I delivered the unpleasant news I had delayed for days, wishing to avoid the discomfort I thought it would cause her. *"You know, we're leaving for New York end of June."* She stopped, captured my eyes, said nothing for a moment, tried not to react. *"Well, I suppose that would be the place for you to go. It's not as if you were meant to stay in Sarno forever. These past four years will be just a chapter in your life. You will move on, grow older, marry an American girl, I suppose, and live happily ever after somewhere, an ocean away."* She made a halfhearted attempt to remain composed, but her strength failed her, stood up and walked away, quickening her pace leaving me a good ten feet behind. I caught up, took her arm, and whirled her toward me. We came face to face, her eyes rejecting mine. She kept looking away, demanding to let her go. I held on tighter until the struggle caused her to find the words lost somewhere in that confusion zone between her heart and mind. She became frantic with forceful bursts of energy. *"Gianni, what do you want from me? Do you expect me to simply bid you farewell, give you my final addio, and close the book on our lives together? As much as I want to move on with my days, it is so dreadful to think that we may never see each other again. You know things will get in the way, you have university to attend, perhaps a job afterwards that will keep you busy for who knows how many years, and we will write frequently for a year or so until we no longer have anything endearing or meaningful to say. We will invent excuses to turn us into distant memories. Then, we will meet by chance years later at the airport in Rome, you on a business trip, and me to visit my parents. We will catch up on all the lost time, you'll show me pictures of your wife and children, and I will have nothing to show you because I hate photos. We will exchange some awkward words as if we had only met for the first time. A superficial kiss or two later and off we would go promising unfaithfully to get together."* She no longer found the fortitude to

MERECÀ

camouflage her more delicate side, which she had succeeded in doing for years. *"I know I'm being incoherent and silly, but the pain of leaving Stella behind in her tomb has made me so weak, so afraid of more pain. Here I am again, walking down that path toward another dreadful moment ... I feel the panic waiting in the shadows, ready to steal away the best of me, and turn me into someone I will despise. I'm not good alone, I admit to it. Tell me Gianni, is there a way of avoiding all this?"*
"Hey, what is going on with you? Why all the ugly predictions? I don't see it like that at all. *I'm already planning my summer trips. I won't let anything get in the way of having you show me around London or touring Rome together. We will be older, able to make decisions without any interference, and who knows, I may not even like you anymore."* The remark was meant to lighten things up, but instead in brought on a torrent of tears and several punches to my stomach and chest. *"You can be so cruel at times! I'm walking through my own circle of Hell, and you are making jokes. Gianni, please hold me, just hold me."* As she burrowed into my arms, she surrendered more truths. *"You may think me needy and girly, but you should know that I have loved you as much as anyone. Stella overwhelmed me. Everything about her turned me on at first ... falling in love came unexpectedly and so irresistibly. You came into my life as the best of men, and I will be the loneliest of creatures without you."*

  She remained unsettled during the walk back to the Marabbecca. *"I don't want to be alone, you fancy staying a bit? My parents are away in Naples, I want you to make me some promises."* "Promises I can keep?" *"Of course, I'll only allow you to make those you can keep."* The more playful she became, the more I wanted to be alone with her. Being the object of some of her attention was a pure joy ... being the object of all her attention had become a welcomed fixation that beckoned for those hours spent locked in her room. We maneuvered quietly through the back door and up the staircase, avoiding the maid dusting down the family portraits flanking the ornate parlor doors. Her body kept a steady beat to the popular Neapolitan tune she hummed while paying attention to her work. It was a familiar sight in the south where women sang while carrying on with all sorts of chores from washing clothes on the rocks along the river, to prepping tomato plants in the San Marzano fields, to the swagger with which the farm girls balanced baskets filled with produce on their heads. We made enough noise to get her attention. *"Signorina Elisa?"* Eli acknowledged. *"Si, sono io."* I had climbed a few steps to stay out of sight. On her last trip to London, she had purchased Simon and Garfunkle's album *Bridge Over Troubled Waters*. I enjoyed the entire album, but the title song said much of how the world around us had become. Eli knew the words by heart. She sang them softly as she laid on her bed, eyes closed, imagining who knows what. *"Gianni, come, lay next to me. Tell me there will always be a bridge between us. Yes, we will lay ourselves down, promise that our hearts will always be connected, and we will be there to comfort each other."*

The perfect teenage storm settled over us that afternoon, numbing us to life beyond the door and the windows of her room. The music had taken hold of us much the way the love story of Lancelot and Guinevere had overcome Dante's Paolo and Francesca. We shunned all formalities, giving nature the freedom to free our senses and passions, and making love came to us in the most unrestrained procession of actions, at times subtle, and at times lustful. We performed, hardly losing sight of each other's eyes, wondering how impossible it would be to disengage, to allow distances to deny us those desires. Eli always found a reason to enlighten. With no words spoken, she bestowed a careful lesson on how poorly instructed men were on the art of satisfying a woman. She guided my hands, fingers, tongue, and lips with the care of a faithful lover. Finally, we gave into our exhaustion, settling into a short, deep sleep. I drifted off with images of Stella in my place … my curiosity taking me possibly to a forbidden place.

   Later, as we sat legs crossed facing each other, I revealed my thought: were a woman's instincts better? *"Eli, tell me, when I think of Stella in my place in this very moment, was it easier to love a woman because you can give each other what a man is incapable of? I mean, I doubt I could have been as prepared as Stella in making love to you. In a few minutes you taught me what to do, and I confess, I wasn't very familiar with much of it, and I doubt my sentiment would have been enough. Not sure why I brought this up." "Gianni, perfectly normal for you to ask. I had tried a relationship with a boy older than me in London. It was a horrible experience. It started well, but then it became hurtful, one sided, all about him and his needs. When it ended, I was happy again. Many of my girlfriends had similar experiences. Then I met Melinda at a party in Soho. It may have been pure infatuation, but my time with her was all about us, not me or her, us. There wasn't a time we were together that wasn't a complete delight. I turned my feelings towards women, but nothing could have prepared me for Stella. Stella had all of me for the first time in my life. She was passion, love, infatuation, and sexuality, she was all that. Let me see if I can make you understand. Today I made love to a man with the heart of a woman. Please don't be offended, this is not an insult on your masculinity, please take it as a compliment. I never would have allowed it if I didn't think I knew you well enough. Another sad experience with a selfish male was the last thing I cared for. I never made a secret of my affections for both sexes, Stella just sent me over the edge, leaning me to one side."* She took my hand to her lips. *"Merecà, my dear Americano, be my lover. If circumstances deny us all else, then be my sweet lover, my dearest friend, my darling companion ... let's avoid having just one title, let's be everything and anything we want to be to each other ... think of how liberating that would be. I will cherish these thoughts until we meet again. You know, I'm willing to suffer the long, cold, and gloomy winters, but our summers in England or Italy will be magnificent, I promise. And I suppose I must shed many tears, for only then will you feel a terrible guilt should you fail to write. You know it will be pure agony waiting for the post, hoping to find a letter from New York."*

    Nothing could have prepared me for the gathering organized by Mimmo that last Saturday in June before our departure two days later. Carminuccio met me on Via Umberto for what was supposed to be a gathering with Mimmo and Raffaele at our favorite pizzeria. On the way there, Mimmo insisted on stopping at the Bar Michelangelo for an *aperitivo*. I thought the

MERECÀ

suggestion and his insistence to be strange since we hadn't made a habit of doing *aperitivi* before a meal. I chalked it up to either maturity seeping into our habits, or to a simple curiosity of whether there was some truth to the notion that having an *aperitivo* before a meal enhanced one's appetite. I never believed it, nor did I entertain trying it out more than once at the insistence of one of my crusty uncles whose taste buds had surely been annihilated from years of drinking wine that had gone to vinegar. Most *aperitivi* were liquors made from strained juices of plants like artichokes mixed with grain alcohol, the product being very bitter with a strong medicinal taste … that day it succeeded in killing my appetite.

  As we walked in, Mimmo led us to a back room where around twenty of my closest friends and classmates were waiting in party mode. Eli was the first to greet me with her brilliant smile, and that silky golden hair bouncing off her shoulders. One by one, they approached with hugs and kisses, smiles, watery eyes, and expressions of disbelief that they would have to do without me. I was humbled when each greeted me by my nickname. I had happily been their *merecà* for four endearing years, despite becoming more and more *italiano*. Questions about ever returning surfaced constantly. I could only answer "*speriamo*" "let's hope". I had no doubts about trips during the summer months, but I wasn't ready to commit. Rehabilitating to the Bronx would take much work, and money was becoming more of a factor in any future plans. Mom and Pop had based their decision to return mostly on the need to jumpstart incomes. I understood that priority, so I bit my tongue to avoid talk of things that were important to me. The atmosphere at the Bar Michelangelo that day was more adult than teenage. There was a tender feeling of how we had come along, of our peculiar evolution not only in age, but as a breed forced from its small-town sanctuary and tossed onto the global stage, a Pirandello generation of actors in search of an author. We could never hope to match the agendas and the imagery of the hippies with legacies such as Woodstock, anti-war protests, Bob Dylan, flowers, and peace signs. Best we could do was to adopt what we could appreciate from that iconic generation as we set out to create our own cultural marker. Sarno was sending me off as a new immigrant back to America, much the way it had done with my parents. Mom and Pop carried with them the teachings and the cultural habits of their generation and put them to perfect use in a new world. I got the unusual, but grateful opportunity to do and experience the same. My conditioning had been as complete as possible within a four-year-old life, and Mimmo, Carminuccio, Eli, Stella and the rest were counting on me to show it off; to empower a small, southern Italian town and grant it one more chance to export its humanity.

    The day of our departure Eli and Carminuccio insisted on coming to the Stazione Centrale in Naples. Eli's father had volunteered his car and driver. I sat in the back with Eli, Carminuccio kept the driver company up front. We followed the thankfully slow caravan of family vehicles burdened with luggage and relatives to see us off. The train would take us to Rome for the flight to New York. I expected and got a peculiar silence from both my dear friends. None of us knew how to manage that moment. I guessed we were each searching for a way of expressing some awkward sentiment, but mundane words would have been completely inadequate. Eli held on to my arm, as was her way, leaning her head precariously on my shoulder, knowing it wouldn't last long. As the train station came into view, anxieties invaded my thoughts knowing I would have no good reason to find happiness. The first minutes were spent bidding *addio* to relatives which allowed the time I craved to be as intimate as I wanted with my dear companions. Carminuccio's honest embrace delivered a series of flashbacks to a sweet and delicate friendship that had developed into a colloquium on our coming of age. The lessons were spontaneous, rooted in an elaborately ancient culture, and welcomed by me in all its capacity. I turned to Eli, who at first seemed unwilling to face what was happening. She then reduced the few steps that separated us in a leap that fused her lips nostalgically to mine in a lover's departing kiss, furious with affection, devotion, and the subdued anger that one feels when circumstances dictate the inevitable. "*So, merecà, this is it, I suppose. This is my dreaded, bugger moment that I thought would*

MERECÀ

never happen. I tried fooling myself into thinking we could keep living our most precious moments over and over with no interference. It was all a fool's dream with this vulgar awakening. I'm doomed to feel only your ghostly presence in the giardino. It will keep me sad for days." She cushioned my face in her soft, unsteady hands, bestowing one final *bacio* as she slipped me an envelope. Mom called out, nudging me back into existence, asking me to join them boarding our coach. While the others took their seats, I remained harnessed to the door, peering out at the framed images of my saddened escorts. As the train slowly inched forward, I fixed on Eli one last time committing that flawless portrait to memory.

    I took to my seat next to my mother. She asked about Eli. I simply told her that I would miss her immensely, and that leaving Sarno was much more painful than I had anticipated. My thoughts occupied my time halfway to Rome when I remembered Eli's envelope I had folded and tucked into my back pocket. Only she could have written a letter that came to life as I read it. *"My Dearest Americano do not believe for a moment that if you are reading this letter, it means I am no longer by your side. I will always be with you. You may also wrongly believe that it was I who had the most profound effect on you, when in truth it was you who changed my life for the better in so many ways. I will forever hold you in my heart, and you will forever have my love. Dante wrote about some of the souls in heaven as being too beautiful to describe with words. You have that beauty ... words would only be an injustice should I attempt to define you. My days will be filled with memories of a perfect friend and a most gentle lover. My dear Gianni, sei la Stella che vive in me, che respira di nuovo nella mia anima. Ricordati, e ritorni, ritorni da me. (... you are the Stella that lives in me, who breathes once again in my soul. Remember, and come back, come back to me.)"* To know Eli was to understand her depth. She could find Stella in anything or anyone she loved unconditionally, bringing her lover back to life. I was contented and at peace with her, knowing that in me she had found one instrument of that resurrection.

About the Author-

John Benny Dolgetta was born in the Bronx to Maria and Giuseppe Dolgetta. His immigrant parents landed in New York as a married couple off the Andrea Doria in 1954. Giuseppe worked as an independent scrap metal collector, while Maria worked a Singer sewing machine as a seamstress in one of the many sweatshops in the Arthur Avenue section of the borough.

John graduated from Fordham Preparatory School High School. Attended Fordham University and graduated with a B.A. in Political Science and a B.A. in Italian Literature. After college he worked for Alitalia Airlines at JFK airport. Four years later he was asked to return to Fordham Prep to teach Italian Language Studies and Political Science.

At Fordham Graduate School he completed his M.A. in Political Science and a Professional Diploma in Education. Eventually an offer came to teach in the Yonkers Public Schools. He accepted and spent the next thirty years at Gorton High School.

John is married to Adelaide, has four children-Maria, Daniela, JoJo, and Johnny. He and his family have settled in the hamlet of Mahopac in Putnam County, New York.

His first book-***Bronx River North***-a high school coming of age story was published in its second edition in 2020.

Author can be reached at:
johndolgetta@yahoo.com
914-330-1727

Made in the USA
Columbia, SC
20 July 2021